PEST

G. SPENCER MYERS

Creator of the Dr. Derk Bryan Eco-Thriller Series

ISBN

Hardcover:978-1-966565-12-3
Paperback:978-1-966565-13-0

Other Books by G. Spencer Myers

Pest:

A man experiences a deadly premonition while fishing in the Florida Keys. A murder in Michigan causes a toxic spill. Dr. Derk Bryan, the Indiana Jones of the EPA, soon discovers that these two disparate events threaten every drop of water on the planet and every important relationship in his life. His laisse faire life on the beach is on a collision course with the maniacal chemical company magnate, Jack Von Lleuwan, and his bodyguard, Jimmy "Gloves Swingle, an ex-wrestler with anger management issues.

Von Lleuwan's newest product, PESTfree© , designed to replace the chemicals that are contaminating food and water worldwide, contains a deadly flaw. As a result, Kate McCardigan, Derk's college sweetheart, becomes a target when she blames Von Lleuwan for crippling her son and others. As the body count grows, Derk Bryan races against the clock to thwart disaster and save McCardigan from becoming another victim.

Praise for Pest:

"Murder leads Derk Bryan, the EPA's most creative investigator, from a chemical spill in West Michigan to Tampa Bay and back to Ohio. Pest will make you laugh and make you cry. Ultimately, you will ask, Will I be the next victim? A must-read book."

- **Ervin Harmon, Book Reviewer, and Critic**

"The engaging narrative of Pest contains much to think about regarding toxicology, environmental awareness, and the balance of nature. . . Pest leaves one wondering how closely the story resembles a true one."

- **Rachel Elaine, Author of Thoughts for Thought.**

The Girl with the Red Nails:

In The Girl with the Red Nails, Dr. Derk Bryan, the Indiana Jones of the EPA, pursues the greedy and the complicit who are fueling an approaching catastrophe.

All roads lead to the doorstep of Pendleton Danswirth III and his billionaire buddies. It looks as if he'll get away with murder and more until an ending that no one saw coming.

Greed, sex, religion and murder drive this eco-thriller. A must read!

Dead Wrong:

A truckload of toxic chemicals crashes into Tampa Bay, a bank president's son and a senator's daughter die after smoking weed at a fraternity party, and the publisher of a weekly entertainment rag accuses the cops of murder. As one of the EPA's top investigators, Derk Bryan refuses to accept the ME's conclusion that the spill was an accident and that these events are not related. With three monster hurricanes on a collision course with Florida, Bryan races against the clock and the bureaucracy to uncover the clues in this ecological crossword puzzle.

Praise for Dead Wrong:

"Using an EPA investigator is unique for a crime novel. I really like Derk Bryan and I really liked this book."

> \-   **Ann Bocock WXEL-TV, "Between the Sheets"
> Summer Reading Series.**

"Dr. Derk Bryan is a hero without a Messiah complex."

> \-   **Buch 1-DM, Online Book Club**

"Impressive characters headline this suspenseful tale with an ecological bent."

\- **Kirkus review**

"… interesting, thought-provoking, and thrilling… There is no doubt that audiences will be anticipating the next adventure."

\- **Gretchen Hansen, The US Review of Books**

We Are Playing Roulette With Your Future:

G. Spencer Myers issues a profound warning to Ian, his grandson, and Ian's generation that involves a threat to humanity so great that scientists have given it a name: The Anthropocene—a human caused extinction.

Using a series of short stories Myers challenges grandsons from eight to eighty to think big and be bold in your ideas in the face of the crisis of your lifetime: Global Warming. In 1980, he became the first person in the U.S. to put 400 sq. ft. of solar panels on a multi-family residence listed on the National Register of Historic Places. Today, he drives an EV and fuels it with sunshine. Having devoted his life to reducing his own carbon footprint, he says, "There's hope. We know what to do." Read it and become inspired.

All books are available at: www.GSpencerMyers.com or your favorite online book provider.

Contents

1

"Son-of-a-bitch!" A pen-sized beam of light pierced the air above him as he fell to the floor.

"Shut up," came a loud whisper through the darkness.

"Goddammit! I shouldn't have let you to talk me into this."

"I didn't. Two hundred bucks did."

"I thought this was his office. Fucking golf balls everywhere."

"I know. Can you reach the light?" A light flickered on the floor several feet from him.

"I think I broke my ass."

"You mean your sacrum."

"Fuck you!" The beam of light took flight again. "Where are you?"

"Over here."

A ray worked its way from the man on the floor to the other's pants and then to his face. Then it circumscribed the area around the man on the floor, then against the walls.

"He's got a frigging golf course in here," said the man on the floor.

"What's happening? Are you in?" a voice corroded by static penetrated the darkness.

"Shit! I can't find the walkie-talkie," said the man with the light.

"On the floor," said his accomplice. When the light hit it, "Over there."

The man on the floor crawled toward the walkie-talkie. The sound of golf balls rolling across the wooden floor was like thunder in an old folks' home. He pushed the send button, "Roger that," but the button wouldn't move. "Fuck!"

"What?"

"Damn thing's broken." His eyes had adjusted to a dim light that filtered in from a narrow window overhead. The ceiling was, at least, twenty feet high. He sat up and fanned the balls away from him with his legs but an electric current shot through his lower body. "Eeesus!"

"You hurt?" said the other man.

"Egocentric fart. Everybody's mother told him to clean up his room." He lay down and brushed the area around him with his forearm. The balls rolled again, and it seemed like an eternity before they bounced off the wall at the other end of the room. "What is this place?"

"Can you make it?"

He shined the light around him. When the area seemed clear he struggled to his feet. "Ahhh!" He massaged his lower back. "Fucker ought to have to walk blind folded through here."

"Hey, did you find anything?" came the voice on the walkie-talkie. "Come back."

The man aimed the tiny flashlight on his friend, then shot a beam on the floor between them. The other man kicked away the balls in his path and joined him. They were inside the office of the president of a Von Lleuwan Enterprises, a leading pesticide producer, and they were standing on a putting green. The pin was in the hole next to them.

"Fucking-a," the man with the light said as he held out the number eighteen flag.

"Shine it over there," his friend said.

"What are we looking for?"

"Files, product lists, experimental shit. Something like that, I guess."

The small light scanned the room, landing upon a set of golf clubs, a desk, a computer and a wall full of books. "No files here," the man with the light whispered.

"The computer," the other man said.

The light hit the PC again. Suddenly a voice came from below them.

"Oh shit, we've got to get out of here." The light searched for the door. Once found, it scoured the floor for a clear path.

The hallway was as dark as when they had entered, and they retraced their path down the stairs, but the light in the corridor leading to the rear exit was off. It had been on when they entered. By the time they reached the door, they heard only a faint moan, resembling a cry for help. They stopped and turned toward the voice.

"No way," said the man rubbing his sacrum. He pulled the other man out the back door by his arm.

The rear exit was illuminated only by the light of a halfmoon. The lights had been knocked out before they got there. They ran for a clump of brush at the back of the property, sidestepping storage containers as they proceeded, then leaped down a brief embankment and forded a small stream to a cornfield. They walked along the edge of the field until they reached a country road. In the tall grass they recovered their bicycles and rode back to the van where their boss waited. They threw the bikes into the back of the truck and sped off.

2

It was past two in the morning when the phone rang in Derk Bryan's St. Pete Beach condo. He got in late after an all-night drive from Key West and was as tired as a slug on a thousand mile journey. At that hour no voice is familiar, and he felt like heavy metal poured onto cotton wadding. A female voice identified herself as Joyce, told him "be in Grand Rapids this afternoon," and left the flight time and number.

He recalled the message from Wallace Twill on his voice mail about the unusual events in west Michigan. The story was bizarre enough that it would have been picked off the wire service and shown up in the St. Petersburg's *Times*, but there was a week's worth of unread papers piled up on his balcony. The story was a only a couple of days old and Michigan is 2000 miles north of the Dry Tortugas, where he had been fishing. Therefore, he hadn't read the news, and he wasn't ready to think about work. He was still enjoying his first vacation in over a year. He collapsed with images of majestic Tarpon dangling on invisible filament fluttering through plains of turquoise.

A bright sun pierced the bedroom blinds. He staggered from bed, hit the head, poured a tall glass of orange juice, and went to the balcony patio to collect the morning newspaper. It was already above eighty, humid, and high tide was filling the bay. He slumped into a chaise lounge overlooking the Gulf of Mexico, and, in spite of his languid status, was buoyed by the familiar trappings of summer on the beach.

Suddenly he felt the kind of panic reserved for those times he realized he was already an hour late for an important appointment. He ran to the answering machine. Thank god, the red light was still flashing. He retrieved Wally's message, scribbled down the details, and sank into his living room couch. "Fuck!"

On the way to the airport he called Wally, and his wife said he had gone fishing. It was a work day, but Derk wasn't surprised. Wallace Twill was only a part-time instructor. Fishing was his avocation. On a hunch he tried Wally's lab at The Training Academy.

"It's Derk. Thought you went fishing?"

"I am but right now there's big trouble in a small town," Wally said.

"Can't the locals take care of it?" Derk Bryan was an independent contractor, but his agreement with the Environmental Protection Agency required that he be available to investigate environmental mishaps involving major crimes. Apparently, this Tuesday wasn't going to include a beer and a grouper sandwich at Frenchy's Cafe on Clearwater Beach, but he wanted to be sure.

"I'm short on details, but a spill and dead body is big news in Zeeland. As soon as I heard about it I figured they'd call you."

Derk had worked for the Michigan DNR and was familiar with Zeeland. It was, indeed, a small town. The entire central business district was comprised of one street. Its claim to fame was that one of the largest office furniture manufacturers in the world was headquartered there. It was just east of The Big Lake, what the locals called Lake Michigan. Only three or four miles separated it from Holland, the industrious Dutch community situated on Lake Macatawa that opened into Lake Michigan. The area was famous for its annual Tulip Festival, wooden shoes, fishing piers, sandy beaches, and a sizable community of Dutch Christian Reform faithful. And the amount of snow in the winter allowed Derk to identify with anyone who lived through the Ice Age.

"Zeeland, that rattles the memory bank. Know anything else?" Derk asked.

"The plant is owned by Jack Von Lleuwan of Von Lleuwan Enterprises. It's not a big plant, a little production, mostly research, but they hold a lot of pesticide patents. Looks like some guys broke in, vandalized the place, and killed an employee. Tied him to a stool in a mixing tank. They didn't know the tanks were on timers, or maybe they did. It happened on the weekend and by Monday the only thing left was his torso."

"Holy shit! But why do they need me?" Key West had 225 restaurants, but none had a grouper sandwich that matched Frenchy's, and he'd been looking forward to one all week.

"The guy on the stool caused the tank to overflow, and some nasty stuff ended up in a nearby stream, 1,1 TT 4," Wally added.

"Cat-A-Lyst®," Derk said. "Highly acidic. Used to be common in making pesticides. Not anymore, but I wouldn't use it for bath beads. You still need a license to use it in anything that might interact with food or people, right?"

"Yes, sir."

Derk knew it was routine to be called when a spill occurred, but this seemed more like an accident than some sinister plot to skirt the environmental code. Someone died but probably not directly due to an environmental infraction. He guessed the EPA was just being thorough. In a couple days he could get back to Frenchy's. As he drove and listened to Wally he wondered if Von Lleuwan had a permit for Cat-A-Lyst® and he wondered for what purpose it was being used? He wondered what the intruders were looking for, and he wondered if any of these events might be connected? Curiosity, an occupational burden and an investigator's best friend. And he wondered how he would be received in west Michigan.

"You there?" Wally asked.

"Just thinking. Do you know what they took?" Derk asked.

"Don't think they took anything, but one thing was unusual. Some fellows on bicycles were seen near the plant over the weekend," Wally said.

"Any connection?" Derk had two bikes, a $2500 Kestrel that he considered the only bicycle with sex appeal and a used ATB he got at a pawn shop with the intention to rehab it and ride the beaches, scoping for coeds in thongs.

"Don't know, but they were nimble as teenagers," Wally said.

"Like stunts?"

"I guess so."

"A lot of people ride bikes, but not to crime scenes," Derk said.

"Thought you'd want to know. Anyway, if the spill wasn't enough, the dead guy was. Something must be awry there. So how was the fishing down there?"

It was a two-headed question. Wally always wanted to know about the fishing, but he was well aware of Derk's proclivity to fish for blondes. They'd known each other a long time. Wally Twill had not only supported his work, he had treated him like a son. Wally wanted him to catch a keeper.

"I'm at the airport. I'll fill you in later." Derk side-stepped the question and pressed "End" on his cellular phone.

He hoped he hadn't been too short with Wally. He had gone fishing on this trip, but he curtailed it and returned to St. Pete before he had intended. Something had told him to go home. Key West was one of the most spectacular venues in the world for sport fishing, and he had hired a guide who took him close to the Dry Tortugas where he landed two twenty-pound tunas and a forty-pound grouper. In spite of all of the bikini-ladened tourists on Duval Street, he had ignored Sloppy Joe's, Rick's, and Dirty Harry's all week. The thrill of landing a prize grouper had felt more rewarding than the temporal splendor of a one-night stand, but even that hadn't been enough. He felt out of balance, as if the status quo was about to be altered. He was proud that in spite of his forty-one years he was a trim, fit, above-average athlete, and still able to excel in most things that involved sun and fresh air. He was an unabashed protector of the environment because it gave him the freedom to work in his most comfortable surroundings, and it had a direct effect upon his quality of life. But a gnawing disquiet pervaded him as he approached the airport. He heard the same distant voice that had told him to cut short his vacation, and now it was telling him that something about this case was going to be unusual.

Pockets of heat huddled above the pavement of the palm and schefflera-lined causeway that formed the approach to Tampa International Airport, a stark contrast with his destination in west Michigan. He geared down his bright red, customized '86 Mustang convertible because the entrance to this airport came at him like a mangled maze of one-chance chutes. If he missed one turn he would end up back on the expressway and halfway to Clearwater. On another day he might have looked forward to that diversion and motored over to Frenchy's, but not today. As he approached another set of overhead signs he sucked in the supersaturated Tampa Bay air and veered into Long Term Parking. He locked the car and headed toward the terminal with a duffel bag and an attaché case. Within an hour he was aboard a non-stop flight to Grand Rapids.

3

Kate McCardigan was waiting in the office of her construction foreman when he arrived at half past seven Monday morning. John Westfield had called her the previous day from a pay phone outside his hotel room in Grand Rapids, but she had been leery about discussing anything on the telephone. She had been pacing for twenty minutes, reading and re-reading the news about the spill and the dead "half" body found in the Zeeland chemical plant. She'd been as nervous as a turtle on the expressway when she dispatched him to west Michigan so her anxiety was now about to bubble over.

"What the hell happened up there?" Kate blurted as John entered.

"Nothing. I told you yesterday," John said. "They didn't find anything."

She tossed the *Dayton Daily News* on his desk. It was opened to the article about the dead man with half a body.

"Are you crazy? What got into you? I just wanted you to find some documents. You didn't have to kill anybody!"

Her foreman's attitude suggested that breaking and entering and murder were routine occurrences to him. "What are you talking about?" He sat down and glanced at the headline of the article: "Body Found in West Michigan Burglary-Murder."

He raced through the article, then read the story word by word, his mouth agape and his eyes the size of cantaloupes. Kate leaned over his desk with her brow as crinkled as an aging Dachshund.

"Who was it, John? For God sakes what happened?" She was propped on her hands and the vessels in her neck protruded like a yard full of mole tunnels.

He stared at the article, dumfounded, like a student pilot searching for landmarks in a dense fog.

"Are you listening to me?"

Kate went around the desk and leaned beside him. When she was so close that the strength of her pheromones could weaken any man's resistance, she placed one hand on each side of his face and turned his head toward her.

"What happened up there?" She applied a little empathy this time.

"They heard some voices and split. That's it."

She retreated but stood next to him. "Did you touch anything? Did you wear gloves? Did anybody see you?"

He stared at the newspaper, but his concentration seemed inward.

"John!" she said.

"Not that I'm aware of," he said and looked up at her. "I thought it was strange that Mat and," he began to say their names but checked himself, "they told me the door was open when they got there, like jimmied open. There was a light on downstairs, but they didn't see anybody. They were in his office when they heard the voices so they just got the hell out of there. I didn't go in with them---I ran com and lookout---but I'm sure they didn't lay a hand on anybody."

His uncertainty was as poignant as the sound of her thumping heart. There was fear in his eyes.

"The police are looking for two guys on bikes." Kate paced in front of John's desk.

"No." He ran a hand through his hair and exhaled a billow of stomach acids. "They rode bikes around the place to check it out before they went in. Figured nobody would pay attention to a couple of guys on bikes. They were all pumped up, used to riding on Saturdays. It was after midnight. How would anybody see them?"

"They were doing tricks," she said. "According to the paper."

He shrunk into his seat. "They owed me a favor. I got 'em jobs here when they were kicked out of school. They traded a weekend of hill climbing for a couple hundred bucks, and I drove one of our vans so they could throw their bikes in the back."

"They're looking for two guys on bikes. They think you killed that guy," she said.

"They were trying to help," he said, trouble etched into his forehead.

"Where are they now?" she asked.

"I gave them the day off," he said.

"You've got me involved in a man's death, and I don't know if I can handle that."

"No, Kate," he said but she interrupted him.

"I've never done anything illegal. Never ignored a building code. Never bribed an inspector," she said. A twisted empathy overlaid her foreman's grimace. "But I was desperate."

"Nothing happened, Kate," he said.

"I've counted upon you since Scott's death, and you've been loyal, but this is different. I don't think you're capable of this kind of thing, but maybe you were trying so hard that things got out of control."

Her foreman took her by the arms. "I'm telling you I'd know if something happened in there."

She backed away from him and resorted to her role as his boss rather than his friend and occasional lover. "Take care of these guys. Keep them out of sight and tell them to be cool. Got it?" Then she returned to her office.

Kate didn't have a lot of friends, but a lot of people, especially men, wanted to be her friend. She was smart, rich, blonde, and beautiful, and she could use those things to her benefit if she wanted, but she knew that those things didn't guarantee happiness. She had the emotional scars to prove it. Now even her closest relationships were adding to her difficulties, and she was oscillating between guilt and self-preservation.

A rare female in a man's world, she was responsible for running a major construction company, left to her by her deceased husband,

Scott McCardigan. Her only child lay withering in a hospital bed, and her foreman was navigating in stormy waters without any charts. Two guys she didn't know could link her to a break-in and a murder, and she still had no irrefutable evidence to incriminate the man she knew to be responsible for her son's illness. As her stomach churned, her mind juggled competing emotions. Her physician recommended medication for her rising blood pressure, but her therapist suggested deep breathing. She sat down behind her desk and practiced inhaling deeply. "One, two, three, four, five, six," she counted before exhaling.

When she picked up the phone she remembered she had a golf lesson in one hour. She wasn't going to make it. As she dialed, her throat felt like sandstone, but she couldn't stem the tears. Her life had turned from charmed to cursed at the end of a spray gun. Her son's pleading, "Why is this happening, mommy?" felt like a fifty-pound weight around her neck, but it didn't make her helpless. Asking John Westfield to help may have been a mistake, but it wasn't a character flaw. She had resources, a few more friends, and she had learned to turn her anger into action. Jack Von Lleuwan was responsible for ruining her son's life, but he wasn't going to get away with it. As her old college friend came onto the line, she wiped the tears from her face and sucked in her stomach.

4

Derk was awakened by a sound that was neither a bell nor a chime, but a familiar combination of each, and a crisp, emotionless female voice that came from overhead. "Please return your seats to their upright position and fasten your seat belts. We have been cleared for landing at the Kent County International Airport. It's 1:30 P.M., and we'll be on the ground in 10 minutes. It's 72 degrees and cloudy in Grand Rapids."

The doze hadn't begun to cut into the sleep deficit he had acquired from the previous night. He was groggy and fighting off one of those low-grade headaches he often developed while trying to sleep in an airplane during the middle of the day. As he regained consciousness he caught a glimpse of a beautiful head of light brown, almost blonde hair, on the woman three rows up and across the isle from him. He didn't have a full view of her face but was certain she was in her thirties and quite attractive. He wondered why he was always seated next to some red-faced, twenty-something, homely, bookish woman on her way home to Cleveland after a week in the sun at her grandmother's home in Venice. For a fleeting moment, he envisioned a huge marketing success for the airline that arranged seat assignments according to age, interests, and marital status. Their motto might be, "We'll help you make the right connection!"

Just then the woman with the beautiful hair turned to hand her pillow to a flight attendant. She was in her late fifties, chunky-cheeked, and had a face that appeared to have been applied by Glidden. With that he returned his attention to the matter at hand and sketched a mental picture of the scene he hoped to find in Zeeland: a routine investigation, a brief report, and a quick return trip. "Conceive it, believe it, achieve it."

He was received at the baggage return by Sandra French. He faked a smile and uttered to no one in particular, "Oh Great! They would have to assign French to this case."

Sandra French was professional, competent, over-dressed, and bureaucratic as hell. She had earned her job through some familial connections in the Michigan House of Representatives. Derk considered her to be the least sexy good-looking woman he had ever known. She was five-feet seven, slender, a blue-eyed blonde, but his criteria included intelligence, political awareness, and a commitment to principle. It had been his impression that environmental protection was just a job to her, not an avocation and not a devotion. He doubted she got frenzied about anything with the possible exception of her hairdo.

She waved as Derk approached and then held out her hand. As Derk reached to shake it, she said, "Hello, Derk, my car is parked right outside."

"Hi-yea, Sandra. How've you been?" Derk said.

Her unmarked green Caprice was parked at the curb just outside the terminal. It resembled an oversized dill pickle. He deposited his bags in the back and slid into the passenger's seat.

It had been warm, clear, and sunny when he departed Tampa. Riding around in an overgrown pickle with Sandra French on a gray, west Michigan day was going to be a challenge, so he focused upon the spill and the halfbody found in Zeeland.

"So, what's happening, French?" Derk asked. "What do we have here?"

"A spill and a DOA in Zeeland. You know where that is?" Was there a note of sarcasm in her voice? She knew he was very familiar with Zeeland.

"There was some debate about whether to call you," she said.

"I heard about the Cat-A-Lyst®," he said.

"They had a permit," she said. Her tone was, indeed, cool. Derk rolled his eyes but didn't react.

"Light contamination of a minor stream. I thought it was a local matter," she added. She didn't seem to want him here anymore than he wanted to be here.

"Except for the body?" he said.

"Hard to dismiss that."

"I heard they broke in, ransacked a plant, and one of them ended up in a mixing tank. The tank overflowed and killed some wildlife. That happen everyday up here?"

"Obviously not," she said.

"By the book. Isn't that the way you do it?"

"Yes sir, Mr. Bryan. By the book."

"Are we headed there now?" Derk said.

A slight snap of the chin was her confirmation. She exited the airport and headed west on 44th Street.

"Anywhere around here a guy can get a good grouper sandwich?"

"What?"

"Never mind."

Suburban sprawl was in full bloom on the south side of Grand Rapids. As they passed through Kentwood, Wyoming, Grandville, and Jennison it was clear that things had changed a lot since his days in west Michigan. The auto parts plants, the furniture manufacturers, the low cost of living, the ubiquitous lakes, and the rolling countryside had made Grand Rapids the second largest city in Michigan. Derk preferred the poplar and spruce to the fast-food restaurants and townhomes.

Forty-Fourth Street became Old Chicago Drive before they entered Hudsonville in the middle of some bountiful farm country. The soil was the color of tar and the flavor of a side salad. Even with the windows down, the aroma of onions stacked in the warehouses that lined either side of the main road made his eyes water.

The plant was located on several acres on the east side of Zeeland a few blocks north of Main Street. It bordered on farmland traversed by a small stream. A small, white metal sign with the words Von Lleuwan Enterprises Plant 1, stenciled in black, identified the location.

A construction crew was erecting a chain link fence around the grounds. When completed, that wire barricade would enclose a chemical plant replete with a plethora of tanks and connecting pipes. Several tank trucks with the words Van Pool Trucking on the doors were parked in a lot next to a corrugated steel building, probably a warehouse. Next to the warehouse was an older, two-story, block building with a flat metal roof. On the door some faded letters spelled "Offic . . . " A partially visible imprint was all that remained of the well-weathered "e." A white Ford van with the name VanderVorst Security Systems was backed up to the office.

They parked next to the van and exited the "pickle." Two men exited ahead of them. One was average build, lightly complected, and wore blue trousers and a white work shirt with the name VanderVorst Security Systems on the pocket. The other was huge, broad shouldered, maybe six-five, mid 30's, with a crew cut and skin as pale as alabaster. He wore a black tie, a navy-blue sport coat, a blue denim shirt, black slacks, and black, pointy Italian loafers. In spite of the eclectic wardrobe and transparent complexion, what caught Derk's attention were his gloves. It was an eighty-degree June day, but he was wearing black, plastic gloves. As Derk and Sandra reached the entrance to the office, the man with the black gloves blocked their entrance, after proffering orders to the alarm installer.

"Who are you, and whattaya want?" His stare was made of coal.

Before Derk could respond, Sandra introduced herself, "Sandra French, Environmental Protection Agency. This is Derk Bryan. There was a spill at this plant, and we're here to investigate."

"The police already did. What are you looking for?" He folded his arms across his chest and his focus fell to Sandra French's cleavage. She stepped back.

"It's routine. When there's a spill we have to file a report," Derk said and tried to slip by him. He smelled like stale mash. The gloves were latex and even on this cloudy day, Derk saw Sandra French's creamy complexion reflected in them.

He blocked Derk's entrance. "Where you going?" He said and pushed him away.

Derk noticed something else odd about him. His ears didn't match, to each other or to his skin color, and one of them was stuck on, like a toupee.

"I'm sorry," Sandra said and reached into her purse for her card.

His hand swallowed hers as she held it out. "Nice," he said, as he undressed her with his eyes.

He separated the card from her as she jerked her hand free. Derk slipped between them. A big plastic hand enveloped his face. Derk stomped on the point of one of the Italian loafers which caused the offensive oddity to hop on the other foot. Derk turned sideways and jabbed his heal into the man's left patella. He fell like a giant maple under a woodman's axe and lay groaning, one hand on his knee and the other over his ear.

"Gloves, what's going on?" Another circus sideshow appeared in the doorway, a tall man with dark hair, a slight limp, and a patch over one eye.

"We're from the EPA," Sandra repeated her story.

"And this man needs to learn some manners," Derk said, readying himself for the coupe de grace.

"Let 'em in," the other man said as he helped Gloves to his feet.

"Where's my ear?" The dust coated his hands as he scoured the floor.

A sizable arc of his ear was missing, the edges shaped like teeth marks.

"Down there," Derk said, pointing to a piece of flesh-colored rubber on the floor. Gloves picked it up and lunged at Derk.

The man with the eye-patch stepped between them. "Get out of here," he said to Gloves.

After the man with the detachable ear left the other one introduced himself as Jack Von Lleuwan, president of Von Lleuwan Enterprises. "Sorry about Jimmy. He's in charge of security, and the break-in and this terrible crime have made everybody edgy. It's probably a little late, but we're installing a new security system." He stepped aside to allow them to enter.

Sandra French handed her card to Von Lleuwan. "I'm Sandra French and this is Derk Bryan."

"The police have gone over everything. What are you looking for?"

Derk appreciated that Sandra had taken the lead. It allowed him to observe the surroundings and evaluate the gentleman's demeanor. These guys were running some major interference, and he wondered why.

"Could you show us where it happened, Mr. Von Lleuwan?" Sandra said. Derk glanced around the room in search of anything unusual.

They followed Von Lleuwan through a couple of offices into a lab. Derk examined the tank where the body was recovered and searched for the lines running into and out of the tank.

"Does this drain lead to the sewer system?" Derk asked.

"This is a very old building. This drain is just for overflow. It ends up outside."

Von Lleuwan fingered his patch. He had revealed a code violation. "This lab is seldom used and never for anything as toxic as the stuff those guys got into, so we haven't had to re-spec it."

Derk made a mental note. That may or may not have been true, but it provided cover for his previous remark. Derk asked a few technical questions for which Von Lleuwan supplied the answers without reservation.

Then he asked, "For what purpose are you using Cat-A-Lyst®?"

"I'm not really sure. It's seldom used anymore. I don't know how those guys found it."

Derk wasn't buying it. Whoever was responsible for this little disaster must have had some knowledge of chemicals, and this chemical must have been readily available. It's doubtful they would have spent a long time searching for something such as this under the circumstances. They either grabbed something that was nearby, or they knew exactly what they were doing. Either way, Von Lleuwan was either incompetent or lying, and he was, without doubt, as odd as a Buffalo nickel.

"What are you working on?" Derk asked.

"I'm not at liberty to discuss that. This is a very competitive business."

"So you're working on something new?"

"We're always monitoring our production and trying to improve our formula. That's our business," Von Lleuwan added.

Derk didn't press him. There were other tactics. "Can you please give me a tour of the facilities and show me where the drain empties outside?"

Derk wondered where the research was being conducted if the lab wasn't in use. Or was it? Derk's intuition told him that Von Lleuwan was concealing something.

He took the tour and investigated the location of the outdoor drain. He flinched at what he saw. It fed into a small stream. Anything toxic would have lethal consequences for the wildlife in that water. Such a flagrant oversight angered him. Small streams led to rivers and they formed lakes. He knew that Sandra French had noticed it too, but he said nothing. He made another note. The rest of the tour didn't take long, and without further altercations Derk and Sandra returned to her cucumber shaped car, and they were on their way.

"Nice work back there," she said.

"Three-ring circus," Derk said. "Let's go by the Zeeland PD. I'd like to get a copy of the police report. Then I'd like to see Wally Twill." He had forgotten about the grouper sandwich and the nagging uneasiness he had felt that morning.

5

Kate needed someone knowledgeable, someone with a creative mind, someone sensitive to her plight, and someone she could trust. She hadn't seen Skip Trace since college, twenty years ago.

She had other friends, but there were two reasons for calling him. For one, he had a photographic memory. She had never seen him lose at bridge, and he was sought for high stakes trivia matches and assistance on term papers. He had a knack for drama, having been in more than one college play, and he had once met Kreskin, who had encouraged him to become a magician. So, he was crafty. He had also been a horticulture major and knew more about pesticides than anyone else Kate knew. But the second was that he had been involved in some serious shenanigans, the kind of stuff that would cost him a fortune in goodwill if it ever became public, and she was ready to play hardball if necessary.

She found Frederick Trace in the white pages. He had been nicknamed him "Skip" for his ability to find almost anything and anybody. He spent part of a semester tracking down a guy who had stolen a dorm friend's album collection and left town. Skip posed as a night janitor in the Administration Building and rifled the admissions' files to locate the guy's home address. Then he posed as one of the guy's ex-girlfriends, called his parents and told them she was pregnant. The kid called back within an hour. Skip threatened to call the police and the kid sent back the albums plus a couple from his own collection. They weren't worth much, but Skip said, "Petty theft gives real hippies a bad name."

He answered on the first ring, "Trace here. If it walks or talks, we can insure it."

The voice was deeper than she remembered. "Is this Frederick, I mean, Skip Trace?"

"Only if it's about sex or money."

"It's Kate McCardigan. Katheryn Ellis, Antioch College," she offered her maiden name to stir his memory.

"We don't go to the same club so this must be about business," he said.

"I need your help." She decided to use the direct approach.

"You dumped Derk and married into money, so I guess you're not asking for a loan." She couldn't tell if he was being humorous or sarcastic. "Your husband died. I'm sorry," he said. He sounded sincere.

"Thank you."

Skip continued unabated, "Left you the only woman in the state running a major construction company. Single, but elusive, and quite the golfer."

Same old Skip, direct and unrelenting. Nothing escaped him.

"I took up golf again out of necessity. Stress relief. You know how it is."

"Third in the state? That's a lot of free time," he said.

Maybe this was a mistake. "I've been lucky," she said.

"Modesty doesn't suit you,' he said. "What's up?"

She shouldn't have expected more after twenty years of silence. "It's my son. I don't want to talk about it on the phone. Can you meet me this afternoon?"

"Got appointments all day."

"How 'bout lunch?"

"You buying?" Skip said.

"Meet me at Elsa's at 11:45. Know where it is?"

"I've only got an hour," he said.

Kate waited in her BMW in the parking lot of Elsa's Mexican Restaurant. It was a neighborhood bar run by a group of local attorneys who formed a partnership with a talented south of the border trained chef and turned it into a popular hangout. Kate chose it because she seldom traversed the east end of town and hoped no one would recognize her. She could still stop a naked jogger on a cold day, and even in her gray tweed Ann Taylor suit she looked as luscious as fresh fruit on a spring morning, but she didn't feel that way. She hadn't been to the salon in weeks and renegade strands kept falling into her eyes. Her misgivings were compounded when Skip pulled up in an aging compact car that shut off with a blue burp.

Why did she feel so anxious, so exposed, so vulnerable? She couldn't help it that she was an only child or that her father was a successful real estate agent. And golf became part of her life when at six they had moved into a sprawling split-level adjacent to the eighth fairway on one of the most prestigious private golf courses in town. She didn't make these decisions. It was true that she left Derk Bryan, but it hadn't been as simple as Skip thought. She had accepted a teaching position in Dayton to be close to her ailing father. Derk had moved to Michigan to accept a job with the Michigan Department of Natural Resources. The distance and the time apart had become arduous obstacles. Scott McCardigan, whom she met at a coed golf scramble, had established a very successful career in the family construction business, was attractive, and fawned over her. They fit together well, and she wanted a family. Sure, she was like her mother, a housewife after a brief career as a schoolteacher, devoted to her family and comfortable with the expectations that wealth brought to her hearth. It was clear that Skip held this against her. He couldn't know the challenges she faced taking care of her ailing son or running a big company in a male dominated industry. He couldn't know about her loneliness, the high blood pressure or that she had been seeing a therapist for anxiety attacks. All he saw were the spoils of her agony and hard work, and he resented it. The truth was she did feel guilty and her brief conversation with Skip served as a reminder. After making the lunch date with him she had called her therapist, Dr. Draper, for an afternoon appointment.

Her greeting was rather formal. "Hello, Frederick. Thanks for coming." Her hand was extended, but her smile was fractured. Her need to trust and her need to protect herself were pulling her in opposing directions.

"Life's been good it appears," he said.

"And you?" she said as he released her hand.

Skip was still tall and thin, and what was left of his dark brown hair had receded above the forehead. But something was different. He still had the awkward gate, tended to cock his head to one side when he spoke, and his nose was long and narrow, too long to allow aging with grace, just distinction. She had met Skip when she joined the Environmental Club at Antioch College in Yellow Springs, Ohio, northwest of Dayton. Yellow Springs was famous for creating a green belt around its borders to slow down crass commercialism and suburban sprawl, and Antioch was famous for Rod Serling, who created *The Twilight Zone*. When she was there, Skip was famous. He constructed a tree house on the lawn in front of the Administration Building to satisfy his course assignment in Independent Thought and Self Sufficiency. The skinny, long-haired erudite in the bellbottom jeans she had known long ago and the man in the kakis, sandals and denim shirt standing before her were one in the same, but something had changed. He stroked his chin as he contemplated his answer. That's it, the goatee.

"Every day vertical is a good day," he said.

They took a table against the back wall by the divider that separated the bar from the dining area. Elsa's was already over half full, and Kate was relieved to find that no one recognized her.

After a few perfunctory inquiries about Skip's business and family, his impatience became evident. She recalled that he had afternoon appointments. They placed their lunch orders, and she forged ahead.

"I need your help. You're the only one I know who will understand."

"What's that?"

"My son lives in a respite for handicapped kids. He'll probably die there. He was poisoned by pesticides."

His sight narrowed, as if he were looking down the barrel of a gun. She removed a small packet of photographs from her purse and laid them on the table.

"This is my son from age three until about three months ago," she said.

The photos illustrated the transition from a vigorous baby to a dark-eyed, distorted, emaciated, sliver of a child with dark, mottled skin. He was dressed in a white smock and lay motionless in a sterile hospital bed surrounded by stainless rails. Skip studied each one, his mouth agape.

"I used to live in Washington Township near the Warren County border. We moved to Oakwood because I thought that the chemicals used in the orchard next to our house had made Trevor sick."

"Did you go to the police?" he asked.

"The police, the Health Department, the EPA. By the time I suspected a connection between the two, the orchard was gone. They were already houses on it. The Health Department said it was too late. They took ground samples, and that was it."

"What made you think it was pesticides?"

"You guys in the Environmental Club. You made me aware." She noticed a tiny gleam in Skip's eyes.

"Was it well water or city water?" he asked.

"Make any difference?"

"Pesticides from agricultural use have been contaminating drinking water for years. Groundwater provides half the drinking water in the United States. I coordinated one of the largest community gardening programs in the country for years, and I wouldn't allow any chemicals unless it was an emergency."

"They checked it."

"Who?" he asked.

"The Health Department." Her answer seemed to satisfy him.

"What did your doctor say?"

She clasped her forehead with one hand. She had covered this territory so many times.

"I know who did this," she said. "I just don't have the proof."

Skip reached for her hand. "Sorry, Kate. I need to know."

"Trevor has nerve damage that affects his muscles. He can't even go to the bathroom by himself."

Skip took another look at the pictures.

"The doctors know what he has, but they don't know how he got it, and they can't stop it. The toxins affected his central nervous system." She clutched one of the pictures and flipped it in front of Skip. "They think it happened over time." She held back the tears. "We couldn't take care of him, so we got help, but he got worse. Then came Scott's heart attack." A small stream of tears trickled down her cheeks.

Skip handed her his handkerchief as she reached for her purse. Between the table chatter and the clatter of dishes, her emotional display had become another part of the noonday din. She wiped her face and took a slug of iced tea.

"I had to take care of the business and Trevor after that. It was too much, so I put Trevor in the hospital. I didn't have any choice." Why was she defending her actions to him?

A middle-aged Latin woman with coal hair wearing a white blouse, black apron, and red scarf passed them carrying steaming plates of grilled steak burritos covered with red sauce, sour cream, and sides of rice and beans. The aroma and the Sangria reminded

Kate of the time Scott took her to that marvelous resort in Sedona, but pleasant thoughts of earlier times too often resurrected painful memories. And more guilt. One of her close friends had confided that Scott once said she had married him for his status and money. He worked himself into coronary condition. "Someone had to pay the mortgage," she could still hear him say. He keeled over at a jobsite after lunch with some big clients. She wondered if her husband's insecurities had killed him.

"I'm sorry about your son," Skip said as she drifted between the past and the present. "If his condition had anything to do with pesticides or chemicals or anything like that, you know I'd try to help, but it doesn't sound like you have much to go on."

"Help me get some evidence on this bastard!" Her bluntness was like a bolt of electricity. He sat up in his chair. "A couple of months ago a woman in Florida claimed that a company named Elgar Industries made her son sick with the stuff they sprayed on the orchards next to her house. She made the headlines when she stole a truck full of ammonia, parked it in their lot, put on a gas mask, and told the manager she was going to clean out their sinuses if he didn't tell the truth about poisoning her son."

Skip was stroking the end of his chin hairs. "I know it's hard to believe," Kate said. "I went to see her because I needed someone to believe me, and she was definitely committed."

"You saw her?" Skip said.

She leaned toward Skip and lowered her voice. "She lived outside of Tampa near some orange groves. I lived next to an apple orchard. Her son was about the same age as Trevor, got the same symptoms at the same time. I got goose bumps just listening to her." Remembering brought back the shivers. She rubbed her hands up and down her arms.

"You believed her?" Skip asked.

"She showed me the reports of contamination of wells and the Floridan aquifer caused by the pesticides in Florida. She said the government knew about it and didn't do anything."

"I believe that."

"She showed me an article about the alligators dying."

"Alligators?"

"The alligators' penises were deformed from all the pesticides used on the vegetable farms around Lake Apopka. They couldn't reproduce. Their population dropped by ninety percent."

"Alligator penises?"

"I checked. It's true."

"Deformities in frogs have been showing up all over the place, but alligator penises?"

She wasn't sure if he were being derisive or it was his nature to be comical. Their waitress interrupted to ask if she could refill their drinks.

"When I got home I did some research on Elgar Industries. It's a corporate shell licensed to do business in Florida. It's owned by a firm incorporated in the Bahamas, and its principal stockholder is Jack Von Lleuwan. He owns Von Lleuwan Enterprises, a chemcial company. And the company that developed the land where the orchard used to be next to our house in Washington Township . . . Clarion Development."

"And Jack Von Lleuwan is involved with Clarion," he finished her thought.

She nodded. "The Orchards, big residential development with a golf course."

"Damn, you've done your homework," he said.

For the first time since they sat down, she felt that he believed her.

"So you're convinced these two incidents, your son and the boy in Florida, are related?"

"I know they are, and so do you. Help me find out how." She leaned forward again, reached across the table, and took hold of his arms.

Her relief was catalytic when he responded. "What do you have in mind?"

6

It was approaching 6:00 P.M. when they arrived at the state police training academy in Lansing. Derk had fond memories of the place the officers in training referred to as "The University." It was where, as an EPA rookie, he had completed his training in environmental forensics. It was home to one of the most sophisticated labs in the state, and it was where he expected to find Wally Twill.

Once he determined that Wally had already left the campus, he walked back to the car to join Sandra French. He had long since metabolized the cheese and crackers served on the flight from Tampa, and although his hands were full of a copy of the Zeeland PD's report on the events at Von Lleuwan Enterprises, his stomach was as empty as an overturned dump truck. Sandra French was still a very attractive woman. For a moment he let down his guard and asked her if she would like to join him for dinner and go over the police report. She told him that she already had plans and asked him to brief her in the morning. He asked her to drop him at Wally Twill's house with no particular discussion regarding the next day's agenda.

Wally's wife came to the front door as Derk climbed the steps to the veranda. "Wally, look who's here!" she shouted back into the house.

He joined Wally in his home lab, comprised of pre-historic forensics equipment, work benches, an old computer, and an extraordinary collection of fishing gear. Wally didn't look up from his desk where he was tying some flies. "Derk! Look at this."

Wally had a series of flies in various stages of completion mounted in a small vice.

"These are killers. Trout can't resist them. How long will you be in town?"

"Don't know."

"We're going up to the Manistee on Saturday for some trout fishing. Join us." He never looked up.

Derk knew the area. The Manistee River flowed from north central Michigan south and west through some of the most pristine real estate on the planet before it dumped into the Big Lake at the little town of Manistee. Some of the best fishing camps in Michigan were tucked down those unpaved back roads. He would have loved the fresh air and the aroma of pine tar, but he had to decline Wally's offer.

"I'd love to, but I don't think I'll be here that long. How've you been, Wally?"

"Other than this bum knee, not bad! You go to Zeeland?" Wally said.

"Yes. How's the knee?" Derk asked. Wally had knee replacement surgery two months ago.

The old man extended his leg about three quarters and massaged the tendons around the kneecap. "I couldn't do this three weeks ago."

"So what do you know about Von Lleuwan Enterprises?" Derk said.

"They sell pesticides. Von Lleuwan holds the patents, and he licenses companies to produce and market them under various names."

"Know if they're working on anything new?" Derk asked.

Wally looked up from the vice securing the flies. He was short, had thinning white hair, full cheeks about the color of ripe tomatoes, and a modest paunch for a man his age, two years past normal retirement. He possessed a cheerful and disarming disposition although he smiled a too much when he talked, but he always had something kind to say. It was difficult not to like him. However, Derk had learned that his affable nature should not be mistaken for a deficiency of acumen. Wallace Twill held a law degree, a doctorate in anthropology, was a champion bridge player, and the best forensics scientist Derk knew.

"I knew you'd ask. They're doing more than just product monitoring, but I don't know what," Wally said.

"The operations manager claimed that that lab is seldom used and never with anything toxic, but the dead man was bathed in Cat-A-Lyst®."

The condition of the body made it a novel situation for Derk, for most experienced investigators, and some chemicals had washed into a nearby stream and killed some fish. That would have normally aroused Wally's interest. On the other hand, each case began in its own unique way, and they were all personal to somebody. Wally squinted, rubbed his leg again, and fidgeted with a small maroon and silver fly. Derk held it in place while he tied it.

"Somebody's not telling the truth, eh?" Wally jested.

"Can you check the files and see if they've ever been sited for chemical violations?"

"Sure."

"Find out what they listed as the purpose for Cat-A-Lyst® on the permit, and get me everything you can on that outfit. And I know you're already on it, but let me know if they're working on anything new?"

"You're onto something, aren't you?" From the corner of one eye came the glint of a proud parent.

"Just a hunch," Derk said.

"Stay here tonight and have dinner with us."

"Thought you'd never ask. I don't have a car. Sandra French is my driver."

"She assigned to this case?" Wally asked.

Derk recognized the ploy.

Wally added, "She likes you, Derk."

"Right!"

"She just thinks you're a little impulsive and politically insensitive."

"Because I didn't get my job through Uncle Bill's connections! She's a total political. No substance," Derk responded.

"Yeah, but she's a "looker!"

After dinner they played a round of gin rummy and talked about fishing, politics, and guy stuff. Wally had always been interested in the details of Derk's life. At times Derk felt that Wally would have liked to adopt him as a replacement for his only son, who died when he was not yet thirty. The affection Derk felt made him think of the contrasts between Wally and his own father. They hadn't talked much in years. He regretted that, but he didn't think it was his fault. Wally could be critical, but he was always constructive, supportive, and nurturing. Wally and Derk's grandfather were the closest things to a real father that Derk had known. Feeling somewhat melancholy Derk excused himself and went to his room to read the Zeeland police report.

At 6:30 the next morning he was awakened by the same eerie, unsettled anxiety that had pursued him for days. He couldn't explain it, but he was subsumed with a despair bordering upon hopelessness. It was the same feeling he had that summer his best friend moved when the kid's father took a job in another town. The following day Scoops, his dog, ran away. He didn't know if he were dead or alive or if he would ever see either of them again. He felt abandoned and the emptiness was more sour than a belly full of green apples. This was more real than that, more grownup than that. And there was the dream, the man without a face. That's all he could recollect except for the emptiness. He still had on his clothes, and the police report had fallen onto the floor beside the bed. Still groggy, he called Sandra French's office and left a message for her to pick him up. He set the alarm and went back to sleep.

7

"What the hell's going on, Jimmy?" Jack Von Lleuwan said. "I put you in charge of security, and people are coming in my plants like they were fucking shopping malls!"

Before Gloves could answer, Von Lleuwan looked at the man seated next to him, "Tommy, what the fuck's taking you so long? I want my goddamn plants secured now, not when you get around to it. I'm in a battle for survival, and I can't have scatter-brained schoolteachers and two-bit burglars threatening a multi-million operation."

Jimmy Swingle, Director of Security for Von Lleuwan Enterprises, and Tommy VanderVorst, the owner of VanderVorst Security Systems, sat across from Jack Von Lleuwan on the patio of his gargantuan split-level on Lake Macatawa, just a few miles west of his Zeeland plant. His home was excessive in every aspect, but it exuded his personality. The 6000 square foot main structure had six bedrooms, a study, a lab, a billiard room, two Jacuzzis, a weight room, and a small motion picture viewing room. Attached was a covered, heated pool and a squash court. He had a collection of Cadillacs from the 1950s and 60s that were housed in an unattached garage, and two other late model Cadillacs were parked in the drive. In Michigan, if you had an ounce of concern for the local economy you drove an American car, but that wasn't Jack Von Lleuwan's motivation. Much of his adolescence had been spent in the back seat of an old Caddy, and they aroused reminiscences of some great days before his accident. To avoid the ice and snow he had an underground passage constructed to connect the garage with the house. He had become extra sensitive to cold since he began spending much of the winters at his pricey, north Tampa residential country club resort. Sales of pesticides to U.S. farmers were over six billion dollars per year, and Jack Von Lleuwan had taken his share.

It was 80 degrees with a slight westerly breeze, and the sky was so clear you could see the entire length of the galaxy. It was the kind of day that made Michiganders leave work early for their golf courses, bike paths, beaches, and fishing holes. Von Lleuwan wasn't happy that he had to deal with these slackers rather than spend the afternoon on the golf course.

Jimmy was squeezing his ear. "Jesus Christ, what is it with your ear?" Von Lleuwan said.

"It keeps coming off." Jimmy was trying a new prosthesis. His wrestling career had been short-lived but costly on body parts.

"I told you to see Doc Caruthers," Von Lleuwan said.

"I'm not having no monkey ear stitched on me!"

"Suit yourself, but you can't go popping everybody who visits us unexpectedly. For Chris-sakes, you've got to cut down on the traffic in my plants!"

There are over three hundred pesticides approved for use on food crops in the United States and hundreds more available for pest control by businesses and homeowners. Not all of them were safe. He knew that, and he knew that concerns over food and water contamination had been forcing the government to stiffen standards. He wasn't sympathetic to the environmental "nay-sayers," but he could see that the days were numbered for some of his largest revenue producers. He had taken steps to overcome the potential loss, including increased security, and he was up to his skivies in personnel problems.

"We'll have Zeeland complete in a couple of days. We'll have a fence around the grounds and every entrance monitored. We'll even," Tommy VanderVorst said until Von Lleuwan cut him off.

"What about Florida?" Von Lleuwan asked.

"The golf course is done, and the second phase of condos has been laid out."

Von Lleuwan interrupted again, "I don't mean that, fuckwad. What about the plant?" He pulled down the patch and rubbed the area around his glass eye.

"We're securing the that now, hi-tech sensors, cameras and everything," Tommy said but didn't look directly at him.

He was interrupted again. "And the Simpson woman?" Von Lleuwan looked at Gloves who was still fidgeting with his false ear.

"She'll never be recognized even if she's found," Gloves said.

Jack Von Lleuwan didn't appreciate the carnage his security director had left behind, but he couldn't help feeling relieved that two of his problems had been resolved. He was used to overcoming obstacles. As a kid he'd survived an alcoholic mother and a part-time father. Jack's mother would drop him off at the country club in the afternoon before she made the rounds, and his dad would take him home at night when he wasn't traveling. As a caddy he carried the bags for most of the town's white, upper-crust men at one time or another. Eventually he assimilated the chauvinistic and privileged attitudes from what became his mentors during his adolescence. He used golf and his contacts to get a scholarship at Algonquin, a small Christian college in west Michigan. He became a collegiate golf champion in his senior year and graduated with a degree in chemical engineering. After college he pursued a part-time pro golf career but also took a job with a chemical manufacturer in west Michigan. He advanced from product engineer to president of his own company in five years through hard work and marriage to the deceased owner's daughter. An automobile accident claimed her and his son, crushed his left leg, and poked out one eye. He was in therapy for six months and wore a prosthesis below his left knee. He now thought it ironic that he was on the board of directors of the ultra-conservative Christian college where he had matriculated. The locally popular Dutch Christian Reform religion did not subscribe to Darwin's

Theory of Evolution, but Jack Von Lleuwan believed in the survival of the fittest. He was a living example.

Von Lleuwan acquiesced the point but didn't let up. "You were downright cordial to those EPA agents."

"They don't need to be around here," Gloves said. "There's nothing for them to find, no prints, and we created a fictitious file on the guy. Besides, it's a local matter, and your guy, Charlie Meeks, is in charge."

Von Lleuwan interpreted the reference to Charlie Meeks in front of Tommy VanderVorst as a challenge to his authority. He had always held Jimmy Swingle in disdain, not because of his few discernible skills, but because he thought Jimmy was a sick fuck. Besides his career choices and physical abnormalities, the guy couldn't keep his hands off young girls. By the time he was sixteen he had more notches on his pistol than a frontier gunslinger, and his propensity for force had landed him in reform school for gross sexual imposition. Because it was a juvenile crime, his record was expunged and the small, needy college that granted him a scholarship for his wrestling prowess was able to overlook it. After a tumultuous five and a half years Jimmy took a student teaching assignment at a small high school in upstate Michigan. During his brief coaching stint he knocked up an overdeveloped fifteen-year old on the girls' soccer team and spent the next three years behind bars.

Upon parole he was assigned to Esther Von Lleuwan, a counselor with the state probation department. It had taken her seven years, three failed careers, and a divorce from an alcoholic to graduate. She was Jack's only close family member, and he felt sorry for her. But he became incensed when she took a personal interest in Jimmy's rehabilitation.

"Do not mistake this man's educational experience for any sign of intelligence or docility," he told her.

"Jimmy is attracted to me, and, my god, he has the body of Adonis," she told her brother.

"Of course he is, but a store mannequin could arouse Jimmy Swingle. You're his ticket to freedom, sweetheart."

The terms of his parole denied Jimmy from teaching, and after a few years he was kicked out of professional wrestling for not following the script. His sister convinced him to give Jimmy a job, but Jimmy's history demanded that he set the rules of conduct with brute clarity.

He told Jimmy, "If you ever harm my sister or embarrass either of us you'll be the definition of deformity."

Von Lleuwan wasn't sure if that was a defiant scowl on Jimmy's face or not, but apparently Jimmy had forgotten what can happen when he failed to heed his commands. Not long after Jimmy joined the company, Von Lleuwan overheard a discussion among some of his employees that his security director had been swimming in the company's secretarial pool. He called Jimmy to the lab and proceeded to get him drunk. He had spiked his drink. He intended to immerse his dick in a solution of Cat-A-Lyst®. That would have forever put a damper on his sexual meandering, but he relented when he thought about his sister. Instead, he tied his brother-in-law's hands and held them in the acidic solution until they resembled blanched potatoes. After six skin-grafts they still looked like something out of a *Friday the Thirteenth* movie. Since the day they healed well enough that he could handle anything without intense pain, he had been wearing black surgical gloves. Maybe it was time for another lesson. He snapped the patch back in place.

"I'm talking about the fuckin' Environmental Protection Agency, you ignoramus," Von Lleuwan said. "Stop thinking with your dick. Ninety days ago all I had to worry about was my business and my handicap. Now I've got the EPA and the police in two states investigating me, burglars in my plant, and one of Walker's spies walking around right under my goddamn nose, not to mention two corpses. When you guys get these plants secured, I want Walker to know that we're on to him. Jesus Christ, Jimmy! You understand any of this?"

Gloves said nothing, but his kettle was just beneath a boil.

Von Lleuwan turned his Darth Vader glare upon Tommy VanderVorst. He needed him to feel that that uncontrollable, sinking sensation that he was smack-fucking-dab up to his armpits in shit and things were way beyond his control. He wanted the little wart to recognize that under the circumstances the fear of Jack Von Lleuwan was far more important to his well being than his fear of God.

"Any of this sinking in or do we need to recharge your batteries?" Von Lleuwan said.

Tommy sat mute.

"That all?" Gloves asked.

Von Lleuwan's stern stare ricocheted between them, but he added nothing.

Gloves headed for the door. Tommy followed like a berated hound.

"Gloves." Von Lleuwan seldom called him Gloves.

Gloves stopped, turned halfway around, and looked over his shoulder.

"Find out who broke into my plant. Tell Meeks that Jack Von Lleuwan wants to know, and I want to know before anybody else."

Gloves shuffled toward the house, ear in hand.

"One more thing."

Gloves stopped again but didn't look back.

"I'm not concerned about Charlie Meeks and the police. It's the EPA, Jimmy. This is not a propitious time to have them aroused. Try some fucking diplomacy. Can you do that?" Von Lleuwan said.

When they left, Von Lleuwan called Arturo Domingo, his V.P. of Marketing, from the phone on his patio. Art was a native of Central America and his father had been an interpreter for several US ambassadors there. Von Lleuwan hired him straight out of college by enticing him with a plan to improve the agricultural yields of third world countries with his pesticides. He paid for his graduate school and introduced him to all the amenities of wealth. After eleven years, Von Lleuwan had grown to depend upon him, and Art had always delivered. He had demanded only an occasional breach of ethics, but the risks had now increased to match the stakes, and he was counting upon him now more than ever.

"It's Jack. Meet me at the club this afternoon."

"I can't until after two," Art responded in perfect English.

"Make it three."

"What's up?" Art asked.

"There's shit all over the fan!"

Jack dialed the club and got a three o'clock tee off. Then he called Huissen's Travel and made reservations for Dayton and Tampa.

8

Kate waited for Skip in the lobby of McCardigan Construction Company. She sat in the receptionist's chair under the golden arches that rose above the counter of a scaled version of an original 1960's McDonald's restaurant. The bright yellow neon created an arcade-like atmosphere although it was only 7 A.M. She wanted to meet him before the business day began. She drummed her fingers on the arms of the chair. She wanted him to believe in her as much as she needed his help, and if he agreed to help she hoped she wouldn't regret it. She had volunteered to convert some of her company's insurance policies to one of Skip's carriers, offered him a rental car, and whatever he needed it. She wondered if she had gone too far. What could he really do?

At Elsa's Restaurant he told her he would help, but it was cloaked somewhere among these laborious lines, "Most of this country's fertile land had been wasted in the past sixty years by, among things, chemically intensive farming, and a lot of people are dying from it. The residue from these chemicals is contaminating most of the usable fresh water on the planet. It took from the beginning of time to 1945 for the Earth to reach two billion people and another fifty years to reach six billion. In our lifetime we'll reach nine billion. There are too many people for the planet to support under these circumstances. So, we end up with all these chemicals, and I have no doubt that your son is a victim of this abuse. Can I get back with you in a couple of days?"

"Good morning," she said when Skip arrived. "Come with me."

The walls of the corridor to her office were constructed of gleaming, almost antiseptic, white tiles. The lighting was florescent but didn't create the usual yellow tint of cool whites. The floor appeared to be brick red terrazzo, but it had an absorbent quality to it. Silence accompanied their steps as they padded toward her office.

"I'm impressed," he said.

"Everything's been made easy to clean with a minimum of effort and cost. Lights are full spectrum. Easier on the eyes, less tiring, and they make the food look more natural. They also cost less to operate."

"What's on the floor?" he asked.

"Recycled glass and tires. Reduces back and leg strain. Increases productivity and quality."

"Hi-tech fast food," Skip said.

"Our offices resemble the buildings we put up."

"Great marketing tool," he added.

They entered Kate's office. "We're putting up about fifty of these a year. Cookie cutter stuff, but it's our specialty. Free standing, pre-fab, hi-tech, fast-food restaurants."

"And environmentally friendly." Once again, she couldn't distinguish his compliments from his backhanded quips.

As she reached her desk a huge, white dog rose, somewhat unsteady, and stood beside her. It was taller than the desk by, at least, a foot. Its lips were furled on one side of its face revealing two rows of jagged teeth. It stared at Skip. Skip's pace slowed to that of melting ice. When he moved the dog moved. With each step toward the desk, the dog advanced. There was an unusual cog in its gears, but Skip didn't take his eyes off the behemoth's teeth. He walked so that the chairs in front of Kate's desk came between him and the dog. He was a big guy, but the reputation of the Doberman pinscher, black, white or any color, was enough to arouse trepidation. Skip kept the chair between him and the dog. The enormous creature was now across from him, huge, white, and drooling from one side of its mouth. If he were to sit down he would be face to face with the creature. He pulled away as the dog limped toward him. In spite of its size and posture there was something subdued about the animal's demeanor. His self-assurance, all of that protective casual arrogance he relished, had evaporated.

"Am I okay?" A whisper from a voice that had turned to hard taffy.

"He just wants to say hello," she said. "Rub his chin."

Skip held his breath. His arms were nailed to his sides.

"Go ahead. You'll have a friend forever. Well, for a while longer."

Skip offered the dog a timid hand.

"He's not well. I'm taking him to the vet this morning," Kate said.

Skip forced a half smile and moved one hand beside the dog's head, leery of being only a heartbeat away from amputation. "A dog a tenth this size took a chunk out of my face when I was a kid," he said.

"He won't bite," she reaffirmed. "Just posturing. Remnants of ingrained breeding and a small stroke that paralyzed one side of his body."

The dog tipped its head, and its drool plopped onto the floor. It had no control of its facial muscles. Repugnant yet sad. Skip pet him on the neck, but didn't place his hand too close to its mouth. The animal enjoyed the attention. Skip stroked its chin as Kate had instructed. Like a rag doll the big, bad animal collapsed against Skip's arm, wagged its tail and whimpered.

A gush of warm air large enough to fill the room rushed from Skip's semi-paralyzed body. He sat down.

"He's about as dangerous as a sedated gerbil," she said.

"What's his name?" Skip asked.

"Hope, after Great White Hope. Scott got it for security when we lived in the country. I think he thought it made his family complete. I'm not a dog person, but Trevor loved it. The Great White Hope has withered away, though, and as you can see, in spite his size and permanent growl, his greatest deterrence now is his reputation."

Hope shuffled to the other side of the desk and lied down next to Kate. She patted the dog on the head.

"He's the last connection to the men in my life," she said, hesitated and exclaimed, "and that is why we're here. Right?"

Skip stroked his goatee. "Doberman pinscher, eh, bred and trained by the Germans as attack dogs. They've earned their reputations. White is rare. Some think it's the product of many rounds of inbreeding. Incest in human terms: uncle to niece, mother to son and such. Kind of makes you cringe, but it's not true. It occurs when a gene is dropped, a freak of nature. Also makes them prone to certain illnesses like blindness. It's a magnificent creature though. Must have cost a fortune," Skip expounded.

Kate shook her head. "Can we get on with it?"

"Nice place," he said as he glanced around her office. The large, plush white divan patterned with yellow and pink daisies was, indeed, feminine. The rest of the furnishings could have gone either way including the thick glass coffee table top that was positioned above a white enameled pedestal and a cherry desk and twelve-foot cherry conference table with matching chairs. One large splash of modern art hung behind her desk. Well-lit photos of buildings McCardigan had constructed over the years were mounted on the wall to her right. She adjusted the lights over the photos from a control panel in a small cherry cabinet on her desk. There was a PC on the matching cherry wood and stainless-steel credenza behind her desk, and a few files were stacked next to the computer. Her desk was clear except for a small, ornate, antique brass clock and a burgundy, leather-covered time manager. A faint but intoxicating fragrance, like a bouquet of fresh lilacs, wafted nearby.

"How we can find out what Von Lleuwan was using on those orchards? The stuff he used here and the chemicals used in Florida must have been the same. Don't they need permits or something?" she asked.

"How unusual. An almost fifty-fifty male-female balance," he said.

"Did you hear me?"

"They're supposed to," he said, studying the photos on the wall. "I could check to see if they filed for any, but it won't be easy to tie them down to these locations or to I.D. the specific compounds."

"What do you mean?"

"Part of the problem in determining risk," he said as he faced her, "is that the approval process for pesticides, and there's over four hundred of them, relates only to their intended proper use and the potential toxicity of the active ingredient in each compound. It doesn't take into effect delayed toxic responses or the interaction with other chemicals in the environment. Recently the government began using more rigorous methods for registration of new pesticides and more sophisticated equipment to test for toxicity, but most of those four hundred chemicals haven't been registered under the new criteria."

"So, it's inevitable that some of these pesticides will end up in the food?"

"You got it, Sally!" he said and refocused on one of the photos.

"And that's why Trevor was exposed," she said.

He got up and moved closer to the photo he was perusing. "Over two billion pounds are sprayed on the food each year and less than one percent reaches the pests," he said.

"What are you looking at?" she asked. Hope raised its head off the floor for an instant, then relaxed.

Skip faced her. "It's been known for a long time that we can switch to sustainable agriculture and use a lot less of this stuff. Since 1945 the pesticide use has increased by thirty times, and the crop loss due to the pests has still increased twenty times. These guys still lose a third of their crops in spite of this stuff. Of the three hundred pesticides approved for use on food, almost seventy-five are possible or probable carcinogens," he said, then glanced at the rest of the pictures on the wall.

"So how do we connect Von Lleuwan with the stuff that poisoned Trevor?"

"These things are just great big deep fryers in a box," he said. "Heavy-duty coronary factories in between the grease fires. That ever bother you?"

"Did you hear what I said?"

"I don't know yet. If he used off the shelf products according to label specifications that's all he has to do. He only needs permits for the new stuff," Skip said, then returned to his chair.

Kate fell back into her chair, running her hands through her hair.

"I'll think of something. Where are they located?" he asked.

"Zeeland," she answered.

"Really! Office furniture capital of the world."

"What's your plan?"

"Don't know yet. Why are you so nervous?"

"You're kidding." She got up but didn't leave.

"You asked me to help. I've got to start somewhere."

As she paced she brushed the strays from her face and noticed some brown roots in the lone mirror in her office. She had been a bleached blonde since she entered college and took immense pride in her appearance, but even that was becoming a victim of her quandary.

"I want to know what you're going to do. I'm not looking for trouble."

As she sat down Hope stirred. She patted his crown. "It's ok, boy." Her words defied the tension that washed over her when she thought about the dead man in the mixing tank. As the dog laid down Kate drifted into the past, searching for memories that would bring her comfort. After Skip left she called Dr. Draper to schedule another appointment.

9

By 9:05 A.M. Skip was aboard a flight to Grand Rapids, and an hour later he was headed to Zeeland in a rental car. He got the Von Lleuwan Enterprises corporate address from a copy of a D & B report Kate had given him.

He pulled off I-196, west of Grand Rapids, to buy a map at a convenience store. Within minutes he found himself in Hudsonville surrounded by the aroma of onions. The map directed him west on Old Chicago Drive. He was already through downtown Zeeland when he realized he'd gone too far. The main street curved its way through the planters, trees, and brick accents that had been added in an attempt to divert people from the mega-malls in Grand Rapids. It looked quaint, but he didn't want to shop there. The convoluted path through town just slowed down traffic and delayed his trip to Von Lleuwan's plant. By 11:30 his shiny black rental car was parked across the street from Von Lleuwan Enterprises Plant 1.

A work crew was completing a chain link fence around the perimeter, and there were two white vans parked in front of a building with the weathered word "Offic" on the door. The name VanderVorst Security Systems was stenciled on the side of the vans in red and blue letters, and an American flag waved in the background. A bald eagle hovered over the corner of the flag.

He exited the car and walked across the street in the guise of asking one of the work crew for directions. He was curious about the extra security. A kid in his early twenties with a brown crew cut, sawed-off body, and a pack of cigarettes rolled into his sleeve volunteered that there had been a burglary and a murder there the past weekend. The scuttle was some guys had broken into the plant intending to steal something. They got into a fight and one of them ended up taking an acid bath.

The crew cut continued, "Everybody in there," and he motioned to the office, "is tighter than a hermit's rectum. They're installing alarms, cameras, lasers, everything. The owner's so frigging paranoid he has a bodyguard. Big dude, professional wrestler. Meaner than a wounded rhino. No problemo for this guy, though," he said and pointed toward a cherry '57 pearl white Cadillac parked in front of the office. "He's loaded. Drives nothing but Caddies. Friggin' sweet, eh? And, he's only got one eye."

Just being on Von Lleuwan's grounds seemed to elevate the kid's social status.

"How long are you going to be on this job?" Skip asked.

"Couple days. Everybody's on overtime. Kicking ass," the kid said.

Another guy with a crew cut came out of the office and headed their way. He was huge, wore a levy suit and black tie with matching gloves that reflected the half-hidden sun as he lumbered toward them.

"That's him," the kid said, looking toward the building.

"Who?" said Skip.

"The bodyguard. Look at his hands. Some say it was a chemical accident. Don't know, but the guy's got a serious attitude. Once broke a guy in two in the ring. Frigging right in two."

Skip moved closer to the fence as the man approached them. The sight of the huge man with the eclectic wardrobe and the plastic gloves glistening in the noonday sun did get one's attention. Skip's chest felt like dried hide. Inside he felt the thumping of a distant drum. He decided to forego a formal introduction.

He turned to face the kid. "I see what you mean. Thanks."

"No problem, Dude."

Skip returned to the rental car. Just as he closed the door and inserted the key into the ignition the gloved bodyguard reached the car.

"Who are you and whatta ya want?" the huge man said.

Skip started the car. Before he could move the man placed one hand on the roof and another on the steering wheel and leaned his head through the open window. A piece of his ear fell into Skip's lap.

"The hell is that?" Skip brushed it away as if it were a tarantula.

"Excuse me," the bodyguard said as he reached between Skip's legs.

"Get off me," Skip shouted. As he spread his legs a large, black plastic glove encompassed his balls. He stuck a hand in the man's face but it slid off the three-day old bristle. Their heads collided. He felt the heat of the uncouth man's breath in his ear. Childhood images of Big Time Wrestling televised live in black and white from the Chicago Amphitheater flashed through Skip's mind. He envisioned the guy dragging him out of the window by his neck, hoisting him over his head, and spinning him around in an apparent prelude to flight that would end, not on the canvas but, against the hood of his car. Skip slid toward the passenger seat as the intruder recovered his prosthesis.

"Get the hell out of here!" Skip said.

"I asked you a question?" The man tried to slip the fake earpiece into place.

"Frederick Trace. I stopped for directions," Skip said.

"Got any I.D?"

Skip's reflexive thought was, "Who the hell are you? I'm on a public right-a-way. I don't need to show you shit," but he wanted to shorten his introductory meeting with this carnival oddity to the bare minimum and retain all of his body parts. He offered the man his business card.

Gloves kept one hand on the door while he studied the card. "Where you headed?"

"I'm in town on business, and I'm looking for a motel. I was told there was a Holiday Inn around here."

"Who told you that?" asked Gloves.

The guy was persistent and not as slow-witted as his appearance suggested.

"I guess I got the directions wrong," Skip said.

"Go down here." The oaf pointed in the direction of Main Street. "Turn right at the first light, and don't get lost around here again."

Thanking the man wouldn't improve their relationship, so he only asked for the return of his business card. As he reached for it Gloves stepped back and stuffed the card into his shirt pocket. He folded his arms and motioned for the insurance salesmen in the shiny, new rental car to move along. Skip didn't hesitate.

Skip felt like a kid who'd just escaped a troll's grasp. His mind and his body were advancing in two disparate directions. Kate's little drama involved some in-your-face, heart-pumping danger from which he should be scurrying as fast as possible. He wasn't sure what to do next. He needed more information, so he stopped at the local newspaper and purchased copies of every edition since the break-in and murder. Then he went to the library to find out everything he could about Jack Von Lleuwan.

On the trip back to the airport the leaden skies began to drip. It was so stuffy inside the car he turned on the air conditioner to keep the windows from fogging. He wasn't sure if it was his anxiety or his keen sense of observation, but through the mist it looked like the same car that was behind him when he left the plant and again at the newspaper office. Maybe it was the guy with the detachable ear. He put his hand on his ear, wondering why he wasn't home writing an annuity for some young married couple or taking his kid to piano practice. Or was it? In the rain he couldn't be sure. He recalled a poster pinned on the wall of one of his corporate clients, "Just because you think you're paranoid doesn't mean they're not after you." On the other hand, events there had piqued his inquisitive nature. He kept thinking about all the security? If the break-in and murder were just isolated events in this quiet town, why would Von Lleuwan go to so much trouble and cost to secure his plant? Post homicide jitters? Maybe. It's a special kind of person who breaks into a chemical plant. There must be something very important in there. Was Von Lleuwan hiding something? Probably. Everyone has something to hide. Who broke in and what did they want? Who was murdered and why? Was any of this related to Kate? He wanted to read the police report, but he didn't want to introduce himself to the local police. Who was this thug with the bagged hands, and was he following him? He looked again and realized that the car had turned at the last intersection.

By the time Skip arrived at the airport he had deduced that some of the answers must be inside Von Lleuwan's plant, but he wasn't going back there alone. A half-cocked idea took shape in his mind, but all of the questions still remained. He even wondered if Kate might be holding something back. He returned the rental car, and prior to his return flight to Dayton he added a connector flight to Tampa. He wanted to meet Eva Simpson.

10

In the morning Derk herd a knock on Wally Twill's front door.

"Derk! There's a beautiful, young woman to see you," Eleanor Twill's voice filled the upstairs hallway.

He wasn't ready for the day to begin, but he tumbled down the stairway to the living room. "French," Derk said. "Damn, you're punctual."

She looked exceptional for nine in the morning. Her hair fell like soft light, and her eyes were like diamonds on a warm summer evening. He couldn't help wondering what it might be like to get all tangled up in Sandra French's warm, wet snare. He tried to imagine the kind of man with whom she would let it all hang out. Tall, dark, rich, politically influential, someone with an inflated self-worth? Some early morning sour grapes and Derk was ready to hit the road.

"You said nine. What's your story?" Her response was just short of a reprisal.

"Give me a minute," he said and headed back upstairs. Halfway up he turned and said, "I'm sorry, have a seat. I'll be right down."

Promptness was a trait that Derk appreciated. On the other hand, his stomach felt like an empty conch shell. He hadn't even had time for a glass of juice. Trying to catch up on his sleep deficit of the past couple of days had caused him to oversleep, and he was restless from a recurring dream involving a faceless man hanging from a ledge. The image startled him. He realized that he was trying to rescue the man.

"Derk, can I get you a cup of coffee or some juice?" came a voice from the kitchen as he descended the stairway again.

"Thanks, but I don't want to keep Ms. French waiting," he shouted just as Mrs. Twill entered the living room. "And thanks again for dinner and the clean sheets."

"Nice to see you again, Derk," she said. She gave him a motherly embrace and a kiss on the cheek.

"It was nice to see you again, Mrs. Twill," Sandra French said and followed Derk out the door.

As they backed out of the drive Derk said, "Let's see what Wally's found. Go by his lab."

"About what?"

Derk ignored the question but in a somewhat commanding voice he said, "French." He paused and then resumed in a kinder tone, "Sandra, would you please stop at a 7-11 or something. I need something to eat."

On the way he tried to resurrect more of the dream. He could make out neither the man's face nor the location, only that he was alone with him, suspended in pitch darkness. Thirty-five minutes and a pineapple Danish later they arrived at the police training academy. Derk was finishing his third grapefruit juice as he and Sandra entered Wally's lab amidst a herd of uniforms.

"I don't have anything for you yet, but I'm working on it," he said to Derk. "I've got a class and a lab to teach this morning. Can you stick around?"

"I thought you were part-time," Derk said.

"Not today," Wally said.

"How long will it be?" Derk asked.

"Soon," Wally answered, looking at his watch. "I've got somebody on it."

"I'm going back to the beach. Call me," Derk said.

Sandra French said, "Goodbye, Dr. Twill," pirouetted and then followed Derk out the door and down the hall.

She caught him and grabbed his arm. "What's going on? If there's any information coming out of this department, it's supposed to be channeled through me."

He turned but kept moving. "I just asked Wally to find out something about Von Lleuwan. That's all." He told her all he wanted her to know.

"Right!" she said. "What do you mean you're going to the beach?"

"I'm still on vacation."

He had known Sandra French long enough to know that she knew that he wasn't telling her everything. He knew that she thought he was too independent, but he was surprised when Wally told him that she actually liked him although it was more a matter of respect due to his zealous dedication. He was somewhat set back when Wally said that she resented his unabashed confidence and his immunity to the consequences of his aberrant behavior. But Wally suggested that her feelings were probably more akin to jealousy. Wally had made Sandra French a topic of conversation after last night's dinner. In Derk's opinion Sandra French had neither his training nor his experience, so she had to play by all the rules. That he didn't hold against her. He thought she was hamstrung by her familial connections, though. She might have been a conscientious defender of environmental laws, but she couldn't do anything that might embarrass her uncle. So she played it straight. He understood this, but he thought it compromised her effectiveness.

"There's an eleven o'clock flight to Tampa. Could you take me to the airport?" Derk asked.

11

The previous evening Kate had left a message on John Westfield's desk that she wanted to see him the moment he arrived. In the morning he poked his head into Kate's office. She was kneeling behind her desk, looking for something in her credenza.

"I want you to leave the Von Lleuwan thing alone," she looked up and said. She hoped her foreman would appreciate a reduction in his involvement as much as she needed to reduce her worries.

"Why?" he asked, filling the open doorway.

"Just cool it for now. Things didn't go very well up there."

"You heard something I should know?" His squint produced a series of fine lines on his forehead. Her lower lip curled slightly, but she said nothing. "Kate, I didn't do anything up there, and the guys didn't do anything either."

She stood up and faced him. "What do you mean? You broke into a plant, and somebody ended up a corpse!" she retorted. She was wearing black gabardine slacks and an off-white silk blouse. The matching jacket was hanging on the back of her chair. Her hair, combed back, revealed her high, prominent cheekbones that were brushed with a little too much rouge. And her eyes were heavily shadowed. She had tried to compensate for her increasingly porcelain tint. Golf had once provided her with a healthy tan, but she would miss today's round, too.

"We didn't do it."

"It's in your best interest to stay low, so just cool it," she said.

His shoulders slumped. "What are you going to do?"

"Nothing," she lied to him. "Who were the guys that were with you?"

His face became a giant hook-shaped question mark.

"And where are they now?" she asked.

"I sent them to Florida with one of our crews. Why?"

"Not the Tampa job. Von Lleuwan's got a plant down there." She closed her eyes and pinched her forehead. The job site was actually in Brandon, about fifteen miles east of Tampa.

"I thought you wanted them out of town."

"Remember the woman in Tampa? Same thing happened to her son. Get rid of them."

Since her husband's death, Kate had come to rely upon John Westfield. He was competent, reliable, honest and her crews respected him. He had been comforting and charming at a time when there was no other man in her life. And he was handsome, with sandy hair, Paul Newman eyes, a chiseled chin, and a rock hard physique. Her female friends called him a hunk. She oscillated between her instinctive need to care for her son and her loneliness, her own need to be nurtured, and she had allowed herself to become more intimate than she would have under other circumstances. She didn't love John Westfield, and she didn't think she ever would in a way she envisioned a mate, so she didn't inflate the meaning of the physical component of their relationship. They were very different people. She drove a BMW. He drove a Gimmy. She lived in a $500,000 house in Oakwood. He lived in a century year-old "fixer upper" on St. Anne Hill. But it wasn't just the money. They enjoyed different lifestyles. John was a straight-forward, hard-working, red-blooded American male who preferred football and hunting to golf and weekends at the country club. Everyone had occasional romantic encounters that were destined to end. They were simply not meant for each other. He must have known that, but his increasingly obsequious nature suggested otherwise. And she had become so self-indulged that she hadn't addressed it with him.

"Not now!" he said. "I'll keep them out of sight. No one knows they're there."

She dropped into her chair, unconvinced.

"I won't do it. But I will go down there and make sure they understand."

"Put the fear of God in those kids. I don't want any loose ends," she said.

"Sir, please put your seat back to the upright position. We'll be landing soon," Skip heard a voice and awakened to a flight attendant's gentle hand on his shoulder.

Before he dozed off he was reading a copy of Marc Lappe's book, Chemical Deception. The condition of Kate's son had personalized Lappe's revelations, and Skip's reaction had progressed from anxiety to anger to fear. Pictures formed in his mind, as if he were a doomed character in a science fiction fantasy. In the dream he was mired on a planet, half of which was devoted to laboratories that ran night and day to create bio-organisms that could assimilate and destroy the toxic wastes that were exhausted by the engines of commerce on the other half. Dreary as could be, the outlook was exacerbated by the already outlawed concoctions, like the PCBs that were excluded from U.S. production in the 1970s, but were still accumulating in most living tissue. It was the rawest kind of Halloween. A stark world of urban silos, like chain smoking machines, rose almost beyond his vision and spewed out the by-products that were opening giant gaps in the protective cover. The landscape was bleak and littered with the poor, desperate souls who were forced to work under the sun's unfiltered rays. The more fortunate were pale, frail, and drawn from a life under cover or underground. What had gone awry? Although the primary biological purpose of any species is to perpetuate itself, in his dream, a sort of slowly growing insanity had taken hold. The chemical stew that he and his own brothers and sisters were cooking seemed unabatable even though it was responsible for the extinction of a hundred different species of life each and every day. Gone. Kaput! And he was standing in the stew up to his waste. Its touch was corrosive, but the fumes were intoxicating, and he could not escape it.

As Skip returned to his senses, the rush of the 747's engines were interrupted only by the whine of the landing gear as it locked into place. The seat belt signs were backlit in red and the flight attendants had taken their seats. Through the cabin window he watched the airplane descend through a rusty pall that was the horizon. His palms were moss wet and his head full of gunk. Was it a premonition or a bad dream?

People sometimes accused him of being fanatical, but Skip possessed no illusion about saving the planet. The Earth was billions of years old. It would survive. His dream served to reinforce the stark reality of evolution. He was haunted by the prospect that he would become part of another extinct species. He couldn't shake it. He knew that a catastrophic event had wiped out the dinosaurs, but he also knew that there had been four other such events in the planet's history, and one of them had exterminated over ninety percent of all life on Earth. As a matter of faith he wanted to believe that he is a member of a cogent species, blessed with the capacity for creativity and reason, but to have faith there must be doubt. And his doubt was shaped by the reality that we are still driven by our hormones and our most primitive instincts. He felt something cool and damp, his shirt soaked by perspiration. The sheer instinct of self-preservation that guides most species away from a collision course with disaster had been repressed or conditioned out of mankind. His dreams emanated from this unsavory cynicism, and Kate McCardigan reminded him that the consequences were very personal. He separated his cans from his bottles, recycled his newspapers, drove a small car, ate no red meat, kept the thermostat at seventy-five, and belonged to the Sierra Club, but Kate's son had caused him to look in the mirror and further question his behavior in the face of encroaching catastrophe. Doing so manifested his vulnerability and left him feeling he was in a free fall. He was afraid he was not in control of his life or its outcome. Regardless of what he did, it might not matter. The conditioned air from the overhead vents formed goose bumps on his arms. He pulled the seatbelt taut and prepared for touchdown.

The heat and the humidity caught Skip by surprise. He opened the top two buttons on his shirt. He wished he were wearing shorts, but he never wore shorts because the sight of his gangly limbs hanging out in public made him feel self-conscious. He looked paler than an empty milk bottle.

He commissioned a car from a rent-a-wreck agency and headed toward downtown Tampa. At a service station near I-275 he bought a county map and called information for Eva Simpson's address and telephone number. He took I-275 north through the S-curve and headed east on I-4. Even with the A/C on fullspeed he perspired like a soldered joint.

At the intersection with State Route 301, he turned south. He was unable to appreciate the lush tropical landscape of Florida due to the overcrowded expressways and oppressive weather. Even the giant palms seemed reclusive against the cloudless sky under the sweltering solstice.

Eva Simpson's address was a double-wide mobile home in Riverview that backed up to the Alafia River. Contiguous to her eastern boundary was a residential golf resort in the late stages of construction. A sign read, "The Orchards, a Residential Country Club by Elgar." He despised golf. Golf courses in this country took up more space than the whole state of Delaware, and in spite of Tiger Woods, they were the almost exclusive domains of wealthy white males. Their maintenance was energy intensive, and they used massive amounts of fertilizers and pesticides that washed into the local water supply. It reminded him that he forgot to write the letter protesting the county's new incinerator. It was going up next to an old golf course where three hundred new luxury homes were being built. The housing project would buy all the power the incinerator could generate, but those things always eliminated recycling efforts and exhausted toxic trace elements. Golf courses and incinerators, a giant mistake to cover up another prodigal indulgence.

Skip pulled up under the empty carport. The lawn needed mowing and the house looked empty. The solar panel on the roof surprised him. His wondered why every house in Florida didn't have one. He knocked on the front door, but no one answered. The air was as still as the inside of a vacuum cleaner. Only the occasional sounds of some construction equipment broke the silence.

He headed for the backyard. The lot appeared to have been cut from an old orchard. Tangelo and pink grapefruit trees circumscribed the house but stopped at her property line. There were several raised garden beds protruding from a sea of weeds. An unmanaged compost pile had sprouted squash plants in a small clearing west of the house. The path from the house to the river was bordered by a jungle of vegetation. He recognized the hibiscus, some Boston ferns, and a few century plants but couldn't differentiate between a variety of palms. At the river, the path, overgrown by a bank of mangroves, trickled into the water. The diversity of plant life was impressive, a tropical garden by northern standards, but the level of disorder was progressive. He would never have allowed this to happen at the garden center he used to manage in Dayton. No wonder this woman complained about the pesticides. She was apparently against any means of control in her garden. He wondered if she might be one of those environmental kooks, a tree hugger.

Judging from the weeds, the uncut grass, and the stack of unopened newspapers at the side door he surmised that Eva Simpson had been away for a while. Given that she was a schoolteacher, an early June vacation was logical, but it seemed odd that she would leave home for a week or two without stopping her newspaper or having a student mow the lawn.

He walked around the house and looked for a window with a view. He peered inside, but nothing seemed out of the ordinary. He didn't know Eva Simpson. He didn't know where she worked, and he couldn't ask the neighbors because there were none, all dead-ends. He returned to the rental car, unsure of his next move.

Skip backed out of the driveway. When he passed the mailbox in front of Eva's house he hit the brakes. As he got out of the car the heat rose from the street like water vapor from a geyser. He was dripping like a leaky faucet. He rolled up his cuffs to just below the knees, then walked to the mailbox. Among a few bills and the litter of junk mail was a letter addressed to Eva Simpson from the County School Board.

Four calls and an hour later, Skip discovered that Eva Simpson hadn't been to school the last week before the summer recess. He had a hunch. In the library he located the articles about her protest of Elgar Industries, her claim that they were responsible for her son's illness, and her arrest for trespassing. He called the P.D. to get some details and found that all the charges against her had been dropped by Elgar.

By seven o'clock he returned to Eva Simpson's house. The sun was still high on the horizon, and it was still ninety-three degrees. He couldn't understand how anyone could function in this climate. He had donned a pair of denim shorts, three-quarter length like the kids wore that he found in a variety store, and loosened his pinstriped oxford shirt another three buttons. He was soaked to his underwear. He wore a pair of dark blue sunglasses because he was self-conscious about being recognized, but he had to get inside her house before it turned dark. In his more impulsive collegiate days he had been involved in some serious pranks, but he had never engaged in breaking and entering. His tank was full of high anxiety.

Even though his risk of being discovered was close to nil, a person's home is sacred ground. His fingers flickered as if attached to electrodes as he broke the glass in the side door and turned the deadbolt. In a moment he was inside. Too easy. Why didn't people secure their homes better, but what troubled him more was that they had to. He heard the echo of his heartbeat against his ribs. An inner voice said, "Get the hell out of here." Time dripped like maple syrup. Skip glanced at the windows to see if anyone was watching, and he reminded himself that the place was isolated, and that he had been inside her home less than thirty seconds. He hyperventilated as he continued through the kitchen into the living room. Nothing notable was in sight. Two bedrooms were off the hallway. One appeared to have been a kid's room that had been converted to an office. The walls were light blue and decorated with kid stuff. A dark blue comforter with multi-colored cars was thrown over a single bed shaped like an Indianapolis racer. Would his son like that? There was a small chair and a desk, on top of which was a computer and a printer. Mounted on the wall above the desk was a large cork bulletin board. A map of Florida was attached to it, and red pushpins were stuck into various points of the map throughout west and central Florida. Its edges were surrounded with articles on pesticide and chemical contamination. Among the manila folders lying on the desk was one labeled Elgar.

Skip sat down, switched on the halogen lamp, and thumbed through the file. The name Von Lleuwan was circled on almost every document. Von Lleuwan had his hands in a lot of shit. Besides chemicals and pesticides the list included import/export, real estate development, and golf courses. She had D&B reports, a list of his companies' patents, and a printout listing permits his firms had obtained from the EPA. "Thank you, Eva Simpson," he whispered.

She had linked Von Lleuwan to Elgar Industries that owned Elgar Estates through some offshore affiliation just as Kate had said. The country club/housing development going up next door had once been a citrus orchard. She had been researching the effects of the long-term use of pesticides on the environment in central Florida, specifically Von Lleuwan's applications. As he sensed that the dropped charges and Eva's simultaneous disappearance were more than coincidental, he collapsed in the chair. A chill, like liquid hydrogen, crept up his spine. Their suspicions may have been true, but neither Kate nor Eva had the proof they needed to go to the authorities. Otherwise, Eva Simpson wouldn't have gambled on that tank full of ammonia. Skip looked around the room again. He was drawn to the teddy bear tossed upon the bed, the baseball bat, glove, and hat propped in one corner. Some toy trucks filled with broken dreams lay collecting dust on the windowsill. His throat turned to parchment as something metallic simmered in his mouth. His anxiety mixed like chemicals in a beaker with his paternal instincts, and the resulting solution turned to fear. He had had only two tangential encounters with Von Lleuwan Enterprises and each involved death or disappearance.

A red light flashed on the answering machine as the telephone rang. It lifted him half a foot off the seat, and his knee hit the bottom of the lap drawer.

"Jesus-milly!" he shrieked. He grabbed his knee and massaged the pain, then got up and hobbled around the room until he heard the voice being recorded by answering machine.

"Mrs. Simpson, this is Miss Whistlethwaite from the Ward Institute. We haven't heard from you in a couple of weeks, and we wondered if something might be wrong. Your son hasn't been very responsive lately, and a visit by you would be helpful. Please give me a call as soon as possible. Thank you."

He hobbled back to the desk, found a note pad and jotted down the names, Miss Whistlethwaite, Ward Institute. The woman from the institute had called her Mrs. Simpson. Other than her son, he had seen no familiar male signs in her house and assumed that she must be divorced or widowed. He also scribbled the words Clarion Development and Elgar Industries on the pad and highlighted them with a big question mark.

He glanced at his watch. Less than an hour of daylight remained. He found a telephone book and looked up two addresses, The Holiday Inn near the airport and Elgar Industries. There was no Elgar Industries, but there was an Elgar Chemical Company. He wrote the addresses on the note pad, tore off the page, gathered up the Elgar file, and left.

The Elgar plant was located in the Port of Tampa off Twenty-Second Street on the east side of Tampa. As he reached the acme of the bridge on Causeway Boulevard that elevated above the harbor, several ships, their hulls brimming with cargo from around the world, came into view. The downtown Tampa skyline formed a silhouette behind them as the sun began its descent. It was a site quite different from anything he was used to in Ohio. But in spite of the panoramic view he felt only the cold, industrial reality of the moment. He was in a strange place twelve hundred miles from home. The climate was oppressive. He was down to his T-shirt. He knew no one here, and no one knew he was here. He was now convinced that Von Lleuwan was responsible for the children's illnesses, but he had no smoking gun proof and only a semi-baked idea of how to get it. He was headed for one of Von Lleuwan's plants, and he couldn't shake the obvious deduction that Eva Simpson had been there and disappeared.

Most people visit Florida to take in the sun and beaches, the game fishing, the amusement parks, or just to get a respite from the long northern winters. They dress down, relax, and enjoy the sub-tropical surroundings. That had never appealed to him until now. He found some temporary comfort imagining he were headed back to meet his wife who was waiting to have dinner with him and plan another mindless day at their beachfront vacation resort.

He parked across from the entrance to the plant. Just as in Michigan, a new security fence that would circumscribe the facility was nearing completion. The two white panel trucks were unmarked, but he recognized the work uniforms with the name VanderVorst Security Systems printed on the shirts. There was a large tanker in the yard with the name Van Pool Trucking on its door. Deja-vu!

The old clunker's A/C system was not adequate for his needs. Skip was down to his underwear. He slinked down and watched as the last of the workers departed. The entire area, as far into the distance as his ground level vantage point would allow, was filled with huge tanks and bulging bins. Of course, this was the Port of Tampa, the largest storehouse of chemicals in the southeastern United States. The scent of ammonia drifted by him, and the air abraded his skin. It was similar to the aroma under his kitchen sink, but this was an industrial grade mixture. An eeriness, like a dark cloud, wafted above the evening tide and reminding him that with each breath he took in six hundred times more chlorine than Moses did during his life. If he stayed much longer he was certain that the contents of his body would dissolve onto the seat of the car, then evaporate as if he'd never existed.

He headed for a motel. As twilight ascended, the pastel neon of Ybor City soothed some of his fears. He was hungry and he had some reading to do, but first he would tell Kate McCardigan what he found. Then he would call his wife. When he awakened this morning, Shirley had most certainly not expected him to spend the night in Tampa. Right now, though, he longed for an air-conditioned room and a cool shower.

13

Derk seemed like a stranger in his own bed, considering the venue of his past two weeks, and he writhed in the cool, dank percale that had become a twisted entrapment. Leery of the figure on the ledge below him, he couldn't will the face into focus. The figure slipped backward into a darkness. Derk lurched for him, but his grip was tenuous. He sensed a familiarity, and the man, yes, it was a man, seemed almost disinterested in Derk's effort, as if resigned to a fate. What Derk felt was not only heavy but threatening, as if his own life were in jeopardy. He felt something wet and slimy cross his lips. He realized he was completely immersed in it, something gooey, something more viscous than water. Why hadn't he noticed it? He reached into the peril with his other hand, not knowing what to expect or how long he would last, as the downpour, slippery as glycerin but colder, chilled him to his core. In spite of his efforts the man was seeping through his grasp, slithering into the abyss, and taking Derk's soul with him. And then there was nothing.

Derk opened his eyes. The man was gone, but the image remained. What demons had been summoned from his past? Or were they premonitions? Or did it have something to do with this new case? He recalled a recurring dream in his youth where he was chased at night through an abandoned town by a robot from outer space. A child's dream, and it waned with the adolescence. He supposed this one would too, but he seemed much more real.

He stretched, rubbed away the grit, and began his morning ritual. He collected the newspaper from the balcony of his condo, where he had trained the deliveryman via a holiday bonus to throw it, and headed for the bathroom. After the sports section he threw some water on his face, patted down some stray hairs, and went to the kitchen to squeeze a glass of orange juice. He finished the metro and bay life sections while stretched on a chaise lounge on the patio overlooking the Gulf of Mexico. The sun was already on full active duty and a steady southwest breeze carried with it the aroma of bacon and eggs. He inhaled the sights and sounds of home.

The tide was low, and some stealthy brown pelicans cruised the shoreline for breakfast. They glided like leaves on a cloud, focused upon the waves below them. Graceful in flight but awkward looking, these genial creatures sometimes ended up in the tackle of the local fishermen who too often considered them pests and killed them. From California to Louisiana, they had not survived DDT, but in Florida there were so many pelicans they seemed omnipotent. They were magnificent in flight, and Derk assumed they must have served as models for our best-designed aircraft. An immature male, distinguishable by its lack of gray feathers, dived toward the Gulf. Before impact its wings parted to break the descent and its head submarined into the water. Moments later it surfaced, bobbed upon a whitecap, its bill empty, and scanned around it. Derk wondered if the pelican had swallowed its catch whole before surfacing, or had mistaken a watery shadow for a mackerel, or had missed its target completely? He'd seldom seen the pelicans catch anything during their aerial assaults, but he had witnessed this scene thousands of times, and he was always awestruck by the spectacle of the hunt.

He loved the gulf, so tranquil and so powerful at the same time. It rhythm, ever constant, reminded him of the interconnectedness of all things and the relative significance of mankind. Or insignificance. Beneath the surface was a bouquet of life so colorful, so plentiful, and so varied that it overwhelmed his imagination. It was from the primordial "goo" of this universal solvent that life had begun, and from which the bounty of the Earth had developed. The oceans were the only things on Earth with the capacity to dilute, reform, and assimilate almost everything that interacted with them. They provided a contrast of beauty and power so awesome they had their own god, Poseidon, not so many generations past.

Life on the beach wasn't always a vacation. He had been there when the red tide killed fish by the thousands and kept the tourists away. He had pruned tar from the feathery bodies of the great blue herons that had washed ashore as a result of the slashed hulls of giant oil tankers. He had friends who lost their jobs due to the decline of the shrimp and fishing industries in Florida and throughout the Gulf of Mexico from pesticides and chemicals spread on the overworked farms of the Great Plains that poured into the Gulf from the Mississippi River. As a diver he had witnessed the despoilment of the Florida Bay and the Coral Reef as a result of the overuse and misuse of the Everglades by agricultural interests, the land-hungry developers, and the uncontrolled population growth.

Two lily-white bathers with coolers and lounge chairs were staking out their place on the beach across the street, innocent and unsuspecting, as they prepared for a relaxing day in paradise. It reminded him that to the tourists on their short stays, the beaches and oceans were still a wonderland. The degradation had been so gradual they didn't notice it. He'd noticed it, and as he watched the brown pelican bob empty-billed on the turquoise waves, it motivated him.

He browsed the last twelve days of the newspapers that were stacked upon the dining room table. At 10:30 he called Wally Twill.

"Police Lab, this is Twill."

"It's Derk. What have you got?"

"An excellent weather report. You ought to go with us."

"What've you found?" Derk asked again.

"About Von Lleuwan? Not much."

"Come on, Wally!" Derk said. His old friend was making an obvious effort to test his patience.

"You should relax more." Wally laughed. "A couple of things. They filed for a permit to work on something that is protected from disclosure. It looks like EPA registration, probably a new product. As you know, EPA doesn't have to divulge, in fact, it's prohibited, from divulging trade secrets."

"What kind of product?"

"Don't know, but word is Von Lleuwan is in danger of losing some of his patented formulas from re-registration and some others when the new law is passed. Sounds like he might be working on a new potion."

"What's the other thing?"

"Von Lleuwan's got a connection in your neighborhood."

"Yeah?"

"Elgar Chemical Company, Tampa, Florida."

"Small world."

"Distribution, import/export. They're suspected of importing and exporting illegal chemicals."

"Like what?"

"Stuff that's banned here, but legal out of the country."

"Did you say Algar or Elgar?" Derk asked.

"E-L-G-A-R," Wally spelled it.

"I'll call you later," Derk said.

"I've got to tell French about this," Wally said as he hung up.

On the patio he leafed through a stack of newspapers until he found the article about the woman in the tanker who blocked the entrance to Elgar Chemical Company. Her name was Eva Simpson, a local high school science teacher. She claimed that Von Lleuwan was responsible for poisoning her son.

Maybe it was coincidental, but he'd been told that if one paid close attention to cause and affect, nothing was coincidental. These were not uncommon charges these days. She could have been inspired by the reports that State officials had known for years that the chemicals used in the orange groves in Central Florida were contaminating the wells of local residents, and they did nothing. Von Lleuwan wasn't immune to such charges, true or otherwise, but the

Simpson woman had been specific about Von Lleuwan. This was brashy action for such an educated woman.

He called the Tampa P.D., got her address, a telephone number, and another surprise. She'd been missing since the day the charges against her were dropped. He called Eva Simpson's home but got the answering machine. He knew one couldn't discern much about a person from a voice on a tape recording, but it was a sane and rational voice. He wondered why he had left his name and number. For some unexplained reason, he didn't think he would ever see or hear from Eva Simpson.

At quarter to twelve he called Wally again. Before Wally could complete his routine greeting, Derk interrupted, "I need the whole file on Von Lleuwan. Can you fax it to me?"

"Sorry. Sandra left with it fifteen minutes ago. Said everything out of Michigan went through her. Aren't you working together?" Wally said.

"Talk with you soon," Derk said.

He had programmed Sandra French's office number into his speed dial. Ten seconds later she was on the line.

"Sandra, it's Derk. I need the file on Von Lleuwan."

"What's up?"

"Just checking some things."

"I need more than that," she said.

"Come on, French. Von Lleuwan is connected to a plant in Tampa, and I'm checking out a connection with a missing woman who thinks Von Lleuwan poisoned her son."

"What's it have to do with Michigan?"

"Quit being such a bureaucrat."

"If there's a connection I want to know immediately," she told him.

These people were worse than cats when it came to protecting their turf. "If you want to know so badly, come down here and look for yourself."

"I'll be there in the morning," she said.

"Sure."

"I'm taking a 7 o'clock flight. Pick me up in Tampa."

"You serious?" She had already put down the receiver. He felt the muscles in the back of his neck cord. Sandra French would be overdressed and out of place, walking around with her EPA rulebook. He'd have to spend the better part of two days coddling her while she dogged his every move. The trip to Frenchy's would have to wait. As he paced between the patio and kitchen the telephone rang.

"Derk," said his mother with tears in her voice.

"What's wrong?"

"It's your dad."

The air was as suffocating as mill dust and his heart filled with ancient lava.

14

When Jack Von Lleuwan told Art Domingo to meet him at three o'clock that meant tee off at three o'clock, not "be at the club at three" or "I'll meet you around three." Von Lleuwan had already been waiting in a golf cart at the starter's table for fifteen minutes when Art arrived on the run at two fifty-eight. Von Lleuwan's underling had donned a red ball cap with the words White Caps in white letters over the bill, a pair of navy blue dress slacks and a blue pinstriped button-down oxford dress shirt. He carried a pair of golf shoes, white saddle trimmed in black, along with his bag, and gasped for air after he slogged the bag onto the cart.

"Cutting it close, eh?" Von Lleuwan said, looking at his watch.

Art slid into the passenger's side of the cart, his normal position when they played together. "I had to make a couple of calls. I knew you'd want to know what was going on at the EPA."

Von Lleuwan could tell his associate was harried, but Jack Von Lleuwan was more competitive than a flock of vultures after road kill. He gave no quarter. Even though he played on only one firm leg and with only one good eye, Arturo Domingo had never beaten him, except during the first three months of therapy after the accident. Art was at his side for everything when he was breaking in the artificial leg. They had played together and against each other, and they often played their own version of bingo, bango, bungo: first on, first down, and low score. At ten bucks per hole and one hundred dollars for the round, each player had $640 at stake. If you weren't competitive and played every week you could drop thirty grand a year. Many had to Jack Von Lleuwan because they either wanted his business or they were masochistic, but after the accident he had never asked Art to pay him, although he figured he would own the title to Art's house if he called the debt.

Von Lleuwan accelerated toward the first tee. "What the fuck's taking them so long?"

"You know these things take time," Art said as he removed his street shoes.

"Bullshit! Not this long."

At the first tee Von Lleuwan motioned to Art to take the first shot. "Go ahead."

Art finished tying his golf shoes and gazed down the fairway, his face a marquis of despair. The first hole at The Pines was picturesque, but it was also a 535 yard, par five with a slight dog-leg to the left about eighty yards short of the green. The fairway was generous but confined on both sides by a thick stand of huge Michigan soft pines. There was a sand trap on the right about 150 yards out and water on the left at two hundred. The green was sufficient but elevated. It sloped to the right and was surrounded by sand traps except for a twenty-yard approach where it met the fairway. It required length and accuracy, as did the following seventeen holes, and he hadn't yet warmed up.

Art took out a Calloway Big Bertha, bent down to place his ball on the tee. He retracted, grimaced, and held his lower back.

"Pace a little too much for you?" Von Lleuwan said.

Art massaged his sacrum, and leaned to stretch, but couldn't touch his toes. He stepped back, placed the club behind his head with one hand on each end, and did a couple of trunk rotations, each of which was accompanied by an "ugh." He took two practice swings.

"Thought you were going to get rid of that bulge," Von Lleuwan said.

His marketing director was thirty-five years old, five foot eight, had black almost curly hair, a smooth mid-tan complexion, and an even disposition. He resembled Lee Trevino or, at least, his cousin. The only sign of physical neglect was an extra fifteen pounds he had been talking about loosing for the past three years, and in recent months, that fifteen had usurped another ten.

"Working for you takes its toll," Art responded.

Von Lleuwan's only reaction was to tweak the patch on his eye. Art approached the ball, exhaled a mountain of air, and brought the club back slowly. As Von Lleuwan watched him, he knew he was concentrating on keeping his left arm straight and his head down as he had instructed him a thousand times. Art followed through with enough voltage to rocket the ball straight down the fairway to within a few feet of where he would have dropped it by hand if allowed, but the ball sailed low and to the right and caught the far lip of the sand trap on the fly at the one-fifty marker. Its momentum propelled it another twenty yards out of the trap to the edge of the fairway within a yardstick's length of a huge oak. There was no rough here, just fairway and forest. It was a miserable lie.

"Sheet!" Art shrieked through his teeth.

"You're falling apart, Domingo," Von Lleuwan said, shaking his head. He stepped from the cart, selected a Yonex driver, and headed for the tee.

There was a slight catch in Von Lleuwan's gate caused by the prosthesis below his left knee. After the pickup had severed the side panel safety beams of his '67 Caddy and crushed his leg, he installed a gym and hired a private trainer to help him strengthen the quadriceps enough to become agile on his feet, but he still couldn't feel anything south of his left kneecap.

Von Lleuwan was aware that Art Domingo's attention was fixed upon him as he approached the first tee. He had on custom tailored, three-hundred-dollar, summer weight, white linen slacks and a $100 red, yellow, and blue sports shirt. His shoes were 100% Australian kangaroo and died blue to match his golf bag cut from the same material. His name had been stitched onto the leather in raised white letters, and the buckles were polished brass. He hadn't batted a lash at the three-thousand-dollar price tag. In addition to woods at about three hundred each, he had a fifteen-hundred dollar set of irons. His putter was a George Lowe "Wizard 600," a collector's item last made in 1960. In Von Lleuwan's opinion, it didn't look right for a guy with eight grand in golf equipment and apparel to shoot twelve-dollar a dozen golfballs, so he used only Title Pro balls at over four dollars each, and he got out a new one for each hole. He didn't view these things as excessive or ostentatious, just the perks of a connoisseur who can afford them.

He placed the ball on the tee and decided to challenge himself today. He would hit over the water hazard and hug the left fairway. If he could drive out about two-seventy, he would try to hook a long iron around the pines and come up on the grassy approach to the green. Normally he would hit his first shot a little right of center so that the long approach to the green required a straighter, safer shot. Even if it were short on the fly he could roll it onto the green. Today's option involved a definite risk, but nothing close to his business challenges these days, and he needed some immediately positive feedback.

What augmented the difficulty was his restricted vision. He could only see with his right eye, the one farthest from the up-field view. It had taken him a long time to conquer the slice that had become the most frustrating residual affect of the accident, aside from the emotional loss. Despite therapy, hours of videotaping, and professional lessons, it took far more concentration than the average player for him to hit the ball with accuracy. Putting had remained the most difficult part of his game. He had noticed that when he stood over the ball with his Wizard 600 in hand, players routinely mimicked him by closing one eye in practice swings. The game was already difficult enough with full sight but almost impossible without it. He used this to his advantage. Anyone who played golf with Jack Von Lleuwan found that he was a man of considerable dedication and courage, and no one wanted to take advantage of a cripple. This cripple shot par, and when he took their money they were more amazed than upset.

Whack! The cosmos seemed to strain against the impact. He cleared the water hazard with a comfortable margin, but the ball stopped rolling a little left of the center fairway about five yards past the two-fifty marker. Ninety-nine of a hundred golfers, including most of the PGA, would have been thrilled with the lie. Von Lleuwan twisted his body, jerked his head, and grunted, "Damn!" He shoved the club into the bag and limped to the electric cart.

They headed toward Art's ball first since he was the farthest from the pin.

"What's taking Sid so damn long?" Von Lleuwan asked. Before Art could answer he continued, "I can't pick up the newspaper without reading some article about another pesticide being linked to cancer. If DDT is still linked to breast cancer and it was banned over twenty years ago, the public isn't going to trust any pesticide. There was a TV program last week about pesticide residuals on fruit, a harmless situation that results in the longest lasting, best tasting, most marketable fruit in the world, and all they did was scare the shit out of ten million mothers. You know, Art, there's a bunch of folks pushing legislation to ban a whole shitload of things."

"He can't push this any faster without drawing attention to it," Art said.

They stopped about ten feet behind Art's ball. Von Lleuwan tossed his own ball beside the cart, got out, and lined up a shot.

"I've got ten million wrapped up in this, not counting his two hundred grand. It's time he got his ass in gear. Eleven years on this. That's long enough. Tell him thirty days. And if he can't do it he'll lose more than his son's Harvard education. Tell the little beauro-twirp that!"

Von Lleuwan took an unmerciful cut at the ball. The report of the club head resembled small arm's fire as it shredded leaves and severed branches before ricocheting off a giant conifer deep in the rough. He was not in the mood for any explanation about EPA committees and approval procedures. He knew that Sidney O'Connor had already used his EPA position to move the approval of *PESTfree©* through the research validation stage of the permitting process. The EPA required in-depth research on all active ingredients used in any substance for which a permit is requested. Its technical procedures in the past may have allowed a lot of chemicals to be approved without thorough examination, but those days had passed. Technical advances made testing more rigorous for new products and many of the old products had been mandated to undergo re-registration. The EPA performed some tests itself, verified objectivity of third-party tests, and subjected the product to an economic analysis designed to balance the potential economic loss from denying a permit with any suspected health risk. That meant that as a result of the lawful use of a pesticide, a certain number of cancer cases might occur per million people, but the economic hardship created by the prohibition of its use was given weight in determining its approval. Von Lleuwan and his friends in the industry had introduced a new bill that would stop the economic impact review and gut the protections of the old legislation. More than a third of Congress received campaign contributions from his cronies and the agricultural interests to get the job done. In the meantime, the EPA had its guard up. Jack Von Lleuwan was aware of all of this, but he didn't want to hear about it today. He had a lot invested in Sidney O'Connor, and it was time that his investment paid dividends.

"He said they were going over the research again. He didn't know how long it would take," Art said.

"What research? That's what he was supposed to take care of. You said we could count on the little twit. The fuck's going on? We can't have everyone in Washington going over that data. You know how that place is. Everybody in a lab coat will know what we're doing before we get it permitted. It's bound to leak."

Von Lleuwan didn't share his manager's faith in Sidney O'Connor. Arturo Domingo had known Sid O'Connor since college. They had dated sisters at the same sorority. Later they came into contact with each other through their work. Von Lleuwan Enterprises had navigated the EPA approval process many times in the past. Sid O'Connor, a twenty-two year veteran of the Environmental Protection Agency, was cordial but not always an ally. In fact, he had worked against approval of two of their products. That was one of the reasons Von Lleuwan had suggested that Art ask him to help. No one would suspect anything. Besides, Sid was broke. He'd married Jill Johnson, from Shaker Heights, and after two kids, two dogs, huge dental payments, four cars, and a big mortgage in the suburb, she told him, "You will never make enough money in that government job to meet my needs." To make a bad situation worse, during the divorce his eldest son was accepted by Harvard at $25,000 per year, and Sid's mother required hospitalization for Alzheimer's disease. Neither her health care plan nor Medicare covered all of the costs. When Sid's ex-wife and her father's attorneys were done with him, he couldn't afford a pay toilet.

At first O'Connor rejected Von Lleuwan's proposal for altruistic reasons and due to the risk of getting caught. Von Lleuwan counseled Art, "Appeal to his logic. Tell him about the economic benefits of *PESTfree©*. Thousands of farmers want to change to less chemically intensive farming but lack the knowledge and can't afford the risk of failure. Tell him about the health benefits. Mothers will feel safe about sending their kids to school when their lunch pales are free of those nasty chemicals. And remind him why he got into this field in the first place."

It was a persuasive argument but not clinching until he sent Gloves to accompany Art Domingo. They presented him with a plan to compensate O'Connor in a way that would mollify his feelings of avarice and with a message that there could be unpleasant consequences if he didn't appreciate its value. One hundred thousand dollars of blue chip stocks were placed into a trust fund for his children's education, available until each of them reached the age of twenty-two, fifty thousand up front and the balance when *PESTfree©* was permitted. And his mother's institutional care was remedied in a manner that couldn't be linked to him. The arrangement was so clean Von Lleuwan worried that he hadn't maintained enough overt control over his man in the EPA, and today's news confirmed that.

Art removed a two wood from his green and white Naugahyde bag with the letters Slazenger emblazoned on it.

"You can't suspect O'Connor. He wouldn't put his own ass in a sling," Art said.

"That son of a bitch, Walker! That's how he found out about us. O'Connor leaked. I'll bet my ass on it. I want to talk with him, myself. Arrange it!" Von Lleuwan demanded. "By the way, does he think there's any problem with the research?"

"You know damn well there's a problem!"

"These government stiffs aren't satisfied until the meringue is on the pie and everyone's eaten a piece. Two universities signed off on it. The fuck's the problem?"

Von Lleuwan threw down another four-dollar ball and blasted it into the woods. A ruffle of dark feathers lofted above the trees.

Art shrugged.

"He knows specifically why we need him, doesn't he? Von Lleuwan asked.

"He's a bright guy. He knows what to do. Besides, he's got a lot at stake," Art said.

Art's response didn't muster the confidence Von Lleuwan was seeking. This time he swung so hard the undercut slammed into the turf behind the ball and severed the head of a five hundred dollar driver.

"Son-of-a-bitch!" He threw the shaft as far as he could. He turned to his vice president and shouted, "You got a fuckin' piece of paper or anything I can write on?"

Art raised one hand to shield himself from his boss's tirade. "You sure you're up for this?"

"Shoot!" Von Lleuwan said.

Art got out of the cart and placed his club behind his neck and repeated the trunk rotation exercise a couple of times. Then he took his stance and loosed a couple of practice cuts.

Von Lleuwan could tell a lot about a man by the way he played golf. He trusted Art Domingo. He was bright, energetic, steady, and loyal. He stretched, but he stayed within his limits. These were qualities that Von Lleuwan appreciated. So it occurred to him as he watched Art approach the ball that he had two options. If he hit it straight and short he would have to use a long iron for his third shot that would involve a hard roll onto the green. There were risks with a hard role onto this green, namely traps and pines. Or he could hit it as far as possible so that his next shot could be taken with a shorter club that would allow him to loft the ball onto the green and minimize the roll. That was the preferred option, and he knew Art Domingo would have chosen it if he were Greg Norman. He was just as certain that Art would get into trouble from the over-swing necessary to hit the ball that far, and he was damned sure that Art was under no illusion that he was Greg Norman.

Von Lleuwan knew what he would do in this situation. He would get out his big Yonex driver, or the new one he would buy to replace the one stuck in the ground twenty yards up the fairway, and smack the shit out of the ball. The goal was to get the ball into that goddamn tiny four-inch cup, and the closer you got to it, the easier it was. If you screw up on the first shot, you have to make up for it on the second. Crush the son-of-a-bitch! That's what he would do.

Art Domingo topped the ball. It rolled about one hundred and fifty yards and came to a rest in the center of the fairway.

"Nice shot," Von Lleuwan said and smirked. The grimace returned to his face. Art wasn't into the game, either. *PESTfree©* was stressing out everyone.

"Come on, let's get out of here. I've got to call Ludema and Waterton, and you've got to arrange a meeting for me with O'Connor," Von Lleuwan said. They didn't even take the time to pick up their balls.

Von Lleuwan found an empty office in the clubhouse and made a long-distance phone card call to Clark College. After sitting on hold for several minutes, a familiar voice answered.

"Dr. Ludema."

"It's Jack Von Lleuwan. Where were you?"

"Sorry, Mr. Von Lleuwan," he said. "Why didn't anybody tell me it was Mr. Von Lleuwan?" he shouted. "I was in the conservatory. To what do I owe the pleasure of your call?"

"Don't pleasure me, goddammit! Is there any reason to worry about the research you did on *PESTfree©?* I mean is there any possible way those freeloading gatekeepers at the EPA can hold this thing up?"

"What's happening?" Ludema said.

"They're reviewing the research again."

"Well, I don't know. I mean I don't think so. Not unless they duplicate the research. You know what we were up against." Ludema's voice bounced up and down as if he were on a pogo stick. "There's a problem, isn't there? Something you're not telling me."

"Look, you little wimp-ass labcoat!" Von Lleuwan said.

He had met Thornton Ludema, Ph.D., head of biological sciences at Clark Institute, when he was the keynote speaker at a conference sponsored by several Christian colleges to recruit students into their science curricula. Clark's image within the academic community was only exceeded by its reputation as an athletic power. The college needed a big name to increase its exposure and attract research money. To most people the name Thor might conjure up images of the ancient German God of Thunder, an omnipotent force. Thornton Ludema, on the other hand, resembled Pee Wee Herman, replete with the sniffly, ache all over, can't sleep a wink, feverish countenance. He was short and thin, with fine features, had a pallor complexion and tiny, almost beady, bloodshot, faint-blue orbs that were hidden behind an aging pair of brackish frames. A thinning wave of pale red hair went wherever it wanted. His only claim to fame was some research that had led to the development of an environmentally friendly method of discouraging slugs in vegetable gardens.

Von Lleuwan had attended a college not unlike Clark. It hadn't escaped him what hypocrites some fundamentalist Christian academicians were. He tested Ludema by asking him to participate in some incidental research studies, nothing of consequence, but over time the grants were like chum to game fish. Then he established a scholarship fund for science students. By the time he needed the research done for the registration of *PESTfree©* Ludema was hooked. The bait this time was a substantial contribution for the construction of Clark's new biological sciences building.

Thornton Ludema wasn't an incompetent researcher, just an insecure one. Sometimes he didn't trust his own conclusions, and he was under great pressure from Clark's Board to produce. But as he was about to conclude a series of successful test applications on the *PESTfree©* microencapsulates developed by Von Lleuwan's company, Ludema discovered some inconsistencies in the time it took for the product to break down in the soil and water. What made this product effective also made it toxic. In the late stages of decomposition the active ingredients of *PESTfree©* were considered harmless. If their chemical bonds decomposed too soon, however, they would become toxic in an aqueous solution due to the high concentrations of the active ingredients at this phase. The present formulation, while theoretically sound, at times, appeared flawed. However, he determined that the levels of toxicity would be minimal and most likely not harmful to people unless this occurred in areas where the water table was close to the surface or where contact occurred with water supplies after inadequate filtering through the soil, as in wells in the immediate area where the product was used. In effect, at its current level of development, *PESTfree©* was, at best, unstable. When Von Lleuwan heard about this he had said, "Your research inconclusive? I doubt that. Come on, Thor, trust yourself. You're a superb researcher. Finish this and let's get that new lab up."

Von Lleuwan insisted that due to the competitive demands of the marketplace, if Ludema didn't complete the research soon and give it a passing grade, it might never make it to the marketplace, and the funds for the lab, of course, depended upon that. Pure and simple extortion, and it worked! Dr. Ludema made a couple of changes in his research notes and deleted the bad news from the final report.

"So how are the plans for the new lab coming?" Von Lleuwan asked.

"What do you mean by that? I did your work for you. I've got a lot at stake here, too," Ludema retorted.

"Don't talk to me about stakes. It's my money that's building your lab, and I don't have this damn product permitted yet," Von Lleuwan said. A considerable silence followed.

"I should never have gotten involved in this," Dr. Ludema said.

"You weak-kneed nerd! You're very involved in this thing and don't you forget it. Check everything again and tell me if there's any way they can find out," Von Lleuwan ordered him. He put down the receiver with a clang.

He started to dial again, chastising himself for not carrying his cellular phone. He refused to take it on the golf course, not wanting to be interrupted. Art Domingo knocked on the door and entered without waiting for an answer.

"I tried to reach O'Connor, but he was out. Be back tomorrow. I'll see you back at the office."

Von Lleuwan dispatched him with a flick of his wrist.

"Hello," a male voice answered.

"It's Jack."

"You done already?" the voice on the other end asked.

"Nah, we quit."

"I wanted to play, but something came up," Clay Van Pool said from the private line in his office.

"I wanted to see how your new graphites played. You wouldn't believe Art. He's so damned nervous he hit the trap on number one and topped his second shot. We didn't even finish the first hole," Jack told his inveterate friend.

"Want to play tomorrow?" Clay asked.

"Can't. Big problems. Clay, you know the guy they found in our plant?" Jack said.

"Don't know his name. Why?"

"I'm pretty sure I know what that was about, one of Walker's men. Gloves is going to send him a thank you card."

"A what?"

"Talk with Charlie Meeks. Will you? Tell him Gloves needs a little leeway. He's sending a guy to pick up a large package. And about those guys who broke into my plant, I want to know who they were before anybody else," Von Lleuwan said.

Jack Von Lleuwan had known Clay Van Pool for years. The relationship between with Von Lleuwan Enterprises and Clay's trucking company had made Clay Von Pool a wealthy and influential man in this small community, and Jack Von Lleuwan never let him forget it. As a result, Von Lleuwan had occasionally extracted a favor regarding zoning or building ordinances in Clay's capacity as a city councilman. Today's request was of a different nature.

"What's he going to do, Jack?" Von Lleuwan heard Clay's half chuckle, a nervous habit when he was under stress.

"Don't know for sure. He just wants to take another look at the body," Von Lleuwan responded and paused long enough for emphasis, "when no one is around."

"Jesus Christ, Jack. He can't do that! You expect Meeks to go for that? What's he going to do?" The trucking executive did not chuckle this time.

"I didn't say he was going to do anything."

"Christ Almighty! The things I do for you," his old friend said.

"You worry too much, Clay."

"I'll talk to him, but goddammit, don't get us into any trouble we can't get out of!"

"Thanks, councilman," Von Lleuwan said. "You're one hell of a public servant!"

<h1 style="text-align:center">15</h1>

Bad things come in threes. A familiar cliché and Derk was far from superstitious, but he couldn't help wondering if he ought to stay off the streets and disconnect the telephone for a few days. He was already involved in a murder investigation and now the news about his father. If he got a call that his dog had been hit by a car he'd be surprised, but only because he didn't have a dog.

His dad's physical status had been waning for months, but his relationship with him had been strained for years. They rarely spoke. In spite of this, his mother told him his father's health had reached the critical stage, and she figured he would want to see him. Derk knew there was more to it than that. If he went now he'd have to make a decision he wasn't prepared to make, but he didn't want to disappoint his mother either.

Exercise might have been a stress reducer, but it was also a way to delay decision making. He opted for a ride up the beach on his Kestrel to burn off some calories while he planned his day. He was changing into cycling gear when the telephone rang.

"Wally?" Derk said.

"No, a voice from the past."

"Skip! How are you?"

"Never better!"

"It's good to hear your voice. Where are you?" Derk asked.

"Tampa, and I couldn't get this close without calling," Skip said.

"What are you doing down here?"

"Business, brother."

"How long are you going to be here?"

"I leave tonight. Let's get together for lunch."

They met at a restaurant near the junction of Routes 19 and 60 on the Clearwater side of the bay. Skip stepped from the entrance of the lobby as Derk entered the parking lot. Skip was wearing an Hawaiian shirt and denim shorts like the kids wear. They fell to his calves and had a picture of a roadrunner on a surfboard stitched to the back pocket.

Skip met him as he exited the Mustang. "Still driving that gas guzzler?"

"I saved this from extinction, recycled it, in fact. Nice duds." Derk smirked as they shook hands.

"Where do you shop around here?" Skip said.

"The middle-aged hip look is you." Skip's attire had always been casual but conservative. He must have gotten sidetracked in some beachside T-shirt shop.

Derk motioned to the outdoor patio that wrapped around the restaurant.

"Still got the motorcycle?" Skip asked.

"Yup and I'm working on another, '74 Shovelhead."

"You and your boy toys."

Derk acknowledged the inference with a raised brow and a back handed gesture. Skip had never challenged Derk's professional commitment but sometimes accused him of over consumption.

"You just come from a Hootie and the Blowfish concert?" Derk said, looking at his garb.

"Where do you get the time?" Skip said, ignoring his satire

"All work and no play. You know what happens?" Derk said.

They took seats and ordered. Skip loosened a couple of buttons on his shirt.

"How's life in the rustbelt?" Derk asked.

"Not bad for those of us who bought Rustoleum at 10 ½," Skip said, took a pinch of a perspiration stained, parrot and pineapple decorated shirt and waved it away from his body. "No wonder it's so hot down here. There must be a gigantic hole over Florida from all the refrigerants you release."

"Come often, use your credit card, but don't stay," Derk replied. "How's Shirley?"

"Fine. Says hello."

"She's with you?" Derk rose from his stool and looked toward the parking lot.

"No, I called her last night. When I told her where I was she wanted to come down and go to one of those topless beaches," Skip said. He bit his lip through a silly grin.

"How'd you end up with such a hot woman?"

"Sympathy, I guess," Skip replied. He made Derk laugh.

"And your son?"

"He's learning to play the piano." Skip beamed.

"That's a challenge." He knew Skip's son was autistic.

"Everything is, but we love him." The depth of his expression exposed part of his soul.

The canvas over the patio shielded them from the sun's intensity. Paddle vans whirred, a nursery of hanging plants cocooned them, a reggae tune drifted in the air, and the mood was upbeat. Friends sharing with friends, life as it ought to be. It was such a contrast with the events in Derk's life the past couple of days. To hear one, especially a dear friend, speak of love with such compassion refueled him. He gave his old friend a hug.

"And you? Still seeing the gal with the petting zoo?"

"The biker gal who bred the tropical birds?" Derk replied.

"No, the one with the tattoo."

"Oh, the pussy on her thigh." He laughed again as he recalled the massage therapist with the eclectic spirit. "Nah, she met some tarot card reader from Gibsonton and joined the carnival."

Skip shook his head in disbelief. He was a devoted family man, and Derk knew what he was thinking. Where did he find these women?

"I'm sorry," Derk said. "She went back to chiropractic school."

Skip laughed and held up his glass for a toast. "It's good to see you again."

Derk couldn't resist the opportunity to ask, "Seen Kate lately?"

"Been awhile."

Derk flashed his eyes and made a gesture with his hands that he expected more.

"We don't run with the same crowd."

"But you hear stuff."

"Only that she's got more trouble than anyone ought to have."

"Like what?"

"Nothing," Skip said and shook his head as if he didn't want to talk about it.

"Tell me," Derk said.

"What's it matter? You two are farther apart now than you were before."

"What do you mean by that?" Derk said.

Skip held up both hands in front of him and shook his head no. He didn't want to talk about it.

"So tell me what brings you to Tampa," Derk said. He had no idea that Skip felt that way about Kate and him. More than that, he was dismayed that he'd never told him.

"A client, a potential one anyway. I'm into commercial stuff now."

"Insurance?"

Skip nodded. "It involves a lot of checking and big risks, but big money," he said brimming with lust. "Ever hear of Von Lleuwan Enterprises?"

The room went mute, the fans stopped, the plants quit photosynthesizing. "What about it?"

"You've heard of him, Jack Von Lleuwan?" Skip said.

He didn't know if his friend was somehow involved with Von Lleuwan or a potential victim. All he could think about was the third thing, the cold, ominous feeling of something bad about to happen.

"What's your connection?" Derk asked.

"Liability coverage. Anything I should know?"

He wanted to protect his friend, but he didn't want to spook him. There was no clear evidence that Von Lleuwan was involved in anything illegal so far. Just a gut feeling. Although it shouted at him to tell his friend to forget Von Lleuwan, there were huge premiums at stake. It wasn't easy to raise an autistic child. And it was an unresolved case. He couldn't reveal information that might compromise a case or prejudice an innocent party.

"What a coincidence." He didn't believe his own words, but it was the only logical explanation. "I'm working a case involving one of his plants. Just started. Don't know much."

"I know what he does," Skip said. "Any chance he's done anything illegal?"

"Too early to tell. There was a small spill. That's all. I'd help if I could."

"It'd be nice to know before we get over exposed," Skip said.

"If there's anything wrong it'll be public knowledge. You'll know it as soon as we do." Why was he hedging? Skip was one of his oldest friends. He tried to ease the guilt. "I'll let you know."

"Thanks. How's your mom?" Skip changed the subject, and Derk felt the 500-pound gorilla fall on him.

<h1 style="text-align:center">16</h1>

Sheldon Walker, III was asleep when the telephone rang next to his bed. The clock radio's digital display read 5:07 A.M. as he answered with a groggy, "Hello."

"Mr. Walker, Mr. Walker, is that you?" an elderly male voice asked.

"Who is this?"

"It's Farley Dickerson, Mr. Walker. At the plant."

"What do you want?"

"There's something here you, uh, need to see. I think you, uh-"

"What is it, Dickerson?"

"Mr. Walker, I think you ought to get down here right away!" We, uh, found something in your office, sir."

"You what?" Between his sleep deprivation and the security guard's stuttering, he couldn't understand what the man was trying to say.

"Found something in your office, sir. I think you should get down here and see for yourself, before anybody else does. I wouldn't even take time to brush your teeth."

Wal-Chem was just one of a multitude of companies involved in the production of pesticides, herbicides, fungicides, and acaricides. Sheldon Winthrop Walker III's grandfather had started Walker Chemical Company in Detroit fifty years ago. It had thrived during the growth of corporate farms since the post-war years and had made the Walkers rich. Sheldon Walker III, Chairman of the Board, had changed the name to Wal-Chem at the urging of a public relations firm in the mid 80's.

Even though Walker and Von Lleuwan fed from the same trough, Sheldon Walker III hadn't considered them major competitors. One anonymous call from an EPA insider quickly changed his point of view. The man said he was attempting to clear his conscious by sharing unusually sensitive information about a new product to which he had provided what some might consider biased treatment. He expected no remuneration for his efforts, but he did require silence. All Walker had to do was say yes to a voice on the phone obviously weighted down by Judas sized guilt. Sheldon Walker III was not going to let such consequential information go unheeded, but he was about to discover the gravity of competing with Jack Von Lleuwan.

As Sheldon Walker, a tall, lean, bookish, sixty-something man, with white hair all awry and donning pajama bottoms, a white T-shirt and a suit coat, entered his office, Manny Poloski, his Chief of Security, was berating Farley Dickerson.

"Jesus Christ, Farley. How could you do that? How could you let those guys waltz in here like that? You know damn well they're not our regular cleaning crew. What to hell were you thinking?"

"They told me they were filling in for the other guys," Dickerson stuttered. "They said the regular guys had been put on some kind of emergency job, but they knew what to do. I didn't know? They were driving a Conway van."

Manny exhaled a bellow of expletives.

"What the hell's going on?" Walker said. "Manny, what's he talking about?"

"What we think, Mr. Walker, is that a couple of guys disguised as maintenance men got past Dickerson last night, and you're not going to believe this. Come over here," Manny said as he walked toward Sheldon Walker's private bathroom, replete with the amenities of a resort spa.

Manny Poloski pulled back the shower curtain and revealed a gross clump of pale, white, reconstituted flesh. It looked like a soggy old, discarded mannequin.

"My God! What's that? Who is that?" Walker said upon closer examination. He held his hand over his mouth and turned away. The limbless, distended, stinking mass lying on the shower floor turned his stomach. It had a head, but it was faceless. There was a dark, matted, pasty substance on its head that had been hair at a healthier time. Raw, frayed openings were visible where legs had once attached. Its arms ended in jagged fashion just above the wrists. The partially dissolved distal ends of the radius and ulna revealed what must have been a gruesome ending for whoever this was. "Who did this and why?" He said, glancing back.

"I've been looking through the film, Mr. Walker. I don't know who they were, but they were in a Conway truck. That's for sure," Manny Poloski said. "I'll call Conway as soon as they open and find out who they were."

"Shouldn't we call the cops?" Farley said.

"I'll do it," Manny said.

"And tell them what?" Walker said, "That you found an unidentifiable, mutilated, rotting carcass in my bathroom. You think I want every cop and reporter in Detroit traipsing through my office. Fucking *National Enquirer* will be in here next! This is a message, to me from someone, and we need to figure out what we're going to do before anybody else knows about this. You guys understand?"

Walker hid an unsettling fear from his security crew. Someone had slipped through his security and violated his personal space. These people were ruthless. He hadn't heard a word from Alerio Alvarez since two days before the newspaper report of the break-in and murder at Von Lleuwan's plant in Zeeland. He sensed that the body in his shower was that of Alvarez. It fit the newspaper description. He planted Alvarez in Von Lleuwan's plant, and told him that nobody would suspect a thing if he got a job in the maintenance department. He was to nose around and get some information on Von Lleuwan's new product. Alvarez ends up in a tank of acid, and now what is left of him is lying on the floor in his own private bathroom. Were these the normal rules of espionage or was Jack Von Lleuwan one cold, merciless, unpredictable son-of-a-bitch?

"But Jesus, boss, we gotta tell 'em. What are we gonna do with this?" Manny asked.

"Your brother-in-law's a butcher?" Walker asked and Manny affirmed. "Put it in a bag and take it down to cold storage for a couple of days. We didn't kill him, and he's not going anywhere."

"You serious?" Manny said.

"Just tell him you need a favor, something that needs to be kept cold for a couple days. Put it in a plastic bag so it doesn't stink and box it up. Nobody will know what it is. You're not doing anything wrong. We'll give it to the cops in a couple of days. Okay? Do it!" Walker commanded.

"One more thing, Manny, Farley." They were frozen stiff by what their boss had just commanded them do so Sheldon Walker had their undivided attention. "Not a word of this to anybody. Understand? Not a word," he said and walked out.

17

Skip was waiting for her when Kate pulled her Madeira flavored BMW 535 into the parking lot of the diner on Main Street near downtown Dayton that he had chosen for their meeting.

"I had a client who only worked on 300 series Beemers because he said the people who drove the 500's and 700's were too cheap. They'd pay forty thousand dollars for the *ultimate driving machine* and then bitch about paying three hundred to keep it running."

"You don't approve of me or my car," she said.

"Forty thousand dollars is too much to pay for basic transportation. Big cars are resource mongers and bigger pollutes," Skip said.

"You asked me here to talk about cars?" she said. As he opened the door to the restaurant she changed the subject. "Nice spot."

"You wanted a place where no one would recognize you," Skip said.

"Now I'll know where to go if I get hard up for a date or I need a dime bag," she said.

"And the best chocolate malts, real malt in them. Let's sit down there." He pointed to a booth in the rear. "This used to be one of the original White Towers. Burgers, fries, and shakes. The cooks in here are something else. I spent thirty minutes in here one morning watching a shorthanded short order cook handle seventeen customers. Served nine of them full breakfasts, twelve coffees, half a dozen Danishes, and seven 'to go' orders. It's an art form,."

She held up her hand. "In the midst of most of the pimps, pushers, and homeless in downtown Dayton, to find such competence is, indeed, comforting. But you've forgotten that I know all about restaurants. Now what did you find out?"

Before he could respond, the waitress arrived with a pot of coffee.

"Coffee, black, and a Danish, please," Kate said. The waitress poured as she looked at Skip. He turned his cup over.

"An egg sandwich over easy with lettuce and tomato on lightly toasted wheat with mustard on the side, hash browns, grilled not fried, light on the oil, and a large V8 with Tabasco. Lemon and a sprig of parsley," he said. The waitress didn't seem to take his last request seriously.

The detail by which Skip conducted every aspect of his life sometimes irritated her. She said nothing, but her impatience must have been evident.

"You won't believe what happened in Zeeland!" he said.

Her heart became arrhythmic at its mention.

"Somebody in that plant was murdered. Then this circus freak comes after me and his ear falls off?"

"You can't do this. It's too dangerous."

"You're probably right. I went to see Eva Simpson, and she's missing," he said.

She felt as if she were hop-scotching through a field of downed utility lines. The cream she had been pouring into the coffee spilled over the top.

He reached across the table with a napkin. "You were right."

"She's missing?"

"I was in her house. I saw the charts," he said.

"You were in her house, and now she's missing?" Kate said. She stopped stirring her coffee and fidgeted with some stray hairs that had fallen onto her face, then rolled the napkin he had given her into a tight wad. First, it was John Westfield, now Skip. More deep breathing. "What if something has happened to her and they find your fingerprints? Did anybody see you?"

"I surrender." He held his hands up in front of him.

"I'm sorry. It's Trevor. I'm going to see him today," she said. "What if we find out what caused Trevor's illness, and there's nothing we can do for him?" His condition evoked feelings from helplessness to guilt to anger, and she was already awash with distress. Skip sat across from her as the innocent victim of her emotional volley. He was sometimes tiring, but he was caring and relentless. She had, after all, summoned his help. She pictured her therapist's hand on her diaphragm illustrating the breathing technique.

"How is he doing?" Skip asked.

"Not well." The corners of her mouth crinkled like tributaries of a large river.

Skip placed his hand upon hers again. "Sorry, Kate. I know you have your hands full. Did you know that my son is autistic?"

"Oh no! I'm so embarrassed."

"Don't be," he said. "Is there any hope?"

She shook her head. Tiny sparrow tracks emanated from the corners of her eyes.

"It's not what we expected as parents, is it?" he said.

She shook her head again and put a hand on her stomach to feel if she was fully exhaling. "This guy is into all sorts of things. I read Eva Simpson's notes and called a couple of people. I even saw Derk."

She lit up like a flashbulb in a nightclub.

"I didn't mention a word about you or anything," he said.

She slumped into her seat. Was there no one she could trust?

"He's a friend, I was in Tampa, I wanted some information. That's it," Skip said.

"You promised," she said.

"I didn't' tell him anything." He sounded sincere, and she needed to believe him. "But get this. He's working on a case involving Von Lleuwan."

She felt like a fly being blown into an industrial fan. "What kind of case?"

"I don't know, and he couldn't give me any details."

"This is scary. Are you sure about this?"

"This guy *is* connected and he hangs with some *dangerous* people, but he's dirty. You know the place next to where you used to live, The Orchards. There's one in Florida with the same name, and guess what? It's right next door to Eva Simpson's house."

She folder her arms around herself to keep from shivering.

"You didn't know that? I thought you went to Eva's house," he said.

"I was, and she told me."

"This will get you. Von Lleuwan's a sort of 'local boy made good.' He serves on the board of the local Christian college where he went to school. A star athlete, he's six two, weighs about two hundred pounds, has black hair and dark eyes. I mean eye. He's got a patch over one of them, the left, from an accident that killed his wife and child and he has a gimp leg --"

"Mmmm?" She squinted.

"A prosthesis, a wooden leg," he said. "But get this. He shoots par."

"What's that got to do with anything?" she said, unfolding her arms

"He was a collegiate champ." He must have assumed that would be important to her since she was a golfer. Impressive as it was, she really didn't care, but Skip seemed so proud of himself. She didn't want to deflate him.

"You have been busy," she said.

"You don't know the half of it."

He had gathered a lot of information in a short time, but except for Von Lleuwan's golf game, little of what he had told her was new or helpful. She needed more substance, something she could use against Von Lleuwan.

"Anything else?" she asked.

As he stroked his goatee, she noticed that the years and the length of his nose made his eyes look like ink spots at the bottom of two deep wells. "I think Von Lleuwan may be working on a new product or has a product that's not performing well."

The heavyset, large-breasted, stringy-haired blonde in the yellow uniform and white apron brought their orders to the table.

"What took you so long?" Skip asked with a straight face, and then each of them smiled. He looked at his watch and after she left he said, "Just under five minutes. Can you believe it?" Kate made a funny clicking sound with her lips and shook her head.

"You know he did it, don't you? He made Trevor sick." Kate's focus narrowed, awaiting his confirmation.

"I'm not positive, but I had a guy I know at the Ohio EPA check all the permits Von Lleuwan ever applied for. He also tried to find out if any of Von Lleuwan's formula were under investigation. Turns out, nothing in particular, but many of his, as well as others, will be restricted when the new law passes or they have to comply with the Delaney Clause."

Kate shook her head. She didn't understand.

"The Delaney Clause is part of a law that was passed in the seventies that made it illegal to put anything on food that is a possible carcinogen. It hasn't been enforced very well. In the early 1990's some environmental and consumer groups forced the government to enforce the provisions that apply to pesticides," he said.

"I heard about that," she said.

He continued, "That led the large corporate producers and users to lobby for an overturn of Delaney. I think Von Lleuwan's into something new, and it may not be safe. It's just a guess, but the answer is in Zeeland."

She spit hot coffee all over the table.

"I know. I know," Skip said, grabbing napkins while looking for the waitress. "Somebody was murdered in that plant. I'm going to need some help."

"No, no help," she said, helping him dry the table.

"I'm going to call Player, Bear, and Dougal Ketchum."

She shook her head no.

He nodded yes.

"No, absolutely not," she repeated but he kept nodding. After a moment of silence she said, "And Derk?"

"Not until I have more information," he said.

She put her hands in her lap and stiffened. "I don't like this at all," she said. She had seen little of Skip and his cronies since she stopped dating Derk, but she knew her old classmates' propensity for the type of subversion that generated maximum publicity.

She couldn't confirm nor deny his request. She began plucking designs in the cream cheese on her Danish with a fork.

Skip slipped the last of the egg sandwich into his mouth and washed it down with the V8. He held up the empty container. "Just a second," he said. "Waitress!" When she approached their table he said, "What a waste. This can costs more than the juice, and it's environmentally irresponsible. That's why we're running out of landfills. Can't you buy this stuff in larger containers and pour it into a glass like everybody else?"

The waitress' head bobbed up and down. "You're right, but I don't make those decisions. Sorry," she said and walked away.

He looked to Kate for empathy.

"Damn it, Skip, what are you going to do?" she said.

"That's what we're up against: ignorance, greed, and incompetence. Ohio recycles less than five percent of its waste, and we rank fourth in the nation in release of toxic chemicals," he said but Kate interrupted him.

"With the guys?" she said.

"It'll be all right," he said and dismissed her concern with a stroke of his goatee. "There'll be some more expenses, though. Let me review the rest of your insurance portfolio."

"No way! I'm not putting those guys on my payroll," she said.

"What's your total worker's comp nut each month?" he asked.

"Come on, Skip."

"I might even save you a few bucks."

"This is my life and my business."

"I can help you, but I need them," he said.

There weren't many other options. "Frederick Trace, you're too much," she said. He may have thought it was a gesture of stress relief, but she meant it. She was twisting the hairs in her face that had fallen like her spirit.

"Have you ever thought about going self-insured?" He began a discourse on the advantages of self-insurance under the Ohio laws covering workers' compensation while Kate threw a ten spot on the table and walked out.

18

The phone in Derk's head rang again, and he leaped from bed, clad in faded magenta boxers and an old yellow Hilly Hundred cycling shirt. He couldn't mitigate the distress of his mother's call. In the dream he was lying prone, stretched to the limit of his grasp, dangling over the dark ledge in a frantic struggle to save the stranger. He paced with his radar more cluttered than an air traffic controller's. Images of the dead body, a missing woman, and an impending but elusive guest flickered before him like silent films.

He fetched the morning paper from the patio and headed to the kitchen for a glass of juice. Halfway he stopped, realizing this was not his normal routine. He redirected himself to the bathroom, and halfway there stopped again. He retraced his steps through the living room to the patio and threw the paper onto a chaise lounge. On the horizon, above the turquoise tide, a cruise ship in tow came into view. Its weary cargo draped from the rails, straining for a view of the tug pulling them toward the safety of Tampa Harbor. People from disparate places brought together by a single circumstance with their fate simultaneously tied to a broken propeller or an electrical short. Was it coincidental? He gave little credence to coincidence so he wondered whose lives would change and how as a result of this simple event. Or was the message meant for him? An old friend once said, "Sometimes things are as they seem to be." On any other day he would have organized his thoughts, prioritized his actions and proceeded with confidence. Begin at point A. A would lead to B and B to C. Or sometimes he worked backward. Today he didn't know where to begin. His father was deteriorating from the effects of Alzheimer's disease, but death was not imminent unless he ceded to his mother's wish. He didn't know if he was more troubled by the prospect of his father's passing or that he needed closure. Alzheimer's was as burdensome for the caretakers as it was for its victims, and caring for a man who had made her life much less fulfilling than she deserved had been a long and demanding challenge for his mother. Was he resentful? No doubt about it. His father's absences had been as hard for her as they were for him. She deserved the relief that his father's passing would bring, but the business of life and death was God's domain. That had been his philosophy, but his mother's call made it clear that it wasn't entirely true.

He replaced the boxers with a pair of cycling shorts, donned his clip-less shoes, grabbed a full water bottle from the refrigerator, and bounded down the stairs to the garage. A hard ride up the beach would clear his head, and in the process, a resolution would appear. At least it was a plan, and he would call his mother when he returned.

19

Platinum clouds dripped like a rung sponge as Skip slogged toward his meeting with Player, Bear, and Dougal Ketchum. The rain turned into a thunderstorm of epic proportions. The firmament cracked like whips prodding a team of fuming steeds, and sheets of Plexiglas rained from the sky. The curbs overflowed, slowing traffic to a knotty crawl. Twice he was forced to a stop by idling cars, rocking in the street, stranded like beached watercraft. He should have turned back and rescheduled the whole thing, but he was counting upon their help even though there was little room to candy coat the news about Jack Von Lleuwan. None of them respected Kate McCardigan, but what had happened to her son could have happened to any of their kids.

As Cornell Drive became Little Richmond Road past Gettysburg, the rain subsided to a steady drizzle. With the spontaneity of a prairie wildfire, the clouds exploded in malaise of color. The horizon temporarily blinded him. As suddenly as it had appeared, the giant fireball receded into a silvery envelope and the clouds compacted against a peach and azure firmament. The sun pried open the clouds as if someone were removing the lid from a boiling kettle, until everything before him was consumed by it. He glanced into the rearview mirror. A serpent of lights slithered down the slope behind him. A bend in the road turned him away from the sun, and a rainbow appeared, ground to ground. It was less than five minutes of raw cinematography but reinforced the sheer delight of being human.

Player's house was a model for conservation, designed after the Urban Integral House in Berkeley during the 1970s. It had a solar water heater, a greenhouse, a gray-water system, a compost toilet, banks of photovoltaic cells, and a windmill. An old, two-story Victorian, it sat on an acre and a half slightly elevated above the road. A covered porch with a spindle-railed banister wrapped it like a

Christmas ribbon. The porch swing, suspended from the ceiling by two steel chains, rocked in the wind as it dripped with the remnants of the passing storm.

The rain had stopped and a clear, blue, pre-sunset sky emerged as he entered the driveway. Vicki, Player's diminutive wife, was planting mint in shallow puddles next to the house. She had on a bright red raincoat and flip-flops.

"Haven't seen you in a while. Go on in," she said in a tone just above a murmur. She was four-feet eleven, petite, pretty but too demure to be called beautiful, and self-deprecating, when you could get her to talk. Her first husband had died in a fiery explosion when a drunken neighbor hit their mobile home and disconnected the propane lines from the tanks he was using to weld metal art in the living room. Her second husband had shot himself while she slept beside him in their bed. She had once told Skip that she married Player because, "He's only four inches taller than me. That's good for my self-esteem."

"Kind of wet for planting," Skip said.

"Keeps the ants away," she said as she spaded through two inches of water.

"You don't say." He had never found logic to get in the way of Vicki's rationale.

"*The Nontoxic Home and Office,*" she said.

"Player's latest library addition."

"You can borrow it if you want," she said, never looking up. "He's in the kitchen."

Skip entered a formal dining room with ten-foot ceilings and old pine floors varnished to a high gloss. A hardy oak library table stood in the center of the room under a glittering crystalline chandelier. A well-worn upright piano leaned against one wall.

"What's the haps, bro?" Player said. He was mixing something in the kitchen sink.

"Not much, chef." Skip referred to him by his current professional title.

Skip had met Player at Antioch College. He'd been part of a group that took squatter's rights on the lawn in front of the Administration Building where they would ponder the universe, critique the establishment, smoke cheap weed, and jam with anybody who showed up. Player was a quick learner, musically gifted, and bizarre. By the time Skip met him he had experimented with every non-traditional, counter-cultural lifestyle known to man. He had been an orderly in a home for musically gifted autistic kids. He had been a delivery driver for the local parts bank, snatching the eyes from the sockets of still warm but deceased accident victims with donor cards. He worked as a paramedic's helper and later as the assistant manager at a porno-theater before enrolling at Antioch to guarantee a handsome allowance from his father. Several more meaningless jobs, a failed marriage, and a few years later he met Vicki while jamming at a local rathskeller where she worked as a waitress.

"Know this dude?" Player said referring to the music.

Player's house was a sensual experience. The walls in the kitchen were pastel yellow, the woodwork was navy, and the cabinets were pecan. The doors had been removed to display the china, stemware, and a myriad of glass jars filled with garbanzo beans, brown rice, lentils, assorted pastas, and a colorful variety of dried peppers. Huge spider plants hung in the windows. An aroma of something recently cooked wafted in the air, and a flute accompanied by a solo piano filled the background.

"Jean Pierre-Rampal," Skip said. "What are you mixing up?"

"One part plaster of Paris, one part flour with a little sugar, and some cocoa. These mice, they're like bitches. They love chocolate, but it's murder on them. Tell me where these guys came from: Bob Seeger, Del Shannon, and Madonna?" Player said.

"Michigan, Michigan, and Michigan," Skip said. Player hadn't stumped him in six months. "Having trouble with ants?"

"Like a plague," Player said.

"Try sprinkling chili pepper, paprika, dried peppermint, or borax where they're coming in. Various combinations of baking soda, borax, and tri-sodium-phosphate also work."

"I know, a non-toxic remedy for every pesticide," Player said.

Skip had told them to try that approach six months ago after he spotted a mousetrap in one corner. Vicki was allergic to cats.

"Okay, try this one," Player said. "Although Donald Byrd was into jazz and Peter, Paul, and Mary were folk singers one of their songs had a common theme. What was it?"

"I'm a leaving on a jet plane," Skip crooned. The answer was jet planes.

Player acknowledged his prowess at musical trivia with a gleeful smile. "So what's with the pow-wow, maestro?"

"Can't a guy just drop by to shoot the breeze and catch some tunes?" Skip said.

"Anytime, but what's up?"

"Kate McCardigan's son, he's in the hospital from pesticide poisoning."

"No shit!" Player stopped what he was doing.

"It's terminal."

Player ran his hand across his face and behind his neck. "Bad karma, man. She must be totally spaced."

"A wreck and she asked me to help her."

Before Skip could elaborate Vicki entered the house with a round faced, heavy-set, bearded man in his early forties. He had shaggy brown hair and a tuft that blossomed from the "V" in his shirt. He wore khaki shorts that revealed a sight Skip had seen on no other living man, totally hairy knees. Except for his porcelain smile, he looked like a big stuffed animal.

"Look at you guys!" Bear said and embraced each of them. He backed up for a second look. "You look great!"

Skip had seen Bear three weeks ago during a party at his house, but Bear made it seem as if it had been years.

Bear sniffed the air as he glanced around the kitchen. "Something's cooking."

"Vicki made bread," Player said. Bear lit up. "She forgot you were coming," Player said.

"Get out of here," Bear said as he brushed the air with one hand.

"You scarfed all her brownies last time you were here," Player said.

"My compliments to the chef," Bear said.

"More like a brownie high," Player added.

"Like the smores?" Skip said. "Your ex-wife, your ex-girlfriend, and your current touch all sitting around the same campfire downing those smores."

"THC in the marshmallows? You're a bad man, Elliot Johnson," Bear said. Player was rarely called by his given name.

Skip gave Player a high five.

Bear produced an insulated, nylon bag that was slung over his shoulder. "Speaking of which, you'll love these," he said.

Skip had helped Bear broker a health food store five years ago for a tidy profit and with the proceeds he became a distributor of a new line of tofu novelty products. Skip could still recall the label. *Tofu on U. Best taste'n healthiest snack you've ever eat'n. Distributed by Tofu Novelties International.* Bear knew everyone in the health food business for five hundred miles. He did the rounds to renew old acquaintances and in the process he built a very lucrative distributorship. He lacked for nothing, but he and Ann were frugal, and he was the most spiritually devoted man Skip knew. There was nothing he would not do for a friend, and Skip was about to ask a sizable favor.

Bear unzipped the bag and handed them something that resembled an ice cream. The dry ice in the bag had made the wrapper as crisp as dried leaves.

"Tofu popsicles?" Vicki asked.

"Tofu ice cream, Vick," Player corrected her, looking at Bear as if for confirmation.

Skip read the packaging aloud, "Double Barrel Banana! What's yours?"

"Current Ripple!" Player said. "Space me, dude."

Vicki rolled against her husband's arm. "CumQuatLy!" she whispered. The others snickered.

"No way. I want that one," Player said. They traded.

"Are these for real?" Vicki said.

"Brand new, adult frozen novelties, low cal, fat and cholesterol free. Try 'em, you'll like 'em," Bear said, sounding like a radio announcer.

They opened their frozen snacks and traded bites. Everyone wanted to lick the CumQuatly, except Vicki. She was too embarrassed after the guys finished a rapid-fire succession of off-color double entendres. After brief critiques, it was decided that Double Barrel Banana was the most realistic tasting, but since none of them could recall having eaten currents or cumquats they couldn't be objective.

They crowded around a counter that doubled as a kitchen table in the kitchen, engulfed in the camaraderie of the moment. The plight of Kate McCardigan and the malaise into which Skip was about to inject them seemed a distant cloud on a passing horizon. Times like this were the best times of his life. When the music stopped the mood changed. Player went to the living room, and Vicki excused herself.

Bear turned serious. "What's going on, Skip?"

"Kate Ellis, Derk's old flame," Player answered from the other room.

"Haven't seen her since the middle-ages."

"She called the other day," Skip said. "Her son is dying from some stuff that was sprayed on the trees next to her house. Throw in a mutilated corpse, a missing person, an ex-wrestler, and a gimp with one eye who shoots par, and you've got it." So much for rehearsal, but he did have Bear's attention.

"Say what?" Bear said.

"Any requests?" came a voice from the living room.

Skip and Bear looked at each other and shook their heads.

"No," Skip said quietly.

"What?" Player asked again but there was no response.

A moment later Herbie Hancock's quirky sounds filled the air.

"*Watermelon Man* from *Head Hunters*, first jazz album to sell a million copies," Skip said as Player returned to the kitchen. "You know what the second was?"

Bear's mouth hung open, and his hands were in the air.

"He told you?" Player asked, having returned to the kitchen.

"Kate's son was poisoned, but what about the dead guy?" Bear said.

"As in corpus delicti?" Player said.

"I knew that would be the tough part," Skip said. His friends awaited an explanation.

"I don't know if they're related or not, but the same guy we think did a number on Kate's son . . . some guy broke into his plant in Michigan last week and ended up in a tank of bad water."

"Acid bath?" Player said.

"They only found half of him," Skip confirmed.

"No way, man." Player turned away. "This is not good."

Skip laid the photos of Kate's son before them. "She went to the police, the health department, the EPA, everybody. Hit a roadblock everywhere."

"Pesticides do this?" Player said as he steepled the hair in his hands behind his head.

"Yea, the kind of stuff I wouldn't allow at the garden center. Ever hear of delayed toxicity?" They shook their heads but didn't stop looking at the pictures. "The bugs are becoming immune to this stuff. It's been around for a long time, and it's beginning to attack immune systems. It's worse for kids, but, hell, we're all at risk, especially as we get older," Skip said.

"This is some ugly shit, man," Player said. He was studying the details of the emaciated child in the photos.

There was a knock at the door, two knocks, tree more quick ones, and then the door opened.

"Dougal, you've gotta hear this," Bear said.

"And hello to you, too," Dougal retorted, then displayed a smile as wide as Wisconsin.

"Damn, that was some storm!" Dougal said. "Anybody see the rainbow?"

"Amazing, wasn't it?" Skip said.

Player gave Dougal a hug and wedged a stool into the group. "Lose some weight?"

"A little," Dougal acknowledged.

Dougal Ketchum was a handsome man, tall and slender with shoulder length hair, a full beard, and an affable manner. He drove an old VW van with a big peace sign painted on the back along with a bumper sticker that read "Think globally, act locally." On one side of the van was a picture of Earth and the word "Home" stenciled below it and on the other side was an air-brushed forest scene with the caption, "There is more water in all the forests on Earth than in all the lakes." His house was full of recycling containers for almost every material known to man. He heated his home with a wood-burning stove, and survived on pita, tofu and sprouts, the latter two he grew in the spare bedroom. He sold his excess production to the produce distributor where he worked as a driver. Single now, but he had been married for nine months to a woman he met at the airport on a return trip from Sweden. She was young, blonde, intelligent, and in search of an American husband. She had never seen his house nor was she accustomed to his lifestyle prior to their marriage. It turned out that Helga not only wanted to become an American, she wanted to become an upwardly mobile one. Poor Dougal. He cherished that woman. Their separation broke Skip's heart, too. He had never known anyone so committed to his principles.

"Might as well bring you up to snuff," Skip said to Dougal.

Bear handed Dougal the insulated bag. "Try one. They're easy on the waste line."

"Excuse me. Can we get on with this?" Skip said. He told him what had happened from the moment of Kate's first call to the trips to Zeeland and Tampa, and everything he had learned about Jack Von Lleuwan.

"I appreciate your concern, but it's a police matter," Bear said.

"They're not doing anything about it," Skip said.

"You're taking about a homicide," Bear countered.

Player shook his head. "No way, man. No friggin' way."

"Damn, this is good. Tastes like banana," Dougal said, licking the last morsel from the wooden stick.

"What do you think?" Bear asked Dougal.

"Look at this," Dougal said, waving a photo of Trevor McCardigan in front of them. "The guy should be stopped just on principle."

"Easy for you to say, you sprout loving hippie," Bear said.

"This stuff isn't necessary. Kills farm workers, and it's building up in people's immune systems like a time-bomb. You guys should see the chemicals they wash the produce in just to keep it looking fresh. How do you eat that stuff anyway? Organics, man. We got some organic carrots in the other day and I did a test. The organics were sweeter. No pesticides, no preservatives, and they tasted better. Something's got to be done," Dougal said.

Bear laughed. "Because organic carrots taste better, that's why we should do something?"

"No, because people are dying," Dougal said. "Under different circumstances he'd be a serial killer."

That was in their face, but it was Dougal's style. Skip recalled the controversy in the Environmental Club over the dumping of untreated wastewater, what Dougal referred to as "industrial potty water," by The Gem City Foundry into the Miami River. They were going to get water samples and then picket, but Dougal was more ambitious. With Player's help he procured a truck into which they diverted thousands of gallons of what they called "industrial potty water." One day while the foundry executives were having a board meeting, a small tanker with the name *Tru-Turf* stenciled on its cab sprayed the caustic run-off onto the well-manicured lawns of every member of the Board of Directors. On each door was posted a note from *Tru-Turf* thanking them for their business. Within five days the lawns were as dead as fossils. The news made the front page, and *Tru-Turf* settled out of court. "In the real world you've got to make an impact, not just study an issue," Dougal said. "We just made an impact!"

Bear responded, "Come on now! We don't know he killed anybody, and if he did it's a job for the cops."

Player looked at Skip, and agreed with Bear, "Hey, man, what can *we* do anyway?"

"What would you like to do? What would you do if this were your kid?" Skip said waving another photograph. Player pushed out his lower lip and nodded his agreement. Skip continued, "It did happen to one of our kids, a friend's kid. In the past there's no doubt what we would have done. Have we become so comfortable and so complacent we can ignore our friends?"

"What this country needs is a good shock-a-buka," Bear said.

"A what?" Dougal said.

"A swift kick to the head that results in a spiritual renaissance, a sort of understanding that everything is connected."

"So what?" Dougal said.

"The natural world is the source of all of our power, creativity, and love, and its energy flows into each of us. We're destroying it, and if we keep it up the human spirit will wither away," Bear said.

"Right on, brother!" Player said.

"Agreed, but what's that got to do with Kate?" Skip said.

"You know when you stand in the middle of a pine forest next to a trickling brook how you feel refreshed and invigorated?" Bear said. "Or on the ledge of a canyon overlooking a desert bathed in silence?"

"Peaceful, man," Player said as he hiked up his bib overalls.

"Or on the beach at sunset as the warm, sandy tide gushes between your toes and the moon lights your path? Connected, my friends, that's how I feel."

"He's right," Player added.

Skip sensed from the expression on Dougal's face that he was growing impatient.

Bear continued, "The suburbs have exploded because people want to be closer to the energizing effects of the country more than they want the life-dulling concrete and glass of the city. The things from which we absorb our energy are being diminished at an alarming rate. We are facing a spiritual crisis that is interconnected with the environmental crisis. Things will just get worse until somebody does something, but this is a police thing."

The music had disquieted, the rich aroma had dissipated, and the retreat into philosophical territory had dispirited the mood. Skip frowned at Dougal Ketchum, who seemed put off by Bear's meandering.

Dougal broke the subdued din. "Shit, fuck, hell, damn! I'll tell you what I think. This Von Lleuwan guy is one bad motherfucker, and I'm not going to sit around and let him poison my food and paralyze our kids. I agree with you, Bear, but by the time the rest of the world gets its shit together, this guy and his friends will have contaminated half the planet. You got a plan, Skip?"

"Right on!" Player exclaimed. He raised his hand for a high-five, and Dougal laid a fat one across his palm.

Bear turned away.

Skip said, "It's sketchy, but it might work. Deception is the key."

"Wait a minute. I've got to hear this," Bear said before he entered the bathroom off the kitchen. A minute later he returned, still zipping his pants.

"We'll pose as journalists," Skip unfolded a loose but creative plan.

Bear didn't object since he wasn't part of the initial plot. The others acquiesced, and everyone agreed to meet as soon as Skip could arrange a meeting with Von Lleuwan.

20

On the third Sunday in January five years ago, two different but related ads appeared in *The Press*, one under "Professional Services" and the other in the "Help Wanted" section. The former read as follows:

Pest Removal. If it's too obnoxious or repulsive for you to handle, we can dispose of it. All enquiries confidential.
Call 1-888-Dispose.

Jack Von Lleuwan remembered the day and the ad with indelible clarity. It was the day he was to leave for Tampa to close on a new house in Carrollwood Estates, an exclusive new residential golf development. He had invited some of his golfing cronies to join him after closing on Monday and to stay a few days to play with him in advance of the Suncoast Golf Classic in Tampa. He wanted to be in the house and at the top of his game when the top names in golf arrived for the tournament so he had been looking forward to this day with the zealous anticipation of a kid on the day before Christmas.

It was the same day that west Michigan was hit by one of the worst winter storms in history. The snow blew sideways for three days. The airport closed. Streets were impassable, and he couldn't go anyplace without a snowmobile, but it was too damned frigid to venture outside even if he had one. The wind-chill dropped to twenty-three below zero. With bags packed Von Lleuwan had nothing better to do that Sunday than to read *The Press* from beginning to end.

In the classifieds he was struck by the unusual wording in the ad entitled, Pest Removal, and the fact that the telephone number spelled out DISPOSE. It didn't say waste removal. It said pest

117

removal. And it had used the word "confidential." With his curiosity peaked and little else to do, he called the number. A recorded message instructed him to leave his name and number and to indicate the degree of urgency. He circled the ad and put newspaper aside.

When he returned from Florida a couple of weeks later, he found three messages on his answering machine. The first was from a gentle-sounding, middle-aged male apologizing for calling the wrong number. The second was from the Police Athletic League asking for a donation. The last one riveted his attention. A strong and mesmerizing male voice left a message:

"Mr. Von Lleuwan, you called about a pest removal problem? We know how difficult it is when you are facing a problem that seems insurmountable, and you'll do almost anything to get rid of it. You've tried everything, but nothing has worked. Your life is being disrupted, and the problem is not going away. We are the professionals in these matters, careful not to let anyone know you've even had such a problem. We can help. When you call again, ask for Eddie."

What troubled him was that he had left neither his name nor his number when he called, and from the response on his answering machine, it was clear that their interpretation of pest control was rather broad. He called back and got the voice mail again. This time he left his name and number and said it was urgent. Five minutes later his telephone rang.

"Hello," he said, a question mark in his voice.

"Mr. Von Lleuwan, Jack Von Lleuwan isn't it?" the voice said.

"Who is this?"

"This is Eddie. I thought I might be hearing from you," the voice on the other end said. It was the same impelling voice that had left the message on his answering machine.

"How did you get my number?"

"Caller I.D., Jack. This *is* the electronic age," the man who called himself Eddie said. "You *are* Jack Von Lleuwan, aren't you? Of Von Lleuwan Enterprises? A very important fellow in the pesticide business, and I gather you are having a disposal problem."

Von Lleuwan was struck by how carefully chosen were his words. "No. I mean yes, I am Jack Von Lleuwan, and no I don't have a problem," he told the insistent man.

"Even important fellows like you have problems from time to time that require discreet solutions."

"I don't know what you're talking about!"

"But Jack, you're the one who called," Eddie said. "You're in the chemical business. We're in the disposal business. You obviously have things that need disposing. Maybe we can do some business together."

"I doubt it."

"You can't tell me that you don't have some irritating stuff to get rid of. It's not easy these days with all the regulations. Why don't we talk?"

What Eddie said was true. He handled stuff every day that required special disposition. If this guy could handle it they had something to discuss. He was both intrigued and leery. Whoever these guys were he suspected they made up their own rules, but this kind of connection might one day prove to be useful.

They met in a seedy commercial district in Detroit. His real name was not Eddie. It wasn't even Fagan Miranda, the name he was currently favoring. He had it changed to Miranda, obtained a fraudulent birth certificate and a new social security number after a seven-year stretch in the federal pen for money laundering and tax evasion under his birthname, Olivio Candilotti. The new corporation had been formed in his attorney's name to escape federal scrutiny, but Eddie ran the whole show. Von Lleuwan found that he could dispose of some of his more toxic stuff in the process of taking out the daily trash. They forged a legitimate business relationship, but the back of Von Lleuwan's mind remained etched with the words from the ad that had initially captured his attention. Alone in his office, with the gruesome image one of Sheldon Walker's spy's remains lying in the local morgue, he was reminded once again of those words: "If it is too obnoxious or repulsive for you to handle, we can dispose of it."

Jack Von Lleuwan glanced over and completely forgot another ad that had appeared in the "Help Wanted" section that Sunday:

Truck Driver Wanted for waste disposal company. Evenings and weekends a must. Some overnight.
Call 1-888-Dispose, ext. 2.

He would later learn from Eddie that a nineteen-year-old, high school dropout from Caledonia by the name of Mason Williams Bonnett, named after the poet and songwriter, got the job with the help of his uncle, a trucker for a local furniture manufacturer. Mason had been living with his uncle since his mother died of drug and alcohol abuse several years earlier.

Eddie said, "This driver I'm sending to help you, I wanna warn you, he's got a face makes kids hide under their mother's apron. One side is like a child, and the other is worse than a bomb threat on an airplane. Caused by fetal alcohol syndrome his uncle said."

"My mother was a drunk," Von Lleuwan said. "Are you sure about him?"

"He's okay. I asked him about it? He said he didn't know what it meant, but his uncle told him it was from coca-cola. You mean coke, as in cocaine, I said? He said yea, I guess so, and she was always drunk. His uncle said if they'd put her in some program instead of jail she'd still be alive and he wouldn't have to take care of me."

"Can I count on him?" Von Lleuwan said.

Eddie told Von Lleuwan, "At first, I didn't trust him either. He's slow and he's weird. It looked like his uncle just wanted to get rid of him, but the old man said he's harmless due to the Ritalin and he can drive anything. So I asked about his face. His uncle piped up that he was bigger than the other kids because he'd been held back three times, but they picked on him nonetheless. What did you do about that I asked him. He said his uncle told him to knock their clocks off, but he got hurt if he tried to fight, and then his uncle would hit him with the newspaper. He said the teacher told his uncle 'it's cuz my hard time learning to read and write and low steam.' The kid was screwy. He said he saw the steam come out of his uncle's teakettle, but he didn't like tea."

"Yes, yes, I understand but can he follow instructions and keep his mouth shut?" Von Lleuwan wanted to know.

"I took him into the yard and he knew more about my trucks than I did," Eddie said. "Gave him a little road test and he could back up blindfolded. And he's smart, too, the uncle said. Say one of the poems his uncle told him. He said the kid's mother used to read poems to him in place of bedtime stores. I wrote it down. Listen to this:

"How 'bout them Tommy Gunners,
Ain't they a lot?
Havin' fun
With they rapid fire shots

Gunnin' them targets,
Up and down the line,
Runnin' 'round shouting
It's Tommy Gunnin' time!

Look at them Tommy Gunners,
Lurkin' in the bushes,
Waitin' for some homies
To shoot in their tushes.

Them slippery fingered Tommy Gunners,
Ain't they some bunch
Riding through the hood
Stealing all the brothers' lunch

How to be a Tommy Gunner?
No sense needed
Run and grab a shooter
No rules heeded."

Eddie said to Von Lleuwan, "He knows more about my trucks than I do and I don't know a single verse of poetry. He's been with me five years. Yeah, you can count on him."

After leaving the big, gruff man with the shiny, black gloves at the Detroit International Airport, Mason's heart was racing. It had been hours since he returned from the Wal-Chem plant, washed out the van, removed the Conway Cleaning signs, returned it to the rental agency, and picked up his own truck to take the man called Gloves to the airport. He was headed home on familiar, almost empty, early morning streets, but his stomach was as twisted as a Ficus hedge. He had done every job Mr. Miranda had ever asked him to do. He had carried stench so nasty it made him vomit and toxins that ate through the soles of his shoes. Another time the fumes were so bad his throat hurt for a week. In spite of it, he was proud that he had called in sick only five times in five years. Most of the other drivers couldn't stay on the job more than a few months. He was unsure whether all of the things he had done were on the "up and up," as his mother used to say. Probably not, but he didn't want to lose this job. He loved to drive. It was the only thing he could do, and he didn't want to go back to living in his uncle's cramped trailer.

Last night's delivery started him thinking that there might be some other job where he wouldn't have to deliver the things that made him sick or made his skin break out in those rashes. He wanted to keep this job, but he decided he was going to tell Mr. Miranda that he couldn't work with anyone like what that man did last night. He hoped that Mr. Miranda would not get too mad. He had seen Mr. Miranda when he got mad, and it scared him.

Mr. Miranda had told him, "I need you to pick up something for a client in West Michigan and take it to a plant in Wyandotte. Can you do that?"

It would be farther than he had ever driven, but he said, "Yes, sir." He didn't want Mr. Miranda to think he couldn't do it. He had been told he would meet someone there who would tell him what to do.

He had gotten up at one in the morning and driven to Zeeland to meet the man with the foul mouth and the funny ear. He didn't understand why he wore those shiny black gloves even in the summer, or why this guy, who was not even his boss, bossed him all the way to Detroit, "Keep it under fifty, kid. Don't slow down if you see a cop. Don't pass, kid. Stay in the right lane."

Mason knew how to drive, but the man kept barking orders. He was the awfulest man he had ever known. "Why don't you get your face fixed? You can't get any pussy looking like that," the man said to him.

The man directed him to a place in Grand Haven he called 'the morgue.' It was an eerie, cold, and dark place with a scary echo, and it had lots of shiny steel beds that you pulled out of the wall. From one of them they took out part of a body. It made him sick in his stomach. He had never touched a dead person. He had never even seen a dead person. He didn't know if it was all right to pick up a dead person from this place, but the man said, "Just drive and do what you're told."

It was cold and clammy, and it smelled worse than some of the guys passed out on the floor that his mother used to bring home. They put the body into a bag and dropped it into a big drum they had picked up on the way. By the time they made it to Wyandott and dumped the body in the shower of someone's office, it looked and smelled worse than a dead dog that had been run over on the road. It made him throw up right there on the bathroom floor. But that wasn't the worst part. What he couldn't understand, what he couldn't accept, was why the terrible man had opened all the drawers at the morgue until he was surrounded by every one of them, some old and withered, a couple of deformed accident victims, and one guy his own age. They were just lying there like ghosts. Then he took out a pocket-knife and cut the ear off one of them, the one who was about Mason's age. He put it in a plastic sandwich bag and stuffed it into his shirt pocket. Thinking about it made goose bumps all over his arms.

"Please don't make me do that again," he decided to tell Mr. Miranda. He was so jittery he repeated the same poem over and over and over:

"Look at them rat runners
Ain't they a sight
Runnin' those rats
Everynight

Running them rodents
Down those shoots
Taking their times

When they reach the loot

Timing those black rats
Timing those brownies
Pokin' them mulattos
In they hinies

Checking those fast rats
And checking them slow ones
Checking those switches
To keep things goin'

For making little marks
On those long paper charts
For recording the tests
On those dumb little pests

If you wanna be a rat runner
All you gotta do
Get yourself a shoot
And an old rat, too

And run that rat
As fast as you can
And check your watch
When he gets to . . . The end."

21

On the seventh circle of arrivals at Tampa International Airport, Derk's patience was waning. Sandra French's flight was behind schedule, and the rule that you couldn't wait at the curb to pick up arriving passengers was beyond irksome. As he circled at a smoldering seven miles per hour, the images in his dream returned. He had latched onto the man hanging beneath the ledge, his bond as firm as a kid's tongue on cold steel. And although the body was ethereal, almost weightless, as hard as Derk pulled he couldn't bring him to safety. The shape of face was familiar but in place of eyes were dark, lifeless pockets. At their depth Derk sensed a dim energy source, but he feared it as if these eyes were trapdoors to his own mortality. His mother's call had disconnected the image as sure as if she had turned off the television in the middle of a crucial scene. She entreated him just to visit his father, but he sensed an ulterior motive and he couldn't do it.

On the tenth pass he saw Sandra French exiting the Delta baggage claim. She had removed the jacket from her navy suit, revealing perfectly shaped spheres in her white cotton blouse. Her hair glistened like a king's treasure. She pirouetted one time, highlighting her sinewy calves, which were as shapely as a lingerie model's. She waved at him. Her smile, like polished pearls, would have mitigated the ambivalence of most men, but not Derk.

He collected her bags without comment and tossed them into the back seat while she cushioned herself in one of the snug leather buckets of his convertible. He laid a layer of polyester and steel on the pavement as he left the terminal.

"It's good to see you, too," Agent French said as she fumbled with her seatbelt.

"Morning," he grumbled.

"A little on edge today, Mr. Bryan?"

"What gave you that idea?"

"Silly me," she said as the clasp on the seatbelt snapped shut.

"Stuff on my mind."

"Is this what I have to look forward to all day?"

"Don't know yet. It's a long day," he said.

"My god, it's hot here. Can we roll up the windows?"

"You're in Florida, tropical paradise. I'll take you back if you don't like it?"

 "I thought everybody had A/C here."

"You'll get used to that extra layer of lubricant. Let's you flow better," he said as he did some gyration with his body. "Did you bring the Von Lleuwan file?" The car had air conditioning, but this morning he needed to feel all of its turbocharged power.

She turned toward the bags in the back seat.

"Good, we've got a lot to do."

"At the beach?" she said, noticing his shorts.

When he reached the main road outside the airport he shot through the traffic like a Grand Prix racer. Her head drifted backward, and she held onto the armrest.

I know what you're thinking, "Men and their testosterone charged toys. They think women are impressed by them."

"My brother's into cars, too," she said. "Do this work yourself?" Derk's car, a customized 1986 Mustang, was an immaculate candy apple red with black leather upholstery. It had a five-speed transmission on the floor, and a dashboard and console that resembled an airplane cockpit. As he slowed to the flow of the traffic around him she pulled a file from one of her bags.

"Little by little over time. The highway patrol uses these in several states. It has a tight cradle, MacPherson struts, oversized rubber, and it flies," he said.

"I noticed." She cranked her neck from side to side.

This woman was not easily rattled.

"I want to read that file, and you might be interested in the article on the Simpson woman," he said.

"Simpson woman?"

"She's missing, and I think she's involved. I want to go by the Tampa P.D. and see if anyone's filed a missing person's report. Then I want to find out about her son, see him if possible. I'd like to know what she knew that got her into trouble," Derk answered.

"What trouble?" Sandra said.

"She thought Von Lleuwan used some chemicals on the trees next to her house, and it made her son ill."

"You've been busy."

"It's my job."

"Did you know he has plant here?"

"In Tampa?"

"And some land investments. Golf courses and housing developments. The one here is called The Orchards. It's in the file," she said as she drummed her fingers on its cover.

"You don't say?"

"There's a distribution center and some suspicion about some illegal stuff flowing through it," Sandra said as she pulled her windblown hair away from her face to behind one ear. "It's on Twenty Second Street. Where's that?"

"Near the port. Wonder if there's any Cat-A-Lyst® there?" He tilted in her direction.

She pulled her blouse away from her moist skin. The wind continued to blow her hair awry. Derk turned on the A/C and rolled up the windows.

"Thank you," she said. "What did you mean, she's missing?"

"She was arrested for protesting at his plant. All the charges were dropped, and she disappeared."

"And you don't think that was a coincidence," she said.

"There's no such thing as a coincidence," Derk responded. "One way or the other, we need to find out what's going on."

"What's the plan?"

"I'm dropping you at the P.D. Find out everything you can about the Simpson woman. She was a science teacher, I believe, but I don't know where? Find our about her friends, relatives, environmental groups, anybody that might know what she was onto. Check missing persons. See if she's turned up anywhere. And her son, find out where he is and what's his condition."

"What are you going to do?" Sandra stiffened.

"Check a couple of things. Here's my cell number. Call me when you find something," he said as he handed her his card. He had taken the Ashley Street exit off I-275 north and was now in front of the Tampa Police Department. He stopped, got out of the car, and ran around to open her door. She didn't move.

"You wanted to help," he said.

"Not like this," she said as she exited.

"I'm sure you can find your way around the P.D."

She shouted as he started to drive away, "Derk, my bags!"

He hesitated, opened the window, and shouted back, "Don't worry about 'em. I'll pick you up later. We'll have dinner and compare notes!"

"But I've got to make arrangements," she said as he drove away.

Derk called information for Eva Simpson's address. He hadn't told Sandra where he was going because he preferred the freedom that a solo act provided. He didn't believe in violating people's Constitutional Rights, but he had exercised some creative investigatory techniques from time to time, and if he were alone there was nobody to question him. Twenty-five minutes later he was in front of her Riverview home. He drove past her house to the entrance of the construction site contiguous to her property. A big wooden sign marked the location: The Orchards, a Residential Country Club by Elgar. He wound his way through the development. The golf course was almost complete as was the clubhouse, the maintenance facility, and acres of new homes. Only a few sites remained under construction. He was looking for fruit trees. There was no orchard, but there were citrus trees scattered throughout the property. The fencerow that separated the Simpson property from the golf course consisted of a hedge of red and yellow Oleander bushes. The sight of the colorful foliage amused him. There would be a bevy of unhappy golfers after frisking the harmless looking foliage for their stray balls. Oleander was both beautiful and toxic.

He returned to the Simpson house. The grass must have been six inches high, and over a week's worth of newspapers were scattered about the front entrance. He shaded his eyes from the glare off the glass to see through the front windows. There was no movement. Then he tried the side and rear windows. No signs of life. He recognized some plants in the garden through a sea of weeds, but most had gone to seed. The signs of abandonment resurrected the same sinister feeling he had upon hearing the woman's voice on the answering machine. Eva Simpson might be gone a long time.

He wanted to get inside her house, but he had grave reservations about breaking and entering. As he approached the side door the decision was made easier by the sight of broken glass. The door was closed but unlocked. Inside he perused each room. There were no signs of damage, and nothing seemed out of place. One room that appeared to have been a child's room, now doubled as an office. There was a map on the wall with stickpins relating to well water contamination in central Florida. He rummaged through the desk drawers, but other than some articles on local pesticide use, he found nothing related to Von Lleuwan. As he left he noticed a red light flashing on the answering machine. He hit the play button. There were ten calls, but only four left messages: one from Alice Drake, one from Ruth Conby and another from Maria Alvarez. Each was brief and expressed her empathy with Eva's protest at the chemical plant. They were behind her all the way. The last woman's voice said, "Mrs. Simpson, this is Miss Whistlethwaite from the Ward Institute. We haven't heard from you in a couple of weeks, and we wondered if something might be wrong. Your son hasn't been very responsive lately, and a visit by you would be helpful. Please give me a call as soon as possible. Thank you."

He reached for the pad and pen next to the telephone and was about to write down Miss Whistlethwaite 's name when he noticed the impressions on the pad from the previous message. He found a number two pencil and lightly shaded the area of the message. It read: Miss Whistlethwaite, Ward Institute, Clarion Development, Elgar Industries. He put the notepaper in his pocket, jotted down the other names, and turned to leave. Half way through the door he returned to the answering machine. He pushed the play button and listened for the date, June eleventh, the day Miss Whistlethwaite had called. That was five days after the Simpson woman was released and not seen again. Who wrote this note? The broken glass suggested that some uninvited person had been in her home. He sensed someone familiar. Then the feel of thc cold, dank flesh of the man in his dream returned.

His next stop was at the office of the county EPA administrator in Ybor City, an historic neighborhood near downtown Tampa. Ybor had once been the bustling cigar-making capital of the United States, a status inherited when the frequent fires and labor unrest caused the industry to flee Key West. What was not long ago a stark, brick cold, urban center for the weird, the wayward, and the transient was now the hippest entertainment district in the city, in fact, all of Tampa Bay. Seldom a month passed without a new restaurant or club being added to the burgeoning night-scene. It had, among other things, placed Tampa on the map as one of the premier venues for a young professional to live in the 1990s.

Al Rodriguez had been the County EPA Administrator for as long as Derk could remember. He tried to keep the politics out of the position and do what was best for the community. He was aggressive and tough but reasonable, the kind of guy who could converse for hours on any subject. Except for Derk's power-mongering Mustang, Derk knew that Al appreciated his commitment to his work. He just didn't like big, fast, fuel-hungry cars, and he made no secret of it.

"Did you know that about one half of all urban space is devoted to the automobile including roads, parking lots, dealerships, repair shops, and car washes?" Al once told him. "If Americans' love affair with the automobile were to subside, many of my problems would be minimized."

It wasn't easy for Derk to be around Al without feeling a modicum of guilt, but behind the wheel of his customized, legendary nameplate, Derk would think about Al's lecture and muse, "We all have our fantasies." He knew it was rationalization. By 2020, half of all the oil resources in the world will already have been used. The days of the gasoline-powered internal combustion engine were numbered, and the country would no doubt benefit from the evolution. Pollution could be mitigated, power could be decentralized and the political clout of many unfriendly governments would falter.

Al was finalizing some instructions to his secretary when Derk entered.

"Come in, Derk," he said, extending his hand. Al Rodriguez was in his early sixties, five foot eight, with thinning brown hair, a slight paunch, and an affable personality. It was hard not to like him unless you had violated one of the regulations he was in charge of enforcing. Al motioned to a chair by a table in the corner of the room. He liked to keep things informal.

"How have you been?" he asked.

"Just got back from the Keys. Did a little fishing. You?" Derk said.

"Just became a grandfather again," Al said, pointing to a photo on his desk of a newborn.

"Congratulations! How many's that?"

"Three, and each is so beautiful! I'm a lucky man." Al rejoiced. "What's up?"

"I'm in the middle of a messy little situation up north and there may be a local connection," Derk said.

"What can I do for you?"

"You know that golf course and housing development going up in Riverview, The Orchards?" Derk said.

"Sort of."

"Ever do any tests out there?"

"What kind of tests?"

"Water, soil, anything?"

"It's possible. Why?"

"Remember, a little while back, a woman commandeered a tanker and blocked the entrance to a plant down at the port?" Derk said.

"Ammonia, I think," Al said. "That would have been a mess,"

"Her name is Eva Simpson. The company that owns The Orchards is Elgar Industries or Elgar Chemical Company. Simpson lives next door to The Orchards. Were there fruit trees there before the development?" Derk asked and then answered himself, "There must have been or she wouldn't have made that claim."

"You think there was something to her accusation?" Al asked.

"I don't know, but she's been missing since the day Elgar dropped the charges," Derk answered. He rubbed the back of his neck with his left hand and offered one of those "I'm not quite sure where to go from here" expressions.

"To answer your question, the Health Department would perform tests, particularly on the water. The Ag Department the soil test for pesticides. What are you looking for?"

"There was an incident at a Michigan plant owned by the same guy who owns Elgar, Jack Von Lleuwan, a major player. There was a small spill up there and somebody ended up looking like beef stew in one of his mixing tanks. They may or may not be related, but I'd sure like to talk with Eva Simpson."

Al Rodriguez shrugged his shoulders. "I don't know if I can help."

Derk recalled the pin map in Eva Simpson's house. "Al, if something were used on the trees near the Simpson house and it got into the well water . . ." he trailed off, thinking to himself.

"If a test were done on the water and it turned up negative, that would be the end of it," Al said, as if anticipating his question.

Thinking aloud again, Derk said, "And if they were using any pesticide or chemical according to the instructions, there wouldn't be any need for a special permit."

"As long as it's approved," Al confirmed.

"Right, as long as it were approved. But what if it weren't? Like an import, an illegal import, or something experimental?"

"Wouldn't make any difference," Al said. "If it didn't show up in any tests, then nothing would have been done."

"Damn! Something's going on, Al. I just know it," Derk said. He pinched his chin as he rose. His mind was already somewhere else. "Thanks for your time," he said as he ambled toward the door.

Derk was disappointed. He had hoped for more from the county's chief environmental authority. The more he thought about it he realized that if the answers he needed were in some past tests related to The Orchards or Elgar, that information would have already been used by Eva Simpson. What next?

He wondered if French had found anything, and he wanted to find the Simpson kid, but it was already two thirty, and his stomach was growling. He hadn't had breakfast or lunch, so he decided to read the Von Lleuwan file at Speedy Brown's on Seventh Street in Ybor City. It was only a few blocks away, and Speedy had the best garbanzo bean soup in Tampa.

A half hour later he left the restaurant disgruntled. The day wasn't going well. Speedy Brown's had been replaced by a sub shop, and he had to settle for a slice of reheated cellulose they called pizza. He was making no progress on this case, his father was dying, he was losing sleep from a relentless dream, and he was conflicted by his mother's wish. As he approached his car a guy was crouched next to the driver's side door, fidgeting with something. Derk could see only his back, but dreadlocks seeped from beneath his cap. He wore baggy jeans and a long-sleeved, oversized denim jacket. A little overdressed for this heat. Derk was used to people admiring his car. Pinstriped and triple clear-coated with polished chrome accessories, it was in show condition. But this guy was up to something much more ambitious.

"Admiring my car?" he said. He was only a few feet behind him.

The kid stood and turned abruptly, trying to conceal something behind his back. Derk guessed it was a Slim Jim, used to open locked cars and illegal for civilians to carry. He wanted to slam the kid against the car but stopped short, worried about damaging the thirty-five-hundred dollar custom paint job. That was a mistake. He ducked and tried to shield himself, but the steel-shafted lock puller smashed his left arm. The blow sent him to the pavement, and a torrent of pain flooded him like a tsunami after an earthquake.

As he started to rise, a voice behind him said, "Leave the man alone and you know who I'm talking about!" That command was followed by a chop to the back of his neck that sent him to the deck again. His mouth filled with a solution of blood and road-tar. A boot to the ribs emptied his lungs, and before the shock dissipated, he heard the two thugs sprinting up Nineteenth Street.

He got to his feet and tried to unlock the door. As the key entered the empty hole that had moments earlier been his lock he fell forward. His left arm hurt so much he couldn't raise it to brace himself from the forward lurch against the door. "Goddammit!" he cried out. Then he noticed a tear in the convertible top on the driver's side. His mood changed from wounded to rage.

He spit out the remnants of the ambush, and a charge of adrenaline numbed the screaming in his arm. He ran to the other side of the car, opened the door, slid in, hurdled the console and started the engine. He gunned it, headed north on Nineteenth Street and turned east at Eighth Avenue. About a block down the street he saw the guy with the dreads heading into an alley. The other was nowhere in sight. He down shifted and took advantage of the turbocharger. The tires screeched and smoke rose in the rear view mirror. He hit the curb on the narrow turn with his right front tire and the blow thrust his ribcage against the steering wheel. On the recoil his foot jammed the accelerator and sent the turbocharger into action again. All three hundred and nine horses responded. His head jerked back, the tires squealed, and the car wrenched sideways. The fugitive tossed the lock puller away and lengthened his stride. Derk tightened his grip and straightened the wheels. Fortunately, there were no pedestrians in sight. He punched the pedal again, ricocheted off a parked car on one side and a brick building on the other. One of his mirrors was ripped from its socket. He winced, thirty-five hundred dollars of custom paint reduced to bare metal. He was closing on him when he reached Seventh Avenue. He slowed enough to avoid a head on collision with a westbound Toyota and then hammered the accelerator as he turned east. The turbocharger did its job. He took aim for the punk winding his way down Seventh Avenue.

By this time the commotion had caught the attention of a couple of Sheriff deputies. The one with its blue light flashing was bearing down from behind him and the other was coming straight at him, less than a block away. Derk was almost upon the kid when he ducked into one of the many bars on Seventh Avenue. Derk slammed on the brakes and pulled the key from the ignition. In a series of moves that would have impressed Edwin Moses he exited the car, vaulted the hood, jumped over a planter on the sidewalk, and opened the door to the bar. At that very moment, the deputy in his rearview mirror had stopped and taken a position beside his cruiser. With both outstretched arms braced on the roof of his car and his hands on his service revolver, with the blue light coruscating off the windows of the nearby shops, he shouted, "Police! Stop right there or I'll shoot!"

Derk complied, raised his hands, and turned around. "I'm with the EPA. They tried to steal—" and before he could finish, the other cop exploded onto the scene, grabbed him under the arms, spun him around, and pushed him up against the wall.

Derk tried to turn and say something, but the officer pushed him harder this time and ordered him, "Shut up and put your hands up high against the wall!" Then he kicked Derk's legs apart and searched him. By the time the deputy had located Derk's wallet and ascertained his identity, the prospective car thief had escaped through the rear entrance to the bar.

Derk gave the deputies a description of the perp and filed a criminal report that included assault, larceny, and attempted auto theft. The deputies said they would turn it over to the Tampa P.D.

"This is Tampa's authority, and they have a special unit working these offenses," one of the deputies said. "They'll catch 'em when they try it again, and they *will* try it again."

They apologized for the rough stuff but not for the ticket they issued to him for reckless driving. "You damaged two cars besides your own and put the lives of others in danger," one of the deputies said. "You should know better. I don't have any choice here."

"Sure you do. Everybody does," Derk said. He was infuriated, but they were correct.

Derk surveyed his Mustang. The sight of it renewed the pain in his arm. He cradled the left arm in his right arm and massaged the area around the elbow. Then he slowly caressed his swollen lips which left a swath of red on his forefinger. He glanced at his watch. It was close to four. He shuffled to his damaged car, found the cell phone and called Sandra French.

"Derk, I found out where the Simpson kid is. The kid's father filed a missing person's report on his mother, and there's more," she said with unusual excitement. "Over near HeeHaw Junction they found—"

"Yeehaw, it's Yeehaw Junction. Can it wait?

"What's wrong?"

"I'll pick you up in ten minutes. Wait outside." Each sentence, each word, each breath was forced.

"Okay, but make it twenty. There's one more thing I have to check. Are you okay?" "No," he said.

22

At 5:15 P.M. the telephone rang in Mat Strong's and Watt Guillermo's motel room.

"Watt?" the caller said.

"No, it's Mat. You here already?"

"I'll be there in an hour. Don't move," John Westfield ordered him.

John Westfield had made a total commitment when he went to Michigan on behalf of Kate McCardigan. Now she had asked him to step aside. On the flight to Tampa he kept hearing his old football coach, "There are three kinds of ballplayers. Those that make things happen, those that watch things happen, and those that don't know what's happening!" It was a risky plan, but he needed to get back into her good graces.

"What's up, boss?" Watt asked as Westfield entered his crew's motel room at 6:30 P.M.

"You know that piece of work you did for me in Michigan?" Westfield said as his young accomplices stiffened. "The job's not done."

"You want us to go back up there?" Mat said.

"No! They've got a plant in Tampa. There's another two hundred in it for each of you," Westfield said.

"Fat fucking chance!" Mat said.

"We're going down there first thing in the morning before they open," Westfield commanded.

"No way. We didn't do anything up there, and we still got in trouble," Watt said.

Mat nodded his agreement. "It's bad news, boss."

"This is about Mrs. McCardigan's son. He's dying. We know this slimeball did it, and we're going help her," the boss said.

139

"And if we don't we're fired?" Mat said. Westfield allowed the suggestion to linger.

Watt kicked at the air and hit the leg of a chair. "Goddammit! You can't do that."

"You're going to lose more than your jobs. I didn't go into that building in Michigan. I didn't touch anything or anybody," Westfield told them. "She knows who you are," he lied to them, "and I had to talk her out of calling the cops. So get dressed."

"You're nothing but a pussy slave," Watt said.

Westfield rushed him, chest puffed, "You want to go at it right here?"

"Fuck you," Watt said and turned away. "How did you talk me into this?" Watt said to Mat.

"I didn't," Mat said.

"You said it was easy money, you dumb gear-head."

"Fuck you. You didn't have to go."

Watt leaped at his friend.

Westfield stepped between them. "Cool it, both of you," he said, fending off their mock attempts to hit each other. "We'll need a van and some tools. We'll get 'em at the construction site and then pick up something to eat. Get your shit together, and let's get out of here!"

They dressed slowly, grumbling at each other.

"Come on, you guys, hurry up," Westfield snapped. "And look like construction workers. I don't want any attention drawn to us this time."

The cussing subsided, but their pace remained lethargic. John Westfield had never been this nervous about the start of the second half of a game.

23

Jason Henderson's young bladder was about to explode. He slid down the embankment into the weed cover where he could squat. He had been holding back nature ever since they left Busch Gardens because his father wanted to cross central Florida before it got dark. He and his family were on their way to visit his grandmother in West Palm Beach.

His dad said, "There's no place to stop out here. There's nothing but swamp for miles." And his mother had tried to reassure him, "Sweetheart, Daddy will find a place to stop as soon as he can. Hold on." But he had reached his limit.

By the time they turned off the highway onto a two-lane rut, the swarm of bugs hitting the car was so thick it had turned the windshield the color of monkey vomit. Jason saw neither a building nor a sign of human life. He was sure this place was full of bugs, snakes, and things he only wanted to see in a museum.

"Faster, dad," he urged. But his father said he had to go slow or he might slip into the ruts and he wouldn't be able to turn the car around without sliding down the bank into what Jason imagined was the slimy, green, gooey, primordial existence of alien life-forms. Except for the weeds brushing against the car doors, there was dead silence.

When he and his dad exited the car the bugs attacked them from all directions. There were so many of them Jason's face hurt from slapping it. In weeds above his waist, he dropped his pants to take care of his business when a frantic rustling in the grass startled him. He jumped forward and fell as his trousers formed a noose around his ankles. He looked back and screamed. A huge, dark, leathery creature was wrestling something in the sawgrass. His dad descended the levy in a single leap, yelling and screaming, flailing his arms and stomping his feet. Jason struggled to pull up his pants as the giant reptile backed away from a bloated mass of flesh with a leg in its jaws. He didn't stop screaming until his father picked him up and carried him to safety. At a convenience store in Yeehaw Junction his dad notified the police, and Jason used the restroom.

24

Derk waited for Sandra French in front of the Tampa Police Department. He was in no mood to be chivalrous. He tapped the horn as she came through the door.

"What the hell happened?" she said, looking at Derk's car. Then she got in and saw his face, "Oh no! You all right?"

"Hurts when I laugh," he said and forced a chuckle as the pain in his arm engulfed him. "Goddamn kids!"

"You going to tell me?"

"Some kids tried to steal my car."

"With you in it?"

"Over in Ybor. One of them hit me with a lock puller, and the other came out of nowhere," he said, wincing and slowly running a forefinger across his lips. "I chased them until a couple of county boys showed up and they got away. Chumps gave me a ticket. Can you believe that?"

"What did you do?" Sandra said.

"Punks try to steal my car and break my arm, and I'm the one who gets the damn ticket!" he said as he shifted into second and entered the traffic cautiously, having had enough excitement for one day.

"I'm sorry about your car. Do you need a doctor?" she said.

"Thirty-five-hundred dollar paint job, gone." He waved his right hand while holding the wheel in his left, grimacing the whole time.

Sandra put her hand on his side. "Anything I can do?"

"No! The ribs," he said, trying to pull back, but the sudden movement was not helpful. "Welcome to Tampa, auto theft capital of the world!"

"Got any aspirin?"

"Sure you don't want to get that checked out?" she said as rummaged through her purse.

"I want to go home, take a shower, and put some ice on this. Can you stay at my place tonight?' he said. "I've got an extra room. It's right on the beach. We'll get dinner and go over what you found out." Sandra acquiesced, but he knew he was putting her in an uncomfortable position. "I'm sure Von Lleuwan is up to something," he added, "and I want to find out what it is. Is that all right with you?" Both the agony in his face and the humility in his voice were sincere.

"Where do you live?"

"Pass-a-Grille at the end of St. Pete Beach. Quiet, artsy, sophisticated. You'll like it." He forced a thankful smile.

They arrived in Pass-a-Grille about forty-five minutes later. Sandra was still talking about the Don Cesar, the magnificent resort hotel at the entrance to Pass-a-Grille, as they approached the historical Hurricane Restaurant.

"It's just like you described, but better," she said, looking beyond the sea oats across a wide sandy beach to the sun still resting on the edge of the Gulf of Mexico. "And this is your front yard."

Derk enjoyed the acknowledgment of the ever-appealing natural ambience of his neighborhood. "There are places like this everywhere, each with its own appeal. Some have mountains, some have rivers, some have plains, and some are deserts. Some have nothing special, just the people and the places where people live and work and raise their kids. And they all deserve to have clean water and air. I'm fortunate," Derk said.

He showered and dressed as Sandra unpacked in the spare bedroom. It doubled as an office with a computer and some file cabinets as well as his library that ranged from *Goodbye to the Flush Toilet* to *Passages*. On the walls were a few tasteful Demarais nudes but the focal point was a glass case with books, articles, and paraphernalia about Bill Veeck.

"Who's Bill Veeck and what's this?" Sandra said as she entered the living room.

"The guy who sent a midget to bat. You don't follow baseball?" Derk said from the couch in the living room. When he turned around, pinched between her thumb and forefinger was a neon yellow mesh bikini designed to cover the most exotic of female real estate with patches the size of half dollars.

"Oh no! She didn't," Derk said.

"Life on the beach is . . . quite revealing," Sandra said.

He reached for the bathing suit, but she wadded the threads into a ball.

"Spacey, I mean Tracey. That's hers," he said and reached for it again.

She held it out to one side. It looked more like brightly colored strings than a piece of clothing.

"Let me explain. It was a trade," he said.

"So you're a cross-dresser?"

"Give me that." He grabbed it from her hand this time. "Tracey Larkin, that was her name. She'd just finished her doctoral thesis on bio-thermal engineering and needed a break, so she came down here to stay at her folks' beach house for a month."

"Her folks' house or your house?"

He smirked, a half-embarrassed acknowledgement that his relationship with Tracey had ventured into carnal territory.

"She talked me into taking her to some biker's event on the beach and when I saw it in one of the shops I said why don't I ever date a woman who wears one of those? She left a message on my answering machine before I left for the Keys about taking my chaps, which she said she wanted to wear to a party, but said she left something in exchange. I guess this is it," he said.

"Souvenirs of the single life," Sandra said.

"It's not what you think," he said, unsure why he felt obliged to minimize his relationship with Tracey. "She's gone." He waved the air. "Off to Antarctica to test some fabric that sustains body heat. Organically based fabrics or something."

"Hey, it's your life. I'm just passing through. So, this Bill Veeck, a maverick like you?"

"Maybe." He was happy she changed the subject, but he didn't like her inference. He held up an ace bandage and a towel he had brought from the bathroom.

"Would you mind getting me some ice from the freezer? There's a plastic bag under the sink." On her way to the kitchen he added, "How about some wine?"

"White or red?"

"Your choice, but there's a bottle of white in the fridge."

She wrapped his arm and they sat in the living room sharing personal histories while the ice pack and the wine numbed him. She told him she had grown up in the Lansing area, attended a local college and became the Director of Marketing for her family's business, a chain of farm supply outlets, until they sold out to a national distributor. Her uncle, the politician, maneuvered her into a position with the State. Derk was surprised to discover that she had been the salutatorian of her high school graduating class and played on the girls' championship volleyball team in college. They walked down to the Hurricane for a late dinner.

"You said you knew where the Simpson boy was?" Derk asked while they waited to be served. "The Ward Institute. Right?"

"How'd you know that?"

"Where is it?"

"Lady Lake," she responded.

"Not far. Did you find out about his condition? Get his doctor's name? Can we visit him?"

"No, no, and I don't know. Is there anything else Herr Bryan?"

"Sorry," Derk excused himself with a laugh.

"Do you want to know the really important stuff I found?" she looked askance. "It's about Eva Simpson," she said and shut up.

She looked at her nails and then at her make-up through a mirror she retrieved from her purse, but said nothing. Her reticence got to him.

"Yes, mam, please tell me what you found out about Eva Simpson," he said.

"There's a guy in MIS, a Sgt. Bardo, who tracks all sorts of things including missing persons. He used to play volleyball and had a pro career snuffed out with a knee injury. That's why he's got a desk job now. He still coaches the Police Athletic League teams and coordinates some programs at the "Y." You'd never know it from his appearance, kind of out of shape. He's tall, though, and I thought he played basketball. But no, it was volleyball. I told you I played volleyball. Anyway, the things you find out about people!" she said.

He feigned interest in her discourse, and she kept going. "So Mrs. Simpson's ex-husband called the P.D. after he got a call from the Ward Institute telling him that Mrs. Simpson couldn't be reached at home or at school. He lives in Spokane, so they don't talk much. He gets back here as often as possible due to his son, but his fear of flying is a major obstacle. Now here's the coincidental part. Turns out Bardo knew this guy from college. He was quite an athlete. Bardo remembered the Simpson case, not because of her arrest but because he read about her in the newspaper, and he lives near an orchard and has a daughter about the same age as Simpson's son."

She rambled with great detail, but he didn't interrupt her. Sandra French may have gotten a late start in this business, but she was accomplished investigator.

"So a couple of days ago a family on vacation finds a unknown female body in the weeds near Heehaw Junction."

Derk laughed. "Yeehaw."

"What?"

"Yeehaw Junction."

"Yeehaw, that's it. Anyway, when an unidentified corpse turns up Bardo runs it against his missing persons' list. He thinks it might be our Eva Simpson," she concluded.

"No shit!" He straightened in his chair. "Sorry. What's the cause of death?"

"Between the bugs, birds and alligators her body was pretty well mutilated, but she died from some sort of poison and was dropped in the bushes," she said.

"When will they have a positive I.D?" Derk asked.

"They're working on it."

"Sandra, have you read the entire Von Lleuwan file, the one you gave me?" Derk asked.

She nodded. "Why?"

"Does the name Clarion Development mean anything to you?"

She shook her head.

He didn't want to tell her he was in Eva Simpson's house without a warrant, but what to hell. He was now sure that Eva Simpson was dead.

"I was in the Simpson house today," he said and noticed the not unexpected expression of reproval on her face, "and I found the words Clarion Development and Elgar Estates written on a notepad. They're owned by Von Lleuwan, and they're residential golf course developments. I don't know the connection, but they're called The

Orchards, and Eva Simpson lived next to one of them. And something else. I swear somebody else was in her house. The glass was broken and the side door was ajar. Maybe she was abducted. I think we ought to tell the locals to dust for prints. Tomorrow I'd like to see the Simpson boy and go to Heehaw Junction," he said and they laughed together. "Right now, I'm hungry." He massaged his ribs.

"You got hit good, didn't you?" She said.

"Maybe they'll give me a bag of ice with dinner," he said.

After dinner they walked across the street to the beach. A full moon reflected off the ripples in the tide and illuminated their way. The warm, salty, Gulf breeze coasted through Sandra's lithesome locks. Derk removed his shoes, and Sandra followed his lead. As he strolled the beach, her body brushed against him and the sand felt cool between his toes. He had relegated his objections to her trip to Florida to work on this case to a distant chamber in his mind.

"Even when you're working here it feels like you're on vacation," Sandra said.

For the moment he had almost suppressed the image of his father lying helplessly in a lonely northern hospice.

25

It was not yet dawn when the construction crew piled out of the van they had borrowed from the site of the latest hi-tech cholesterol factory they were building in Brandon. Although as calm as an old-folks home after midnight, the Elgar plant was well illuminated and the superheated air reeked of turpentine. John Westfield alternated between holding his breath and hyperventilating. His blood pressure was in the danger zone, and his anxiety was approaching the end of a burning fuse. He had instructed the guys to don dark clothes, but when Mat slipped off his windbreaker he was wearing a bright red Cincinnati baseball jersey.

"Damn moron, why don't you just wear a neon sign?" Westfield said and stopped short of Mat's chest with a backhand. "Take that off, you dumb fuck," he said.

Then he shouted at Watt, "What the hell are you waiting for?" Westfield knew that Watt had been given his nickname by the guys on the football team for his ability to disassemble and reassemble small motors, auto electrical systems, radios and VCRs. So Westfield had instructed him to circumscribe the plant and report on the security just as he had done in Michigan. Mat stripped to his bare chest while Watt went to the back of the van. He removed a bright yellow mountain bike.

"Jesus fucking Christ! Put that thing away. You guys are dumber than bark," Westfield said.

"It's faster," Watt said.

"Faster my ass!" Westfield shouted. Then just above a whisper he said, "These commercial security systems are designed to turn on enough lights to illuminate Yankee fucking Stadium, set off sirens that will awaken the deaf, and alert every cop within three counties. Use your damn heads for a change."

As he leaned the bicycle against the van and walked away, Watt said, "What's up your ass?"

"My foot'll be in yours if you don't get moving," Westfield replied.

Westfield and Mat waited in the van. Watt returned a few minutes later.

"Well?" Westfield said.

"We need to put out the lights. There's a camera on the roof that won't be worth much without them. The office appears to be unsecured, and there's no dog. I don't think the fence is hot because I didn't see any power to it. We can cut a hole on the other side and get in without being seen," Watt summarized, and then added, "asshole."

"Can either of you shoot worth a damn?" Westfield asked as he pulled a leather gun bag from the back of the van.

"What the fuck you talking about?" Mat reacted.

Watt's hands flew into the air as he walked away, "I'm out of here."

"Slow down, you dimwits. It's for the lights," Westfield said. He removed a pellet gun.

"Don't look at me. I couldn't hit the ground if I fell off the roof," Mat said.

"I'll get the lights," Westfield said, "When they go out you guys cut the fence and head for the office. Let's go."

Things didn't go badly all at until they were inside the building. Immediately, lights came on and the wall switches wouldn't turn them off.

"That's a bad sign," Watt said.

Then a calm female voice came from a loudspeaker no one could spot. The emotionless voice said, "The Van Ostrom 2000 Security System has been activated. Any attempt to leave the premises will result in severe injury or worse. Please wait for security personnel to disarm the system." It stopped them like a rear-end collision.

"What the fuck's that mean?" Mat said.

"How do I know, asshole?" Watt retorted.

"Damn it! You're the electronics expert," John Westfield shouted at Watt. "You said everything was okay."

"What kind of injury? What is she talking about?" Mat said. "Look, there's another camera." He pointed to the corner of the room.

John and Mat leaped toward the camera. As if they were puppets on a string, they snapped back after one large step.

"Lasers?" Mat shouted.

"Why would they put lasers in a place like this?" asked Westfield.

Watt circumscribed the room without leaving his position, looking high and low in each corner.

The ubiquitous female voice returned. "Please remain still. Any movement will result in serious injury or worse. Please wait for security personnel to disarm the system."

"Oh shit! Motion detectors," Watt exclaimed.

"You dumb Dago. You got us trapped in here," Mat yelled.

"Hey, muscle-head, you're here with me," Watt said.

"Shut up," Westfield ordered, and none of them moved another inch, frozen in various awkward positions.

"Are we just waiting here for the cops to show up and take us to Butt-fuck City?" Watt said.

The stoic female voice announced again, "Please remain still. Any movement will result in serious injury or worse. Please wait for security personnel to disarm the system."

Mat stumbled but caught his fall.

"Don't move!" Watt said.

"I didn't," Mat said and they each looked at Westfield.

"Neither did I."

"It's a fucking recording! It's bogus. Nobody's gonna show up here," Watt exclaimed.

At that moment the front door, ajar as a result of a forced lock, opened and a diminutive, bookish man of thirty-five with thinning brown hair and thick glasses, who stood less than five feet five in his stocking feet, entered with a briefcase in one hand and a cup of coffee in the other.

"Who are you guys?" The dispatcher raised his voice.

Upon realizing that their unexpected guest was neither the police nor a security guard, John Westfield spoke up, "We're from the cleaning company. That's our truck outside."

To their complete surprise the wimpish newcomer dropped his attaché case and the hot coffee, leaped on the desk closest to their exit, and donned a karate pose. Legs bent, arms raised, and with hands crafting the air, he focused upon one and then the other and retorted in what Westfield presumed was the most authoritative voice he could muster, "The fuck you are!"

"The what?" Westfield replied.

Watt said, "There's no lasers here. He walked in and nothing happened."

Moments later, John Westfield and his crew, looking like the entire backfield of the Tampa Bay Buccaneers, turned the Elgar plant dispatcher into a floor mat. Then they scampered through the fence and were half way to the van when the middle-aged karate student hobbled into the yard. Watt sped away on his bicycle, and Westfield and Mat skidded down the road in the company van with the name McCardigan Construction stenciled on the back.

26

Since the incident in Zeeland, the employees of all Von Lleuwan facilities had been instructed that in the event of any security breach they should call Mr. Swingle, Director of Security, who would report to Mr. Von Lleuwan and then notify the police. As a result, the dispatcher at the Elgar plant had called the plant manager who in turn reported the incident to Gloves who then informed Jack Von Lleuwan.

"It's Sheldon Walker," Von Lleuwan told Gloves. "That son-of-a-bitch is relentless, and Sid O'Connor set him up. Did you get hold of him?"

"The little nerd is on vacation, but get this," Gloves said. "They were driving a marked van and one of them rode a bicycle."

"Get that surveillance tape up here immediately," Von Lleuwan ordered.

"Should I have Charlie Meeks make some calls?" Gloves asked.

One of the calls was to McCardigan Construction Company in Moraine, Ohio. With photos of the three men in hand, Gloves waited at the Mr. Spud construction site in Brandon. *"If it has eyes and can be deep fried or baked, we've got it,"* was Mr. Spud's motto. You could get them with blue cheese, salsa, malt vinegar, mayonnaise, chutney or the hot sauce of the day. Gloves had tried all of them, but he preferred them in a greasy cup smothered with catsup. The thought of it today made him sick. He was still hung over from his trek through the titty bars last night.

He had caught up with two of the intruders the previous afternoon, but they got away while he was being tossed out of the bar for touching one of the mother and daughter tag-team members. It was after midnight, a weeknight, and there were more dancers than customers in the club. It was the forth strip club the construction workers had visited. The place was a thick shroud of cigarette exhaust and the only the illumination was supplied by a few candles, a light over the bar, and the spotlight on the skinny, naked, twenty something, red head who clung to a brass pole on the center a stage like a climbing vine. The two construction workers were quickly escorted to a table in the corner for a lap dance.

A half dozen shots of Jim Beam with Ybor Gold chasers had emboldened Gloves. Three women in peeling lingerie sat at a table in the corner but he couldn't take his eye off the pretty, fully clothed one. She couldn't have been more than eighteen, but she resembled one of the older women. Her ivory complexion and red lip-gloss glowed like neon in contrast to her skin-tight purple jumpsuit. Her hair was full and in perfect place, and it framed her shy, pasty face. She was slender but had breasts the size of full moons. She said nothing, but in exaggerated movements took occasional drags on a filtered cigarette and coughed out the exhaust.

Gloves ordered drinks for the girls and another Jim Beam, straight up with a chaser, as the DJ called out a round of double entendres to introduce the next performer. She went by the name of Maggie May and danced to a Rod Stewart tune. Gloves put an arm around the women who were on either side of him, but his libido was focused upon the younger sitting across from him. She lit another cigarette before the half smoked one was extinguished. One of the girls licked his ear, but he pushed her away. Gloves reached across the table and took the hand of the younger woman into his latex grip.

"What the fuck's on your hands?" One of them said. The younger one tried to pull away.

"Dance for me," he said and started to get up. She slipped from his grasp.

"She doesn't dance, but I do," the woman next to her leaned toward him.

"Who are you, her mother?" Gloves said.

"So. what!"

"Son-of-a-bitch!" he said and sat down. The resemblance was no coincidence. The mother was rough but not unattractive, fit for thirty-five, but her face looked as if the cigs, the booze, the late hours, and the beatings had taken their toll. The other dancers moved to each side of the mother and daughter. Gloves laid three one-hundred dollar bills on the table.

"I'd like the lady to dance for me," he said again.

"I'll dance for you," another said, her triangular smile shaped like the eye of a Halloween pumpkin. "Hell, I'll dance 'til we close for half that!"

"Who asked you?" he barked. He put another hundred on the table. "I'm not going to hurt you, sweetie," he said. "I just want you to dance for me."

The mother glanced at her daughter and then at the money. The young woman folded her arms around herself and pulled her legs up to her chin. Her mother put an arm around her.

"For another hundred you've got both of us!" The mother exclaimed. None of the others seemed a bit surprised. The daughter made an effort to pull her arm away, but her mother held on. "Put up or shut up, big guy!"

The phallic gatekeeper tripped the latch and freed its erotic host. Gloves placed another large one on the table and reached for the ladies' hands. The older woman kept herself between him and her daughter as he was led to a black, cloaked doorway in the rear and side of the stage. A stocky, bronzed stud with a marine cut drew back the curtain. As they entered a short, dumpy man about fifty with Coke bottle lenses left with one of the dancers. In Gloves' periphery he noticed that the two young construction workers he was following to the club were up to their zippers in the dancers' body parts. He was taken to a room that contained a carpeted deck, a stool, and a stand with a half-full box of Kleenex on it. A single bulb covered a revolving red, yellow, and blue filter that dimly illuminated the little cubicle. It smelled of cheap perfume, stale perspiration and spent semen.

The younger woman stepped onto the platform. She sat down and leaned back, one leg bent at an angle to the other that she had fully extended. The long hair at the back of her neck fell forward and covered her face as she dipped into her lap.

"Show me something," Gloves said.

The young woman raised her arms perpendicular to her body, titled her head back, and shook her hair from her head. Her hands went over her head and as she slowly lowered them, she swung her head to one side and whined a seductive "meow." A bubble formed on her wet lips, and she made a circular motion with her tongue. Her hands and her forearms came to a rest on the floor along with one leg. The other rose behind her until it was straight overhead and her back was arched. She slowly reclined, as would a serpent slithering down a tree, then ran her hands up and down her body while circumscribing her breasts. Then she did it for him again. This time she stopped to massage one breast, then the other. Then she concentrated on just one. She closed her eyes and thrust back her head, her lips barely parted. One hand dropped to her crotch. She writhed, fondled, and purred.

Gloves was as hard as pig iron. He loosened his belt and removed his shirt.

"Are we enjoying ourselves yet?" the young woman said.

She peeled the jumpsuit from her shoulders, revealing her ivory breasts. It reminded Gloves of fresh fruit parting with its shrink-wrap. He removed his trousers from one leg. The older woman, who had faded into the woodwork, whispered something as she left.

"She's not your mother, is she?" Gloves said.

The jumpsuit descended below her furry "V," exposing a canyon of delight that weakened his remaining propriety. He didn't care that she had done this before. She was naked now, massaging her inner thighs and undulating on the carpet in front of him. His pants were on the floor. He removed his gloves. Completely erect, he arched back and stretched both legs onto the platform, brushing against the young lady. She was squatted, masturbating in front of him. His leg touched her again. She moved her leg sideways. "No, no, Tiger," she said. "No touching."

His moans were barely audible above the deep base from the main stage. He stroked himself slowly at first and then faster, but she was thwarting his ultimate satisfaction. He reached his leg behind her and pulled her to him.

"No," she said again jumped back.

He stood, grabbed her around the waist, and laid her on the platform. He forced himself into her and pushed, spreading her delicate thighs further and further apart. His hand stifled her attempts to scream. She scratched, but her slender arms were like the tender branches of a wispy willow against his sides. Eventually the alcohol and the erection were no match for the vigor and depth of her fingernails. He removed his hand from her mouth to swat her hands away from his shoulders. She shrieked, and the door burst open. A stocky bouncer came in swinging. Gloves forced himself deeper into the girl, but the bouncer caught him with a right hook. The blow sent Gloves backward, pinning the girl's legs under him. She screamed again. The bouncer's next punch knocked him off the platform. Gloves rolled and came up on all fours. His giant erection, aimed at the bouncer like a harpoon, gave him pause. Gloves lunged toward the bouncer's midsection. With the angle in his favor he drove him against the wall. A giant "Ahhhhh!" followed and his hand raked across Gloves' head, detaching a piece of Gloves' ear. Startled, the bouncer hesitated and lowered his guard. Gloves hit him with a hard right to the head and then a left and another right to the gut, and the bouncer crumbled like a sack of potatoes falling from a produce wagon. Gloves reached down to pull up his pants, but the stripper jumped on his back, screaming.

The girls in the hallway were calling, "Alphonse, Alphonse!" and another hard body appeared at the door. Gloves twisted his torso violently, tossing the stripper to the floor. Alphonse charged him, but was met by a jab that instantly deviated his septum. He went down like a curtain. Then Gloves pushed the girls who had collected at the door out of the way and burst for the exit, dragging his pants by one ankle. With the girls shouting, "Call the cops. Call the cops," everyone in the place still sober enough to walk scrambled out. Gloves ran barefoot out the front door carrying his shoes and a hard-on.

"Oh shit!" Gloves glanced up from the *Penthouse* magazine he was studying. There they were, the two dimwits in the photos taken by the Elgar security camera, wheeling through the gravel at the rear of the construction site. He hadn't expected the bicycles. They were headed east, leaping the ruts in the landscape left by the bulldozers and the backhoes. The nearest crossroad was a quarter of a mile away.

He shoved the van into first gear, crossed Kingsway, and headed into the parking lot. He was over the curb before he realized the error of his ways and slammed on the brakes. Through a thick, rising cloud of dust he got a bead on them as they rode toward the backyards and open fields already two hundred yards away. Even if it were possible it would be too conspicuous to follow them. He waited to see which direction they would go, hoping they would turn north and he could intersect them at Route 60. He wound his way toward the rear of the job site and kept them in view as long as possible. They zigzagged around swimming pools, clothesline posts, hibiscus bushes, and storage sheds. They rode up and down drainage ditches and flew over landscaped moguls, then disappeared behind a house. They appeared to be headed in the direction of a strip shopping center on Route 60.

By this time a trailer had backed into position to load a backhoe, blocking his exit. Gloves hammered the horn and tried to negotiate around the truck. No luck. He resisted the urge to get out, extract the driver from his perch, and move the damned truck himself. He waited in a hurry.

Five minutes later the view to the road was clear. He pushed the van as fast as it would go. It swerved back and forth, ricocheting off the ruts and through the gravel. A plume of dust and cinders rose a half block behind him. He bounced over the curb as he exited the construction site onto Kingsway. Two cars swerved to avoid him. He raced north to the busy intersection of Brandon Boulevard with State Route 60, and turned east without waiting for the signal to change. His ill-timed turn caused a middle-aged man in a sub-compact to shift lanes so quickly he was struck in the rear by two teenagers driving a compact four-wheel drive SUV. As Gloves looked into his rearview mirror, the small car spun out of control and one of the kids exited through the front windshield. Gloves winced and eased off the accelerator. People in every direction were gawking, but no one seemed to have noticed him. Trouble would surely ensue if he stopped, so he accelerated slowly for about a block and then sped east in search of the two free-wheeling construction workers. At the same time he buckled his seat belt.

He didn't see them on his first pass down Brandon Boulevard so he retraced his route, careful to stay clear of flashing lights that had converged back at the corner of Brandon Boulevard and Kingsway. When he reached Seffner-Valrico Road the second time and they were still not in sight, he turned south. He drove about a mile without spying them, then retreated, crossed the highway, and headed north on Seffner-Valrico Road. He cursed the damned backhoe operator again and wondered how anyone could disappear so fast on a bicycle.

Seffner-Valrico Road's undulating humps, like the back of a dragon, obstructed Gloves' view. He still hadn't spotted them after descending the last hill. Thinking he had lost them, he slammed the steering wheel so hard it cracked. As the road opened onto a longer, unobstructed flat stretch, through the overhanging branches of the trees that lined the residential roadside, he caught a glimpse of two figures bobbing in the distance. If they are the two guys I am chasing, Gloves said, "Some-bitch, those guys can fly!"

The tires squealed as he jammed the pedal to the floor. Within a minute he was a half block from them. In his zest he had almost forgotten that he had no idea what he was going to do when he caught them. He hadn't counted upon the bicycles. He presumed they would return to their motel after work and he would corner them there. "So much for the best laid plans of men and mice," he repeated a line from one of the few serious literary recollections of his collegiate life. He had read John Steinbeck's novel in its entirety during his junior year and had always had a soft spot for Lenny. He slowed and continued to follow them at a distance, hoping to avoid discovery.

The terrain had become rural, and he had to find a place to stop them where he wouldn't be disturbed. While he waited for his opportunity, he watched their workout in awe. On the open road he clocked them at almost thirty miles per hour. They rode into ravines and drainage ditches at high speeds just to gain some elevation from which they would propel themselves into flight. They would jump the shrubs and short fences, do 180 degree turns in the air and stop on a mark. He didn't know much about cycling, but he had been an athlete for years and thirty miles per hour on a mountain bike was "frigging humming!" The Italian looking one with the dark complexion, was shorter and had thick, dark hair and a scar on his forearm and chin, probably from a bad landing, Gloves smirked. The other was fair-skinned but well-tanned with a wave of brown hair seeping from his helmet. Although he was less stocky than his riding companion, he was a sturdy six feet. In spite of their condition and athleticism, Gloves felt that riding bicycles was a far cry from professional wrestling. Besides, he was going take them by surprise.

He was becoming anxious. He hated Florida, not just because the cops were probably after him, but the windows were rolled up, the

A/C was on full blast, and he was still dripping like a possum on a spit. He trailed them for a couple of miles in search of a propitious place to complete his work, but there were no turnouts, side roads, or open fields without fences where he could force them off the road or, at least, into semi-seclusion.

He approached within a hundred feet. The guys on the bikes were bearing down so hard he didn't think they would notice him, but they slowed and moved onto the highway's apron. They waved for him to pass. He got a little closer but didn't go around them. They slowed even more and moved farther off the road, onto the gravel. He moved onto the shoulder of the road and slowed to match their pace. They stopped and turned to face him. Gloves was less than twenty feet behind them when it became apparent that one of them recognized something about the van and shouted to the other. Their faces turned as ashen as parchment, and they stood up on the pedals.

"You're going to try to outrun 200 horsepower," Gloves said. "Your asses are mine."

They were weaving and searching for some off road escape, somewhere that a bike might go that his truck could not. There was nothing but an embankment down and across the road from them. He decided to ram the backs of their bikes and run them right into the hill. They might be damaged but they could still talk, and all he needed was information.

As he speeded up they surprised him and crossed to the other side of the road. He couldn't follow because he was approaching a bend in the road, and he had to be alert for oncoming traffic. A roadside sign across the street read *Public Boat Launch Ahead*. The bicyclists pedaled in that direction. The lake was visible through the trees on his right. As they crossed to Gloves' side of the road again he accelerated. They pushed the pedals with relentless effort, but he was almost on their tail. Their contorted faces reflected in their mirrors as they headed into the curve. Aware that a public facility lay just around the bend, Gloves slowed to look for traffic before toppling them.

He was only twenty-five feet behind them, close enough that they couldn't cross the road in front of him without being hit. They were standing on the pedals as they came around the sharp bend in the road that opened onto the entrance of the public boat launch. The sign at the acme of the curve in the road had issued a warning for drivers: *Beware of vehicles on the road.* Gloves accelerated and pulled within a few feet of their rear wheels. They looked back at him.

At the same time, David Kinder was backing his boat trailer onto the road. When Mat Strong and Watt Guillermo turned around they were facing the inclined propeller of Kinder's new seventy-horsepower Mercruiser that was attached to his brand new eighteen-foot bass boat. Mat's head was dissected by the propeller. Gloves slammed on the brakes and swerved around them, but Watt's bike caromed off his front fender. When Gloves stopped, in the rearview mirror, he noticed a sizable welt forming on his temple, but the sight of Watt's half severed torso hanging from a hook on the end of a post at the corner of the bass boat made him upchuck all over the steering wheel. The blood on the pavement was slaughterhouse thick. He hadn't intended upon harming them, only to question them and, maybe, rough 'em up a bit. His was pissed off that they had made him look bad by breaking into Von Lleuwan's plants, his domain. Now, no one could talk to them, and Von Lleuwan was going be mad as hell. The vomit on his hands gave him the cold shakes. He wiped them on the seat and drove off.

27

Derk felt as if he'd been torn, in the middle of the night, from the comforting billows of a deep sleep and plunged into an icy crater. Movement of his left arm was paralyzingly painful. The more he kicked the deeper he sank, as if his very thoughts had become a propellant. He couldn't breathe. The frigid depth was pulling him down to a destiny as inevitable as the day gravity will pull the earth and the sun and all the planets into a black, lifeless abyss. He lay in his bed, drenched in the dankness of his own expirations, conscious but unable to move and unaware of where he was until some feeble rays of dawn filtered through the slits in the blinds. The image on the ledge below him had been real. His grasp was still not secure and, in spite of the danger, he thought one final lurch could bring the man to safety. He held firm and pulled. The face revealed itself, his father, and then he slipped through his fingers. He screamed, and sat up in bed. Startled by the voice, he rolled away from the sound. When his sore ribs hit the frame of his waterbed, he cried out and fell like a side of beef onto the floor. He looked around and realized he was alone. The voice he'd heard was his own. Reaching for a light on the bedside stand, he knocked over the digital clock. Not yet four o'clock. He crawled back into bed and collapsed.

He was awakened again around seven by the clunking of cupboard cabinets. A caffeine-stained aroma seeped through the cracks in the bedroom door. His swollen arm made it difficult to negotiate the frame of the waterbed, but once vertical, he retrieved an ace bandage and two Advil from the bathroom. Then he straggled to the kitchen for a bag of ice. Sandra French was drinking a glass of juice and reading the newspaper. She had on gray gym shorts, an oversized green and gray Michigan State T-shirt and a pair of white sneakers. Her hair was combed back, revealing an energetic, youthful smile.

"Good morning. I got a glass of orange juice and started some coffee. Hope you don't mind?" she said with more cheer than he could digest so soon on this day.

He looked up long enough to reply, "Get what you need." He was holding one arm with the other.

"You all right?" she asked.

"Been better," he mumbled.

He took a box of plastic bags from one of the cupboards, opened the freezer, and tried to remove some ice-cubes. The trays fell to the floor, spreading shattered ice like glass crystals.

Sandra bent down to assist him.

"I got it," he said as he reached down to retrieve a couple of the stray cubes. Pain shot through his body. "No, I don't." He slumped against the kitchen cabinets.

She rose to steady him, but he pulled away. "I'm all right. Do you mind putting some ice in a bag?"

He put the sports page under one arm and took her half-empty glass of juice to the patio. From the balcony the sight of his damaged car added to his distress. "Ouch!" he cried out.

"What'd you do?" Sandra called from the kitchen.

"Nothing," he said and sat down.

Joining him on the patio, she juggled a bag of ice from one hand to the other. Her long legs and lean, muscular arms were a bit pale but a few days in the Florida sun would take care of that. She had an earthy, ruddy, naturally clear complexion without the lipstick and make-up. Her hair was pulled back into a ponytail and secured with a rubber band, exposing her high cheekbones. She was distractingly sensuous.

"What are you looking at?" she asked.

"Thanks," he said, reaching for the ice. "Going for a run?"

Sympathy draped her. "Is there anything I can get for you?"

"A new car."

"Anything else?"

"Call my mother."

"Now?" she said.

He shook his head. The ice slipped from his grip as he tried to wrap his arm with the ace bandage.

"Let me help," she said. She wrapped the icepack against his arm. "I want to go for a walk on the beach. Do we have time?"

"I want to see the Simpson kid today," he said. "We have to leave by nine."

She glanced at her wristwatch. "I'll be ready."

"Hope so. You're driving," he said.

Derk reclined in his chaise lounge. He wanted the morning sun to warm his body while the Advil dulled his senses. If he could just avoid being punched or run into today, it had to be better than yesterday. In any event, he could no longer postpone seeing his father.

As planned, they were ready to go by nine. Derk settled into the passenger seat as Sandra looked over his battered muscle car with dismay.

"It's this or my motorcycle. Your choice," he told her.

On the way, he dialed his insurance agent and made arrangements to pick up a rental in Tampa. Lady Lake was located in central Florida, about an hour and a half northeast of Tampa.

"You'll like this place. It resembles Michigan: small towns, rolling hills, lot of lakes, and nice golf courses," Derk said, not sure why he was concerned that she like it.

They exchanged notes on the case as they drove and arrived at the Ward Institute at noon. The yard was lined with oleander and crammed with Sabal palms, known to Floridians as cabbage palms, yuccas, sago palms, majestic live oaks and a huge, aging banyan tree that filled the sky above the oval shaped drive.

"It's just like she described it," remarked Sandra. "Shaped like an octopus. Each tentacle is for patients with similar problems. This place is for people who are too sick for home care and not expected to get better."

"Doesn't look that bleak," commented Derk.

"I made arrangements for us to see the Simpson boy and talk with a Saraphina Whistlethwaite, the physical therapist assigned to him."

"Can't we talk with the kid's doctor?" asked Derk.

"The hospital says she knows it all. Her doctoral thesis is on physical therapy for those suffering from the effects of toxic poisoning."

"That's a mouthful."

"Apparently, she's aware of the mother's effort to affix responsibility for his condition. He's been there over two years."

Derk and Sandra sat in the lobby while Miss Whistlethwaite was paged. Fifteen minutes later a pudgy black woman in her late thirties wearing a white smock and a charming continence held out her hand and introduced herself.

"Mr. Bryan, Miss French, I'm Sara Whistlethwaite. I'm told you'd like to chat wiss me 'bout Billy Seempson."

Derk was caught off guard by her accent and her dialect. Each of them was familiar but not in concert. Miss Whistlethwaite asked if they would like to join her in the cafeteria for lunch in that she was on a tight schedule. They agreed and asked if they could first see the Simpson boy.

On the way to Billy's ward Miss Whistlethwaite said, "You look puzzled. Is there a question?"

"It's your accent, delightful, but unusual," Sandra said.

"Which part, the Jamaican or the Spanish?"

"That's it!" said Derk.

"I'm sorry. I hope I didn't offend you," Sandra said.

"To the contrary. I'm quite used to it. Besides, it was the fault of my mother and father. She was Spanish. He was Jamaican. Me grandfather was English, the bloody bloke. I've been in the States for fifteen years, but it's stuck with me like tarpaper. The accent, I mean," she replied. "The Simpson boy, he's just down the hall, and he's not in very good shape I should warn you."

Derk wasn't prepared for what he saw. The emaciated, jaundiced boy lying in the hospital bed was about ten, no older than twelve. His feeble body shook intermittently. The boy seemed to notice him, but his gaze fixed upon the therapist. For a moment he would cease shaking and lie still, and his eyes would dart around the room suggesting that his mind was disconnected from his body. Suddenly, his pupils would constrict, and he would shake again, sometimes violently, and then stop. His hair was dark and thin, and his cheekbones were high and prominent in a manner that suggested what had once been a handsome young lad, but the skin was now drawn so tight it was as if it had been shellacked onto his face. His limbs were free, but there was a loose constraint covering his mid-section, and there were high rails on the sides of the bed. He wore a white hospital gown and plastic diapers. Miss Whistlethwaite went to his bedside and put her hand under his backside. Then she placed her hand on his arm and spoke to him as if he were perfectly healthy.

"Billy, you have a 'cup la' visitors," she said. Her unusual pronunciation required Derk's complete attention. "They're going to have lunch with me. Is there anything I can get you?" she asked, but he didn't respond. "Do you have to go to the bathroom?"

The Simpson boy said nothing, but the therapist seemed to recognize some kind of response.

She said, "I'll get someone to take you to the bathroom." She patted his forehead and brushed back his hair with the docility of a doting mother.

In place of the boy in the hospital bed the image of Derk's ailing father flashed. His throat filled with dried canvas and he felt sorrow drip from his face. The therapist must have noticed his tears. She motioned for Derk and Sandra to leave the room ahead of her.

"I had no idea," Sandra said. She turned, looked at the child again and began to say something, but the remainder of her thought went unspoken.

Derk rubbed the moisture from his face and massaged his wounds. He didn't imagine this day could be as bad as yesterday. "I need to make a call," he said and excused himself.

"You can do that at the nurse's station," the therapist said and pointed the way.

At the nurses' station Miss Whistlethwaite directed an attendant to Billy Simpson's room and Derk called his mother. There was no answer.

"Why doesn't she get an answering machine like everybody else?" he said.

"Who?" Sandra said.

"My mother," he said, gently rubbing his arm again. The Advil was running its course.

Miss Whistlethwaite waved her hand toward another wing of the building, "The cafeteria is this way," and they walked down a long, institutional corridor. "What did you do to your arm?"

"It's nothing," he said, "but I could use some Advil. I gather you were told about our interest in the boy?"

"It's about a case you're working on?" she said.

"We're with the EPA," Sandra answered.

"His mother thought he was poisoned by something sprayed on the trees next to her house," Derk said. "What is his precise problem and can you confirm his mother's accusations?"

"I grew up in Jamaica, and we have wonderful, delicious fruits of all kind, but it's just a little island and the people there are getting sick from all the chemicals. It's worse here. I am only a P.T., but I see more kids with these symptoms all the time. Let me give you some background." She stopped, turned, and faced him.

The therapist was built like a stump and was on the homely side. Her skin was as dark as Cuban coffee but its sheen was luxurious and her smile was like crystal. She was articulate, but couldn't restrain her despair as she explained what had happened. "Three thousand new chemicals are produced each year. We know that many of these are very dangerous. As of 1990 only about two thousand have been tested for carcinogenicity and not many more have been since then. Half tested positive. That means they cause cancer. There have been over six hundred pesticides approved since the 1940's, and a lot of them are very dangerous, particularly to kids and fetuses, but also to older peoples."

She had an unusual trait of making certain words plural. Derk guessed it must be left over from her heritage. He kept rubbing his arm.

"Someone should look at that arm," she interrupted her discourse. Derk concurred with a grimace. "We know that children whose yards have been treated with these chemicals have four times the risk of getting cancers. We know from independent research studies that there are pesticide residues on fruits and vegetables much more than the government reports. We know that these kids have less poorly developed immune systems and they eat proportionately more of these foods, and so their risks are higher. These chemicals, they're on everything. Peas, pears, berries and in the juices. All the things kids eat. Now the drugs they are using to treat sick cows like

BGH, Bovine Growth Hormone, are ending up in the milk. In fact, eighty-two different drugs have been found in milk and only thirty-two have been approved."

Derk was anxious for her to get to the point so he added, "Yeah, cows don't eat corn naturally, but that's what they're fed, and without the drugs they couldn't tolerate the corn. Nonsense, isn't it?"

"He's right, Miss French," she continued, "Even chemicals that were banned years ago, like DDT, are still showing up in mother's milk, and women with the highest exposure rates are getting more breast cancer. There's been a possible link detected between some shampoos used to kill lice and the incidence of childhood brain cancers. Some common household products such as no-pest strips, termite treatments, flea collars and pet shampoos have been linked to higher brain cancer in kids. In fact, brain cancers among white kids under fifteen increased almost one third during the past twenty-five years."

"We know about a lot of these things," Derk said. "Right here in central Florida a lot of people can't drink the water from their own wells due to the chemicals used on the fruit trees over the years. Bromacil, Aldicarb, ethylene dibromide, and various nitrates have washed into their wells. It's a damn shame, excuse me, but that's why we're here, to see if we can do something about it." He was making a diplomatic attempt to hurry her along.

They reached the cafeteria, got trays, and entered the line. Sandra passed the salads, the fruits, the vegetables, the red meats, and was now standing in front of the desserts with only a diet cola on her tray. The therapist laughed.

"I didn't mean to spoil your appetite," the eruditious doctoral candidate said.

"Is Jell-O okay?" Sandra squinted at the Jell-O and then looked at the therapist.

"Sure, if you don't mind a little pork in your diet."

"What do you mean?"

"Gelatin is made from porcine products," the physical therapist replied.

"I didn't know that," Sandra said.

"Really," Derk confirmed. He was amused. It was Sandra French's job to know this stuff, but the pudgy, little Spanish, Jamaican physical therapist with the British accent was a walking encyclopedia of toxicology. "People like their food to look good even though they don't know what's in it or on it. It's all about shelf life in America."

Saraphina added, "As grim as it sounds, it's even worse for the people who grow and harvest the foods. They work around much higher concentrations of chemicals than we digest, and when they get sick they can't complain or take the time off for fear of being fired. We need better laws."

They made their final selections and slid their trays in front of the cashier. Saraphina had taken the turkey hotshot with dressing and iced tea. Derk settled on baked white fish with steamed rice, broccoli and a bottle of water. Sandra found a banana to go with her lime Jell-O and diet cola. Derk paid the cashier and followed them to an empty table as far from the cafeteria noise as possible.

After they were seated Derk asked, "So how does this relate to the Simpson kid? You think he was exposed to some of these chemicals?"

"Probably, according to Dr. Whitesell, Billy's doctor, but the problem is it's not that easy to tell," she responded and took a few bites of her turkey hotshot. "I know it's not so good for me and it's fattening, but I love gravy on mashed potatoes. Once in a while won't kill me." Her self-deprecating manner was accompanied by a snicker. Derk smiled, a reaction that was both empathetic and patronizing. She had not answered his answer about Billy Simpson.

"Sorry," she said covering her mouth with one hand. "Billy Simpson is a little over ten years old. We think he came into contact with something toxic when he was much younger or even when his mother was pregnant. You noticed that he's very thin and discolored?" Derk nodded. Sandra was staring at Sara, almost trance like. "It's his liver," she continued, "and the shaking, it's from neuromuscular damage. He doesn't have much control of his body. That's why I work with him. I don't know how much good it does, but I think it helps him just to get some attention and have someone touch him. His mother hasn't been here for a while," she said. Her sadness suggested dim prospects for the boy's recovery.

"Can you be more specific?" Derk inquired.

The therapist took another large bite of the turkey and mashed potatoes and washed it down with iced tea. Sandra picked at her Jell-O, one small spoonful at a time.

"We've not been able to trace many cancers in the natural environment to the suspected chemicals because the event that triggered them occurred years ago, maybe even decades. In this case it probably occurred when he was very young," she said.

"I know what you mean," Derk added. "People were still getting skin cancer long after the atomic bomb was dropped over Japan."

She continued, "You're right. Most of the chemicals that can cause cancers exercise their influence over a long time. Many carcinogenic chemicals travel through the placenta in pregnant women and start cancers in the fetus that show up later, even after adolescence."

"And many of the chemicals about which we should have the greatest concern have the longest latency periods," Derk added. "I gather that's what happened to Billy Simpson?"

"Are you saying you can't pin it down?" Sandra asked.

Saraphina took another mouthful of mashed potatoes and a long slurp of iced tea.

"Do you mind if I get a little technical? It may help you understand what we think happened to this boy," she said.

"Sure," Derk said, but what he was thinking was why not? She had to get to the point some time.

"The liver's primary function is to filter out all kinds of harmful substances in the body. It uses various detoxifying enzymes to help metabolize various toxins. It converts them to alcohols or mild acids or links them with a kind of shuttle molecule called glutathione that is easily excreted from the body. If the body's stores of this enzyme are reduced, the liver's ability to fight off harmful chemicals can be severely mitigated. In addition, the liver of a fetus or of an infant is too immature to completely fight off harmful chemicals. We found that Mrs. Simpson took mega doses of ascorbic acid, vitamin C." She paused and asked, "Are you still with me?"

Derk said nothing. He understood the chemistry involved. Sandra responded, "Pretty much."

"She took vitamin C during her pregnancy and gave this vitamin to her son after he was born. Normally vitamin C is very healthy for you and non-toxic because it is water-soluble, and if you take too much, what you don't use just washes through the body in a couple of hours. Large doses of vitamin C will deplete the supply of glutathione. Somehow, someway, somewhere, the Simpson boy, maybe even while he was still inside his mother, was exposed to some harmful chemicals, maybe even the pesticides his mother said were sprayed on the trees next to her house. As a result of the delayed toxicity and his impaired ability to fight off the toxins in his body, the boy became very sick. This is what Dr. Whitesell thinks happened. Mr. Bryan, this boy's life was taken away from him before he even had a chance."

Her conviction was sobering, and her conclusion was troubling. Derk had long dreaded the day this would happen, but it was Sandra French who spoke, "You're saying we're all at risk, pregnant women, children, the elderly . . . everybody."

"Now you know what we're up against," Derk stated like a preacher to his congregation. "Miss Whistlethwaite, when was the last time you saw Mrs. Simpson?"

"At least a couple of weeks, maybe more," she responded. "She used to be so regular. Has something happened to her?"

"I'm afraid there may be some more bad news. The police over in Yeehaw Junction found a body that fits her description. We're going over there this afternoon to find out," Derk told her.

"Oh no. What happened?" Saraphina asked.

"We don't even know it's Mrs. Simpson, but it doesn't look good," Sandra said. "We'll let you know."

"By the way, can you please tell us how to get in touch with Dr. Whitesell?" Derk said.

Saraphina sat motionless, dejection stamped on her face like an old license plate. Derk knew that the nature of this facility meant she was around death all the time, but he guessed she never got used to it. He shared her despair. Death was much closer to him than he wanted to admit. He would place another call to his mother before he left.

"The nurse's station has his office number," she muttered. "It's in Tampa."

Derk motioned to Sandra, "Let's go."

"Thank you for your time and good luck with your studies," Agent French said.

"I'm just sad for the boy," Saraphina said without getting up. "He's been through so much."

"He's lucky to have you. Goodbye," Derk said, and they left.

At the nurse's station they were given Dr. Whitesell's telephone number. Derk called his mother while Sandra called the doctor. Still no answer at his mother's house. "Where is she?" he said aloud. He paced in front of the nurse's station, cupping his elbow of his injured close to his side.

"We can see him at five o'clock today," Sandra told Derk.

Derk frowned at his watch. It was almost one o'clock. "We can't make Yeehaw Junction and Tampa. Let's see the doctor," he said.

"Your arm's really bothering you, isn't it?" she said.

"Among things."

As they were leaving the grounds of the institute, Derk said, "How'd you like to tour the Port of Tampa?"

"What's there?"

"Cruise chips, chemicals, storage tanks, more chemicals, some distribution companies and more chemicals."

"Like in Elgar Chemical?" she said.

"Exact-a-mundo!" Derk said.

"What authority do we have there?"

"I'd say it's time for an impromptu safety audit, and since we're going to be in the area with a little time to kill, why not?"

They stood in the parking lot beneath a row of stately royal palms. The air was dead calm and so hot the palmetto bugs bounced off the pavement like popcorn. Each of them began to drip the moment they left the air-conditioned confines of the hospital, but neither said anything about the weather.

"That's harassment, there's no provocation, and it's not our job. That's the county's responsibility. Besides, I know about you, Derk Bryan," Sandra said.

"There's got to be a link here with the Michigan case. The name Von Lleuwan is written all over it, and Elgar's one of his companies. I want to know what's going on there," he responded. "And what do you mean, you know about me?"

"We don't have any reason to go in there," she said.

"They've been suspected of distributing illegal pesticides for a long time. Wally said that. You said that. It was in the report," he said.

"There's no proof."

"Yet!" he said. "And what do you mean, you know about me?"

"I'm as upset as you, but you're letting the Simpson kid get to you. It's our job to bring the bad guys to justice, not go looking for trouble or create trouble."

Derk puffed. "So I'm a trouble maker."

"You're an activist. You think government should take an active role in the lives of its citizens. I don't. I think we should stay out of people's lives. Let them do what they want. When they cross the line or step out of bounds, then we've got to do something, but not until then," Sandra said. She wiped her brow and drew a pinch of her blouse away from her wet body.

"You mean when the spotted owl, the Key deer, the green turtle, the bald eagle and, hell, hundreds of other species are near extinction, then we should step in and to do something? Go after the bad guys, as you say," Derk said. He wiped his neck and forehead with a handkerchief he pulled from his back pocket.

"Can we get in the car? I feel like a soggy sandwich," she said.

She turned the A/C up to maximum and headed for Tampa.

"So, you think it's okay to pour unlimited amounts of pesticides and herbicides and fertilizers and all kinds of stuff onto the soil each year even if it's contaminating most of the water from the Great Lakes to the Everglades, ruining the fishing and the shrimping from Texas to Florida and destroying the wetlands in the process. That's okay as long as we don't step on free will!"

"The natural environment is self-limiting," Sandra said. "The theory of supply and demand applies to the natural environment, as well. Free enterprise and the price mechanism in the free market place ultimately maintain the balance for human endeavors and their impact upon the environment. To do it any other way artificially distorts the process and slows down and stretches out the negative impact part of the curve. The planet isn't in trouble. It is huge and diverse and self- rectifying. Species have been dying forever, and they'll continue to die. That's evolution. You think we can save ourselves from evolution, from these ultimate changes? You're a dreamer. We're too small and insignificant in the overall spectrum of this huge and complicated cosmos. Free will, it is mankind's greatest gift and his greatest nemesis I'll admit, and once in a while somebody seriously abuses his or her privileges and harms some innocent people in the process. Then it's our job to correct the situation and to bring the bad guys to justice. That's all. In the meantime, we should let people exercise their innate creativity and enjoy themselves. That's what we're here for."

"Wow, French, I had no idea," Derk said. "It's not that I agree with you, although there's more than a kernel of truth to what you said. It's your conviction. I had no idea you'd given this so much thought. Would you really leave the whole planet up for grabs? I mean the water, the air, and the soil to the highest bidder?"

"It already is," she responded. As they reached a stop sign she said, "Which way?"

"Turn left here and go south until you get to nineteen. Make a right and I'll take you through the Withlacoochee State Forest. Thank God, it's not for sale. If you were in charge, the damn thing would be covered with fast food restaurants and parking lots," he said.

"You know I didn't mean that."

"It sounds like a philosophy that lacks any purpose other than to be able to shop at Saks or drive the biggest car or own the most expensive home. In the long run we all end up with the same amount, zero. It seems to me that there has to be some more important point to life, survival of the species, if nothing else."

"A guy who drives the kind of car you do ought to be careful about what he says. It compromises your credibility." There was a smirk at one corner of her mouth.

"I didn't buy that car new. I restored it. As a matter of fact, I recycled it," he said and watched her smirk expand. "All right, you found my sensitive spot. At least, one of them."

"What made you such an environmental crusader?" she asked.

They were passing the sculpted lawns of one of the most renowned country clubs in the state, home of many women's collegiate tournaments. An occasional cirrus cloud floated with the softness of down high above them while the Ruellia wilted in the infernal heat.

"I don't know. Probably my grandfather always telling me to turn off the lights," he said.

"That might cause you to conserve energy, but it didn't create your intensity. When you're on a case, you're driven," she said. "Where'd that come from?"

Her question stimulated some introspection and he flashed back to his childhood. "My grandfather I guess. One day we were sitting out in his little aluminum rowboat, and things were kind of slow. We'd already moved three or four times. He was usually very patient, but he looked over his bifocals and gazed across the lake. It wasn't a very big lake. You could see three shores from where we sat. And he said, 'Too damned many people!' Then he stood up, pointed to one end of the lake, and panned along the far shore. 'There were only fifteen to twenty cottages on this lake when I was your age. Look at them now, probably more than three hundred, and the goddamn fish ain't worth keeping if you caught 'em. Things gotta change. Know what I'm saying, little buddy?' He always told people I was his little buddy. I just shook my head. I'd never heard him cuss before. I figured he was just mad because the fish weren't biting. Then a powerboat went by kind of fast and rocked the boat. Grandpa darn near fell out of the boat, and he knocked his reel overboard trying to keep his balance. That made him even madder. 'They find a good thing and they use it to death. Damn kids!' he said, pulled up the anchor, and we left right then and there. He never took me back to that lake, and every time the fishing was slow anywhere, he'd say the same thing, and it seemed that the fishing was never the same after that."

"You spent a lot of time with your grandfather?" Sandra asked.

The light behind Derk's eyes turned on. "He's the one who taught me about the balance of nature. He said if people didn't put so many pesticides and fertilizers on their lawns or pour their used oil into the lake or use it for a latrine it would support an abundance of wildlife. If they didn't take more than they put back, the lake wouldn't suffer from over fishing. If they didn't build more homes than the natural environment could support, then it would stay healthy and everyone could prosper. It was common sense, but as Grandpa often said, *Common sense ain't so common.* Later I found out he lifted that quote from Voltaire, but it didn't matter. I was even more impressed that he had read Voltaire. He played the banjo, was great at cribbage player and an ace at horseshoes. And he was a real rebel rouser. Grandma said he wrote stinging letters to the county commissioners and once in a while he got so upset he asked her to drive him to commission meetings so he could give them a piece of his mind. And they listened because he knew what he was talking about."

Realizing that he had been monopolizing the conversation Derk ran his finger across his lips to make a motor sound. "Sorry. I'm rambling."

"He sounds like quite a guy," she said. "And now I know where you got it."

Derk squinted at her.

"Your intensity."

Derk laughed. He couldn't deny her observation. They passed a couple dressed in racing gear on bicycles and Derk craned to examine their rides. "Mmm. Nice," he said.

"Why did you leave DNR?" Sandra asked.

"Too damned much politics."

"That's government. You didn't know that when you started?"

"I thought I could make a difference."

"Youthful idealism, but I heard it was more than that."

"Grandpa died just before I started college, but he had inspired me. I studied natural history, anthropology, and biology. I even joined the environmental club." The memory forced him to laugh. "We did some crazy stuff. It's a good thing we didn't get caught. After school I got a job with the Michigan DNR. I'd been there about three years and hadn't done anything important when someone began asking questions about the tumors in Lake Michigan fish."

"I remember that," she said.

"I wanted that case. Three months into it the chief investigator resigns for a job in the private sector, and they gave me the job. There I was, a twenty-five year old kid with his first major assignment and an opportunity to show the world what I could do. I worked night and day."

"Way back then," she said. One corner of her mouth opened slightly when she smiled. It was endearing.

"I was probably trying to prove something to my dad, but I didn't know it at the time," Derk answered.

"You don't talk much about him."

Derk tried to remove the anguish that thoughts of his father summoned by grinding his forehead with the back of his left arm, but the pain shot through him. "Oh, damn," he said.

"Be careful."

He digested his discomfort. They passed another group of bicyclers stopped along the roadside.

"So what happened?" she asked.

"It became apparent that most of the game fish in the Big Lake had tumors and they were toxic if you ate too many. I wondered if this might have been caused Grandpa's cancer. He ate no red meat, said the biggest and strongest animals on the planet were all vegetarians. So he practically lived on fried fish and turnips." Sandra puckered, as if she'd just burped some citrus. "Really, turnips *and* parsnips," he said, then stuck out his tongue and shook his head. "He lost a third of his weight before he died and had to be fed with a straw. It was terrible."

"I'm sorry," Sandra said.

"If it's true what they say about the benefits of fish oil, Grandpa shouldn't have gotten cancer. He should have been mined."

Sandra laughed, but caught herself.

"It's all right," he said. "Anyway, I got carried away looking for the culprit."

"Loose cannon," she interjected.

"Is that what they're saying?"

"Some, but there's been changes."

"You don't have to candy coat it. I had lots of energy but no tact," he confessed. "Hell, everyone was involved. We're all part of the problem, but nobody wanted to point responsibility. Too many heads would have to roll."

"That's the politician's job," she said.

"It's everybody's job," he said, "and nobody takes responsibility."

"You get so personally involved, Derk," she said.

"It is personal," he said, "but I guess I must have thought if I dug deep enough I could find out who killed Grandpa. It didn't seem fair that something as simple and benign as fishing had killed him."

"I'm sorry about your grandfather," Sandra said again.

"Thanks," he said.

"It's nice to see you smile," Sandra said. "You've been so grim since I got here."

"There's tooth marks in my heals."

"I didn't want to say anything, but I heard you scream last night."

"I thought that was me." The face in his dream returned. "Which reminds me, I've got to call mom again." His cheeks turned a shade of porcelain.

"What is it, Derk?" she asked.

"A family matter." Derk held his aching arm close to his side.

"You've certainly earned your reputation," she said.

"What's that?"

"Relentless but stubbornly independent."

"You going to talk about this case or not?"

"Hold onto it if you want, but something's bothering you."

"I've been beat up, my car's been wrecked, people are getting acid baths, and somebody is poisoning little kids. What do you want from me?"

"You usually wake up in the middle of the night screaming when you're on a case?" she said.

"Depends," he said. Her eyes widened, obviously waiting for him to expound. "Upon who's sleeping in the next room."

"Touché," she said. "I didn't mean to pry."

He stared at her vitamin complexion, almost able to see his reflection in her crystal blues. "My God, you're beautiful!" he thought.

Her eyes caught his, but she said nothing. That felt good. Then they focused upon the scene unfolding above the dash in front of them. They were passing through a stand of cypress that stretched as far as the eye could see on one side of the road. On the other side a large herd of black stallions grazed in a huge pastoral dale encompassed by a weathered picket fence and a driveway that creased the meadow down to an enormous stone ranch house flanked by a long stable. A lone giant live oak draped with Spanish moss stood lonely against the azure sky while a flock of cattle egrets searched for sustenance in the shadows of the gallant steeds.

"It's so beautiful here," she said. "And to answer your question, things are going on that probably aren't coincidental, but I haven't seen any proof that Von Lleuwan is involved in anything illegal. You're ready to search his plant, but we don't even know what we're looking for. People attack him because he's so visible. The Simpson woman thought he was responsible for her son's illness, but you heard the physical therapist. There's no direct link between Von Lleuwan and her son. I don't want to search his plant until we have a legitimate reason. We need to do something about your arm."

Five minutes ago he would have been disappointed with her answer, but not now.

"Can you stop at the next convenience store? I need some ice," Derk said. "Got any Advil?"

A few minutes later they pulled into a convenience store. Derk got out of the car to get some ice for his arm and something wet to wash down the aspirin she had found in her purse. He turned and handed Sandra his cellular telephone. "Why don't you call your friend in missing persons and see if they have a positive I.D. on the body in Yeehaw Junction?"

She was still on the telephone when he returned with a bag of ice and a bottle of water.

"Thanks again, Sargeant."

Derk slid in beside her.

"It's a positive. Eva Simpson, all right."

"Anything else?"

"She didn't die there. She was taken there and dropped."

"How do they know?"

"No personal belongings. No purse, no car, nothing."

"Cause of death?"

"They're not sure. She could have bled to death. The body was a mess. It had been out there for a while. Long enough for an alligator chew off one of her legs. There was a lot of internal bleeding, especially abdominal, and some burns in the esophagus," Sandra said. "Maybe from something she drank."

"Or was forced to drink." Derk made a small guttural sound and placed his hand to his mouth. "Any leads?"

"Nothing yet."

"Her car wasn't at her house. Have they found it yet?"

"How do you know that?" she asked.

"I was there."

"Oh, I forgot. No, he didn't say, and I didn't ask," she said. "Why?"

"Just curious. That's all. Let's get going. I know Von Lleuwan is involved in this, and we're going to get your proof, damn it!"

She handed him the cellphone.

He held the ice against his arm with one hand and dialed the cellphone with the other. "Mom, I've been trying to reach you. Are you all right?"

"Yes, but your dad's not," came a maternal reproval from the other end.

"I know. I know. I'm coming up." Her pain had enveloped him. "But I still can't do it."

Dr. Bernard Whitesell's office was inside a four story, brick building on physicians' row, Dr. Martin Luther King Boulevard in Tampa, about four blocks east of St. Joseph Hospital. His office was on the third floor along with three internists, a cardiologist, an ear, nose and throat specialist, and a podiatrist. Taped to the elevator was an out of order sign.

At the top of the stairs, Derk said, "I'd never go to a podiatrist that made me walk up three floors."

They arrived twenty minutes ahead of their scheduled appointment. It was fortunate that they did. The doctor, dictating instructions to one of his nurses as they entered his office, seemed eager to leave.

"You have my number at the lodge, but don't call unless it's an emergency. I mean a serious emergency, one that Dr. Thornhill can't handle, and I don't know what that would be. I want to know the results of Mrs. Guenther's tests, but you'll not be able to page me. They won't let us take our pagers or cell phones or any form of communication with us on the trail, but then that's the purpose of this trip: to get away from everything. Leave the message at the lodge and I'll call back. Oh, call Dr. Ledsforth and let him know the results of Mary Finnegan's lab. Willie Smith will be in for his treatment on Thursday. Betty can handle that," Dr. Whitesell recited instructions until the nurse interrupted him.

"May I help you?" The nurse asked after sliding open the glass window.

"I'm Mr. Bryan and this is Agent French from the EPA. We have an appointment to see Dr. Whitesell about Billy Simpson," Derk said.

"I'm sorry, but the doctor is on his way to a very important meeting. Could we reschedule this?" she said. The doctor slipped behind her and attempted to conceal the nametag on his lab coat.

"Dr. Whitesell, we need to ask you a few questions about Billy Simpson," Derk said.

"My nurse wasn't aware of my five o'clock meeting when you called. Can this wait until another time?"

"I think your wilderness trek can wait just a few more minutes. This is official EPA business," Derk insisted and moved to open the door to the nurse's station.

"Okay, but please make it brief," Dr. Whitesell acquiesced and directed them to his private office at the rear of his suite.

Dr. Whitesell was in his late fifties, tall, distinguished looking with white hair and bold features, although his eyes were kind of beady and too close together for him to be called handsome. He replaced the lab coat with a perfectly tailored suit coat, then sat down behind a large Victorian black cherry desk while Derk and Sandra took seats across from him on a cushy tan leather divan. In addition to the requisite wall of diplomas, a blown-up color photograph of the doctor sky-diving covered another wall and matching male and female marble torsos stood upon four-foot high stands in opposite corners of the room. Track lights highlighted a series of nineteenth century lithographs mounted on the opposite wall. They featured ancient athletic endeavors. On his desk were a telephone, an art deco lamp with brass clock, and a pair of airline tickets. The air was cool and freshly filtered.

"What can I do for you?" the doctor said.

"It's about Billy Simpson," Derk began. "He's your patient?"

"Yes."

"What's his diagnosis?"

"He has cancer of the liver." The doctor stopped mid-sentence and asked, "Why do you want to know?"

"It's official business," Derk responded and laid his card on the doctor's desk as he continued, "You were saying cancer of the liver and ...,"

"And lesions on the basal ganglia of his brain. Have you seen him?" Dr. Whitesell asked.

"On the what?" Sandra asked.

"Basal ganglia," the doctor repeated, "Have you seen him, the Simpson boy?"

"We just came from the Ward Institute," Sandra said.

"Then you noticed the spasms and his weak condition. He's a very sick."

"Miss Whistlethwaite said you thought that he may have ingested some pesticides or chemicals that caused this condition," Derk said.

"It's possible but difficult to prove. There are all kinds of things that could have afflicted him, something he ate, drank, or inhaled. Could have come from indoors or outdoors. In his case he lived next door to an orchard, at least during his prenatal and early childhood days, and those orchards use a variety of pesticides."

"Did he show traces of toxic residue?" Sandra asked.

"Yes, but we couldn't trace them to anything in particular."

"Were any tests conducted on the site for contamination?" Derk asked.

"Nothing was found. She was an organic gardener so it didn't come from anything she was using."

"How about the water?" Derk asked.

"Negative." The doctor shook his head one time.

"How about the orchards next door?"

"Mrs. Simpson was sure that it came from them. She was suspicious of all chemicals used on food, and the orange farmers use a lot of them. When we asked they gave us a list of the pesticides and other chemicals. It was routine, and none of them seemed to be the source of the problem, but there's no way to tell for sure. I can't prove it, but I suspect this was, or is, a case of delayed toxicity. This boy had a suppressed immune system and a compromised liver that couldn't filter out the damaging effects of the bromacil, the aldicarb, and the other chemicals used on that orchard. Toxic residues of these substances and others have been found in the water supply in various parts of the state. Over time, possibly in conjunction with other chemicals in his environment, they caused the development of cancer in his liver and in the lesions in his basal ganglia which led to the loss of body control. It will kill him."

Neither Derk nor Sandra said anything. The doctor got up and extended his hand, "If there is nothing more, I do need to get going."

Derk rose, followed by Sandra, and they each shook his hand. Derk asked, "Have you seen Mrs. Simpson lately?"

"Not in quite a while. Is there anything else?"

Derk said, "No," but he had hoped for more.

The doctor guided them through the door of his office. "I'm sure you can find your way out," he said and went back into his office and closed the door.

Derk didn't say anything until they were stopped at the entrance to Dr. Martin Luther King Boulevard waiting to enter the steady stream of rush hour traffic.

"Which way?" Sandra asked.

Derk leaned his head to the right. Sandra seemed focused upon the traffic, eager to take her place in it.

"Which way?" she repeated.

Buried in thought, he waved his hand to the right.

"Derk, which way should I go?"

"Down to Dale Mabry, turn left. Go to the expressway and turn right. Get off at the Passe-a-Grille exit," he said without breaking his trance.

Sandra mumbled something occasionally on their way to his house. Her words bounced off him like sleet on a tin roof. They were just south of downtown St. Pete when he came back to life.

"Do you believe in euthanasia?" He asked her.

"It's my dad. He had a stroke and he's on life support," Derk said. They had walked to the beach at Pass-a-Grille, not far from his condo, and were sitting on a wooden bench in front of the concession stand. The gulls circled overhead in expectation of some discarded morsels, but they were only drinking beers wrapped in brown paper bags. The blazing sun had just begun its evening descent into the cobalt bay.

"I'm sorry," Sandra said. "I thought something was happening. Every time his name came up you didn't want to talk about him. You're not close?"

"We don't talk much."

"What's the problem if you don't mind me asking?"

"Mom wants to pull the plug."

"And you don't want her to?"

He shook his head. "It's not her job."

"So you and your dad. What happened?" She asked.

"It's a long story."

"Something must have happened, something significant, to separate you this much. I know what happened to me," she said.

"Nothing in particular." He shifted in his seat and rubbed his hand through his hair. "He just didn't give a damn. When he *was* around he was always critical, and he treated mom like shit."

"Were you ever close?"

Derk took a long swig from the paper container. "Don't think so."

"What your father would want?"

"Mother says he told her nothing artificial," Derk said, "but I think he'd want to be around just to be a burden to us."

"That's pretty cynical," she said "but we went through it with my grandfather."

He was watching one of the gulls over his head snatch a piece of cracker from the hand of a passing beachcomber. "Yeah?"

"I guess my dad had a lot of issues with him. They argued all the time. It wasn't until after Grandpa died that Grandmother told me about his past. My Grandfather came from a prominent family that owned the farm supply business. He had strong opinions and had always wanted to run for office, even when he was still in school. Although he took over the family business, he always fought for the rights of working men. He thought that the large companies abused their power, and he was a youngster when they tried to break the unions. He worked on a lot of political campaigns, sat on all kinds of boards, and was away from home a lot. Dad didn't care much for politics, probably because it kept Grandpa away. He said Grandpa neglected his family and his business. Maybe dad just needed more attention. Maybe he thought his brother was Grandpa's favorite. I don't know, but it divided them. In fact, I think Dad joined the other party just to spite him."

That made Derk laugh.

"Anyway, Grandpa stuck with it until he got my uncle elected. According to Grandma it was his crowning glory. After that he went back to the business and spent more time with everybody. He was a happy man, but it was too late for Dad. The damage had been done. He still thinks the only reason I got this job is because of my uncle."

"Doesn't sound like a morality play, but I know you're trying to make a point," Derk said.

"We seldom see our parents as ordinary people with aspirations and dreams and frailties. They're supposed to be superhuman, able to do everything. It's hard for us to appreciate the difficult choices they have to make to balance their responsibility to their families with their personal aspirations. You know, to be self-fulfilled, just like you and I."

Derk tipped back his head and emptied the bottle, then exhaled. The subterranean creases in his face eroded as if, for a brief moment, a burden had been lifted. A gust of sandy, Yucutan wind surged across the beach. Sandra turned leeward and shielded her face. As she brushed away the strands of hair that had lodged in her mouth her sculpted, sunlit face formed an erogenous shadow behind the bench, a glimpse of which Derk captured from the corner of one eye.

"You may have something there, French," he said, "but have you ever had the grouper sandwich at Frenchy's Café?"

Derk convinced her to go with him to Frenchy's Cafe on Clearwater Beach. A shower, two more Advil, another ice pack on his arm, and a glass of chardonnay mollified the agonizing developments of the past few days. By seven-thirty, Sandra French was standing in his living room wearing a lightweight rayon print that fell just above her glossy Liz Claiborne pumps. Her long, finely combed blonde hair glistened in the twilight. Her lips gleamed like rubies and a small handbag at the end of a long strap fell to her side. She looked like a model in a store window.

"You look gorgeous, French, but I'd change the shoes," Derk said.

"They match perfectly," she said, looking at her shoes.

"Tennis shoes, sneakers," Derk said.

"I don't dress like you, Derk." He was wearing tan shorts, an Hawaiian shirt, and motorcycle boots.

"Really, gym shoes, unless you've got boots," he said.

"I'll have to change my whole outfit!"

"Exact-o-mundo!" he said. "We're going on two wheels."

"Your motorcycle? No way. Besides, you can't drive. What about your arm?"

"It's feels much better," he said as he extended and rotated it to test the affects of the assorted painkillers. "You'll love it, the wind in your face, and we'll catch the sunset on the way. Change your clothes and come down to the garage. I want to show you something."

When Sandra joined him, Derk was rubbing a cloth over his bright red Kestrel bicycle. She caressed its smooth fiberglass architecture. Its chrome gears sparkled like surgical steel. Hanging next to it was a fat-tired black bicycle with purple accessories and equally shiny hardware. On a special stand stood a partially assembled motorcycle. Everything was clean, neat, and organized. Then Derk uncovered his favorite motorcycle.

"Is it a Harley?" she asked as Derk backed the bike onto the driveway.

"Yupper, a forty-nine Panhead."

"Looks mint, my brother would say." She circumscribed it.

"Kind of takes your breath away, doesn't it." His pride swelled from her admiration of it. Its high gloss, jet-black sheet metal and chrome accessories shimmered in the twilight.

"Looks like something on the cover of one those drugstore magazines," she said and stroked its soft, sleek seat. The chalk-colored leather hugged the sloping lines of the frame down to the rear wheel, made a nearly ninety degree upward turn, and clung to the fender as does liken on tree bark.

"Custom calfskin, soft as a baby's butt. They don't make these anymore."

She looked into the garage as if she were searching for something. "It might be as soft as a baby's butt, but it's even smaller. Where do you sit?"

He went into the garage and came back with a pad that he placed upon the rear fender. She pushed two fingers into it, squeezed it, and tried to move it around. It may be cushy and cling to the fender like a barnacle on a ship's bottom, but she was clearly unconvinced.

"It's not as comfortable as it looks," he said, handing her a helmet. He pulled the passenger highway pegs into riding position and climbed aboard. The fashionable scooter came to life on the first kick.

Sandra reluctantly straddled the seat behind him, and they were on their way.

They rumbled up Gulf Boulevard through Treasure Island and Redington Beach, crossed the bridge at Sand Key, and entered Clearwater Beach. Summer vacationers filled the T-shirt shops, beach resorts, and restaurants on each side of the road, and their heads turned as the powerful V-twin announced itself with its familiar "po-tot-a, po-tot-a." They cruised the strip along Mandolay to the original Frenchy's Cafe. They sat at the bar, Derk's customary venue, conversed with the waitresses, also from Lansing, Michigan, and shared stories about their hometowns.

Derk pointed to the license plate on the wall above the bar, *Ann Arbor Railroad*. "See that. Frenchy's from Michigan, too," he said.

The gal behind the counter lifted her arm to high five Derk, but he couldn't raise his arm. Sandra took his place, and then shouted, "Go Blue!" after slapping hands with the waitress.

Derk said, "Thought you went to Michigan State."

"I'm a big-time Michigan goodwill ambassador! So live with it!"

"They win more than the Spartans. That's for sure," he said.

She playfully punched his arm, his good arm, and he fell half off the stool, groaning and feigning injury. She caressed him as if to relieve his pain, then cradled him in her arms. Her touch was as fragile as silk crystals.

When she was sufficiently apologetic he said, "It's the other arm."

She dropped him. His injured arm hit the edge of the bar. The pain shot to the tips of his fingers. "Damn!"

"Serves you right," she said and one of the gals behind the bar gave her a high-five.

"Come on, now. I'm supposed to have home court advantage," Derk said.

Sandra agreed that the Cajun-grouper sandwich was the best she ever had. It was served with a side of crisp, almost burned, salt-free potato chips that she couldn't stop eating while she complained about the calories. They drank draft beer, shared stories about their work, and somehow got into a debate with some other patrons about the best party schools. The depth of the debauched orgies that were exposed had them laughing so hard Derk slowly retreated to the door.

As they left, the horizon swallowed the setting sun. Lured to the beach by the moonlight, they removed their shoes and joined the couples strolling, hand in hand, in and out of the rhythmic tide.

"I love the feel of the sand gushing between my toes when the tide goes out," Sandra said.

"Ever been buried up to your neck in the sand?"

"Standing or sitting?"

"Standing, that would take some trust," Derk said.

"And a very deep hole," she said.

They walked on and the discussion evolved to failed relationships and evaporated love. Sandra told Derk that she wasn't dating anyone in particular, and Derk told her that he hadn't met anyone who'd knocked his socks off for quite some time. Then she confessed that she had been dating an aide to a Michigan State senator for about two months, but the senator was likely to lose in the coming election, so his life was uncertain after that. If they broke up, she wouldn't suffer. The senator had never been an ally of the Michigan DNR's environmental efforts, nor was his aide.

The conversation took them all the way to the Adam's Mark Hotel and back to Frenchy's Cafe.

When they returned, "Thanks for bringing me," Sandra said, "I know why you like this place so much."

"El gusto es mio," he said.

"Mmm?"

"The pleasure is mine," he said and kissed her hand, surprised at how relaxed he felt with her. Derk wanted to give her a hug but held back.

After she put on her helmet, he turned to brush the hair from her face.

"I'm glad you came," he said.

She kissed him on the cheek, and he cruised back to Pass-a-Grille with aroused contentment.

29

After the tee off on number two, Art Domingo relayed Sidney O'Connor's response to Von Lleuwan's request for a meeting.

"Patience is a virtue," O'Connor said, "Your boss needs to mellow out."

"Mellow!" Von Lleuwan reacted. "I'll squish that son-of-a-bitch like a bug on the blacktop. Then he'll know mellow," he said. His next shot skipped twenty yards beyond the green.

He kept pulling on his ear. The ringing in it made him regret that he hadn't defrocked Jimmy Swingle when he first met him. He had skipped the trip to Dayton and gone straight to Tampa where his over-sexed muscle-head security guard got him in a headlock, messing up his hearing in one ear. He had gone to Tampa to find out how, in spite of a brand new security system, three guys had waltzed into his plant and overrun one of his employees. And he wanted to know what goddamn stupid kind of mayhem his director of security was planning for him next. He hadn't been in the Elgar plant five minutes when he had to be restrained by three of his own employees after getting into a fracas with Gloves.

"You dumb fuck! You got close enough to whiff their asses, but they ended up mulch on the backend of somebody's bass boat," Von Lleuwan said.

"It's not my fault those guys ran into that boat," Gloves said.

"Someone must have dropped you on your head when you were a kid."

"You weren't there. You don't know what happened. Besides, I took care of that EPA snoop for you."

"What's that on your head?" Von Lleuwan said. It had the shape of an ear but looked like something from a costume store. Some kind of brackish green slime seethed from it.

"Super glue. I'm not getting a fucking monkey ear," Gloves said.

197

"Christ, it looks like some kind of fungus. Get rid of it. You have a week to find the other guy and don't fuck with the EPA."

Gloves moved within a nose length of Von Lleuwan. "Or what?"

"I'll throw you out on your other ear." Although Gloves was built like a demolition dump, Von Lleuwan possessed no fear of the bloated imbecile.

"You one-eyed fag," Gloves said.

"I'm the fag that bailed your perverted ass out of the slammer."

"You heartless bastard. I'm in this shit because you lied to me."

"You knew what you were doing."

"Fuck you. You didn't tell me those chemicals would kill her," Gloves said.

"You didn't have to drown her."

"You said it might scorch her cords a little, keep her from talking, but you knew."

"That was your doing, not mine."

"She went into convulsions and dropped dead right in front of me. You're the chemist, not me."

"You got that right. You're an ignorant child molester," Von Lleuwan said and pushed Gloves out of his way.

The plant supervisor and his staff had huddled outside the office and stepped back as Von Lleuwan went for the door.

"You killed that guy in the tank, too," Gloves said. "That was no fucking accident. You set the timer after I left."

Von Lleuwan turned and shouted, "Shut the fuck up," and lunged a knee toward Gloves' groin. Instead of striking the target, the hard surface of his artificial leg hit Gloves' shin, just below the same knee Derk had hit several days ago. On the way down Gloves lurched for Von Lleuwan's leg and latched onto the leather strap that secured the brace to Von Lleuwan's quadriceps. The brace came lose and Von Lleuwan tumbled on top of Gloves. They wrestled on the floor while

Von Lleuwan's staff looked on. Gloves' wrestling prowess prevailed as he secured Von Lleuwan in a debilitating headlock.

On the outside chance that the rumors about Gloves and one of the company secretaries were true Von Lleuwan said, "You've dipped your pen in the secretarial pool for the last time. When I tell Esther you're done." He knew his sister would dump the oaf in a heartbeat.

Three of Von Lleuwan's employees entered and pulled them apart. Gloves hovered over Von Lleuwan who was still on the floor rummaging for his false leg and massaging one ear.

"Fuck you and your sister," Gloves said and backed away.

"If you ever do anything like that again, I'll feed your shriveled scrotum to the pike in Lake Macatawa," he said, looking up at Gloves.

"Just find the other guy and bring him to me."

"And then I'll flatten your gimp ass for good," Gloves said.

Von Lleuwan returned to Michigan with a head rash and a cauliflower ear. He met Art Domingo at The Pines for an update on *PESTfree©*. Unable to concentrate, he was six over after nine. Down two stokes to Art, Von Lleuwan left him on the eleventh tee and went to his office without changing his clothes.

Skip Trace and Elliot Johnson had been waiting in the corporate office of Von Lleuwan Enterprises for forty-five minutes. For his first interview of the president, Skip had donned the power uniform, a navy suit and white pinstriped blue oxford shirt with a red and blue tie. As a chef and a musician, Player wore a suit as often as a Key West taxi driver. He had on a pair of green gabardines that shined in the seat, a brown tweed sportscoat and a paisley tie. Skip couldn't look at him, and he couldn't make him wait in the car. He needed Player to run the audio-video equipment. Having rehearsed their lines for the tenth time, they grew tired and resorted to their ongoing game of musical trivia.

Player said, "Name everyone who ever played with Fleetwood Mac and cut their own album."

"Stevie Nicks, Lindsay Buckingham, Dave Mason, and I know, at least, one other guy. Don't tell me. Tall guy, dark hair, played a guitar. Had some big hits," Skip said. "Work on this while I think about it. Who played with Cream, Blind Faith and Billy Cobham?"

Player reeled off a list of candidates as a man in loud golf attire entered the lobby. His eye patch was askew, he sported a noticeable limp, and the finger buried in one ear cocked his head to one side like a dump truck turned on its side. Skip looked at the receptionist and a slight twitch confirmed her boss's arrival. So this was the rich and famous executive who brewed up some of the most ominous chemicals known to bugs and man. Hardly, and no way this guy shot par. And responsible for sick kids, missing persons and the mastermind of a commercial empire? Fat chance. Maybe this was his brother or an assistant. Skip had an appointment with the chief executive, Jack Von Lleuwan, but this guy looked like he had escaped from an institution. He had no idea they were waiting for him.

Player whispered, "Bad timing, man."

Skip turned to the receptionist and asked in a low voice, "Is that Mr. Von Lleuwan?

Player rose, shaking his head. "Bad vibes! I'm out of here."

Skip held out his arm. "Wait a minute."

The receptionist had risen to assist her boss, "Are you okay, Mr. Von Lleuwan?"

The eccentric executive flashed a scornful glance, shook his ear, and disappeared into an office with a sign on the glass that read, *The Presidential Linx.*

"Are you sure about this?" Player sat down, adjusted his tie, and rubbed the tops of his shoes against the backs of his pant-legs.

"He often meets important clients at the club, and he has a demanding schedule as you might well imagine," the receptionist said.

They were here now, but it almost hadn't happened. As they waited for their appointment, Skip flashed back to their meeting at Bear's house. Player wore dreadlocks and had a Bob Marley CD playing when Skip arrived. Dougal Ketchum came with a protestant mood and a handful of Gill Scott Heron tapes. Bear passed out pamphlets illustrating the involvement of several organized religious groups in the environmental movement, and he tried for the hundredth time to get them to join his church. Player passed around a joint that got that them into a good mood while Skip laid out his plan. They would pose as journalists for a European magazine and challenge Von Lleuwan to defend himself. Skip hoped this would cause him to unveil something they could use against him. It was such a simple and optimistic strategy that no one volunteered to join him on the interview.

"I've got a crop of sprouts ready for harvest," Dougal said.

"We can do this," Skip said. "It's just acting."

Player said, "You're the actor and the master bullshiter."

"But you're the only one with video experience," Skip said.

"Not me," Player said. "Wrong dude, man."

"I'll do the talking. I'll cover your time off, and I'll get you that new camera you told me about. Come on. I need you."

"What's she paying you?" Bear said.

"I rewrote a couple of policies. That's all," Skip said. "Come on, guys. This is the something we always wanted to do."

Dougal said, "What are you call this fictitious rag?"

"*The Journal of European Agriculture,*" Skip said. "The foreign angle is less suspicious."

"How 'bout *The European Journal of Organic Gardening,*" Player said.

"You must be getting to him, Dougal," Skip said. "He's really into the organic thing."

"Keep it simple," Bear offered. "*The Journal of Organic Agriculture.*"

"If you want it simple and organic, call it *Turds and Whey,*" Dougal Ketchum said.

"Okay. That does it. I'm going as a freelance writer for *Mulch Magazine* and Player will be the cable network rep," Skip said, looking to Player for confirmation.

Player offered only acquiescence, but that was enough. Skip needed just one of them to make the ruse convincing.

Player rubbed his shoes against his cuffs. He had on old, black, greasy chef's shoes.

"Stop it," Skip said as he patted Player' knee. He whispered, "Mr. Von Lleuwan, I'd like you meet Elliot Johnson, internationally renowned writer, crack photo-journalist, and part-time grille cook," and rolled his eyes through his thick brows.

The telephone on Mrs. Huizenga's desk buzzed. She mumbled something. They looked at her like guilty kids about to be called into the principal's office. "He's ready to see you now."

They followed her to Von Lleuwan's office.

Player blurted out, "I don't think any of them did. Clapton, Winwood, Bobby Reich, Ginger Baker. It's a trick question. Isn't it?"

Skip shook his head in three different directions and then reminded himself to relax. In a low voice he said, "Bob Welch."

"What?"

"Bob Welch. Sang with Fleetwood Mac."

Player shook his head. "Yeah, I've got another for you."

"Can it wait?" Skip said.

"Are you sure it's all right? He didn't look like he was feeling well," Skip said to the Mrs. Huizenga, according to the nameplate on her desk.

"A little jet lag from a business trip, that's all," she said with unconvincing cheer.

As they entered Von Lleuwan's office, Skip reminded Player to fetch the recording equipment. Von Lleuwan was bent over a golf ball, putter in hand, talking to someone on the speakerphone. Skip was struck by the enormity of the office. It must have been forty yards long, and the ceiling, at least twenty feet high, was retractable. The office was an audacity. The carpet looked like grass and the putting green *was* real grass. A number eighteen flag protruded from it. Golf balls were scattered everywhere. A floor to ceiling net covered the wall behind the 18th hole. At the other end of the room was the tee and a blue and white golf bag with a full set of clubs and four different putters. Behind it, in a glass case, was a complete set of antique, wooden-shafted clubs in mint condition. Next to that case was a display of the trophies he had apparently earned over the years and a few photographs of Von Lleuwan posing with golf legends. His desk was along one wall and a lone bookshelf covered some of the space behind it, although there was a paucity of technical publications and reference materials occupying those shelves. His desk was bare except for a telephone, a clock, and a golf magazine.

Von Lleuwan was concentrating on a ten-foot putt while talking in a high voice. "Charlie, I think it was Walker's guys again in Tampa, but I don't understand the connection with McCardigan. Probably a cover? Gloves . . ." He stopped when he became aware of the group's presence and walked over to pick up the handset on his desk, "Gloves is checking into it. Thanks for your help. Gotta go," he concluded. As he put down the receiver he glanced at his guests and looked askance at Mrs. Huizenga.

"Your one o'clock appointment, sir. Misters," she started to say.

"Mr. Dinsmore, Frederick Dinsmore, and this is," Skip said as Player rushed into the room carrying two duffel bags, "my A/V assistant E. J. Briggs." Deception required confidence and a schizophrenic ability. Skip approached the executive with enthusiasm and offered his hand.

A question mark remained on Von Lleuwan's face as he shook Skip's hand. The receptionist turned and left. Player dropped one of the bags and waved his hand.

"E. J. Briggs, bro. What's the haps?" Player said way too enthusiastically.

"Gentlemen, sorry, but I just returned from a business trip, and I've had a lot on my mind. Weren't you going to call me?" Von Lleuwan said. He rested the golf club between his legs and fidgeted with his ear. Von Lleuwan had agreed to the interview only after Skip mentioned the Discover Channel, and Von Lleuwan had instructed him to call when he returned from his trip to Tampa. Skip called back when Von Lleuwan was out of town and fabricated a story for the receptionist's favor to secure the time on his calendar.

"I thought you wanted to get together when you returned so we flew in today." Skip paused but not long enough for Von Lleuwan to object. "We're on a deadline, and it would be a shame not to have your input for this story."

"Who are you with again?" Von Lleuwan asked, watching Player unpack the video equipment.

"*Mulch Magazine.* Actually, we're freelance journalists, but the story is for *Mulch.*"

"Never heard of it."

"I'm not surprised. It's a European publication dedicated to alternative gardening. As someone who has been involved in this industry for a long time we wanted your opinion."

"What's he doing?" Von Lleuwan asked. Player stopped setting up the tripod.

"I'm sorry. Remember I told you about the Discover Channel?" Skip said. "Did you see that piece on pollution in the Antarctica last year? E. J. did some of that filming."

There really was a piece on pollution in Antarctica, but Player had nothing to do with it. Skip had been in sales for years. The cardinal rule of handling an objection was first to ignore it. If it came up again, answer directly and keep on trucking. He had his Peterbilt up to tenth gear, but Von Lleuwan still seemed unconvinced.

"You must be some kind of golfer. I've never seen anything like this." Skip made a panoramic gesture. "Please take a seat and get comfortable. Can I ask you a few questions before we start taping?" Player returned to his preparations.

"How long will this take?" Von Lleuwan looked at his watch.

"Not long," Skip said. "How long have you been in this business?" He began with some non-threatening questions.

"Almost twenty years," he answered. "but the company has been here a lot longer." He kept glancing at the camera. "Where are you guys from?"

"*Mulch Magazine.* You haven't heard of us because this is our first foray into mainline agriculture, and the magazine is European," said Skip.

Skip gave Player a sign to stop to mitigate Von Lleuwan's concern about the camera. He moved in front of Von Lleuwan's desk and motioned for the executive to take his seat. Familiar territory. As Von Lleuwan shifted his weight in that direction, allowing his artificial limb to catch up, putter still in hand, Skip began to sit.

"May I?" he said and assumed a chair in front of Von Lleuwan's desk.

He was now turned away from Von Lleuwan and Von Lleuwan was forced to come around his desk to look directly at him. Once there he took his seat, probably out of habit.

"What got you involved in this business?" Skip continued.

"Married the boss's daughter."

"You're modest, Mr. Von Lleuwan. From what I hear you've accomplished a great deal. You have introduced a number of important products, and in spite of the controversy over some, you have made a significant contribution to your field over the years." There was nothing like a little praise to soften up a big executive. "You're involved in research and development as opposed to manufacturing?"

"Mostly. We think it's our strength."

"But you do some manufacturing?"

"Some specialty products. Small volume items," Von Lleuwan said as his shoulders dropped, and he slowly sank into the deep leather contour of his chair.

Von Lleuwan's nonchalant reference to toxic chemicals as small volume items, as if he were manufacturing machine parts, annoyed Skip. They were more dangerous than live ammunition. Player now had the video camera rolling.

"How many patents do you hold?" Skip asked.

"Fourteen."

"All pesticides?"

"Eleven of them. Actually, ten. One fungicide. And one on the way. We're a small outfit. We have to specialize. We had a guy with us one time whose expertise was in fungicides, but we only developed one. He left and we didn't replace him. Too costly." The CEO was loosening up. Skip removed a small microphone from his coat pocket and held it in front of Von Lleuwan. "Do you mind?" Von Lleuwan didn't object, nor did he acquiesce. "It fits on your tie. You won't know it's there. See, I've got one," he said, displaying one clipped onto his power tie.

He laid the microphone on the desk. Von Lleuwan juggled it in his hand while panning the room. He glanced at Player and the video camera and again at the microphone. Then he angled his head slightly left so that his sighted eye looked directly at Skip. "Okay, Mr. Dinsmore, what is it you want to know?"

Skip concealed his glee. He *was* on a roll.

"People all over the world are worrying," and as he begun he pinched his microphone, indicating that he wanted Von Lleuwan to pin the microphone on his shirt, "worrying about the chemicals in their food, their water, their air, their workplaces."

Von Lleuwan fidgeted with the mike.

Skip walked to Von Lleuwan's side of the desk. "May I help you with that?"

Von Lleuwan handed him the miniature microphone and Skip clipped it onto the chief's Polo sport shirt. He continued as he returned to his seat, "There are some twenty-five thousand registered pesticides worldwide, and many are known to contain carcinogens. Are people's fears justified?"

"Since 1950 we have increased the world's production of grains by two and a half times with only a fifteen percent increase in the number of acres under production. This couldn't have happened without the use of chemical fertilizers and sophisticated pest controls," Von Lleuwan answered.

Skip turned to Player and made a circular motion with his finger. Player, already filming, gave him a thumbs up sign.

"There's evidence that these increases have come at a significant cost to the environment. How do you respond to that?" Skip reworded his question.

"All pesticides must be approved by the government and used according to the manufacturer's specifications. The dangers are miniscule, absolutely miniscule." With paternal sureness he added, "You know it's very appealing and romantic to think about people living in communes, teaching their kids at home, and growing their vegetables in backyard gardens, but you can't feed six billion people that way."

"You're not denying that it has come at a cost?" Skip said.

"The most trite prattle from the unenlightened, back to nature groupies is that we ought to grow everything organically. Plants don't distinguish between the nitrogen from clover and the nitrogen from manufactured processes. The yields from organic farming are half of those from modern farming methods. And the United States has only about one third of the organic nitrogen needed to support current crop output. The rest of the world may have only twenty percent. People need to get real."

"Some would say you're playing roulette with people's health. The U.S. banned DDT, chlordane, and heptachlor and yet, residues of chlordane and heptachlor have been found in indoor air samples twenty years later. Isn't is possible that many of the chemicals used today will be found to be toxic in the long run?" Skip said.

"It takes years of testing and millions of dollars for the government to approve a pesticide. The criteria is much more rigorous than ever," Von Lleuwan said.

"So, anything developed today is safe," Skip said. "Is that what you're saying?"

Von Lleuwan pursed his lips. His head listed slowly from side to side.

"So there's little need for new pesticides?" Skip reworded his question.

"What do you mean by that?" Von Lleuwan asked.

"If most of the new ones are safe, and, of course, they're effective or you wouldn't develop them, there can't be many more left to develop. Can there?

Skip's efforts to confuse and irritate Von Lleuwan were succeeding. Skip motioned for Player to zoom in for a close up.

The executive slumped into his chair, pinched his lips, and shot a bead of contempt at Skip. "Occasionally the target of our efforts develops a tolerance for the application, and we need to design a new formula. New product development is an ongoing process, but that doesn't mean they're unsafe."

"So, what you're saying is they don't all work as planned?"

"What a minute!"

Skip continued, "Over 500 insects, 270 weeds, and 150 plant pathogens throughout the world are now resistant to pesticides in spite of the twenty-five thousand different attempts to control them. Am I close?"

"I wouldn't know," Von Lleuwan said.

"It's also my understanding that the government doesn't guarantee that a pesticide is safe. Registration simply indicates that it poses no unreasonable risk if used as directed. It's obvious from your own government's reports that that's not necessarily true. Wasn't that what gave rise to the suit that caused the enforcement of the Delaney Clause?"

Von Lleuwan stiffened. "That's not what happened."

Skip maintained his offensive. "Delaney may cause the removal of quite a few chemicals from the market, even some of yours. Does that mean that some of your products aren't safe?"

"Absolutely not! What are you talking about?" Von Lleuwan reacted. "All of our products have been registered by the EPA, and they're absolutely safe when used as directed."

Von Lleuwan's lips twitched. A bead of perspiration formed on his forehead, and his visible eye had grown to the size of small bolder. He leered at Skip.

"In my opinion, Delaney was a gross overreaction, and I'd like to see it replaced. The testing capabilities today allow the government to split hairs finer and finer, and you, I mean some environmental zealots, think that any residual is too much. No one has ever died from DDT. Enforcement of Delaney harms farmers, producers, and consumers, especially when there are no reasonable substitutes for the banned products. Now, that's the truth if you're willing to listen."

"But it's the law now and if your government re-registers many of these older pesticides, they're going to ban those that are known carcinogens. That effects some of yours, doesn't it?" Skip said.

"Minimally." Von Lleuwan turned away from the camera, nodded his affirmation, and turned back to face Skip with a smirk.

"I thought you said all of your products," Skip said as he noticed a perpendicular change in Von Lleuwan's mood, "were perfectly safe." He wasn't sure what happened to provoke the change, but it was as sentient as a shark in the pool. "Is this going to move the industry in the direction of more natural pesticide methods and environmentally friendlier approaches?" Skip glanced at Player to see if he recognized the change. Player shook his head and mimed something that Skip didn't understand.

Von Lleuwan squinted as if he were looking through the slats in a window. His head rolled like a toy raft and he pursed his lips as if he were resigned to what was coming. "You seem to know a lot about it. What do you think?"

"I think you're a realist. Earlier I heard you refer to some new product in development? You've been one of the leaders in this industry for years. Are you working on something that will be both effective and environmentally friendly?" Skip asked, still wondering what had caused the change in Von Lleuwan's mood.

Von Lleuwan didn't answer immediately. He maintained a confident grin, teetered his chin and chewed on his lower lip while exchanging glances with Skip and Player. His expression had changed from discontent to the look of a kid who was contemplating telling a secret. Then, as if someone had just parked a cement mixer on his foot, Skip realized that his sources had been correct. Von Lleuwan was, indeed, working on something very big.

Skip also knew from years in the field that at these moments, the first one to talk loses. He tilted his head, sealed his lips, and never took his eyes of Von Lleuwan. The pause was parturient.

Von Lleuwan gazed across the room, his stare fixed toward the eighteenth hole. Then he looked at Player and again at Skip. He repeated the pattern while fidgeting with his microphone. Skip looked at Player, who had his camera focused upon the executive, and then back to Von Lleuwan. The camera! Skip turned around and slid his index finger across his throat. Player turned off the camera but not the recorder.

"It's off," Skip said. "Now talk to me."

Von Lleuwan disconnected the mike and placed it on the table in front of them. He cocked his head to one side, ran one hand through his hair, and tugged on his ear. His chest heaved and then relaxed like a bellow releasing its load. In his bright golf attire, dark hair a mess, he was one odd-looking duck.

"Mr. Dinsmore, in this climate of governmental regulation and consumer skepticism, however misplaced it may be, the development of a pesticide that could be applied strategically and safely, do its job as required, and then dissolve harmlessly in the environment would be quite an addition to anyone's arsenal. There's no disagreement about that."

Outside the clouds had dimmed the sun's thrust. The dark walls made the huge room feel more like a catacomb. In the silence, Skip sensed his own internal organs at work. Von Lleuwan had, indeed, developed some kind of new product, and it must not yet be approved or he would be salivating all over his Polo shirt. He couldn't announce it to the public, but he was dying to tell somebody, especially the diehard, hardcore environmentalists with which he had associated the two journalists in front of him. Skip had no idea it would be this easy. On the other hand, he wasn't there yet.

"We've heard that before," Skip said. "DDT was supposed to be a breakthrough. Malathion and many others. Look at them now. There's always some drawback. If it isn't apparent at first, it will turn up over time. A 1991 geological survey found traces of herbicides in the rainwater from twenty-three states? Newton's Law, sir: 'For every action there is an equal and opposite reaction.' The better your pesticide works, the worse the problems it causes. You think you've got something better than that? A lot of people would like to know about it."

Skip's challenge created a palpable tension in the room. Player loosened his tie but said nothing.

Von Lleuwan moved forward in his chair, placed his forearms on the desk, and faced them with a determined glint and a black patch. "What would you say about a product, a pesticide let's say, that you could apply one time? It would release slowly, similar to a time-release vitamin, be ninety-nine percent effective, and then break down harmlessly in the soil?"

"You've field tested such a product?" Skip asked.

Von Lleuwan nodded. Arrogance had crept into his expression.

"And there are no contra-indications?" Skip asked.

Von Lleuwan shrugged with a barely perceptible inference. "Nothing we can't overcome." He shook his head again and replied, "No, none." He leaned back in his plush leather chair, enveloped by smugness.

Hints of the evidence he sought rushed at him like a money train, but there was nothing he could bank that would link Von Lleuwan to Kate McCardigan's or Eva Simpson's sons.

"How long have you been working on it?" Skip was searching for a time frame.

"A number of years and we're close to production."

"Does it work on all fruits?" Skip asked.

"Everything we've tested so far," said Von Lleuwan.

"How about strawberries?"

"We haven't tested them, but we think so."

"Apples?"

Von Lleuwan nodded.

"Citrus?"

"Most likely. We've tested oranges. No problems." Von Lleuwan slapped one side of his head with the palm of his hand.

Skip couldn't wait. "Impressive. Different fruits and different growing climates. You've actually tested the product in places as diverse as Michigan and Florida?"

"Ohio," Von Lleuwan volunteered, "but what does it matter where we tested it?" He sat up. Deep furrows of suspicion dug into the small space between his eye and the patch as he leaned forward. He put his hands on the edge of the desk. "I think you guys understand that what I've told you is confidential. It doesn't leave this room. Are we clear on that?"

Skip responded, "It's not approved yet?"

Von Lleuwan shook his head no.

"This will revolutionize the industry. When can I tell my readers about it?"

Von Lleuwan pushed himself back into his seat, simmering in executive diplomacy. "We've invested a bundle on this, and it will undoubtedly reduce consumer fears and shake up the entire industry. But any new product, and especially one as important as this, requires EPA approval, and we can't announce it until the entire process is complete. I guarantee you that when the time comes, you'll know immediately." He moved forward in his chair again. "In the meantime, I trust that I can count upon your complete confidence."

Skip looked at Von Lleuwan and then at Player with a "where do we go from here?" expression and then back at Von Lleuwan. "Of course, absolutely," he said.

A brief silence followed. Von Lleuwan got up and walked over to line up a shot with his putter.

"Well, gentlemen, if that's all, I've got a lot of work to do," Von Lleuwan said.

Skip turned toward Player. His expression communicated, "What do we do now?"

Player, who hadn't said anything since hello, answered, "Excuse me, sir. Skip, I mean Mr. Dinsmore, said that Discover might be interested in this footage. What would you think about a documentary on the development of your new product?"

Skip jumped in, "From beginning to end. Where you got the idea? How you make it safe? Where you tested it?"

Von Lleuwan held up his putter and waved it back and forth as he shook his head.

"It would be great publicity," Player said.

"That's for our marketing department," Von Lleuwan said.

"Marketing department!" Skip said. "Excuse me, but I doubt you have the kind of marketing apparatus that can generate this kind of exposure. We could be back here in a couple of days."

Von Lleuwan puckered his lips and pecked the air, like a mother hen pondering the possibilities.

"If we get right on it we could be ready immediately after its formal introduction. You wouldn't have to wait for a reaction from satisfied farmers. We could go directly to the places where you tested it and interview them," Skip said.

"And we'd have final approval?" Von Lleuwan asked.

Skip confirmed with a single nod.

"What will you need from us?" Von Lleuwan asked. He looked at his watch and flinched, apparently recalling a prior commitment. He pulled on his ear again as he headed for the door. Before Skip could answer, he said, "Tell my receptionist, Mrs. Huizenga, what you need and she'll put you on my schedule." He opened the door and left.

Ten minutes later, Skip and Player were in the rental car, laughing, exchanging high fives, and heading toward the Kent County International Airport.

30

In the moonlight, hermit crabs scurried across the hard pack as Derk shuffled along the Pass-a-Grille shoreline seeking answers he couldn't find in his sleep. The intermittent swish of the tide and the "coo" of an occasional gull were the only audible sounds. Most kids want their fathers to be proud of them and to love them. For as long as he could recall, he would have relished the day his father had just shown an interest in him. He had booked an afternoon flight to Michigan to see his parents, and he was searching for that single event that had changed the course of his relationship with his father. He didn't want his father to be gone from his life, but he knew his passing would bring relief to a lifetime of disappointment for him and his mother. All her life she wanted to be focus of his attention and when he finally came home he developed Alzheimer's Disease. She had spent the past two years waiting on him like a handmaiden.

Derk's dream had been replaced by other issues. The Von Lleuwan case was more frustrating than the Sunday *New York Times* crossword puzzle. He had bits and pieces but nothing concrete. And there was the stroll along the beach with Sandra French, the quiver her kiss aroused, and her breath on his neck during their ride home.

At 3 A.M. he was walking the beach. Halfway to the Don Cesar, he realized that he had allowed Sandra French, a woman he had never respected and with whom he thought he had little in common, to burrow her way into his fantasies.

Back in the condo he poured a glass of orange juice and read a couple days' worth of *The Times* that had gone neglected. He was halfway through the first newspaper when he dozed off amidst the incandescent glow of Sandra French's sinewy, blonde body curled beneath the covers in the next room.

He wasn't sure what he was going to do when he got to the Elgar plant. He had risen at 7 A.M. and reread the Von Lleuwan file. He was thinking about the pins in the wall at Eva Simpson's house, her son, the residue of an old orchard next to her home, and her protest of Elgar Chemical Company. There had to be a connection, and it just might be at Von Lleuwan's plant in Tampa. He left a note for Sandra to join him for lunch.

He stopped for breakfast at the Ballast Point Pier on Interbay to extricate the growl in his stomach and to formulate an acceptable ruse. He cruised downtown on the Panhead in the early morning salt air as the scantily clad rollerbladers went through their routines. The expansive homes and manicured lawns conformed to the winding balustrade that separated Bayshore Boulevard from the bay. The most enjoyable seven-minute stretch in Tampa, it was like riding into the cover of *Tropical Homes and Gardens*. In complete contrast, minutes from the serenity of this multi-million-dollar view, across the southern tip of the steel and glass that formed the central business district, lay the chemical stewpots of The Port of Tampa.

As he entered Elgar's parking lot, a trey of steel-toed truck drivers and hard-hatted warehousemen surrendered envious glances at his glittering steed. He parked the bike, laid his denim jacket across the seat, took a business card from his wallet, and put it in his denim shirt pocket. It took more than credentials to get this job done. Even without a suit and tie and a car from the motor pool, he was still an agent of the Environmental Protection Agency. He hitched his trousers and headed his denim-clad officialdom straight for the Elgar office.

He was greeted by a thirty-something Spanish gal with plump cheeks and a homely smile. She was stationed behind a desk just inside the door. The room consisted of a large open space divided into workstations by a series of partitions. Surveillance cameras were positioned in the corners at the ceiling. Upon arriving, he had noticed that the property was surrounded by a chain-link fence, and that the windows were covered with ornamental iron grids, similar to the plant in Michigan. A sign of the times or did Von Lleuwan have something or someone specific about which to worry? Maybe they were normal and appropriate crime prevention measures, but they reinforced Derk's suspicion of Von Lleuwan.

"*Buenas dias*, may I help you?" she said without rising from her seat.

He lowered his survey to her level, "*Mi nombre es Derk Bryan. Soy de EPA.*" He handed her his business card. "I'm here for an inspection."

Her head shifted backed, doubt enveloped her face.

Derk offered a disarming smile, "I know. I'm usually in a suit and a tie, but last week I ruined a three-hundred dollar suit during an inspection in Mulberry, and the government's not buying me a new one."

"What do you need?" she asked.

"Routine inspection, mam," he said. "It won't take long."

"I'll get the plant manager. *Tu esperas, por favor,*" she said.

He spoke enough Spanish to know that she either wanted him to wait or she was stalling him.

"*Permisso, senora*, you don't have to bother him. This will only take a few minutes."

"Well, all right, but you have to wear the safety helmet and the glasses," she said. She reached for the helmet and the safety glasses on top of the filing cabinet behind her.

"*Gracias.* I'll put that in my report," he said. She offered a kind of wounded thank you. He took the safety paraphernalia and started through the office. The sight of the rear door was in view. After a few steps he returned and said, "I really need to see the shipping and receiving manifests. Could you have someone get them for me while I'm looking around?"

"Well, I uh, that's Mr. Lombardo's job, our accountant, and he's not here this morning. The plant manager will have to authorize it," she said.

"Look Miss …?"

"Concepcion," she responded.

"Concepcion, I know you're just trying to do your job, but withholding information and obstructing a federal agent in the performance of his duty is a federal offense and can result in fines against you and your company. Mr. Lombardo must have an assistant who can collect the necessary information for me. Right now I am holding you responsible for getting it. *Comprendes?*"

"Yes." She perked up. He had gotten her attention.

"Bring 'em to me in the warehouse, please," he added and headed for the back door. As he exited, he noticed her pudgy little body scurrying through the maze of partitions.

He crossed the yard to the warehouse. Apart from the warehouse were a variety of steel storage domes. He passed a man on a forklift and another backing a Vander Pool Trucking Company rig up to the loading dock. The warehouse was a two-story, L-shaped corrugated steel structure that was abutted by a four-foot concrete dock with a steel apron on the upper twelve inches.

The aroma from the huge anhydrous ammonia storage facility to the south wafted through the yard, enveloping his sinuses and stinging his eyes. Derk donned the safety glasses and the plastic helmet, leaped to the top of the dock, and scurried into one of the open bays. Even though he thought his ruse had been convincing, he was impelled to comb the facility with celerity before someone in authority confronted him.

Soon he found himself in need of something to wash the sting from his throat and his sight. He looked for a water cooler or a restroom as he passed through the rows of steel and fiberboard containers stacked on wooden pallets. The powdered ingredients appeared to be separated from the liquid ones. He looked for any chemical that might be esoteric, restricted, banned, or out of place for the region. The obvious were DDT, Chlordane, Heptachlor, Malathion, aldicarb, lindane and numerous others that could have been imported or exported illegally. He didn't think Von Lleuwan would be careless enough to leave such chemicals around in clearly marked containers, but he had seen it happen. He wanted to see those shipping records, but if they were doing something illegal someone would have tampered with them.

He came to the end of one row, turned the corner, and headed down another aisle. He wasn't used to the aroma. It tasted like spoiled shark, and made him nauseous. Something wasn't right here. He would call Al Rodriguez later. At the end of that aisle he turned and headed toward the end of the building. Ahead he spotted a sign over a door that read, "Men." He had walked to the far north end of the building, there was no one in sight, and he could only hear the whining of the electric lift truck at the other end of the warehouse. There was no air conditioning in the building. It was oppressively humid, reeked of noxious fumes, and the lighting was dim. How could anyone work under these conditions? Only every third overhead light was lit, and most of the bay doors were closed. Through his tears his vision had become compromised in the dim light. He moved closer to the barrels and stopped to read some of the labels on the shipping containers. His vision was so clouded he could barely read them, but he didn't want to remove the protective glasses. They provided almost no protection from the noxious air, but he couldn't convince himself of that. He understood why the warehousemen wore masks and goggles.

He headed for the bathroom to rinse his eyes. In a nook outside of the restroom he noticed several twenty-gallon fiberglass containers. They weren't stacked in neat rows with the other products. He walked over to examine them. Each appeared to have been opened. He turned them around to get a look at the labels, removed his glasses, and dried his eyes with the back of his hands. Bingo! A skull and crossbones and the lettering on the label: 1,1 TT 4®. He put the safety glasses on again and rounded the corner for the bathroom. He held his head under the faucet to flush away the burning sensation. Then he dried his face, used the head, and went in search of Miss Concepcion and those shipping records.

He was a few steps outside the restroom and not yet adjusted to the darkness when he heard footsteps and a deep, burly, familiar voice behind him, "You again."

As he turned, through the mottled rays, a large blur moved quickly toward him. Then the lights went out.

He awakened to an unintelligible din of voices. Through a dim, filtered light he could see what appeared to be the tops of trees swaying in the wind. He had no idea where he was, but with consciousness came intense pain. The pounding he took from the car thieves was a distant memory compared with the thunder blasting inside his head. As he writhed toward lucidity Derk felt cold, hard concrete and a rawness in his throat. He had felt this way only one other time. As a youngster he had fallen from the loft of his cousin's barn during haying and was knocked unconscious. He was in a coma for two hours and in the hospital for two weeks with a black eye the size of a pomegranate. As consciousness evolved, the swaying trees above him took on human form, and the warmth of his mother's voice emerged. She reached down and held his head in her healing hand.

"Derk, are you all right? What happened?"

The voice was familiar, but it wasn't his mother's. He was too groggy to respond.

Again, the voice said, "Are you okay?"

Another female voice spoke. "Look, his glasses are smashed." It sounded Spanish. "Must have hit his head. Let's call an ambulance."

How did he get in Mexico?

"He's out of it." He heard a man's voice. "He looks like the guy on our team that got hit by a softball. Out so cold he didn't know where he was all night."

"Did you see anything?" Derk heard the voice that resembled his mother's say. Was she talking to him?

Someone's head shook. It looked like a woman but a man answered, "I saw him jump onto the loading dock and go inside, but that's all."

"See anyone else in the building?" The woman with his mother's voice asked.

"Nobody unusual," the male voice answered.

"How about you, Miss Concepcion?"

"Nothing. Not until we came out here," the woman called Concepcion said. Her head seemed to be rotating. Was she looking for something? "Look, he's coming to!" she said.

The voice jogged Derk's memory, but it was too dark to recognize anyone. He panned the barrels, the concrete floor, the sign over the door that said, "Men," as his lungs filled with a pungent aroma, ammonia. His jaw ached and he had an 18-wheeler sized headache.

A savory fragrance with a ponytail helped him sit upright. He was propped against her, one hand held his and the other rested on his back.

"Derk, it's Sandra." She tried to lift him. "Can you get up?"

It hurt to move.

"We need an ambulance," Sandra said.

Derk shook his head, but he didn't know why.

"Let's get him out of here," Sandra said.

They stood him up. His arms draped over Sandra and one of the dockworkers.

"How far to the closest emergency room?" Sandra asked.

"There's a hospital not far," said Miss Concepcion.

Out of the dark, acerbic atmosphere of the warehouse he squirmed for them to let him walk on his own.

"Are you okay?" Sandra asked.

As he returned to consciousness, he felt as if he had been used for target practice by an Olympic discus team. The office routine came to a complete stop when he entered. He careened through the maze with Sandra on one arm and the dockworker on the other.

"Thank you," he said as they reached the receptionist's area.

"Can you walk to the car?" Sandra asked.

Derk waved his head. He turned and looked at Maria Concepcion who was standing behind her desk with the folder in her hand that she had taken to the warehouse. "Miss …," Derk addressed her.

"Concepcion," she replied.

"The file?"

She came to life like microwave popcorn. She handed him the manila folder and said, "I made copies for you. I'm so sorry." She looked around as if she were searching for someone.

Did she know who hit him? As he and Sandra left, the buzz from the Elgar employees permeated the room. Outside he slouched at the sight of his motorcycle. He longed for the comfort of four wheels and Corinthian leather.

"We'll get it later," Sandra said.

She guided him to the rental car. He leaned against the car and massaged his right jaw.

"Will you be disappointed if we miss lunch?" he said. Sandra smiled. Then Derk walked to the Harley.

"You sure you can drive?" she asked.

Gloves checked into a fleabag motel not far from the plant and demanded an 8 A.M. wake up call. When the telephone beside his bed awakened him, he put on the same maroon shirt and denim trousers he'd worn the previous night, donned a fresh pair of latex gloves, left the keys on the dresser, and departed. His first stop was to find a pair of shoes, and then he would get a new "do," something less recognizable to the local beat patrol, and a bandana to cover his ear. When he arrived at the Elgar plant a little after nine, Miss Concepcion didn't comment on his new appearance. Two small clumps of hair tied by rubber bands remained at the back of his shaved head. He wore a headband, below which a purple bruise was ripening on his cheek.

"It's not my job dealing with inspectors and all that!" she told Gloves.

He didn't know about what she was talking. He only wanted to know if anybody was looking for him, especially the police.

"No," she said and waved some inventory files in front of him. "This isn't my job either."

"Who's bike's in the yard?" Gloves said, ignoring her pleas.

"Probably the man from the EPA," she said, pointing toward the warehouse. "That's who I'm talking about."

Gloves headed for the warehouse. Minutes later he returned as a leggy blonde from the EPA showed up. He stayed out of sight as the blonde and the receptionist headed for the warehouse. Then he slinked out of the plant.

It had been a full day for Gloves, and it wasn't yet noon. He wanted to go back to the titty bar to find the ear that had come loose from the spirit gum during the fight with the bouncers, but Von Lleuwan had ordered him to go to some construction company in Ohio to look for the other guy who'd broken into his plant. His head was pounding from a hangover and he didn't want to drive, but people in uniforms would be canvassing the airport. He took a company van and headed north.

The skies to the north turned steel gray as Derk tried to start his motorcycle. After one feeble kick he slumped over the bike, caught the rear fender with one hand, and collapsed on the tank. Sandra hurried to his side.

"Leave it. We'll get it later," she said, helped him into the car, and closed the door. "I'll be right back."

Sandra stood in front of the receptionist's desk with hands on hips. "Miss …?" Everyone stopped.

"Concepcion," the receptionist answered.

"That man out there," she pointed outside, "represents a federal agency, and he was injured on your property by someone or something while doing his job. That's his motorcycle. If something happens to it before we get back, I'll have the IRS, the FBI, the EEOC, and the ASPCA in here before you can call Jack Von Lleuwan on your speed dial. Is that clear?"

Sandra didn't wait for her to pick her chin off the desk. When she returned to the car, Derk was half asleep.

"Derk, Derk," she said and shook him, "Don't fall asleep."

He sat up and rubbed his face. "Shit!"

"Tell me how to get to Tampa General," she said.

The right side of his face had already turned the color of a bruised cantaloupe. An emergency room physician determined he was damaged but not broken, gave an ice pack, some painkillers, and told him to take the rest of day off. He fell asleep in the car on the way back to Pass-a-Grille and, except for the time it took to get upstairs and into bed, he didn't awaken until seven-thirty that evening.

He was disoriented when he woke. With the sun in its waning hour, he thought it must be morning. He felt pain, heard the sounds of someone in another room, and began to connect the dots. He sat on the edge of the bed in a pair of boxer shorts. Sandra entered the room wearing MSU running shorts, a white T-shirt, and gym shoes. Her hair was tied into a ponytail revealing her flushed cheekbones. Her makeup was diluted from perspiration. Derk held his swollen mandible in his hand and tried to open his mouth.

"How are you feeling?" She asked.

"Okay, I guess," he could not form the words clearly. He felt the warmth from her well-defined thighs. She was developing a colorful sheen. "Been running?"

"Yes." She kneeled and cradled his face in her hands. Her touch was soothing and her scent was sweet. "I'll get you some more ice," she said.

He sandwiched her hands against his face and tried to thank her, but the words came out contorted. He leaned forward, put his arms around her waist and kissed her. She seemed surprised but she didn't resist. A moment of sympathy he surmised.

She stood up, her arms on his shoulders, and his hands on her waist. "Derk Bryan, what am I going to do with you?"

He pulled himself up with her assistance and put his arms around her. "I've got some ideas."

Derk slept in the next day but called his mother as soon as he woke. He asked about his dad and how she was doing and assured her that he would be up in a day or two. In spite of his physical pain, he felt worse inside. He told himself this wasn't his fault, but the guilt was creeping up on him.

Sandra had already traded her morning cup of java for a run on the beach. When she bounced up the steps to the condo, Derk was sitting on the patio in his maroon undershorts, feet propped upon a rattan footstool. He was unshaven, his hair was awry, his left arm was still black and blue, and he had an ice pack attached to his face with an Ace Bandage. He was reading the newspaper and sipping orange juice through a straw.

"If appearances are any indicator, you may have gotten into the wrong line of work, soldier," she said. The Frenchy's Cafe tank top that Derk had loaned her was saturated. She wiped the perspiration from her face with a bath towel.

He motioned her to come closer and pointed to a copy of the St. Pete *Times* he had picked off the floor from the stack of old newspapers.

"What?" she said.

He ran his finger across a headline on the inside of the second section of a four day old edition. It was about an accident in which two young men who had worked for McCardigan Construction Company had been killed. The vehicle that struck them had been traced to Elgar Chemical Company. Sandra read the article, occasionally glanced at Derk, and nodded. While she read, Derk unwrapped the elastic bandage and removed the icepack. He was full of anticipation in spite of a throbbing, nearly debilitating headache. Sandra pulled up a chair and sat down.

"The guy with the gloves," he said. He stretched his jaw to loosen the muscles while keeping his right hand on his face.

"What are you talking about?"

"The guy who hit me!"

"You saw him?"

"I remember the voice," he said, "Same guy who hit me in Ybor City." He started to get up but the imaginary axe in his head impositioned him.

"The big thug in Zeeland?"

Derk managed to pad into the house and back to the patio. Then he retraced his steps. He came over and stood in front of her.

"He said *leave the man alone and you know who I'm talking about.* I told you it was Von Lleuwan. I want those son-of-a-bitches!"

"We'll get 'em. We'll get 'em."

He paced between the living quarters and the patio. Sandra walked into the living room. Derk went into the kitchen, stopped in front of the sink, and rinsed his glass.

"Another thing. Call that Sarge in Tampa and ask him to check something." The words came out as if his chin was lodged in a vise.

"What's that?"

"Did they find Cat-A-Lyst® in Eva Simpson? I saw some at Elgar."

Something else was on Derk's mind. McCardigan Construction Company and Kate McCardigan. He didn't mention it to Sandra. Instead, he went to the bathroom, hoping that a hot shower would loosen him up, but it just made him more aware of the insult to his body that the colossus with the black hands had caused. It was personal now. He put on a T-shirt and shorts and returned to the living room. Sandra French had just put down the receiver.

"Guess what?" she said. "That security guard is our man. His name's Jimmy Swingle and the Tampa P.D. is looking for him right now. Sexually assaulted a dancer and punched out a couple of bouncers in a topless bar downtown. Everybody remembers the gloves. Guess he was just warming up for you."

Derk bobbed his head in acknowledgement, and even that hurt.

"Here's some irony," she added. "Couple of days ago some guys broke into Elgar and got away in a McCardigan Construction Company van. Same place where the two guys killed in the accident worked."

"Shitting me! What's McCardigan got to do with this?"

"What do you know about McCardigan?"

"Long time ago," he said, then drifted into the patio. He leaned against the railing and surveyed the beach below. A couple in their sixties, dungarees up to their ankles, walked barefoot and hand in hand toward the Don Cesar. He imagined they had been happily married for thirty years, and he envied the intense love they must share to have maintained such a long and committed connection. That hadn't typified his relationships.

The beach could cause one to reminisce about love or about love gone by, like Kate McCardigan. In spite of having come from different places and having been headed in different directions, she was never completely out of his mind. The scent of her hair in the store checkout lane, a glimpse through the window of a passing car, the sound of a familiar voice in the next room. Sophisticated but simple. Inexperienced but not insecure. Precocious but not arrogant. Athletic but not aggressive. Beautiful yet approachable. Maybe what he felt was reserved for the innocence of youth. More mature now, he could consider that option. Maybe it had not been love, only consuming infatuation. A friend once said, "Get over her and move on with your life." He had moved on, but he sometimes wondered if anyone could live up to the image in his head?

He had married once. Ginny was active, attractive, committed to her work, and everyone liked her. He knew he had been too demanding and too focused upon his own needs, but he also knew she wasn't the one. There were other relationships, some shorter, some longer, but nothing lasted.

His meandering was interrupted by Sandra French, "Bardo will call us back about the Cat-A-Lyst®. One more thing. They dusted Simpson's house and all they came up with was an insurance salesman from Ohio. I wonder if she had a premonition?"

"What?" He pondered the odds of coincidence and collapsed in a lounge chair on the patio.

32

As Kate waited for John Westfield in his rickety old swivel chair, her life was beginning to resemble the gloss pealing from her chipped nails. She had asked him to back off, and he hadn't. She stopped flaking her nails when she noticed the football trophy collecting dust on his office windowsill. It reminded her of the frequent analogies he regurgitated from his playing days.

The last time she saw him he said, "My coach once said there are three kinds of players. Those who make things happen, those who watch things happen, and those that don't know what's happening." Then he told her, "I don't know what's happening, and I don't like it!" He had hiked up his pants, puffed out his chest, and announced, "You got me into this mess, things didn't go your way, and now you're discarding me like a dead battery. I'll take care of things, all right, but we're in this together." Then he left.

Her relationship with John Westfield had been one of more than convenience. He had been there when Scott died and again when she put Trevor in the hospice. He had helped her through the work transition without arrogance or resentment that his new boss was a female. He was a capable foreman, liked by everyone, and had been described as a hunk by her female friends. Their relationship evolved into intermittent erotic encounters so extraordinary she felt guilty. It bothered her that she could feel so physically euphoric, but not emotionally committed, not in the way a woman knows whether the man in her life is the man for her life. She knew that John Westfield adored her and would do anything for her. She knew that since Scott's death the area between dependence and guilt had narrowed. She hoped she hadn't taken advantage of his sincerity and generosity. She was truly conflicted until she got the call from the Zeeland police department. She couldn't be John Westfield's lover and his boss. She was ready to do something about it, but he was late for their morning appointment.

Impatient, she returned to her office. Five minutes later he knocked on her door, entered without an invitation and approached with a peck on the cheek.

"Close the door," she said, before his pucker bloomed. "What the hell is going on?" She stood with her desk between them.

His lover's enthusiasm evaporated.

"Two of our guys were killed in Tampa, Mat Strong and another guy named Guillermo."

He deflated on the couch, obviously unaware of the news.

"I got a call from the Zeeland police," Kate said. "They faxed me pictures of the three you and asked if you worked for me? Then these two guys are run over by a truck and you waltz in all hoochy-coochy. What's . . ."

"Oh no," he said, head in hand. He looked up at her. "It must have been the cameras."

"That's how they take pictures."

"Wait. I wasn't in the Zeeland plant." He rose. "Let me see those."

She pushed the pictures on her desk toward him.

"Oh shit! These are Tampa," he said and turned the color of bone china.

"You were in the Elgar plant? In Tampa?" she said. She saw the panic on his face. "You guys broke into Von Lleuwan's plant, they know who you are, and two of you are dead. What the hell were you thinking?"

"I thought we could find something for you," he said, pacing and wringing his hands.

"I told you to leave it alone," she said and sat down, despair flowing across her like sap. "I should never have gotten you involved in this," she said, almost in a whisper.

He sat down, looked at the pictures again, got up, paced and then sat down again.

She had never seen him like this. He was frightened but it wasn't like a kid caught with his hand in the cookie jar. He was in big trouble, and he knew it. So was she, but she hadn't broken into anything or anywhere. She sucked in her stomach and cracked her neck from side to side, a trick she learned form her chiropractor.

"Well?" she said.

"What?

"Did you find anything?"

He shook his head, his eyes full of detest, as if he couldn't believe she had asked him that question.

Kate ran her hands up her body, all the way through her hair. "Can't you do anything right?"

Her foreman stopped pacing and stiffened. His expression turned venomous. "You cold-hearted bitch. I'm not gonna to be your slog anymore," he said. "You're on your own."

"John! I didn't mean," she called out but was interrupted by the slamming of the door. Her phone rang. Her receptionist reminded her that she had a golf lesson in thirty minutes. She started for the door to retrieve her foreman when her receptionist buzzed again to tell her that she had a visitor.

"What is it, Skip?" she said as he entered her office.

"Cheer up. You're about to get some good news!"

Skip detailed how the guys met and planned the interview, how they selected the name for the magazine, and their trip to Von Lleuwan's office.

"You should see it. His office is a damned golf course," Skip said. "Golf is the most prodigal, sedentary, stress-inducing, resource-mongering and environmentally offensive avocation known to man, and that pompous SOB designed his entire office around it."

Kate had never thought of those sculpted, sweet oases as sources of energy abuse and pollution. She had been raised on a golf course and identified it with civility and peacefulness. She viewed golf as the ultimate challenge to her concentration. To play well, very well, one had to be physically fit and mentally focused. They were on different planes when it came to golf, so she could ignore his misplaced discourse. What she couldn't dismiss this morning was his rambling.

"Damn it, Skip. I'm tired of your drivel. My foreman just walked out on me. Two of my crew are dead. I have a kid in terminal condition, and the guy responsible for it is still free. What did you find out?"

"I thought you were concerned about these things."

"I'm concerned that somebody poisoned my son. Do you have anything important to say or not?"

"You don't see the connection between these things, the chemicals on your golf course and the chemicals on the orchards that are killing your son?"

"I don't eat the grass, and I don't lick the golf balls."

"A pesticide is a pesticide is a pesticide. It doesn't matter where you use it. It ends up in the food, the soil, the water, or the air. Ever notice that pesticide and homicide have the same ending? We've deluded ourselves into thinking it's okay for farmers and golf courses and homeowners and anyone to dump this stuff on our food and our lawns, and it won't make any difference. If you don't understand this you'll never appreciate what happened to your son."

She allowed Skip to finish, but she wasn't fazed. "Did you find out anything or not?"

Skip arched his back, tucked his head under one arm, and started to say something. Instead he turned for the exit. In her doorway he said, "Von Lleuwan is working on something that was probably responsible for your son's illness. We're planning another meeting. I'll keep you posted."

"Wait a minute." She went after him. "Everything's okay then?"

"Other than the police are looking for me," he said, already half way down the hall.

She hurried to catch him and hooked his arm in hers. "What happened?"

He turned and left.

33

Skip arrived at the garden center ahead of what Bear had already dubbed, *The Green Team.* He had a hat full of memories of this place, and he wanted a few minutes to reminisce and meditate. The garden center was a twenty-acre park contiguous to the Stillwater River and north of downtown Dayton. A single paved road traversed the grounds and ended at the headquarters in the middle of the park. It was only ten minutes from Skip's house, and it was a one of the most tranquil places in the city, a literal forest that bound a plethora of gardens filled with roses, xenias, and marigolds in full bloom and plots of beans, peas, and sweet potatoes nearly ready for harvest.

He had helped transform the Center from a rather inconspicuous, underutilized garden club to the focal point for community events and into one of the largest community gardening plots in the country. Each spring hundreds of people vied for one of the small plots where they could nurture their own piece of the "Good Earth." It provided them with an opportunity to experiment with square foot gardening and to raise fruits and vegetables that were free of pesticides and every other which thing that the farmers, food processors, and supermarkets added on the way to their tables. It was a place where people could teach their children how and where their food was grown and give them the satisfaction of working with their hands. As important as the nourishment that had ascended from this ground were the relationships that had began and prospered. Man's roots were in the soil, and working the land brought people together. The breakdown of the collective more, consisting of hard work, honesty, and communal sacrifice, had coincided with the diminution of the family farm. Change is inevitable, part of evolution. He adapted. So did others. But this place provided Skip with a moment of clarity. In contrast with the world of Jack Von Lleuwan, this was the way things could be.

He hadn't told his friends about the call he got from the Tampa police, and he wasn't going to tell them. They found his prints in Eva Simpson's house and wanted to know when he had last seen her. He'd forgotten that he'd been finger printed for some insurance licensing. He told the police he was a friend of a friend and had never actually met her. When he asked why they wanted to know, he was told that they had found her body in the bushes in central Florida. Their questions shook him up, and he would have dropped this whole thing with Kate, but Congress had just passed a new law on pesticides that absolutely infuriated him. In addition, the outcome of his meeting with Von Lleuwan had made the possibility of nailing the son-of-a-bitch real. He now wanted to get this guy as much as Kate did.

It was still more than two hours to sunset, and there wasn't a cloud in the sky. It was T-shirt weather, but Skip was in his suit slacks and dress shirt. He had just come from a meeting with a family that needed an annuity plan for their first child. The others arrived in unison at seven o'clock. Player rolled up in a 1974 rusty pickup that he got from a friend in exchange for painting his house. His bleached out, hairy legs seemed to drop out of his cut off denim shorts like peeling, birch limps. He wore a pair of purple-tinted, wire-rimmed sunglasses and a weathered Deadhead T-shirt. Bear arrived in an old station wagon full of product samples and catalogs, looking rather preppy in his tan slacks and red Polo shirt. Dougal Ketchum looked unusually trim and fit in neatly pressed stonewashed denims and white gauze shirt. He had trimmed his beard, and there was a hop to his step. They joined Skip at a picnic table under the shade of a huge silver maple at the riverbank. A light breeze rustled the leaves overhead.

Player, in animated fashion, described the meeting with Von Lleuwan. "The dude was in a bad mood, and he looked kind of freaky with that patch on his eye. He kept asking, *Mulch* what?"

"I told you we should have called it *Turds and Whey*," Dougal said.

"Right on, bro," Bear said.

"Up yours," Player said continued, "Skip should be on Broadway."

Skip said, "When you pulled that Discover thing out of your ass I thought you were toking." Skip gave him a high-five.

"You guys really did it?" Bear said.

"We know something big is going down," Player said.

"But you pulled it off?" Bear said.

Player said, "Skip had this dude in his palm."

"We've got another meeting planned," Skip confirmed.

"Well done," Bear said, "but look out for O'Toole." The others waited for clarification. "O'Toole's Theory," Bear said, "He said Murphy was an optimist."

"Negativity, man" Player said.

"What are you going to do?" Dougal said to Skip.

"Did you hear about Delaney?" Skip changed the subject.

Bear and Player's drawn faces indicated they were out of the loop.

"HR 1627 just frosted it. Gone. Kaput!" Skip said.

"I heard," Dougal said. "Delaney prohibited chemicals that leave residues on food if they have the tendency to cause cancer. It was our best defense against the stuff Von Lleuwan makes."

"The new bill gets rid of zero tolerances. States can't even pass laws that are tougher than the federal ones," Skip said.

"That sucks a big one!" Player said.

"Yeah, the chemical companies and the growers wanted to get rid of Delaney because it became law when they couldn't measure real small amounts, residues the producers considered harmless," Skip said.

"Stuff that was killing us but we didn't know it," Dougal added.

"So, what about it?" Bear asked.

"The point is, things are getting worse, not better," Skip said. "The new tolerances will be set according to some 'lack of harm' standard. People will die, it's guaranteed, from eating this stuff, but they're trying to tell us that the benefits are greater than the risks."

"Benefits to whom?" Player said.

"The pesticide producers, the greedy twits. Ten to one says they buy nothing but organic!" Dougal said. Player high-fived him.

"Should we have expected more?" Bear asked.

"I guess it never was about safe food, just cash flow. Guys like Von Lleuwan make the rules as they go along, and our kids are the innocent victims," Skip said. "The question is, like Dougal said, what are we going to do?"

The leaves of the maple overhead dispersed the sunlight like silver pellets on the picnic table. A dark-colored beagle snatched a Frisbee in flight in the meadow across the road as a man with a rotor-tiller in the back of his pickup intersected their view. Skip noticed but said nothing. His remarks had muted the group. Player gazed at the ground and shuffled his feet. The brief silence was interrupted only by the call of a mallard attempting flight from the river below them.

"We've read about it, we talk about it, and we know it's real. We sort our cans and bottles, read labels, and write our congressmen, but it keeps on happening. Our friends are dying and everyone who should help has turned away. What if it were one of our kids?" Skip said.

Heads shook. There were murmurs.

"You're right," Dougal said. "We can't let this half-blind gimp get away with this."

"Hell no," Player responded. "He's fucking with the *Green Team*!"

"The Green Team?" Bear said.

"Yeah, the Green Team," Player repeated.

The changes in Delaney may have inspired his friends to action. Or maybe it was the odds, the idea of David versus Goliath. Maybe it was Player's notion that were a team, *The Green Team*, that clicked with them. Or in spite of being very different people, they were as much a family as close relatives. They had survived some very hairy schemes together. And they trusted each other with their lives. Whatever it was, it caused Player to hold up his hand, waiting for one of his brothers to join him. Dougal high-fived him first. The others followed. Then Dougal lit a bowl of herbs and passed it around. It had become a sort of ceremonial 'peace pipe' that they shared on special occasions similar to the rituals of the native Indians who had occupied this same land two hundred years earlier.

"Each generation carries the torch for freedom," Skip said. "Our parents' generation fought a war in Europe and the Pacific. We came of age at a time when each of us was compelled to fight for civil rights, woman's rights, sexual rights, environmental rights, even the right to choose the wars we want to fight. The right to explore and choose your own path, and hell, just the right to be, to exist without being hassled. Today I think there are more opportunities for everyone, more sexual freedom, more environmental awareness, and a greater tolerance of everyone and their ideas. But it's obvious that the struggle is far from complete, and I am proud to be going into battle with you guys."

Dougal said to Skip, "Well said, Mr. Lincoln." And Bear gave him a hug.

"What is it?" Skip said, noticing that something was still nagging Player.

Player was pinching the creases in his forehead. "Do any of you guys know who played with Cream, Blind Faith, and Billy Cobham?"

34

Skip's call to set the time for the next interview with Jack Von Lleuwan found the pesticide magnate in a buoyant mood.

"Mr. Dinsmore, I was just thinking about you," Von Lleuwan said.

"You seem to be in a good mood," Skip acknowledged.

"Why not?"

"Is that because congress just got the FDA off your back?"

"Oh, you mean HR 1627. Abso-fucking-lutely!"

"Sounds like the pesticide producers' retirement act to me."

"You're too cynical. Delaney was too rigid."

"You mean you won't have to worry about your favorite recipes for the next ten years. That's a lot of golf balls."

"Lighten up, Dinsmore. I was just beginning to think this interview was a good idea," Von Lleuwan said.

"I admit I'm eager to see if this new product is better than your other stuff."

"Well, Dinsmore, you're going to get your chance."

They set the date, and Skip looked forward to it with the zest of a boy who knew he was getting a new bicycle for his birthday.

The entire *Green Team,* buoyed by success of Skip's initial meeting, arrived at the Von Lleuwan plant in Zeeland in their rented van at nine in the morning. Skip planned to tell Von Lleuwan that The Discover Channel would air the interviews if the news was potent enough and that more people were needed to handle the extra demands of filming. He maintained his professional demeanor with a charcoal blazer, a button-down, blue oxford shirt, paisley tie, and navy slacks. The crew dressed down. Skip didn't think Player could get more casual than he was on their first visit, but Player surprised him. He showed up in a pair of faded denim jeans worn through at the knees and a T-shirt that read, "Don't pull on my ears. I know what I'm doing."

Bear and Dougal Ketchum wore denim trousers, sport shirts, and clean sneakers, and Dougal donned a ball cap that said *One World* on its crest.

Mrs. Huizenga, walking down the hall, recognized Skip when they entered. "Mr. Dinsmore, nice to see you again." But one look at Player turned her as sour as an Osage orange.

"It's a low budget crew, Skip said. "They're not going on TV. Mr. Von Lleuwan is. Is he ready for us?"

"I'll tell him you're here." She returned to her desk, made a brief telephone call, and then

proceeded down the hall to make some copies or something.

The group huddled around Skip in anxious anticipation.

Dougal fidgeted. "I've got to see his office. I hate golf."

Bear said, "I can't picture a guy with one eye and a gimp leg as anything but handicapped. How did you handle that?"

"Relax," Skip said.

Five minutes passed. No Von Lleuwan. Ten more minutes. Nothing. By then they had taken seats in the lobby. Every few minutes one of them would get up and walk around, then sit down again.

"Skip, I've got one for you," Player said. "Whose singing did Jimmy Buffet say made him *'hang on every line*?"

"Damn it," he said in a raspy but hushed tone. "Don't call me Skip. It's Dinsmore, Scott Dinsmore."

Player shrugged. "Sorry."

"Patsy Cline. *Miss You So Badly*, 1977, *Changes in Latitudes, Changes in Attitudes*," Skip answered Player's trivia question.

Bear and Dougal Ketchum laughed and shook their heads.

Player said, "You try him, smart ass!"

Bear held up his hands. "Not me."

Von Lleuwan came down the hall with a well-dressed, middle-aged Latin gentleman. They were absorbed in a discussion. Dougal nudged Player with his elbow and cleared his throat. The others looked toward Von Lleuwan.

"He's taller than I thought he would be," Dougal whispered. Bear agreed.

Von Lleuwan looked far more professional and authoritative than the first time Skip was here. A blue lab coat shielded a white dress shirt and polka-dotted, navy tie. Upon seeing them he strode straight for him with one hand extended.

"Sorry, gentlemen, I was in the lab," Von Lleuwan said and shook Skip's hand. "I'd like you to meet Mr. Domingo, my Director of Operations." Von Lleuwan seemed to be taking charge today.

Arturo Domingo didn't offer his hand.

"Mr. Domingo thinks our meeting is premature, but when I told him about *The Discover Channel* he changed his mind. What's the name of your magazine again?"

"*Mulch Magazine*," Skip answered.

"Oh, *Mulch*. I kept thinking *Muench*. I knew it was European. By the way, Art here used to be a vegetarian. Didn't you?"

Art Domingo's pearlies showed through his attempt to disguise a frown. "A long time ago," he replied.

Skip introduced Player as Mr. Briggs, Bear as Mr. Bear, and Dougal Ketchum as Mr. Ketch, members of his crew. "Mr. Von Lleuwan, the Discover angle is a real possibility and they want some outdoor shooting. That takes a special crew, and these are my prime time guys."

They stopped at the receptionist's desk. Mrs. Huizenga exchanged his lab coat for his suit coat.

"Gentlemen, I was going to drive, but I didn't plan upon expect such a large contingent. Could one of you drive, too?" Von Lleuwan said.

Skip exchanged some quick facial communication with Dougal. "No problem. Why don't you have Mr. Domingo join us? He can ride with Mr. Bear and Mr. Ketch," Skip said.

"I'm up to my neck with stuff," Art Domingo said.

"Great idea," Dougal said and moved to Domingo's side, placed his arm behind him and prodded as he pointed in the direction of their van. This got the entire group moving. "Vegetarian, eh. Is that a conflict of interest here?"

If doubt were a commodity Domingo's displeasure was overt enough to be cut with a cleaver, but he allowed a deep breath to escape and accompanied them to the parking lot.

They split into two groups. As Skip was about to climb into Von Lleuwan's Cadillac El Dorado, he said, "Oh! I almost forgot," and walked back toward the van.

He reached into the van, grabbed a pair of sunglasses, and in a low but firm voice he said, "Dougal, don't spook him."

As their abbreviated caravan moved through the West Michigan countryside north of Zeeland, they slowed to allow a twelve-point buck to cross the road in front of them. The early morning haze had lifted. The sky was crystal clear and the temperature was rising, forecasting a splendid summer day. Skip surveyed the landscape, a mostly flat area replete with tall, aromatic conifers, vibrant vegetation, and some of the lushest nurseries he had ever seen. There were few cars on the road. He assumed that the area's farmers had long since gotten to their fields and the nearby auto parts plants and furniture factories were already well into their first shifts. In spite of the urgent task at hand Skip said little for several minutes, mesmerized by the simple, seemingly undeveloped, beauty of the prodigious West Michigan landscape. An unenlightened visitor to this paradise might be lulled into thinking that all this talk about air and water pollution must be over exaggerated, but Skip knew better.

He glanced at Player who seemed absorbed by the rich leather and luxurious comfort of the El Dorado. Power everything and all the readouts were digital. The control displayed not only the speed and elapsed trip time but the number of miles remaining in the tank, the outdoor temperature which was currently seventy-nine degrees, and the tire pressure. There were separate readings for front and back seat temperature, and there was a display for the time in every time zone on the planet.

"Hey man, how much this set you back, forty, fifty big ones?" Player asked Von Lleuwan.

"Imagine it's a little out of your league."

"Is that a TV?" Player asked, pointing to a screen just to the left of the rear view mirror.

"CD Rom," Von Lleuwan said and plugged a compact disc into the dash. Men playing golf appeared on the four-inch color screen and the hushed voice of the announcer filled the climate-controlled cabin.

"Is that live?" Player said.

"Highlights from the U.S. Amateur championships. You know this new kid, Stix Johnson?"

Player shook his head. Skip closed his eyes and tugged on his goatee. He knew less about golf than liposuction, and the subject always annoyed him.

"He's pretty damn good, amateur champ the past two years, and he has a name that makes equipment manufacturers salivate. He's better than I was at his age."

"Where we headed?" Skip said.

"Not much of a golfer, eh, Dinsmore. It takes discipline and concentration to play golf well," Von Lleuwan said. "Otherwise, I suppose, it's not much fun."

Skip's focus narrowed, but he said nothing. Von Lleuwan was in a levitated mood.

"Through some of the finest apple orchards in the country," Von Lleuwan said. "I'm going to show you what the growers do now so you can see how *PESTfree©* changes things. Then we're going to take a little drive down to blueberry heaven." He sang the words blueberry heaven like an old 50s melody, *Blueberry Hill.* "Wow! Did you see that putt?"

Skip turned away from him and looked out the window. The guy had only one eye and one good leg and his products were killing babies.

He faced Von Lleuwan and said, "Player will drive if you want to watch TV."

"*PESTfree©*, so that's what you're calling it?" Player said.

"Apropos, don't you think so, Dinsmore?" Von Lleuwan said.

Skip bit his lower lip and twisted his goatee. Was Von Lleuwan baiting him or was he lost on his own planet?

"How much further?" Skip said as they turned east onto State Route 45.

"In a few minutes we'll be on the northwest side of Grand Rapids, nothing but orchards all the way to Sparta and east to Rockford," Von Lleuwan said. "You ever play golf?"

Skip shook his head. He liked the man better when he was a disheveled, loudly dressed, reluctant interviewee. He needed to loosen Von Lleuwan's self-confidence.

Player interjected with some light conversation, and the next few miles passed without incident. They turned off the expressway onto Fruitridge Road. It was appropriately named, nothing but apple orchards. Skip rolled the window down and allowed the aroma to usurp him: Spies, McIntoshes and Romes. It reminded him of autumn excursions with his family to the orchards south of Dayton for freshly squeezed cider.

He rolled up the window and looked behind him. Bear was following in the van about ten to twelve car lengths behind them. Art Domingo was turned half-around in the front seat, making insistent gestures with his hands in the direction of Dougal Ketchum. It was too much to hope that they were exchanging pleasantries.

"So what riled Domingo up?" Skip asked Bear later that day.

"Domingo had barely dented the leather when Dougal lit him up," Bear said. "Dougal told him he was surprised they were going ahead with this new product after the passage of HR 1627, and Domingo said, why wouldn't we? Dougal said he'd heard the lobbying was intense and asked how much *they* spent on it? It wasn't so much the question, it was the tone of his voice."

Domingo said, "What are you suggesting?"

"A lot of people are going to die because of that bill," Dougal said. "Don't you ever feel guilty?"

"What is *Mulch Magazine?*" Domingo said.

"We don't work for *Mulch*. We work with Skip, I mean Mr. Dinsmore." Dougal said. "I run a produce warehouse, and Bear has his own business, so whenever he needs us we're free to go."

"You know Dougal, no need for subterfuge, and he pounded away," Bear told Skip.

"This new poison, what do you call it?" Dougal said.

"You don't drink it," Domingo said. "It's a pesticide, and it's called *PESTfree©*. It's perfectly safe when used properly."

"Like all the other stuff you've been pouring on the food for years, but this one's better because it breaks down in the soil?" Dougal said.

"You couldn't stop him?" Skip asked.

"I wanted to, but here's what the guy said, *That's what it's supposed to do and that's a revolutionary step forward*," Bear told Skip.

"Supposed to?" Dougal said.

"That's a figure of speech. Thought you were journalists," Domingo said.

"That's not a figure of speech. You don't know if this thing works or not, and you're ready to coat the world with it?" Dougal said.

"The muscles in the guy's face twitched like plucked guitar strings," Bear said. "I thought he was going to punch Dougal out."

"What do you mean?" Domingo raised his voice. "We spent years on this. It's been thoroughly tested, and it's about to get EPA approval."

"Where, how?" Dougal said.

"Several universities and we did our own research," Domingo almost shouted at him.

"Come on. Names, dates?" Dougal said.

"What difference does it make? Who are you guys and what is *Mulch Magazine* or whatever you call it?" Domingo said.

"You couldn't change the subject or anything?" Skip asked Bear.

"Mr. Domingo, I'm sorry, I told him. We're just here to do some filming. We were told you'd take us to a place where they use the old product and then to a place where used *PESTfree©* so we could see the difference. Mr. Ketch just wants to know where that is? Domingo thought about it for a moment and turned to face me."

"Jack just told me you guys were coming twenty minutes ago," Domingo said. "Frankly, I'm not in favor of this whole thing. You'll just have to see when we get there."

"He side-stepped the whole question," Bear said.

"You said it's for fruits. Like apples and oranges?" Dougal said, continuing his interrogation.

"Domingo just nodded his head," Bear said.

"Apples in the north, oranges in the south, and it works in both climates?" Dougal asked.

"Yup," was all Domingo said.

"He was a little more relaxed when I asked the questions so I told him that they grow a lot of apples in Ohio where I live, and I asked him if they had to test the product for variances in different states," Bear said.

"There's not much difference between Michigan and Ohio, but we did some tests in both states," Domingo said.

"Oranges and apples are different," Bear said. "Is it hard to get somebody to take a chance on a new product?"

"We used our own fields first," Domingo said.

Dougal blurted out, "You own orchards in Florida?" And before Domingo could answer Dougal said, "Oh, yeah, Scott mentioned you had a plant in . . . Tampa, isn't it?"

"Domingo mumbled something without turning to face Dougal," Bear said.

"And a golf course that used to be an orchard. Oranges, I presume. And that's probably where you did the tests in Florida?" Dougal said.

"Domingo couldn't sit still in his seat, and his lips fluttered," Bear told Skip and strummed his lips with his forefinger. "So I said, Dougal, what was the name of that woman who lived next to the golf course where the orchards used to be? The one who claimed that something sprayed on the oranges crippled her son? Domingo turned harder than marble."

Dougal said, "She said Von Lleuwan did it. Tied herself to a load of ammonia and threatened to sanitize his whole plant. What was her name?"

"Most people will get right in your face and deny something they didn't do, but Domingo didn't flinch. Looked straight ahead. That's when I knew you were right!" Bear said.

"He didn't say anything?" Skip said.

"Nope, and Dougal looked at me and said, something's not kosher here. That's when Domingo exploded, starting shouting and waving his hands."

"You ignorant vegetarian scum," he said. "You can write all the cute little articles you want about backyard gardens, but you don't know squat about feeding a hundred million people everyday. I don't have to put up with your slander, not from some insignificant, unenlightened, and tendentious bunch of scribblers from *Mulch Ragazine*."

"He's got a colorful vocabulary. I'll give him that," Bear told Skip. "Then he turned around and didn't say another word."

Skip watched from the Cadillac as Art Domingo sat back in his seat. He had stopped waving his arms, but the rigid, sullen expression on his face was an obvious reaction to the ever-constant challenge created by living in Dougal Ketchum's contentious world. Skip knew that a smiling, compliant Von Lleuwan Enterprises' operations manager would be too much to expect after thirty minutes with Dougal Ketchum, so he had been ready to settle for neutral disinterest. Now that expectation had been depleted as surely as the ozone layer over the South Pole. He guessed there would be little use for much subtlety from this point forward.

"I don't know much about your new product, but now that the Delaney Clause has been torched, it doesn't sound as if there's much need for, what do you call it, *PESTfree©*?" Skip challenged his host.

"You jest, Dinsmore!" Von Lleuwan responded.

"How so?" asked Skip.

"I'm going to show you," he said, motioning ahead of them.

A half-mile up the road they turned into a drive leading to a large farm. The house, its sheds, and the barn were circumscribed by orchards except for a view from the road.

"The Loudermilk farm, been in the family for seventy-five years," Von Lleuwan said, the arrogance overt.

"Big spread," Player said.

"Over three hundred acres."

Farm implements, including tractors, wagons and a fertilizer, were scattered about the grounds. A couple of sprayers were being filled in the barn. A shiny new, extended cab pickup was parked next to the house. The two-story, wood-framed house sported a large screened-in gallery. It dwarfed a smaller single-story structure behind it. The back of a late model sedan protruded from the garage of the smaller home. An elderly woman, probably Loudermilk's mother or mother-in-law, was hanging clothes on a line next to the little house.

"This one of your test sites?" Skip said.

"No," said Von Lleuwan. "It's Ben farm." Von Lleuwan waved to him.

A sturdy, red faced, graying man in his mid-fifties motioned them to park next to his pickup. Von Lleuwan skipped the introductions and hurried them into the barn where the conveyors, sorters, and processing equipment were being made ready for the new season's harvest.

Von Lleuwan stopped to announce, "Gentlemen, in less than ninety days this place will be as busy as a beehive in a flower garden. Mr. Loudermilk runs quite an operation here, and we're not going to get in his way." He kept moving.

Rows of empty crates were stacked almost to the top of the back wall outside the barn. Beyond them was the Loudermilk orchard and the heart of Michigan apple country. Skip sucked in the aromatic fragrance while Von Lleuwan reeled off production numbers for Michigan fruit as he strolled ahead of them.

"These farms are so productive a major baby food manufacturer located a plant nearby," he told them.

Then Von Lleuwan stopped next to a tree that was dripping with fruit, reached in and held an apple in his hand without plucking it from the tree. It was still green but portended a pale reddish hue.

"This is what it's all about. Looks delicious, doesn't it?" Von LLeuwan said. He pirouetted on his firm leg. "Look around you. See any bugs, aphids, rodents, limb or foliage diseases?" He paused slightly between each malady. "No, of course, not. Ben is ardent about pest control." He looked at Ben.

Mr. Loudermilk said somewhat gravely, "Herbicides for the weeds, rodenticides for the critters, insecticides for the bugs, fungicides for the blight and scabs, and a few other things. Everyone likes good-looking fruit, firm fruit, and this is the best in the world." Then he smiled.

"But healthy?" Skip had experienced enough of the Von Lleuwan's road show.

Von Lleuwan's laugh was dismissal.

"There's forty different chemicals used on apples including captan, endosulfan and chlorpyrifos, some of the most toxic things known to man," Skip said. "And you can't get them out of the apples. Feeding applesauce to a kid is like serving him toxic pudding."

"That's a little strong, don't you think, Dinsmore?" said Von Lleuwan.

"*PESTfree©* replaces all of them?" Skip said.

"The answer is most of it. In time we'll be able to kill all the little pests."

"And there's no residue?" Dougal Ketchum asked.

"Breaks down harmlessly," Von Lleuwan retorted.

"So how do you account for the woman?" Dougal said.

"Your tests confirm this?" Skip interjected.

"When it's approved by the EPA, it will change agriculture forever," Von Lleuwan said, staring at Dougal.

It was a statement powerful enough to defuse the most die-hard environmentalist. Regardless of how Skip felt about him, if it were true, and he had little hard evidence to prove otherwise, Von Lleuwan was absolutely, smack-dab on target. Von Lleuwan turned and headed back to the car.

"Ask him about the woman in Florida?" Dougal said to Skip.

As they passed through his barn Mr. Loudermilk offered each of them an apple. Skip wiped it on his shirt before taking a bite. When he walked by the sprayer, he coughed up a mouth full. Von Lleuwan had not answered his earlier question.

"Is this one of the places you tested *PESTfree©*?" Skip said.

Von Lleuwan turned and offered a condescending scowl. He was adjusting the patch over his eye. "What is it with you guys?" The strap caught on one ear. He removed it, exposing a solid blue glass eye with a star on it. It was frigging weird. "I already told you."

Skip interrupted him, "I thought you were going to take us to one of your test-sites."

"That's not really necessary. It's a place just like this, a fruit farm. It could have been any place. In fact, we tested several locations," Von Lleuwan said, as he rubbed his eye and then replaced the patch. He turned and headed toward his car where Art Domingo was waiting. Skip and the others followed.

When they arrived Domingo said, "I thought you were going to take some pictures."

Player, the only one of them holding a camera, said, "Hey man, this isn't the place."

Von Lleuwan, in an obvious attempt at diplomacy, said, "Gentlemen, this was our first stop. Now we're going to the other orchard."

"One of the test sites?" Dougal asked.

"A blueberry farm, similar to one of the sites we tested. Bushes instead of trees. Different fruit, different pests, same results," Von Lleuwan said. Domingo opened the car door while Von Lleuwan went to the passenger side.

"Blueberries," Skip said. "There's almost twenty chemicals used on them. How many does *PESTfree©* replace?" He stood in front their rented van, his friends next to him with folded arms.

Von Lleuwan squinted into the sun and told them, looking over the top of his car, "Most of the sites we tested are no longer in production. I'm showing you what *PESTfree©* can do." His hair was awry, his demeanor combatant. All that was missing was a loud golf shirt. "Are you guys coming or not?" He got into the car.

Skip walked over to the Cadillac and Von Lleuwan rolled down the window. He leaned down and stroke a few strands of his goatee. "You tested in Florida, didn't you," Skip said.

Von Lleuwan shot a troubled glance at his operations director.

"So what about the woman in Florida?" Skip said.

Von Lleuwan's grin was paternal. "When I get back to the office I'll look for a site that you can visit. Is that okay with you, Mr. Dinsmore?"

Skip stood up. "Want us to call you?"

Von Lleuwan dispatched them with flip of his hand and road off.

"I guess he wants to call *us*," Player said and Dougal gave him a high-five, followed by a low one about knee high.

"You guys ever going to grow up?" Bear said as they loaded into the van.

35

The morning after walking out of Kate McCardigan's office, John Westfield slept an extra hour, worked out with some weights on his back porch, and jogged into the Dayton's high profile downtown entertainment strip, the Oregon Historic District, to pick up a copy of the morning newspaper. On the way home he stopped for breakfast. He read *The Herald* and watched the city jump-start itself through the window of the White Tower at Fifth and Patterson. It was a perspective he seldom witnessed because he was normally well into his workday by this time. Today, however, he was contemplating his future.

He returned to his house on St. Anne Hill, mowed the lawn, and spent the day doing minor repairs around the house, the kind that put the finishing touches on projects that had been put off because there was never enough time. Just before sunset he showered and dressed and walked down to the Trolley Stop for a sandwich and a beer. The band, a funky, rhythmic blues quartet, was just setting up as he was finishing dinner. A half dozen Rolling Rocks and two sets later, half an hour past his normal sack time, a possibility of an arrest warrant had been relegated to a distant spot in his mind. He walked down to the Oregon Express and back, occasionally pausing to ponder the window displays of the neighborhood's unusual boutiques. He imbibed the funky sounds of a jazz quartet that drifted through the open door of the Night Owl. The aroma of bratwurst, sauerkraut, and deep-fried eggrolls from the food carts wafted in the air. The humid, urban air refracted the light from the old fashioned street lamps into subdued tones against the dark red cobblestone alleys and buildings. He strolled the historic neighborhood in a semi-besotted state, but his thoughts were clear. By the time he returned to his Queen Anne home he knew he had to call Kate in the morning and discuss the terms of his departure from the McCardigan Construction Company. Then he would get to hell out of town.

He awakened in time to catch her in her office.

"We need to talk. I'll be down at eleven," Westfield said.

"Okay, but I've got an appointment out of the office at noon," she said. He heard her say, "Are you okay?" as he put down the receiver.

He went for a morning jog followed by breakfast with *The Herald* at the White Tower as he had done the previous day. At quarter to eleven he was feeling somewhat melancholy as he locked the back door and headed toward his truck for the trip to Kate's office. He paid no attention to the white van that had been parked across the street from his house since six-thirty that morning.

36

Derk awoke feeling as if someone had driven a Mack Truck into his head and left with the engine running. He lay in bed for two hours waiting for the Advil to deafen the turbines. On top of that, he was feeling guilty. He couldn't dismiss Sandra French's simple wisdom. He had to see his dad. He made two calls. The second was to his mother for an update.

"Yes, he needs you," she said. "I know you're hurt, but your dad is dying."

Derk had first called the hospice where his father was staying. Dying was his mother's term. It was a kind of self-fulfilling prophecy, or maybe the grant of a wish he couldn't condone. His father was on life support, the nurse said, but he could survive indefinitely. It was his mother that needed him, but the throbbing in his head was debilitating. He couldn't read the newspaper without becoming nauseated. He drifted in and out of consciousness all day.

One time he overheard Sandra French call her boss in Michigan. "We're making progress. We're trying to link Von Lleuwan to another murder in Florida. By the way," she said, "we're pretty sure the guy in Zeeland was no accident." She gave the number where she could be reached and said, "I'll be back when I'm back." After that he thought he heard her say, "Derk Bryan! What have you done to me?"

She entered his bedroom and sat beside him. "Need anything?"

He felt like a flickering light bulb but mumbled, "No."

"There's nothing in the Elgar files about Cat-A-Lyst® and nothing about McCardigan Construction," she said. "I called Bardo and Wally. Nothing new." Before burning out he heard her say, "I'm going for a walk and some lunch."

She hadn't returned when he rose to use the bathroom. The telephone rang as he ricocheted down the hall between his bedroom and the bathroom. Sandra entered the condo, ran over, and steadied him against the wall.

"Stay here. I'll be right back," she said.

She answered the phone. "It's Bardo," she whispered to Derk.

Derk maintained his equilibrium, heard her say "Got it" a couple of times, and stumbled toward the bathroom.

She came over and took him by the arm. "Let me help you."

"That would be a little awkward," he said without cracking a smile, his speech still slurred.

Sandra laughed and let loose of his arm. "You'll let me know if you need any help in there?"

Even in his physically compromised, speech-truncated condition he recognized a double entendre and his libido lit up like a Fourth of July sky.

Sandra was seated on the couch in the living room when he finished his business. "I'm okay," he said when she started to get up. He brushed her cheek with his hand as he passed behind her. "You're a sweetheart," he said and he sat down next to her.

Her response was a sympathetic smile.

"Where'd you go?" he asked.

"For a walk. It's so peaceful and relaxing here. The shops, the galleries, the little guest houses. So laid back."

"Looks good on you," he whispered. He was looking at the unclothed parts of her body.

"The tan, you mean." She held out and rotated one arm. "Yeah, but I burn like confetti. I have to watch out." She folded her arms together as if to deflect his compliment. "I saw a horseshoe crab shell on the beach and it made me think of you."

"How so?" He was still languid.

"It looked like a soldier's helmet. Maybe from a troll who patrolled the seashore."

"A troll?"

"When you live in the midst of the discards of everyday urban life, you tend to assume that a certain level of grime and ugliness is normal, like shaving your legs or combing your hair. It's not. This place is so pristine, so natural, and you are its defender."

"Thank you," he said and patted her thigh with his hand. He slumped deeper into the couch.

She patted the back of his hand and got up. "Nature calls."

After she got up, he reclined on the couch.

On the way out of the bathroom Sandra said, "You were right about the Cat-A-Lyst®. She must have been forced to drink it."

Then he heard the chime of wine glasses gently colliding in the kitchen. He was almost asleep when she returned with two glasses of orange juice.

"Did you hear me?" she said. He mumbled something probably not discernible. "Let me help you back into bed." He didn't resist.

She helped him take the two Advil he had wrapped in his fist, then brushed back his hair and kissed his forehead. He gurgled like a baby with gas and drifted into dreamland.

It was dusk when he woke. Filtered by the Venetian blinds he could see a quarter moon rising through his bedroom window. As the cobwebs cleared he inventoried his injuries. The jaw was stiff, but the headache had been reduced from a hard throb to a dull moan. He sat on the side of the bed and rotated his arms. He'd felt better, but tomorrow he thought he could travel. He took a hot shower and put on a pair of shorts and a T-shirt from Daytona Beach Bike Week, 1994. He smelled bread baking. It made him hungry. Sandra was in the kitchen wearing a Progress Grocery apron from New Orleans. It reminded him of the addictive aroma of muffaletta that spilled onto Decatur Street from one of the many delis in the French Quarter.

"Smells good," he said. His speech had almost returned to normal.

"Figured with your sore jaw you couldn't handle anything too tough so it's oyster stew, French style," she said.

"What's French style?"

"Anything I make."

She made him laugh. The discomfort in his jaw was subsiding. He leaned over the soup simmering on the stove. "Mmm Mmm!" he said and put his arm around her. "You're full of surprises."

When he let go of her, the ladle in her other hand impeded him, and she encouraged him to come closer. She kissed him lightly on the cheek. "So are you. You must be feeling better."

"Much, but I'm famished."

"Ready when you are," she said and pulled some wheat rolls from the oven. "Oyster crackers," she said, placing them onto a serving plate.

Derk's only sounds during dinner were the occasional murmurs of a well-satisfied customer. Sandra did most of the talking.

"I know I told you, but you weren't too coherent. Your intuition was correct. Bardot said the Simpson woman was full of Cat-A-Lyst®." He held up one thumb to note his satisfaction with her findings. "On the other hand, I didn't find a trace of it in the Elgar records."

He mumbled something unrecognizable through a mouthful of bread.

She continued, "Wally called. He wishes you well. Said he found out that Von Lleuwan is seeking approval for a new pesticide. Word is it's supposed to be something revolutionary. Strangest thing, he said the body that was found in Von Lleuwan's plant is missing. Disappeared from the morgue."

Derk sat back in his chair, shaking his head. Sandra began clearing the table. He rose to help but was entranced by the weirdness of this case.

"I'll take care of it," she said as she put her hand on his shoulder. "What do you think about that?"

"Un-frigging-believable," he said softly and slipped into deeper thought. He headed for the patio.

"One more thing. Wally said be cool when you talk with Kate. What did he mean by that?"

He didn't respond. Sandra joined him a few minutes later. The evening air was humid, but the intensity of the south Florida day had diminished with the setting sun. A full moon was making its predictable but spectacular, nocturnal ascent. A light zephyr that came in with the tide filtered through the screens with the constancy of a slow paddle fan.

"Tell me about McCardigan Construction," she said.

He looked at her as if he wanted to say something. The lines in his forehead had become tire tracks, his gaze introspective. A light discoloration consumed one side of his face but the swelling had dissipated. He turned away and looked across the beach, barely noticing a gull eclipse a beam from a light-pole on the street. He wondered how the meeting with Kate would go? "Hello, this is agent Bryan. I'm with the EPA." No. "Hello, Kate, this is Derk. How are you?" Too friendly. "Hello, Kate, this is Derk Bryan. I need to talk with you." Nothing resembled what he wanted to say. Nor did the words encompass the exhilaration he felt as he imagined the words he wanted to hear from her. Nagging at him were serious questions about this case that begged a response. The personal ones, however, kept interfering with the professional ones. What was her involvement with Von Lleuwan? Did she ever think about him? Was she in trouble? Would she want his help? How was Skip involved and what did she know about that? If she were mixed up in this case, Derk's emotions were going to be tested.

"Did you hear me?" Sandra's tone was insistent.

"I'm sorry. This is something I have to do myself."

"What's McCardigan Construction?" she said. "I'm entitled to know."

This time he faced her as he spoke. "I've got to do this alone."

"It's about Kate McCardigan, isn't it? You think she might be involved?"

It surprised him that she knew her name, but he said nothing. He left the room.

Sandra followed him and stood beside the countertop of the pass-through between the kitchen and living room. She placed her hands on top of the counter. "Why won't you talk to me?"

He took a deep breath, dropped his head, and rubbed his face and the back of his neck. The words wouldn't come out. He walked toward the bedroom. At the doorway she got his attention.

"I know about you and Kate McCardigan," she said.

He turned toward her. "You what?"

"Wally told me."

"You don't know anything."

He went into the bedroom and closed the door. She entered without knocking. Derk pitched underwear into a travel bag.

"You still love her, don't you?" she said.

Sandta wore a proud but covetous expression. Her body was rigid. Her fists were clenched at her sides. "Lord hath no wrath like a woman scorned," Shakespeare had said. He had made a mistake. In the past five days he had trashed his car and been assaulted twice, the second time in a warehouse that she had advised him not to enter. His response had been childish and self-indulgent. This same woman, who had always found him to be politically insolent and self-centered, had chauffeured him, nursed him, fed him and tolerated him for most of those five days. Now, somehow, she was beginning to find him appealing. She was hurt and jealous. At least, that's how it looked. He opened his arms for her.

"I'm sorry," he said and expected her to embrace him.

She withdrew a step.

"So, talk to me," she said.

His ego sagged with his shoulders. "Oh boy."

He told her about Kate, how they met, the environmental club, and their little group. He hadn't seen her in years, but his friends had kept him informed. She had married Scott McCardigan and had a child, a son he thought. When her husband died she became the only female executive of a major construction company in her area. He spoke with some pride about her prowess in golf. He sat with his feet extended on the bed and his back against some large cushions. Sandra sat on the edge of bed and listened.

"She might be involved in this, and I'm not sure how to approach her," he said. "You asked if I still loved her. No. Maybe. I don't know. Old emotions. Didn't you ever have a relationship that was hard to get over?"

"It's been twenty years."

"I know. Doesn't make sense, does it?"

She placed her hand on his knee. "Have you called her?"

"I've got to see her," Derk said.

"Okay. When are we going?"

"Alone."

"We're on this case together," she said.

"Do I detect a note of jealously?"

"This woman probably has critical information on a capital case. Not of you, you conceited, self-centered," she didn't finish the line, but this time she didn't back away from him.

He slid off the bed. "Don't go away. I'll be right back," he said.

Moments later the light from the outer rooms disappeared and Derk entered the bedroom with two glasses of orange juice and a candle.

He held one out for Sandra and proclaimed, "You're in Florida. How about some juice?"

She took it. "Well?"

"We'll go up together, but I have to talk with her alone." He held out his glass, a compromise and a toast.

She kissed his glass with her own, but her effort lacked commitment.

"Smile," he said.

She forced a grin through pursed lips.

"That's not a real smile. Like this." He made an exaggerated expression. Then he contorted his face in numerous ways until her resistance subsided. "There. Takes less muscles and slows the age lines." She grinned widely at that suggestion. "Besides, your smile lights this whole room."

"Thank you," she said.

"Bottoms up," he said. They finished their drinks and put the glasses on the dresser.

"One more thing, partner, someone else I know might be involved," Derk said.

Sandra's mouth fell open.

"The insurance salesman from Ohio, probably an old friend of mine."

"Who are you, Derk Bryan?" she said.

"I saw him the other day and he mentioned Von Lleuwan. Something about insurance," Derk said. "God, I should have known better. I'm really worried about him."

Sandra patted his thigh affectionately. He lit a candle on the nightstand and turned out the lamp. Their silhouettes danced in the flickering shadows. He put one hand on top of hers. She turned it over and gripped his hand softly at first and then firmly. He put the other hand around her shoulders. They embraced. He let go and then she reconnected with a sense of urgency. They brushed cheeks, smelled each other's hair, and buried their chins in opposing shoulders. Nothing was said. When he found the perfect fit, he held her motionless for a long time. Occasionally they would look at each other, gently kiss and embrace again.

"Can you tell?" Derk broke the silence first. "I'm hug deficient."

"You hug good."

He squeezed her again, then relaxed. "Did you know that four hugs every day are absolutely essential for normal bodily functioning, six for growth and eight for high level-health?"

"You really know how to charm a woman, Derk Bryan!"

The tension drained from his body. "Let's get more comfortable," he said.

She sat up and stiffened. He knew what she was thinking. He shook his head, smiled, and then held out his hands to indicate he wanted her to move.

"Ahh!" she said.

He cupped his hands under her legs and shifted her onto the bed. Then he lay down beside her. All that needed to be said was communicated through wanting eyes. They embraced again and their body heat fueled a petting frenzy as untamed as two teenagers at a drive-in movie. He withdrew, gently kissed her lips and forehead, and asked her to turn away from him. As she rolled over, he blew out the candle. He wrapped his arms around her and held her as close as syrup on an ice cream sundae. The intensity slowly diminished and as might two caterpillars in a single cocoon they fell asleep, fully dressed on top of his waterbed.

He dreamed of a fire he was unable to extinguish. Somehow, he had become locked in a passionate embrace with a woman whose face he didn't recognize. Instead of embracing the ecstasy, he was cursed by an uneasiness that the wind through the open window was blowing the curtain into the flame. He pinched the flame, but when his attention returned to his lover the candle re-ignited.

His restlessness eventually awakened him. The moonlight was screened by the blinds. The digital clock pulsed out 1:30 A.M. He took the candle's remains to the kitchen sink. When he returned to bed he removed everything but his shorts. His effort to turn down the covers without waking Sandra was unsuccessful. She rolled over and shielded her eyes from the moonlight that formed tiny ribbons on the back of her hand. She arose and stumbled to and from the bathroom. He heard her legs hit the bed-frame with a thud and an "ouch," and then the soft snap of something elastic before she nestled next to him under the sheets.

As if his body were a magnet, she clung to him. Her lips met his. Tongues probed. Arms and legs intertwined. His breath shortened. She searched for more exotic real estate, turned and twisted, and got on top of him. She slipped off his shorts. They rolled over, and he was now above her. As aroused as he had ever been, she guided him into her. Her mouth was so close they shared the same air. Time became suspended as he reached a rhythm with her as steady and powerful as the evening tide. He hoped the pleasure would never end as he waited for her orgasm. Then, as if on cue, he followed. She lay in his grip and after a while collapsed in a warm, moist pool of their mutual efforts. Neither of them had said a word the entire time. He fell asleep, exhausted and satiated.

The door to his bedroom was ajar as he tiptoed down the hall. From the slight motion of the waterbed, he could tell she was waking. He stopped to savor her undulating outline. She seemed to be surrendering the cool, redolent sheets with difficulty. He tarried a bit longer while she stretched. Then she glanced at the bedside alarm, its red digits glowing eight three zero, and leaped from bed. She noticed his ogle through the crack in the door, recovered her underwear, and held it against her breasts as she tiptoed past him to the bathroom.

Derk packed his bags and was transporting them from the bedroom to the living room when Sandra emerged from the bathroom. A single white bath towel was all that separated her from him as she slid by him. His mood was grave as he inhaled her, but her damp hair, brushed back from her face, and her fragrance, like cosmic energy, almost over-powered his resistance. She met him with an embarrassed grin. Any normal guy would have willed that towel to the floor, but this was not one of those times.

"We've got to go," he said and pecked her on the cheek.

"And good morning to you too."

"Dad's dying, my friends are in trouble, and I've got to go."

"You mean we've got to go."

Ten minutes later they were back in business suits and on their way to the airport.

"Talk to me," Sandra said, using the mirror on the sun visor to apply her makeup.

"I've got to go to Michigan."

"I thought we were going to Ohio."

"I promised Mom I'd be there two days ago."

"Your dad?"

"Yes. I mean no," Derk said. "I called Kate this morning. She told me the guys who were killed in the accident in Tampa worked for her. She didn't really know them, her foreman had hired them, but they worked on one of her construction crews. Just before the accident she got a call from a cop in Michigan. She's sure he was from Zeeland, and he asked her to I.D. the guys. Next thing she knows, they're dead. And she hasn't talked with Skip,"

"Who?"

"The insurance salesman," Derk said, tearing through traffic with both hands wrapped around the wheel.

"Slow down," she said. He eased off the accelerator. "I'm confused. What about going to see Kate? What about Von Lleuwan?"

"When I pressed her she said he used to own some property next to her house but that was all," Derk said. "Then she changed the subject. She'd been under a lot of stress, problems at work, and her son was ill. She apologized, thanked me for calling, and asked me how I'd been doing. In other words, she sidestepped it. I told her I was sorry about her husband. I hadn't talked with her about it, but I sent flowers and a note when it happened."

Sandra interrupted him. "Save the foreplay.

"Touchy this morning."

"You couldn't have had anything to do with that?" She sneered at him, her nose pinched between her now tanned cheeks. She stuffed the coiffing tools into her purse and snapped it shut.

"Finally, she admitted that she had someone checking into the relationship between her son's illness and Von Lleuwan, but she didn't want to talk about it over the phone."

Sandra tilted her head to one side and smirked.

He slapped the steering wheel. "Damn, I should have known."

Sandra exhaled, a rush of frustration, and shook her head.

"I'm talking about Skip," Derk said. "I thought it was coincidental or I would have said something." He tightened his grip on the wheel and hit the gas again.

"She's involved, your friends are involved. Anybody you haven't told me about?"

"I'm sorry," he said with considerable sincerity. It was meant as a blanket apology, for what he was about to do as much as what he had done.

She ignored his apology. "We need to talk with them."

"I know Player, Bear and Dougal are mixed up in this, too," he said. "She wouldn't have called them unless she didn't have anywhere else to turn. She's in big trouble. They're all in trouble."

"Thought you said there was nobody else, and *we've* got to find out," she said.

He ran his hand across his forehead. It felt like the work of plowhorses. People were dying and old friends were involved. The prospect of seeing Kate was clouded with trepidation.

"So what's the plan?" she asked.

"We're going to Michigan," was all he told her.

They dropped the rental car at the agency and took a shuttle to the airport. He asked the shuttle to stop at the Delta terminal. The driver removed Kate's bags and was about to get Derk's when Derk put his hand on the driver's arm and motioned him to leave his bags in the van.

"USAir," he told the driver.

Sandra grabbed Derk's arm. "What's going on?"

"I'm sorry, but I've got to do this alone." He gave her a quick hug and turned for the van.

"You can't do this. You promised."

"I've got to sort this out," he said and glanced at Sandra's watch. "You've got a flight to Lansing in thirty minutes. I'll call you as soon as I have something."

"Absolutely not!" she shouted and ran after him. "Where are *you* going?"

He jumped into the van. She was inches behind him, hands on hips, steaming like a charging bull, with only an eighth inch of plate glass between them. He rolled down the window.

"It's all going to happen in Michigan. I'm sure. Check out who called Kate from Zeeland."

It had been more than just the most exhilarating sex he'd had in a long time. She had tilted his axis, and guilt, like an arrow from Paris' bow, afflicted him. Unlike Achilles, he would survive but there would be consequences.

As he drove away he stuck his head out the window and shouted, "About last night. It was wonderful!"

He heard her announce to everyone within earshot, "Men, goddamn men!"

37

Derk called his mother from the terminal. "I'm in Dayton. I should be there tomorrow."

"You sure? The life is draining out of him," she said.

"Yes, Mom. I love you," he said. He thought she was exaggerating, but the guilt hooked him like a scorned lover's barb. More than ever, he wanted to know what had happened in his childhood even though going to Michigan under these circumstances was like bad-tasting medicine.

The clock over the auto rental sign read one-thirty when Kate McCardigan came through the revolving door. She was wearing a navy dress, a somewhat raggedy pageboy, and a sulky demeanor. The lean curves of her youth had filled in to form a mature but more sensuous woman. He wiped a dewdrop of melancholia from his bruised cheek, dropped his bags, and opened his arms.

"You look terrific," he said.

"You too."

"It's been too long," he said as he released her. He wasn't sure why he expected some coy teenage response from their dating years. It didn't come so he changed the subject. "I didn't expect to see you here."

"I had some things to do out of the office," she said and motioned toward the exit. "I'm parked right outside. What did you do to your face?" She swiped renegade hairs from her brow.

"Got hit by a train," he said.

"Tough job."

"Some days are worse than others," he said.

In the car she abandoned her formality. "Derk, I'm really glad you called. I wasn't sure what to do."

"What's going on?"

The adolescent innocence with which he was familiar had been replaced by weary gloom. She sucked in half the air in the car before answering.

"It started after my son was born. We're going to see him now," she said as they exited the airport. "I can't prove it, but I think he was poisoned by the pesticides sprayed on the orchards next to our house."

He had heard the story before, but from Kate it was like a sucker-punch.

"We used to live in Washington Township. There were a lot of orchards there, but they've all been developed. That's where it happened. He's dying, Derk."

As the image of Eva Simpson's son reformed, the pieces of the puzzle fell into place. "You lived at The Orchards."

"How'd you know?"

"I'm sorry about your son." He put a hand on her shoulder and she momentarily leaned her head against it. Her sorrow tugged on his sympathy like a puppy dog, and the warmth of her cheek on his hand conjured up old images. "You didn't deserve this, but you're not alone."

She backed away abruptly. "Derk, what do you know?"

"Your son? He's ten or eleven?" Derk said.

"Twelve."

"Lost a lot of weight and muscle control?"

She confirmed each of his depictions.

"I saw a kid in Florida with the same condition. He grew up next to an orchard that was developed into one of those golf course condominium projects," he said.

"You saw Eva's boy?"

He nodded.

"It's Von Lleuwan Enterprises," she said. "Jack Von Lleuwan is behind this."

"I know," Derk said with a painful expression. His intuition about Von Lleuwan had been correct, but this was a high price to pay for such satisfaction.

She told him about her son as they drove south on I-75 through Dayton and then east on S.R. 35 toward Xenia.

"What about Skip?" Derk asked.

Guilt accompanied her response. "He's trying to help me connect Von Lleuwan to Trevor."

"Where he is?"

"I don't know," she answered. Something suggested she was feigning ignorance, but before he could press her they arrived at the Patterson Home.

The sign said it was for children. The two-story, brick structure featured a huge portico with Greek columns that rested on five well-manicured acres. Inside, the waiting areas were furnished with modern furniture, colorful tapestries, and Persian rugs. It was hi-tech and kid friendly, and, given the number of people roaming around in hospital garb, the staff-to-patient ratio seemed high for a hospice. This was not a hospital. Few of these children would ever get to appreciate the worldly rewards of the tax bracket it took for their parents to afford such care.

One glance at Kate's withering son and Derk understood her despair. Her son's symptoms were similar to Eva Simpson's boy, but either more advanced or he was having a poor day. He couldn't tell whether Trevor recognized his mother, but the sound of her voice settled him. His skin was mottled, Derk now understood, as a result of weakened liver and kidney functions. The bones in his face almost penetrated his emaciated skin. His dark, sunken eyes revealed a listlessness that was an inevitable prelude to a release from the burdens of this world. Derk's dream reoccurred and his father took the child's place in the hospital bed.

They left arm in arm. When they reached her car Derk asked, "Could you use a hug?" He needed one. She didn't refuse his open arms. Her mist turned to a drizzle. A drop of rain formed on Derk's cheek, too, but he wiped it away before she noticed.

He took the wheel back to Dayton. Once she had composed herself, he asked again about Skip. "Did he find anything?"

"He told me they posed as journalists," she said.

"They?"

"Player, Bear and Dougal," she said, again confessing.

"Why didn't you just go to the police?"

"No one paid attention."

"Jesus, Kate, this is no college project. Where are they?"

"I don't know. I told you."

He pulled off the road and slammed on the brakes. He grabbed her arms, wanting to shake the truth loose. He relaxed his grip and gazed straight ahead. A fully loaded semi rocked the car as it roared by them.

"There's more," she said. "My foreman and some of his crew broke into Von Lleuwan's plant. The police contacted me and right after that the two kids you asked about were killed." Her body tightened as if she were expecting him to accost her.

"You've been pretty busy," he said.

"I need your help, not your sarcasm," she said.

She had a point, but he had trained himself to question everything that didn't make sense.

"Why did they break into Von Lleuwan's plant?" he asked.

"They were trying to help."

"You said you didn't know them very well?"

"My foreman put them up to it."

"What did the police say?" Derk asked, but he was thinking about her foreman.

"I already told you."

"About your foreman?"

"Oh, no! Maybe that's where he is," she said. Her jaw looked like a Bartlett pear. Another eighteen-wheeler shook the car as it passed them.

"What are you talking about?"

"He called yesterday and said he had to talk with me, but he never showed up. Maybe he was arrested," she said. She folded her arms around herself.

"Your story has more twists than a carnival pretzel."

"I called his house twice and he wasn't there. I'm worried, Derk." He could distinguish concern from fear, but she displayed each of them.

"Where does he live?" Derk said.

"St. Anne's Hill."

Derk pulled onto the highway. They exited onto Linden Avenue which deposited them onto East Third Street. It was about a mile and a half to John Westfield's home in the St. Anne Hill Historic District. Derk knocked on the front door, but no one answered. Kate waited on the porch as he went to the back of the house. Other than a pickup parked in the driveway next to the house, there were no signs of life. Kate met him halfway down the driveway.

"That his?" he asked, noticing the truck's hood was ajar.

Kate's head bobbed once, and her hair fell into her face.

"Does he have another car?"

"No," she answered.

Derk lifted the hood. Several wires were torn from the distributor cap. As they walked away he noticed a red smear on his hand. He faced her with his outstretched hand turned palm up. "Blood," he said.

Short of examining one's checkbook or erotic zones, there are few things more intimate than spending time in another person's home. Since their college love affair, Kate McCardigan had become a widow, the president of her own company, the mother of a terminally ill child, and a player in a deadly game. As appealing as the prospect was of being close to her again, a cloud of ambivalence hovered as he entered Kate's house.

"I work in a man's world, and I'm pretty good at guarding my emotions, but I'm frightened," she said. "I need to change, but I don't want to be alone." She led him upstairs to her bedroom.

A giant dog lay in one corner on a cushion that had been covered with a couple of oversized towels. It was a Doberman, but he'd never seen a white one. The dog glanced at him, its angry canines exposed, but it seemed more interested in Kate. It started to rise, but lacked either the interest or the energy and collapsed on its makeshift bed, one eye maintaining a leering sentry.

Kate walked over, kneeled and stroked its nape. "It's ok, boy."

The dog whimpered, wagged its tail once, and dropped into a pool of slobber.

"She's not well," Kate said, her expression as forlorn as the dog's. "Nothing is these days."

Derk offered his best expression of empathy and took a seat on the edge of the bed. Kate changed her clothes in the bathroom while he studied the dog's labored breathing. Although this dog probably couldn't break a soap bubble, he knew what to do with sleeping dogs.

When Kate entered the bedroom, her hair was blown but still damp, and she looked as drawn as saltwater taffy. Even so, her pheromones rekindled distant fires, and he was beckoned to what ly beneath her flimsy robe.

"I've been such a wimp," she said, plopping down on the bed next to him.

The only things separating him from euphoria were two plies of sheer rayon and a modicum of self-restraint. He rubbed his hands on his knees and summoned some of that resistance.

"You've endured more than most people can handle," he said.

"I don't know about that." She put her hand on his.

Silence accompanied by wanting glances elevated his tension. He put his arm around her and she leaned into his hungry body.

"Why don't I fix dinner while we wait for the police," she said.

He wasn't hungry, but it was a rational diversion. She took his hand and led him downstairs.

Dinner consisted of broiled chicken with steamed wild rice and fresh spinach with buttered mushrooms. A bottle of chardonnay reduced the tension. They were halfway through dinner when the police dispatcher called and told them that an officer was on the way. When the doorbell rang, they found a young rookie officer by the name of P. J. Dutton waiting on the porch.

Derk introduced himself, explained what he thought had happened to Kate's foreman, and provided a description of the man called Gloves. Kate filled in the details about John Westfield. "Blood on the hood?" the officer said. "Might be an accident. Have you called the hospitals?"

"It's not an accident," Derk said.

"Then we'll have to get someone over to dust for prints."

"Are you paying attention?" Derk said.

"There aren't any prints!"

"How do you know?" The officer became as rigid as his nightstick.

"Why do you think they call him Gloves?"

"Maybe you should come downtown," the officer said.

"I don't want to go downtown. I'm investigating a murder. Why don't you just do your job?"

The officer, who introduced himself by telling them that he was already on his fifth hour of overtime as a result of several auto accidents, responded, "Look, I don't care who you are and this is out of my jurisdiction. I'll turn it over to the daytime dicks. They'll follow up with you."

"Hope we didn't put you out," Derk said as the officer left.

"I don't think he believed us," Kate said after she shut the door.

"They've got bodies on the highway, and we really don't know what happened to your foreman," Derk said. "Maybe I was too rough on the kid, but your foreman's disappearance wasn't a coincidence?" She leaned against him like a cub bear seeking the security of its mother.

He helped her clear the table and load the dishwasher. She rambled, probably to cover her own anxiety, and he let her go on because he enjoyed the sound of her voice. His intuition told him to maintain emotional distance, but he struggled to gain the resolve to sever the frayed threads of distant longings. They *were* miles apart. Her lifestyle was far removed from his condo on the beach and even further from the bed they shared in that old house in Yellow Springs. She ran her finger across her lips and made a "bubble, bubble, bubble" sound.

"It's okay. It's nice to hear your voice," he said.

She caressed his jaundiced chin with the back of her hand. Her touch was beyond medicinal.

"What really happened?" she asked.

"You know that train I mentioned at the airport? He works for Von Lleuwan, and he likes to hurt people. I don't mean to frighten you, but if they think you're involve . . ." He let the thought linger.

"But I don't know anything. Skip is the only one who does." She leaned into him again.

She felt like sexual putty. He surrounded her as he spoke. "What does this Westfield guy know?"

"Nothing."

"But he *is* linked to you, and he *was* in Von Lleuwan's plant. They'll want to know why." He held her away from him. "What does Skip know?"

"Von Lleuwan is working on a new pesticide, something very important. Skip thinks it might be what we're looking for, what caused Trevor's illness."

He knew she hadn't told him everything. Again, she hugged him, but he grasped her hands and let them drop to her sides.

"If Von Lleuwan finds out that Skip is connected to you, he'll end up in one of their mixing tanks." He scanned the room for a telephone. "We've got to let him know."

"He's not in town."

"Where is he?"

She shook her head. "I don't know. I mean he's in Michigan, probably Grand Rapids, but I don't know where they're staying."

"Why didn't you tell me?"

"All I know is he's supposed to meet Von Lleuwan in the morning. They're going to film a test site. I'm sorry," she said.

"Damn!" he said and paced the kitchen floor. "We'll call Shirley."

She handed him a piece of paper from a drawer. He dialed but only got Skip's voice mail.

"Got a phone book?" he said.

She went to the living room and returned with the telephone directory. He thumbed through it and tossed it onto the kitchen table.

"No, yellow pages."

With the devotion of a pet beagle, she fetched that, too. He turned to the airlines, put his finger on an entry, and dialed. On the first call he learned that there were no flights to Grand Rapids that evening. On the third call he made a reservation for a 7:40 A.M. flight. Next he called Sandra French and left a message on her answering machine. Then he called Wally Twill and asked him to find out everything he could about the product Von Lleuwan was trying to get approved, particularly the location of the test sites.

"Where are you now?" Wally asked.

"Kate's house."

"What's going on between you and Sandra?"

"What do you mean?" Derk asked.

"She's not happy, and it sounded personal."

"I think Kate's son was a victim of Von Lleuwan's latest formula. Dig up everything you can on this," Derk said.

"Wally interrupted him, "It's called PESTfree© and they're going to approve it next week."

"I've got to hurry, then. Call French, Sandra," he corrected himself, "and ask her to pick me up tomorrow at the Grand Rapids airport, quarter to nine."

Wally didn't respond.

"One more thing. Check with the Tampa P.D. and the locals and see if you can find out if anybody knows where this guy they call Gloves, Von Lleuwan's bodyguard, is right now. Let Sandra know. She'll understand. I'll talk with you tomorrow."

He stared into the darkness through the kitchen window.

"Well?" Kate said.

"There's nothing more I can do now. I'll go to Grand Rapids in the morning and try to find Skip and the others." He brushed by her.

"Where are you staying?" she asked.

"I didn't make any plans."

"Stay here, Derk," she said in a way that no man would mistake for a simple neighborly gesture. He stopped and turned around. She took his hands into hers. "I want you to stay with me. Not for old time's sake. Not because I'm lonely or frightened, and I am," she said as she put his arms around her. "I just want you to stay."

The scent of her hair and the want in her embrace made the invitation difficult to reject. The press of her sensuous curves and the need in her voice, words he had wanted but never expected to hear, created an emotional welling that was linked to a lifetime of unrequited longing. The woman he had never stopped loving was subsumed in his embrace as if she had become shipwrecked in his own personal harbor. He wanted to kiss her, run his hands through her hair, hold her off the ground, and spin her deliriously while telling her how long he had waited for this moment. He wanted to carry her up stairs for a night of exhausting passion to be repeated at dawn and followed with a quiet breakfast as if they were young lovers experiencing the lust of life together for the first time. But they were not young lovers, and they were separated by years and miles and events. The presence of a new intimacy was on his mind, and his friends were in trouble. The reality of all this diffused his response. He held her close, kissed her hair, and buried her face in his shoulder.

It was pitch dark outside and through the open door of the screened patio adjacent to the kitchen, Derk could hear the staccato of raindrops replacing the sounds of crickets in Kate's backyard. She closed the door to the patio, turned off the kitchen lights, and took the remainder of the wine in one hand and Derk's hand in her other.

38

The stress of running a modern corporation is beyond the endurance of most people. Others thrive on it. How they manage the inevitable problems in the course of everyday business will determine their fates. They read management books and executive biographies and, similar to chemists, welcome the challenge of determining and applying the proper doses of Theory X and Theory Y management styles to achieve the desired formula for financial success. The goal, of course, is to entice enough of the workforce to embrace the company's goals as their own and then manage the distracting problems as they occur. Jack Von Lleuwan was, of course, familiar with Theory X and Theory Y, but he had his own simple theory of management. Problems in business, he proffered, you do not manage. You get rid of them. As if they were grounds of dirt on the workshop floor, you sweep them into a dustpan each day and toss them into the dumpster. Problem solved. The morning after the second meeting with Scott Dinsmore and his guileful band of journalists, the dirt on Von Lleuwan's shop floor had risen to his waist.

"I want you to make it difficult for those guys to get an interview with a farm animal," Art Domingo told Von Lleuwan. Dougal Ketchum's obstreperous attitude had really pissed him off. "Call *Mulch Magazine* and tell them that you'll call every one of their advertisers and inform them of this magazine's callous, biased and unprofessional reporting if they don't can those assholes immediately."

"I'm not happy with them either, but they might be useful," Von Lleuwan said.

An hour later Von Lleuwan's operations manager returned. "Those sons-a-bitches scammed us!" he blurted out. "*Discovery Channel* had never heard of them, and there's no *Mulch Magazine*."

Von Lleuwan had just returned from one of the storage buildings behind the plant where he had concluded interrogating the recent, past foreman of McCardigan Construction Company. The chat with John Westfield had left him distracted. He was trying to recall the accusations that a woman by the name of Kate McCardigan had made a number of years ago after he had tested *PESTfree©* in Ohio. To his complete surprise, she had turned up again and one of her hired hands was tied and gagged in his warehouse. His problems were compounding: Sheldon Walker, Eva Simpson, Sidney O'Connor, and now Kate McCardigan. He couldn't sweep them away fast enough.

"They're what?" Von Lleuwan said.

"Bogus! Dinsmore and his whole crew," Art said.

"You sure?"

"Absolutely," Domingo said very animated.

"Motherfuckers!" Von Lleuwan exploded.

"I made some calls," Domingo added. "No one's ever heard of them. *Mulch Magazine* is bullshit."

Von Lleuwan had a pretty good hunch about what they were doing and who put them up to it, but he didn't say anything to his operations director. The fewer people with whom he shared his thought on the matter, the better.

"I'll take care of it." Von Lleuwan composed himself and reached for his Rolodex. Problems, too many problems. Time to call the cleaning crew. When Art left, he turned to an entry with the number 1-888-Dispose written beside the name, Eddie.

Jack Von Lleuwan thought he had personnel problems, but he was more than a little miffed by those at Midwest Waste Haulers.

"I need you to pick up packages in Grand Rapids and Dayton," Von Lleuwan said. He and Fagan Miranda stood in front of urinals in an I-96 rest stop between Grand Rapids and Lansing.

"It takes four guys for one job. To do 'em on the same day I gotta split 'em up," Miranda responded. He was impeccably dressed but kept plucking at a scab on his nose with his little finger.

"Your only threat is Gloves and he's all doped up from an ear infection," Von Lleuwan said.

"You said there was four or five of 'em." Miranda's Long Island accent was thicker than momma's spaghetti sauce.

"They'll be in vans. Run them into one of your big carriers, band them shut, and blow in some insulation," Von Lleuwan said.

"Fuckin-a, might work!" Miranda seemed astounded by Von Lleuwan's ingenuity. "But I gots another problem. One of my guys is sick. Son'bitch!" he cried out as he caught the end of his pecker in his zipper.

"How the fuck does a hit man call in sick?" Von Lleuwan said. "Goddammit!" Distracted by Miranda's little problem, he soiled the pant leg on his artificial limb.

"My cousin, he gots the clap. Barricaded himself in. Says he'll shoot anyone who opens the fuckin' door," Miranda said.

"You surround yourself with these dumb fucks?"

"Says the penicillin don't work no more. Gots only two choices. Three shots every day right in his cock . . . or absolute rest for thirty days. And he can't go out in the sun. No fucking sun. Makes you go crazy he said," Miranda said. "Nobody goes near him."

Von Lleuwan tucked in his pants, zipped up, and joined Miranda at the sink. Miranda had dropped his drawers to rinse the end of his cock with cold water. He had drawn blood.

"The fuck you lookin' at?" Miranda said.

Von Lleuwan turned his head away. "Tell him he gots *three* choices," mimicking Miranda. "If he doesn't get this job done, you'll dip what's left of his cock in a bucket of that slime you haul away for me."

"Won't do it. Said his uncle dissed the treatments and cut off his own cock, clawed it off with a wire brush," Miranda said.

Von Lleuwan looked to the heavens and raised his hands up in the air. Why am I surrounded by such incompetence?

"We go after him, he'll kill somebody," Miranda said, tucked in his trousers and closed the zipper with the dexterity of a skilled surgeon.

Von Lleuwan sat on the edge of on the sink and fidgeted with his brace. "Give me a hand here."

Miranda reluctantly put an arm behind Von Lleuwan and cradled Von Lleuwan's leg with his other hand, allowing Von Lleuwan to blow-dry his trousers under the hand drier.

"So, what are you going to do?" Von Lleuwan asked.

"Call AccounTemps," Miranda said. "The fuck you think I'm gonna to do?"

39

Kate McCardigan wasn't used to second guessing herself, but this morning she was experiencing a confidence crisis. Her son was dying. Her foreman was missing. Her friends were in danger. And her company was behind on an important contract. The words "if only" kept haunting her. She replayed events in her life in search of a scenario that would have led to a different outcome. The only one that made any sense, the only decision that would have remedied the entire problem, involved Derk Bryan. After dropping him at the airport in Vandalia, she took Frederick's Pike into town to avoid the congestion on the freeway, made a brief stop at the vet's office, and headed toward her headquarters.

The aroma of Derk's aftershave lingered in her car. He was more than the handsome and idealistic young man she had known and with whom she had become so infatuated many years ago. He was still bright and confident, but he had followed his chosen path and had become a successful defender of his dreams. For that she was impressed and thankful. And he was still a "hunk" as her friends might have said. She kept thinking about last night, standing in her kitchen consumed within his comforting arms. She couldn't help but think how her life would have been different if she had married Derk Bryan instead of Scott McCardigan. She wouldn't be alone now. Scott worked himself to death. She also knew she probably wouldn't be living in a big house in Oakwood, driving a luxury car, or going to the country club for dinner. She would not be surrounded with many of the familiar comforts she had nor would she have lived in that big country house by the orchard, and, therefore, Trevor wouldn't have gotten sick. Of course, there wouldn't have been a Trevor. Reality can be a carnivorous flower, and what-if thinking only spurred guilt. When she tried to divert her thoughts from Derk, images of John Westfield and Skip and his friends replaced them. What had she done? She had become so self-absorbed that she had managed to get her best friends into trouble. The doubts were many, the answers were few, and within an hour she was supposed to meet with the facilities manager for the Mr. Spud chain. He was going to ask why she was so far behind schedule on construction of the new Florida store. She was so deeply engaged in introspection as she entered the parking lot of her construction company that she paid little attention to the guy with the red-orange porcupine cut in the military fatigues and Bruce Lee T-shirt and the man in the secondhand, three-piece suit sitting in an unmarked van at the rear of her parking lot.

The parking lot was big enough for twenty to thirty cars, but it was separated into two parts. An island with low-lying shrubs separated the back of the lot from the paved portion, and the van was parked on the gravel at the rear. The gravel drive extended around the side to the back of the building where the extra construction equipment was maintained. The entrance to the building was on the corner of the other side and as result no one could see the lot directly from the lobby. A concrete sidewalk wound its way through a well-landscaped and manicured lawn from the parking lot to the offices. Red, yellow and gold marigolds lined the sidewalk. Arbor vitae separated the lot from the grassy approach to the building. Kate stopped on the paved portion in front of a sign that read: "Reserved for Kate McCardigan."

As she got out of her car, one of the men from the van walked toward the sidewalk that led to the McCardigan offices. He had a scar that stretched from the corner of his mouth to his ear, wore a pinstriped suit, and carried a noticeable limp. The van continued around the median as she acquired her briefcase and slung her purse over her shoulder. Then she opened the rear door to fetch her ailing dog, lethargic from the medication it received at the vet's office. The van stopped behind her car. She prodded the dog and it stumbled. When she turned, the man with the limp was facing her, trying to conceal something in his hand. In her peripheral vision she noticed a multi-colored, punk rock commando approaching from the van. Hope turned, imitated a growl, and flashed its vicious-looking dentures. The younger man came to an abrupt stop, pirouetted on one foot, and whirled a one-eighty. He elevated the other leg perpendicular to his body and in one fluid motion kicked at the dog's head. Hope fell sideways as its right leg buckled, and the blow glanced off it. The man lost his balance, hit the pavement, and rolled on the ground, screaming. The dog collapsed onto Kate. Like a chain reaction from a rear-end collision, she fell onto the man in the pinstriped suit and knocked the gun from his hand. Its discharge was thunderous. Dazed, she lay on the ground with her assailants, before inventorying her body parts for signs of new orifices or spurting blood or pain. The silence was broken only by a rushing hiss.

40

Skip Trace was in the shower when the telephone rang at 7 A.M. Player answered it without getting out of bed.

"Tell Dinsmore the plans have changed. My Security Director, Gloves, I mean Mr. Swingle, will meet you in Middleville. Follow him. We'll meet in Yankee Springs and go from there. Write this down," Jack Von Lleuwan said without identifying himself, but Player knew the voice.

Player scrambled for a piece of hotel stationery onto which he scribbled the directions.

Before Player could double check the route, Von Lleuwan said, "You guys better be on time." Then he hung up.

Skip came from the bathroom wearing a pair of sandals and a white Hilton towel. He was combing his hair.

"What an asshole!" Player said.

"Who?"

"Von Lleuwan. Guy needs to get laid more often."

"What do you mean?"

"Same time, new place," Player said. "We gotta meet some dude in Middleville and follow him to Yankee Springs."

"Get directions?" Skip asked.

"Sort of. He was in a shit mood," Player said and handed his hieroglyphics to Skip.

"What's this?" Skip pointed to Player's scribbling.

"Some place called Middleville."

"I know, but where?"

"Gas station at the four corners. Only light in town, he said."

"Who are we meeting and what's he driving?" Skip asked.

"Relax, man. It's just some security dude," Player said. "He'll know us by our van."

"Shit! Not him. Did he say anything else?" Skip asked.

"He hung up. Must have a cob up his butt this morning," Player retorted. "You look a little on edge yourself."

"This guy we're meeting thinks I'm an insurance salesman," Skip said.

"You are an insurance salesman," Player responded.

"We're in trouble if he recognizes me," Skip said.

"So what do we do?"

"Call him back and make something up," Skip said.

"What if I can't get a hold of him?"

"I don't even want to think about it," Skip said and returned to the bathroom. A minute later he appeared in the doorway frothing at the mouth into which he was pumping a bright red toothbrush. "Call the guys and make sure they're up."

At exactly eight o'clock with all of the members of the Green Team anxiously assembled in one of their hotel rooms, Skip called the asshole.

"Mr. Von Lleuwan's office," Mrs. Huizenga answered.

"I need to speak with Mr. Von Lleuwan."

"Well, good morning, Mr. Dinsmore. How are you?" she asked.

"Is Mr. Von Lleuwan." Skip wondered how such a turdball as Von Lleuwan could have such a cheerful and courteous assistant. "Very well, thank you. Is Mr. Von Lleuwan in?"

"I don't expect him until later. I thought he was meeting you."

"That's the problem. Can you get in touch with him?"

"I don't know. I can try him at home. What seems to be the problem?"

"Can you try to get a hold of him right away and have him call me at the hotel?" Skip asked. "He's got my number."

"I'll try," she said.

"Please call me back if you can't reach him. I'm at the Airport Hilton, room 27. Thanks. Bye. Oh! Call me right away," he urged her again.

"I will," she said.

"What if the dude's gone?" Player asked him.

"We've got to meet with him," Dougal Ketchum said. "It's our chance to nail the bastard."

"If he recognizes me who knows what he'll do," Skip said.

"What's he going to do? There's four of us," Dougal said.

Bear added, "Sit in the backseat. I'll drive. He won't notice you."

"How 'bout a disguise?" Player added.

"Sure. What's Von Lleuwan going to think about that?" Skip replied.

The telephone rang. "Mr. Dinsmore, I'm sorry I couldn't reach him. He already left," she told him.

"Does he have a cell phone?"

"It's not on yet. Can I leave him a message?" she asked.

"No," he said and hung up. "He's gone. Let's get going. I need to stop at a convenience store."

Bear drove. Skip sat in the rear with Player. As they headed west on 44th Street, Skip removed his tie and suit coat. Player reached over and unbuttoned the collar of Skip's shirt. That was about as casual as he could get for the moment.

They went south on State Route 37. In Caledonia, Skip took a chance on a well-stocked convenience store. A few minutes later he emerged wearing a purple baseball cap with yellow letters on the crest that said *Bite Me* and a pair of mirrored sunglasses. In the van Player jabbed Dougal in the shoulder with his forefinger. Dougal turned, looked at Skip, and tried to hold his laughter. That diverted Bear's attention, as well.

"Bite me!" Bear said. "You can't get anymore inconspicuous than that."

"They had three hats in there. One was lime green with red letters that said *Fuck Off* and the other was yellow with brown letters that said *Eat Shit & Die*," Skip said.

"Nice lenses,too," Dougal said. "You look like a washed-out seed salesman on speed."

"Bite me," Skip said.

Skip didn't say anything more until they reached the outskirts of Middleville, a lazy little town between Hastings and Grand Rapids, Skip asked, "Did we pass the Thornapple?"

"The what?" Bear said.

Skip surveyed the landscape on each side of the van. "This place is revered for its sucker fishing," Skip said. "They walk the river in hip boots to spear them."

"Where do you get this stuff?" Dougal said.

It was nearly half past eight. The sun had yet to burn off the morning haze, and the sky had not yet given notice of its intent to rain or shine. They passed the only real restaurant in town, the only supermarket, the used car dealership, a car wash, and a few other businesses before rounding the bend on State Route 37.

"There it is," said Player. "The station on the corner."

"Stay low, Skip. I'll handle this," Bear said.

Bear turned into the gas station that doubled as a convenience store, and parked beside a white van. A burly bald man got out and approached them.

"Nice 'do," Dougal said, noticing the two tufts of hair at the back of big guy's skull.

"Shit! That's him," Skip said and pulled the hat over his brow.

Bear rolled down the window. "Are you from Von Lleuwan Enterprises?" Bear asked.

"You Dinsmore?"

Bear motioned to the rear and said, "Where we headed?"

Gloves leaned in the open window. "You guys journalists?"

"Yes, and you are?" Bear asked.

"Your escort." His speech was slurred and he appeared to be looking through clouded glass. The aroma of kerosene and onions reached the back seat. His face contained the residue of four days' growth, and part of one ear appeared to be attached with fishing line. It looked dead.

"I understood Mr. Von Lleuwan is going to meet us. Do you mind telling us where we're going?" Dougal Ketchum asked.

"I know that guy," Gloves said looking at Skip.

"You might, dude," Player said. "Read *Mulch Magazine*?"

The man drifted back, hitting his head on the doorframe.

Bear glanced at his watch. "I don't mean to be rude, Mr. . . . ." Gloves didn't answer. "Mr. Von Lleuwan wanted to meet us at nine."

"What's his problem?" Gloves pointed to the man wearing the ball cap and the mirrored glasses.

Skip put his hand to his throat and in a deep, distorted voice said, "Laryngitis."

"Follow me," Gloves said and lumbered back to his van.

They continued on State Route 37 toward Hastings. Outside of Middleville where the highway made a sweeping curve to the east, the van went straight onto Yankee Springs Road. The *Green Team* followed about a block behind it. The landscape was rural as they approached the Yankee Springs Recreational Area.

Dougal filled his lungs with the piney aroma of the conifer littered landscape. "We're not in Ohio anymore," he said.

"Yankee Springs, my lads. Al Capone had a place on a lake out here," Skip said.

"Damn! Dirt roads," Player said.

There were homes tucked in groves of giant oak and hard maple but they were few and far between.

"Imagine this area fifty years ago when the roads were rutted paths and the game was so thick you could trip over it. The curse of civilization," Dougal lamented.

After a few miles, the van they were following turned west onto Chief Noonday Road. The scenery was unchanging, but in places the trees overhanging the road formed tunnels and the light from the overcast skies sprinkled through the canopy forming shadowy raindrops on their hood. It seemed more like evening than morning. A few more miles down the road the distance between the two vans increased. Their van weaved like waves of grain on the prairie.

"What's wrong, Bear?" Skip said.

"I don't know," Bear answered and held the wheel tighter.

They were now almost a quarter of a mile behind Gloves.

"Don't let him get too far ahead," Dougal urged.

Bear pushed the accelerator. The weaving worsened, then pulled the van hard to one side. He had to slow down. In the distance Skip saw something flash.

"He's turning," exclaimed Player.

"I think we've got a flat," Bear said as he pulled to the side of the dirt road. He and Dougal jumped from the van.

"Nothing here," Bear called to the others.

"Over here," said Dougal Ketchum. Everyone joined him next to the right rear tire.

"That thing's flabbier than your ass," Player said to Dougal.

"Just what we need," Skip said. Throwing up his hand in disgust, he knocked the mirrored sunglasses half way up his forehead. He looked up the road for a sign of the other van.

"Think he saw us?" Player asked.

"Probably not, the dimwit!" Dougal said.

"A foul one, too," Bear added. "You smell that guy? If he'd gotten any closer I'd have to burn my clothes."

"What's the deal with his ear?" Dougal said, looking at Skip.

"Damned thing fell in my lap," Skip said. "Looked like he sewed it on."

"He's a walking sideshow, that dude," Player said.

"There damn well better be a spare," Skip said as he straightened his sunglasses. From the rear he heard the clank of tire changing tools as a raindrop splattered on his nose. "Jesus! What next?"

Gloves noticed the van behind him slow down, but the Percodan he'd been popping to numb the pain in his ear had effected his reaction time. He assumed they would stay on his tail, insistent upon making their appointment with his boss, and he was distracted by the groans of the man on the floor behind him who was returning to consciousness.

He turned onto a dirt road, the path designated by two well-worn ruts in the soil. The van swerved up a sandy incline through trees that bordered each side of the lane for a distance of three or four city blocks. At the ridge, the road opened into a meadow filled with alfalfa and milkweed. A large truck idled with a ramp leaned against its bed. The rear doors were open and waiting. It was just as Von Lleuwan said it would be. His job was nearly done. Rounding up John Westfield had significantly increased his stock with Von Lleuwan.

In less time than it took to introduce a tag team, this whole mess would be behind him. There would be no one else to chase. No more witnesses. No more trouble. He wouldn't be able to return to Florida, but neither its weather nor its women appealed to him.

The plan, according to Von Lleuwan, was simple. He would put John Westfield in the van and escort the bogus writers to a secluded spot in Yankee Springs. There, *The Disposal Team,* as Von Lleuwan had referred to the guys in the truck ahead of him, would take care of the rest. He would mosey on back to town in Von Lleuwan's good graces and pack his bags for the trip to Cancun with his wife that Von Lleuwan had promised him.

It felt good to be on the winning team. He hadn't felt this good since he had been allowed to beat The Prowler in a tag team match in Cincinnati five years ago. Gloves was used to playing the big, dumb, ugly, unscrupulous guy, a stepping-stone for those with sculpted abs and movie star faces. He understood his role, but he craved the applause.

The idea of an extended paid vacation in a warm, tropical place with great room service was a just reward, but he knew Von Lleuwan didn't respect him and it still bothered him that his wife had been responsible for getting him the job. He might not have been the brightest person on the planet, but he had a college degree. He'd even been a teacher, a coach, actually. That is until Melissa's uncle got jealous that he'd banged his niece. Her uncle was probably the only man in town who hadn't yodeled in the canyon of her delight. Regardless of what happened here, maybe it was time to find another job, this time on his own. If he could avoid putting Von Lleuwan in another headlock, he would, no doubt, be a terrific reference. He would wait a couple of months for things to cool off, and then he would begin his search. Indeed, he was near his destination and he was feeling pretty good about himself as he approached the open doors of the large truck parked ahead of him.

As he stopped the rain formed little splotches on his windshield. He waited for the two men in white coveralls to approach. He lowered the window and a soft breeze from the west moistened his face. He wiped the wetness from his cheek with the back of his hand. Little bubbles rolled across the latex surface. In the distance, he heard the sound of something that resembled a compressor. He could only see into the back of the truck, and it was empty except for some banding equipment.

The two men in coveralls looked as if they had been stamped from the same slab of cold, rolled steel. Each was stocky, a smidgeon under six-feet tall, had black hair, an olive complexion and bore an expressionless face. If he had never been beaten in an actual match by his opponent, Gloves imagined himself stronger, quicker, and more cunning. Like a conditioned animal, he viewed everyone as prey and he looked for a weakness or an advantage. He learned to do this from Larry the Louse, the best wrestler he had ever known. As these drones approached he felt uneasy, but not because he thought they might be physically superior to him. They said nothing to each other and displayed no emotion. One stopped in front of the van while the other came to the open window.

"You Gloves?"

Gloves tilted his head to one side as an acknowledgment.

"Your hands," the man said.

"What's that?"

"Let's see your hands."

He resented it, but he held up his hands.

"Roll up the windows. You'll have to get out through the back."

Gloves rolled up the window. The man's aloofness only augmented his concern, but he would follow their instructions and get the hell out of there.

The man in front of the van jumped into the back of the truck and directed Gloves' approach to the ramp. Then he picked up one of the banding machines and moved all the way to front of the box. Gloves spun the wheels in the soft, wet sand, eased off the accelerator, and lurched onto the ramp. He gave it some more gas, and the van leaped into the back of the truck. The man in the coveralls motioned him toward the front and with a final, succinct drop of his hands, like a symphony conductor, directed him to kill the engine.

Gloves took one final look at John Westfield who was lying on the floor, gagged, his hands and feet tied together. As he lifted himself out of his seat to make a rear exit, he heard a clunk against the side of the van and then a cranking noise. Through the front and side windows he saw nothing. The same noise came from the other side. He put his hands on the roof to steady himself as he climbed across his captive. Westfield looked at him and struggled within the duct tape that bound him. He tried to roll into Gloves' path, but Gloves nudged him out of the way. Gloves heard something sprayed onto the windows and looked back. The only light was now diffused through something that appeared to be a kind of rubbery glue that was rapidly covering to the windows. His unease turned to panic. The van was becoming a steel cocoon. He reached for the handle of the rear door and pushed. Only a crack appeared. He pushed with his shoulder. Nothing. Again he pushed as hard as a lineman pushing against a blocking sled. The door did not give.

"The fuck's going on?" he yelled. "Let me out of here!" He slammed against the back door.

He heard the clank of the truck's doors shutting and lost his balance in the total darkness. He could neither hear nor see anything except for the groans beneath him. He backed into Westfield's legs as he retreated to the front of the van. In some strange way, the knowledge that he was not alone became a temporary source of comfort, but he kicked him anyway. He lost his balance, stumbled forward, and crawled to the front seat. He pushed against the door. No luck. They had banded the doors shut. He tried to roll down the window. It wouldn't budge. He was trapped inside a tomb on wheels, and he couldn't see a goddamn thing. He expected the truck to start moving, but nothing happened. He couldn't understand what they were doing or why? He shouted again and again until his voice became hoarse, and he banged on the doors and the side of the van. No response. Exhaustion stopped him. John Westfield was squirming on the floor behind in him. If he remained cool they would eventually have to open the van, and that might be his only chance.

Then a deafening grind and a flash of light came from overhead. The high-pitched vibration of metal being sawed in the dark, enclosed cabin caused him to recoil like a salt covered slug. He ducked down for fear of being lacerated. A circular saw completed its cut through the roof behind him, and he heard the blade being retracted. Through the hole the light, which poured in like a spotlight, illuminated John Westfield's curled, fetal frame. Seconds later the light dimmed as a tube was inserted into the hole and the sound of the compressor he had heard earlier returned. Suddenly the air was filled with soft, dense, sticky globs. They hit his arm and his face, and when he tried to cover one part of his face, they hit another. The blobs hit against the insides of the van, against the backs of the seats, the windows and the floor, and soon his body was covered with a layer of the tacky stuff.

He pushed the door again, harder this time! Nothing. He pounded the side window with his fists, harder and harder, until his hands ached. The glass gave only slightly. The gluey substance sprayed on the outside kept it from breaking. He needed something heavier and sharper. He reached around the seat for something metal, anything that could break glass. A glob of insulation hit him in the mouth. He gagged and spit it out. He wiped his tongue with his hand, but his hand was covered with insulation. He coughed and spat, coughed and spat. He tried to duck behind the seat to avoid direct hits but to no avail. He ran his hand on the floor around the seat. It was thick with blown insulation. There must have been, at least, a foot of it. He snagged Westfield's pantleg. There was no reaction. And fear rocked him like a forearm to the chin. He reached under his seat. Nothing! He leaned across the seat to the other side and reached under the passenger's seat. His fingers hit something and pushed it away. He leaned farther until his face was buried in the cellulose fibers. The dust was so thick now he could barely breathe. He knew it was there, something solid. He had felt it with his fingers. He held his breath, leaned over and scoured the floor again with his fingers. There it was, a long round iron object, probably a tire iron. He found the sharpest end and jammed it against the window until his strength abated. Finally, a whole opened in the glass. The blower continued and with each breath his lungs filled with the cellulose dust. He couldn't last much longer. He jammed the pointed end of the tire iron through the hole and pried. The hole became larger and larger. He slammed the glass with the palm of hand. "More, more!" he said to himself as he felt the glass give way. He lay across the driver's seat, placed his foot against the window, and kicked as hard as he could. After four or five thrusts it gave way. He booted the corners of the window to make the hole large enough to wiggle through. Then, he crawled head first across the seat and forced his abundant girth through the splintered glass.

He cried out as the jagged edges of the glass sliced his waste. He dropped through the window like a fat pig, gasping for air. There was a light above the van coming from a hole in the roof, but he stayed on the floor where the air was cleaner. He rolled under the van to minimize the sediment. There he waited just inches below the suffocated body of John Westfield.

The sound of the compressor forcing the asphyxiating material into the van nearly drowned out the rhythm of the steady rain hitting the truck. Gloves continued to choke on the insulation dust and hoped he could hold back his coughing when the two goons came to open the rear doors.

It seemed longer, but it wasn't more than ten minutes when the compressor stopped. The sudden silence startled him. He listened for movement or the sounds of their voices. His hearing was numbed from the whir and whine of the blower. Then he heard the sound of the latch being lifted from its housing. He rolled from under the van, crawled to the rear of the truck, and leaned against the doors to right himself. The door swung open. He caught his balance and adjusted to the diffused light through the overcast skies just enough to see the image in front of him. The man in the white coveralls tried to slam the door shut, but he was too late. Gloves lowered his shoulders and, with the force of a charging rhino, blasted the door into his captor. As the man in white rolled backward, Gloves leaped from the tail of the truck into full view of the second man in white who was now standing about six feet directly in front of him.

Other than their tools and the element of surprise, these assassins had brought no other obvious weapons with them. At the sight of Gloves' balding, fiber-Mated, bloody body gasping for air, the second man reeled back. As the first one up-righted himself, Gloves thrust a forearm under his chin, driving his mandible upward with such force that the blow severed his tongue and rendered him unconscious. Red gushed from his face.

The second man rushed Gloves, and as Gloves turned, he rammed him with a shoulder block. The force sent them rolling backward onto the wet sand. Gloves flipped the man over his head as they went down. He jumped to his feet and turned around. As the man in white righted himself, Gloves leaped toward him. Gloves' sharp palm to his chin stunned him. Then Gloves applied a headlock, and with one powerful torsion move to the neck, silenced him. Match over!

He felt a jackhammer on his chest, barely able breath. His eyes stung, and his wounds screamed. The bloody perspiration and the rain matted the insulation and sand to his body. He looked freshly butchered, rolled in batter and ready for deep-frying. He was spent, but he reached into his pocket and popped another Percodan. He had one more match!

Skip and his friends had to remove most of the equipment and baggage from the van to pry the spare tire from its grotto in the floor. The steady rain soaked them to the bone while they made the repairs.

Skip said, "I've known you guys for a long time, but I didn't know you knew so many four-letter words."

They piled into the van and threw cinders for a quarter of a mile as Bear tried to make up for lost time. He decelerated to make the turn that Gloves had made less than a half hour earlier as a huge truck came barreling onto the road. Bear swerved to the left but not in time. The impact drove the van across the highway but didn't overturn it. Skip's head ricocheted off the side window, but the seatbelt kept him in tact. Stalled in the middle of nowhere in a van that had been instantly cross- ventilated, his friends seemed to have suffered similar fates, but no one admitted to any serious injury.

Massaging his neck, Dougal said, "Another three months at the chiropractor! Who the fuck was that?"

The driver resembled an enraged pit bull, but Skip, who had taken a front seat after the repairs, recognized the bald head. "Damn security guard," Skip said. "Will it start?"

Bear didn't respond.

"Don't let him get away," Skip said, coaxing Bear, a hand on his shoulder.

Bear cranked the engine and accelerated slowly. "Hear that?" Player said. Everyone craned toward the right side of the vehicle.

"Something's rubbing," Dougal said.

They jumped out of the van. The right front quarter panel was a crinkled tin can pressed against the tire.

"Did any of you dudes notice he went up there in one ride and came back in another?" Player said.

Bear and Dougal used the tire irons to pry the fender from the tire while Skip and Player walked up the hill from where the truck had come. Just over the ridge, two men in white jumpsuits lay lifeless on the damp sand.

41

Derk waited at the Kent County International Airport baggage return until his arms ached. He headed for a rental car. It was half past nine in the morning and a light rain was falling. Outside the terminal Sandra French was waiting at the curb.

"What are you doing out here? I've been waiting for you," Derk said.

"If you ever do that again, I'll . . . you lied to me," she said.

"I didn't mean to."

"Yes, you did!" she said.

"Wait a minute. I'd planned to go together, but after I talked with Kate I didn't think she'd open up if you were there."

"This is a criminal investigation."

"I'm dealing with a lot of history here. I wasn't trying to deceive you if that's what you think," he said.

"Is that an apology?"

"I had to move on this and I had to do it alone." The rain dripped down Derk's forehead as an officer pulled up next to their car and motioned them to move on.

Derk threw his bags in the back and jumped in. "Kate told me a lot. I think I know what's going on, and some friends of mine are in trouble. Can we get going?"

As she pulled away from the terminal the sprinkle turned into a steady drizzle.

"It's not a woman's life-long burden to placate men for their character imperfections," she said. She chomped her bit and ground her teeth.

Great sex could create a powerful bond, but it couldn't overcome deceit and mistrust regardless of the circumstances under which those things occurred. "In spite of how it seems, I'm a man of considerable principle," he said. "I want you to believe that."

"Same old Derk Bryan if you ask me," she said.

"Insensitive rogue or successful loner?" he said.

"I hope there's some middle ground," she said.

He placed an affectionate hand on her arm and changed the subject. "Do you know who made those phone calls to Kate?"

She withdrew her arm. "No."

"Can we get going?" he said and waved his hand in front of him.

"You expect a lot, Derk Bryan," she said and increased her speed. Now the steady drizzle had become a downpour. The rain hit the window like ping-pong balls being shot in rapid succession, and the skies had turned drum gray.

"Take the same route we did the last time," he said.

"I know the way," she snapped.

Such virulence after of a night of splendor meant only one thing. He had messed up. Standing in kitchen in the dark with Kate McCardigan, a bright, beautiful, and successful but lonely and somewhat desperate woman, had convinced him that at this time in his life, and maybe even when he was younger, he and Sandra French had more in common than he and Kate ever did.

He put his hand on her arm again. "I'm sorry. I didn't know a better way to do it."

He couldn't tell if it was the sincerity in his voice or the worried expression on his face, but she placed her hand on his without diverting her attention from the road.

"You just used up your points. You're back to zero," she said.

It was almost ten when they arrived at Von Lleuwan's Zeeland plant. The sky was the color of burnt cinders and the rain had not subsided. Given the number of law enforcement departments in search of the big, burly security guard, Derk hadn't expected him to greet them at the front gate nor had he expected it to be wide open. They parked next to vintage a Cadillac in cherry condition. The receptionist greeted them outside Von Lleuwan's second floor office.

"Sorry, but he's not in," she said.

"When do you expect him?" Sandra asked.

"He's scheduled to meet some people out of the office this morning."

"Skip Trace?" Derk interjected. The name didn't seem to mean anything to her. "Skip Trace. He was going to meet Skip Trace and some other men."

Mrs. Huizenga looked at Sandra who appeared equally dumbfounded.

"He was meeting with a Scott Dinsmore and some journalists," she said.

"Tall man, dark hair and a goatee? Short guy with a beard?" Derk asked.

"His name is Dinsmore," the receptionist said with the certainty of a tenured librarian.

"Where?"

"I don't know, but Mr. Dinsmore called this morning saying he wasn't sure he could make it. I have his number at the hotel," she said and pointed at her message pad.

"Use your phone?" Derk asked and reached for the receiver before she could say, "Sure."

The hotel desk clerk told him they had checked out about eight.

"Damn it! Excuse me," he said. "Can you get hold of Mr. Von Lleuwan?"

"I can try," she answered.

"It's an emergency."

Moments later she had him on the line. "Mr. Von Lleuwan, there's some people here from the EPA that say they have to talk with you right away," she said in a single breath. Her professionalism was unwavering.

Derk whispered, "Tell him to get back here now."

"He asked me to make an appointment for you," she held her hand over the phone and told Derk. "Yes, Mr. Dinsmore called this morning and said he wasn't sure he could meet you. I tried to reach you," she said to Von Lleuwan.

"They what?" Von Lleuwan shouted loudly enough for everyone near the desk to hear.

Derk reached across the desk and grabbed the telephone. "Mr. Von Lleuwan, this is Derk Bryan with the EPA. How soon can you get back here?"

"I'm waiting for someone," Von Lleuwan answered. "Can you make an appointment?"

"Jack, there's a warrant out for that circus character you call a security guard, and if I have to leave without seeing you, there'll be one for you, too."

"What to hell are you talking about?" Von Lleuwan shouted.

"I'm talking about some journalists and something called PESTfree©," Derk said.

"I guess I could break away if these guys don't show up."

"Sounds too much like maybe." Derk looked at the clock on the wall in the lobby. "It's ten-fifteen, Jack. I'm leaving in thirty minutes," Derk said and gave the telephone back to the secretary.

She looked at Derk. "He hung up."

"He's probably in a hurry," Derk said and winked at Sandra.

While they waited, Sandra went to the restroom and Derk called his mother.

"I'm in Zeeland."

"When will you be here?" she asked.

"Are you okay?"

"Yes dear, when are you coming?"

"As soon as I take care of things here I'll be over. Has anything changed?"

"Do you want to meet me at the hospital?"

"I really want to see you first, Mom," he said and looked around to be sure that no one else could hear him. "Mom, was there something that happened when I was a kid involving Dad and I had a hard time getting over it?"

"We'll talk about it when you get here."

"How old was I when dad and I ---?" He didn't complete the question.

"When your dad and you what?"

"I've been thinking about things."

"We'll talk when you get here."

Before he hung up a tall, trim, middle-aged black man named P. Oliver, according to the name tag on his Michigan State Police uniform, stood in front of Jack Von Lleuwan's secretary.

"I've got to go, Mom. See you soon," Derk said.

In a pleasant but resolute tone, the kind you would never mistake for indeterminate, the officer asked to speak with the owner of the Cadillac in the parking lot.

Mrs. Huizenga looked at Derk. "Not mine, officer," Derk said.

The officer displayed a quiet intensity. He glanced at Sandra.

"She's with me," Derk said.

"Probably Mr. Von Lleuwan," Mrs. Huizenga answered. "He has several Cadillacs."

"Is he here?"

"No. Can I help you?"

"Do you know where he is or how I can reach him?" he asked.

"I think he's on his way." She looked for confirmation from Derk and Sandra. "These people are waiting, too."

"And you would be?" He held a rain-spotted trooper's hat in his hands. He was six-foot six with the leanness of a long-distance runner and the upper body of a cleanup hitter. His hair had grayed over the ears, and if he smiled he would probably appear charming. He obviously wasn't here to solicit for the Police Athletic League.

Sandra held out her credentials. "I'm Agent French with the Michigan EPA and this is my colleague, Mr. Bryan. May I ask why you want to see Von Lleuwan?"

"Pop Oliver, nice to meet you. Are you expecting him soon?"

"We just talked with him officer, well, at least, Derk did, and we're expecting him in about?" Sandra said, looking at Derk.

"Half hour," Derk said, stroking his chin. A toggle switch in his memory turned on. "Poppy, Poppy Oliver!"

"Do I know you?"

"Benton Harbor, forty-six points in the semis. You got thrown out protesting a call," Derk exclaimed. "You were screwed." He held his palm out for Poppy as if he were shaking the hand of an NBA star.

"You were there?" he said. Derk nodded. The officer's hand swallowed Derk's palm.

With the status of a coronation, Derk announced, "Sandra, this guy had the smoothest fade away you've ever seen. Six-six and played guard."

"You'd have scored sixty a game if they'd put you inside," he said to Poppy.

With the closest thing to a smile since he entered the officer said, "I hadn't thought about it for a long time." Then he said, "So what's going on here?"

Derk motioned for the officer to walk down the hall with him. "Did you know a guy was found dead here a week ago?" Derk said.

"Read about it. So what?" the officer responded.

"A burglary gone awry," Derk said. "Turns out there was a spill out back so we were called in. Small matter but this guy, Von Lleuwan, is a piranha. His bodyguard is on a rampage, and some people I know are in danger. We'd like to have a little talk with him. What's up with you? Von Lleuwan got some unpaid parking tickets?"

Derk had never seen a two hundred fifty-pound scowl with a gun. "Anything you can tell us?"

"Let's wait and see," Officer Oliver said and walked back to the secretary.

"Do you have a key to the Cadillac?" the officer asked the receptionist.

"He keeps it with him," she said.

The officer looked at his watch and took a seat in the waiting area. Derk and Sandra joined him.

"You look good. Still play?" Derk said.

Officer Oliver shook his head but said nothing. So much for small-talk. Sandra read a magazine while they waited.

When Von Lleuwan arrived he went into his office without saying a word, his sneer chiseled by the site of Derk accompanied by a large black man in a police uniform.

"Is that him?" Officer Oliver asked.

"Yup," Derk said.

"Please tell him that I want to see him," the officer said to the receptionist as he headed toward the office. Derk and Sandra followed him.

Without knocking, they entered Von Lleuwan's office. Derk heard the secretary's voice on the intercom trail the smack of a driver against a golf ball.

"Are you Jack Von Lleuwan?" the officer asked.

"Why do you want to know?"

"It that your Cadillac outside?"

"Both of them, but I haven't had a ticket in a long time." Von Lleuwan fumbled an attempt to place another ball on the tee. Trepidation covered him like graffiti.

"Do you have the keys to them?" the officer asked.

"What's this got to do with the EPA?" Von Lleuwan said.

"Someone was seen putting a body in the back of a car in your parking lot," Officer Oliver said.

"Son-of-a-bitch!" Derk whispered aloud and rushed from the room with the image of his dead friend lying in the back seat of Von Lleuwan's car.

"Who said that?" he heard Von Lleuwan retort. Sandra was behind him.

In the parking lot, the rain shined dollar-sized pancakes through the floodlights onto the hood of a late model Cadillac.

"There's nothing in there," Derk shouted. He stood next to one of Von Lleuwan's cars. The officer had just exited the building, but it was raining so hard he didn't seem to hear Derk.

Officer Oliver directed Von Lleuwan to open the door. The officer glanced inside, saw nothing, then motioned to the trunk. Von Lleuwan opened the trunk. The officer shook his head.

"I told you," Von Lleuwan said.

"Over here," Derk shouted. He and Sandra had already sloshed their way to the antique Cadillac he saw when they entered the lot. They stood on opposite sides of it, and the officer's cruiser was parked behind it. Derk yelled, "It's locked." The water streaked his face. Sandra's hair had become a mop.

"Open it," Officer Oliver said after Von Lleuwan hobbled over to the car.

Derk looked in, backed away, and shook his head. "Nothing here," he shouted above the gale like gusts.

"The trunk!" the officer said, pointing to the back of the car.

Derk slid between the bumpers of the two automobiles. He tried to shield Sandra from the force of the storm. Von Lleuwan sidled into the narrow place between his Cadillac and the police cruiser. Poppy Oliver stood opposite the EPA agents on the other side of the car. As Von Lleuwan fumbled for the trunk key, he mopped the moisture from his unencumbered eye. Thunder cracked above them as a large truck entered the front gate.

Von Lleuwan fell forward as the key slid through the hole where the lock used to be. He looked as if he had just lost his fortune on a draw to an inside straight, and he stood like a scarecrow under a waterfall unable to lift the trunk door. Sandra was repelled when she leaned forward for a closer view. Her reaction confirmed what Derk had suspected from the terrible odor that hung in the air. The anonymous caller must have been correct. Derk held his ground, pulled in opposing directions by anticipation and revulsion.

"Open it!" the officer said. His deep, commanding voice and the steady downpour competed with the sound of the diesel accelerating toward them. Skittish anticipation kept everyone's attention riveted to the trunk.

As Von Lleuwan lifted the trunk door, the stench from a bulky lump rolled in dingy, white freezer paper overpowered him. He lost his balance and fell backward against the police cruiser.

"Look out!" Derk yelled and reached for Sandra. They stumbled and fell backward. He crawled and dragged her on the wet pavement away from the flying debris and the harrowing sound of three tons of metal colliding with flesh and bone. He heard a yelp. When he turned around, Von Lleuwan was collapsed on top of the decaying corpse in the trunk of his antique car.

The blare of the truck's horn rose above the sound of the water pouring off the roof onto the parking lot. Under one of the spotlights at the corner of the building, Derk cradled Sandra's shivering, drenched body, while the headlights from the truck dimly illuminated a stream of blood on the pavement that was slowly draining the life from Jack Von Lleuwan's enterprises.

The receptionist, who had been watching through a window in the lobby door, rushed out screaming.

Officer Oliver climbed into and reversed the truck enough to free Von Lleuwan. Then Derk helped him carry Von Lleuwan into the lobby.

"Do you have a blanket?" Sandra asked Mrs. Huizenga who alternated between her attempts to comfort her boss and her revulsion from the blood clotting the lobby floor.

"Do something, do something. He's dying," she said.

"You have a blanket upstairs?" Sandra said and led the receptionist away.

"Call an ambulance," the officer directed Sandra.

"Loosen his belt," Derk said to Poppy as he removed his own belt.

"Recognize the guy in the trunk?" the officer asked.

Derk had only glanced at the body, but given its advanced state of decomposition he assumed enough time hadn't passed for it to be any of his friends. "No."

Derk wrapped belts around Von Lleuwan's lower limbs and tried to prod him to consciousness. Derk's knees were saturated with Von Lleuwan's life fluids.

"Von Lleuwan, stay with me," Derk said. "An ambulance is on the way."

Von Lleuwan moaned.

"I'm going to check the driver," the officer said.

"Who's the guy in the trunk?" Derk said after the officer left.

Von Lleuwan mumbled incoherently.

"Where's Skip Trace?" Derk said, but Von Lleuwan rolled his head from side to side. "I mean Scott Dinsmore. Where is he?" When Von Lleuwan opened his good eye Derk knew that he recognized the name. Von Lleuwan muttered something and collapsed.

Derk stood and through the lobby window he watched Officer Oliver climb down from the truck Gloves had been driving. The officer shook his head at Derk, an indication Derk interpreted to mean that the ex-wrestler's days as a security guard had come to an end.

Sandra returned to the lobby. "This is the best I could do." She had what looked like a green curtain in one hand. She kneeled down and placed it over Von Lleuwan.

"He knows where they are but he's not talking," Derk said, looking down at the executive.

Von Lleuwan groaned and writhed. It was clear that he'd lost more than most people do in a lifetime and he was suffering intense pain again, but Derk felt no pity.

"Where is he?" Derk shouted as he bent down and grabbed his arms.

"Derk, look!" Sandra said.

The officer stood at the rear of the truck and waved for him to join him. Derk rushed again into the pouring rain. The doors to the truck and the van within it were open. Something like confetti, although more industrial in nature, grayish-white and fluffy, fell from the van and turned to flurries as it was caught by a wet, swirling wind. Derk raised his hands to shield his eyes, but it was the sight of a lifeless hand on the floor that startled him. He reached in and brushed the face clear of debris.

"Know him?" the officer asked.

John Westfield's tongue, stiff as a Popsicle stick, protruded from his mouth, which was filled with the grayish-white stuff that had taken away his breath.

"I can guess," Derk said.

The officer stood next to the van shielding himself from the rain as he waited for Derk to expound.

"John Westfield, Kate McCardigan's foreman."

The names may have aroused the officer's curiosity but more likely just added to the volume of his day's paperwork. The 250-pound scowl returned. "If I wade through there," he said as he pointed into the insulation filled van, "am I going to find any more surprises?"

"Hope not," Derk said. The back of his neck felt like a wire brush as the cold, harsh uncertainty of that prospect settled over him. A sobering fear arose, similar to the time he had the premonition that his cousin had died. He hoped that Skip and the others had contacted Kate. He ran through the lobby, where Sandra was elevating Von Lleuwan's knees and Mrs. Huizenga was holding his head, to make a call.

"Is she there?" he asked the woman who answered his call to McCardigan Construction.

"I haven't seen her today. Who's calling?"

"Derk Bryan, EPA. She may be in trouble."

"Her car wasn't in the parking lot, and there's a white van with Michigan plates out there. It's not ours."

He scribbled the number on a pad he kept in his pocket. He called Kate's home and her cell-phone. No response. Then he returned to the lobby.

"Look out!" he ordered Mrs. Huizenga. She had put a suit coat under Von Lleuwan's neck.

"What is it?" Sandra said.

Derk straddled Von Lleuwan. "Where is Kate McCardigan?"

Von Lleuwan turned his head away.

"Where is she?"

Sandra tried to pull Derk back.

Derk grabbed Von Lleuwan's head and turned it toward him. Officer Oliver entered the lobby as Derk shook the fading executive. The officer reached down, grabbed Derk and separated him from Von Lleuwan. Derk spun around and shouted at Poppy Oliver, "He knows. He knows where they are."

He lurched at Von Lleuwan. Officer Oliver restrained him by one arm with a vice like grip.

"Slow down, fellow," the officer ordered him.

Derk led Officer Oliver to a window with a view of the parking lot.

"This is one of the bad guys," he said and pointed to Von Lleuwan. "He's so bad one of his own people tried to kill him." He turned the officer to the carnage in the parking lot. "He kills little kids. Everywhere he goes people turn up dead. He knows where Kate is. He's got her. You understand? He's got her. She's not at home, she's not in her office, and she doesn't answer her phone. He knows where she is, and I need to find out now!"

"What are you going to do, kill the guy?" the officer said.

"Give me a minute. Go inside and make call, go to the bathroom, smoke a cigarette. I don't know. Write some reports," Derk said. "Take them with you," he added, motioning to Sandra and Von Lleuwan's secretary.

"No, you can't," Mrs. Huizenga protested. Poppy took her by the arm and started toward his cruiser.

Derk handed Sandra a small piece of paper and said, "Have him run that plate. Will you?"

The rain immediately began to blur the number written on it.

Before the officer could position the women in the patrol car, retrieve his clipboard filled with police forms, and return to the building, Derk had loosened the tourniquet on Von Lleuwan's right leg. Von Lleuwan had lost so much blood he was oscillating between a blurry consciousness and the dimness that precedes the afterlife.

Derk leaned close to Von Lleuwan. Beads of rain spilled onto Von Lleuwan's face. As the drops trickled across his mouth he gurgled, shifted his head and gasped. Derk cupped his head in his hands.

"You hear me?" Derk said.

Von Lleuwan moved slightly.

"You've been hit by a truck. Understand?" Derk said. "By your own man. You must have really pissed him off. An ambulance is on the way but if I remove this tourniquet, you won't last sixty seconds." Derk began to loosen the tourniquet on the other thigh.

Von Lleuwan's sighted eye opened like a tollgate.

"Where is she? Where's Kate McCardigan?"

Derk feigned loosening the tourniquet some more. Von Lleuwan's attempt to roll was futile.

"Where is she? Where's Scott Dinsmore?"

"Eddie," Von Lleuwan whispered. Derk leaned closer. "He'll call." The breath seeped from him and he collapsed.

Derk tightened the tourniquets. Something beeped, but his attention was diverted by the flashing lights and the siren of the ambulance as the rescue squad entered the Von Lleuwan Enterprises' parking lot. Poppy Oliver waved the driver to pull up to the lobby. Sandra and Von Lleuwan's secretary burst from the cruiser. They met Derk as he exited the building.

"Is he alive?" Mrs. Huizenga asked.

"Get anything?" the officer asked.

Derk tossed his hands up, but said nothing.

Derk and Officer Oliver helped the paramedics place Von Lleuwan and the ex-wrestler in the back of the ambulance. As they closed the door Derk heard the beep again. He climbed into the ambulance and followed the sound to the blood soaked remains of Von Lleuwan's trousers that the medics had to cut off to get at his injuries. Inside the left front pocket he found a pager displaying a ten-digit number. Having lived in Michigan for a long time he recognized the area code. Officer Oliver and Sandra French waited, water drizzling down their cheeks, as he jumped from the ambulance.

"Run that plate?" Derk asked the officer.

As Officer Oliver handed him a crumpled piece of paper onto which was scribbled an address and a telephone number, the parking lot filled with the flashing lights of two more patrol cars.

42

Officer Oliver removed his service revolver, loaded a fresh clip, and re-holstered it. The gun elevated the gravity of the situation to the weight of molten iron. Derk took a deep breath, emptied his lungs, and turned in his seat to face Sandra.

"You ready?" Derk said.

Sandra acquiesced with a frown. Her reservations were understandable.

"It's your call," the officer said.

"Let's do it," Derk said. They stepped from the State Police cruiser and headed for the entrance of Midwest Waste Haulers.

It was Derk's experience that a path always led from the crime to the perpetrators. He didn't always recognize the clues at first glance because they were sometimes blurred, sometimes obstructed, and sometimes obliterated. Occasionally they fell into his lap as if manna from heaven, like the white van in Kate McCardigan's parking lot. When Poppy ran the plate, it was registered to a Detroit outfit by the name of Midwest Waste Haulers. Their telephone number matched the number on the pager Derk found in Von Lleuwan's pocket.

As the ambulance departed, a beat-up van limped into Von Lleuwan's parking lot. Bear jumped out and began a regurgitation of the morning's events, and Player couldn't stop talking about the big bald guy.

"Do you know where Kate is?" Derk asked Skip.

"No."

"And she hasn't called?" Derk said. Skip shook his head.

"Damn it, Skip. Why didn't you tell me?" Derk said.

"I promised Kate," Skip said.

"Not to tell *me?*"

"The cops didn't help her," Skip said.

"Jesus, Skip, this isn't some college prank. Your promise got her in big trouble," Derk said. "We've got to find her." He motioned to Officer Oliver he was ready to leave.

"I want to go," Skip said.

"You don't have enough bruises yet?" Derk said, giving Skip a quick top to bottom scan. Derk turned and said to Officer Oliver, "Let's go."

"Wait," Skip said, then handed Derk a wadded up handkerchief.

"What's this?" Derk asked.

"Evidence," Skip said.

"Let me see that," Officer Oliver said.

The storm had diminished. Sandra and Mrs. Huizenga stood in the parking lot with the others, focused upon the wad of white cloth in the officer's hand. As he unfolded it, a piece of ear with remnants of some frayed fishing line and a clump of insulation fell into a puddle on the pavement.

Mrs. Huizenga shrieked and Sandra steadied her as she jumped back.

"Is that what I think it is?" the officer said.

"The missing part from the big guy in the ambulance," Derk said and waved in the direction of where the ambulance had just been. For the officer's benefit, Derk quickly connected the dots from Skip and Kate to Von Lleuwan to Midwest Waste Haulers. "She's in Detroit," Derk said.

"You want me to drive?" The officer volunteered.

They headed for the cruiser. "I'll let you know what happens," Derk said to his friends.

"Better call the locals," Sandra said, joining them.

"Do that and they'll call the FBI. They'll surround the place, rush in with their guns blazing, and someone will get killed, maybe Kate," Derk countered.

"Don't be a rogue on this," Sandra said.

"Thanks for your concern," he said.

"You going to let him do this?" she said to Officer Oliver.

"Where I grew up they pumped out this toxic stuff all day long. When the factories closed the drums from the paint lines and the plating operations leached into the ground. My friends played there, and now they've got cancer and birth defects. My brother died of leukemia. Does that tell you where I stand?" he said as the rain drained off the lid of his State issued chapeau. On the way to Detroit he radioed headquarters and told them that he was headed east on I-94. Just prior to reaching their destination, he called for backup.

An unmarked State Police car was waiting outside the entrance to Midwest Waste Haulers when Derk and Poppy arrived. Midwest Waste Haulers was located in a warehouse district near the Port of Detroit. The site, a full city block in size, was encompassed by ten-foot-high sheets of rusty corrugated steel. An equally tall chain-link gate stood open at the entrance. A two by three metal sign that draped precariously from rusty baling wire spelled out the corporate moniker in faded red and black letters.

Derk and Poppy exited the cruiser and got into the unmarked car. Officer Oliver briefed the two officers on the situation, and then asked, "What can you tell us about this place?"

"It's worse than a damn dump in there. It's hard to see because of the fence, but there's no cars in the drive and no sign of life other than some lights in the office. That's the office," one officer said, pointing to an aging single story, wood-framed building visible through the open gate. "There's another exit in the rear."

Derk could see a postage stamp piece of blacktop in front of the office, probably visitors' parking, but it was empty. Two old trailer homes stood on the other side of the office. Derk surmised that employee parking and maintenance must be in the larger, two-story structure that hovered behind the main office.

"Get some local backup," Officer Oliver said. "Let's surround the place."

"Unmarked cars and no lights," Derk said.

The officer immediately pinched his face into a suspicious frown.

"Do it," Officer Oliver told him.

Derk and Poppy returned to the cruiser. "Tell them you're here to look for leaks. There's been a complaint about some fumes," Derk said to Sandra.

"I'll back you up," Officer Oliver said to her.

"I'll cover the rear," Derk said.

"That's not a legal search," she said.

Poppy deferred to Derk.

"Can you do it or not?" Derk said.

"No problem," she answered.

As she and Poppy entered the front door, Derk scurried to the rear of the building. The officer had been correct. It looked like a dump or a salvage yard for car parts. Broken and rusted automobile frames with hoods, wheels, and miscellaneous parts stripped from them stood like aging skeletons in an auto parts bank. There were boats, pieces of boats, scrap metal of every description, piles of wire separated by color, and barrels, hundreds of barrels, many of which were leaking their contents through perforated cardboard and rusted seams. They sat in red, green, and blue pools of slime. Lumber, bricks, broken concrete blocks, and a myriad of building materials were scattered about the yard. An unsavory aroma filled the air. There were a dozen code violations within plain sight, the sort of violations that could persist only as a result of oversight or bribery. Within the chaotic stench, Derk looked at blood dried on his suit trousers and sensed danger. He never carried a gun, but within this dank, pithy, hostile environment he longed for greater security.

There was a door near the rear corner of the building. Under these gray skies the light should have been on, but the bulb was broken, giving the appearance that this exit was not in use. One of three sets of double doors to the maintenance shop was wide open. He counted six, no, seven three or four-year old pickups, two beaters, a late model luxury car, and a subcompact sedan in the garage. The boss and his secretary were probably on the property. Several very large trucks were parked in service bays at the far end of the building. A couple of mechanics were buried under the hood of a giant tractor-trailer. As Derk hurried through the shop and approached the rear entrance to the main office, the radio blared a familiar rhythm and blues tune, but it was competing with some discordant heavy metal sound from outside. He had missed it on the way in. The sight of the wine-colored BMW in the yard, however, confirmed his fears. It was parked across the lot from the maintenance building between a dump truck and a twenty-foot closed bed.

He exited the maintenance building and tried to dodge the puddles as he crossed the lot. One of his wingtips filled with water when he landed in one unusually deep pool. Dirty water splashed up his pant-leg. Somebody was going to pay for this. He ducked between two old trucks and sneaked behind Kate's car. She was in the back seat, and something was tied around her head, maybe a blindfold. The car was slowly rocking from the heavy metal sound that penetrated Derk to the cartilage. In the side mirror he saw someone seated in the driver's seat, a young male he surmised from the hairdo. His red and orange head was bobbing up and down to the deafening syncopations. Derk moved around to the passenger's side of the car and spotted no reflection in the right-side mirror. He was one on one. He stayed low, used the car as a brace, and crept around to the driver's side. As loud as the music was it was now overwhelmed by the pounding in his chest. If the kid so much as glanced to his left, Derk's cover would be blown. He prayed that the door wasn't locked and that the kid had no gun. He reached for the door handle and jerked.

43

Kate had felt this helpless only one other time in her life, when Trevor's doctor told her that whatever had happened to her son would probably take his life. The difference here was that there was no opportunity to delay the inevitable by engaging any of the five psychological stages associated with death, the first of which was denial. Her hands were tied. She was gagged and she was blindfolded. And the music practically incapacitated her ability to concentrate. She had no idea where she was nor could she identity her abductors. Once the car stopped she sensed her demise was imminent.

Then she heard one of the men yell, "Get the fuck off me!"

She tried to scream, but the wad in her mouth muzzled her. She could barely breathe through the congestion caused by her tears. She shook her arms and jumped up and down in her seat in an attempt to loosen the dog's leash they had used to bind her hands. Nothing budged.

Even if she could escape, she couldn't see anything and each breath contained within it the remnants of her previous attempt. The man with the wild hair had kicked her so hard she felt her ribs collapse against her lungs. They had all been lying on the ground in her parking lot when the gun fired. The older man, whom the kid called Banker, was trapped under her dog and the kid was writhing in pain. After she realized she hadn't been shot, she made a break for her office. The kid scrambled on all fours toward his partner. With a brush of his hand he slid the gun toward the older man. Banker grabbed the gun, twisted, and fired in Kate's direction. The revolver's retort and the sound of the bullet ricocheting off the building in front of her stopped her like an elevator that had quit between floors.

"Get this dog off me, bitch!" the man shouted.

The one with the wild hair rose and massaged his hip as she retraced her steps. The man in the suit worked himself free of the

322

giant Doberman, but not until the other had applied a couple of kicks to its midsection. Hope recoiled and moaned. Kate ran to his side, kneeled, and hugged him.

"Into the van," the man in the suit ordered her.

Kate tried to get Hope back on his feet. The younger man circled the two of them and then kicked the dog in the head. "Friggin' dog!" he shouted. Hope's head bounced off the pavement without a whimper. Its body slumped into slumber. Kate jumped to her feet and swung at the man as hard as she could. The blow caught him on the arm and spun him around. His momentum allowed him to pirouette on his unharmed leg and, to her complete surprise, his foot landed between her breasts just below the sternum. All of the air in her world escaped. She lay on the ground, writhing and gasping, unable even to cry.

"Get up and get in the van!" the man in the suit ordered her.

She had fallen upon her dog, and she reached for him like a child's doll. When she could speak she looked up at the two assailants and declared, "Not without him!"

The two men looked at her, their mouths draped open. The one in the military fatigues who had just inflicted more physical pain than she had felt in her whole life, assumed some kind of Kung-fu position and shouted, "Now, lady."

"Wait, kid," the guy with the gun said. "We can't leave the dog. Take 'em both. Now get in!" he ordered and waved the gun toward the back of the van.

The men lifted the animal into the back of the van. Kate got into the passenger's side ahead of Banker and the kid went around to the driver's side. That was when he must have noticed the flat tire. "Well, fuck me. Come here, old man!"

It took the three of them to move Hope from the van to the rear seat of Kate's car. Then they folded down one seat and jammed the dog into the trunk. Kate sat in the back seat. The younger one drove while Banker parked the van at the back of the lot.

"Everybody knows about Jack Von Lleuwan. They probably arrested him already," she told them. "Everybody knows, everybody knows. Let me go now and it'll be easier on you," she told them.

They ignored her until the man in the suit reacted, "Lady, we don't know any Jack Von what the fuck's his name, and if you don't shut up I'm going to let The Kung-fu kid practice on you some more!"

They stayed off the main highway until they were south of Bowling Green, Ohio. Then they tied her hands, gagged and blindfolded her, and laid her down in the back seat ahead of her dog.

<h1 style="text-align:center">44</h1>

Derk opened the car door and grabbed the man in the driver's seat.

"Get the fuck off me!" the man yelled.

As they hit the ground, the man rolled over Derk. He jumped to his feet before Derk could upright himself. Then he crouched, whirled, cocked, and uncoiled. He was a thin five-five or six but quick as a Cobra, and the impact on Derk's chest was like an air-hammer. Derk was slammed against the car door and the handle opened a gully at the nape of his neck. Woozy and gasping, a kaleidoscope of colors rushed toward him like some creature from the primordial, a rainbow of whirling limbs. Another jolt. It left the taste of rubber and blood in his mouth as his head ricocheted off the car's side panel and hit the ground. One more thrust from the creature's indomitable fury and he would enter the dreamland from which one never awakens. He reached into his suitcoat pocket, formed his hand into a gun, and pointed it in the direction of the beast.

The wild thing stopped, slumped its shoulders, and as deftly as before, pirouetted on one foot. Its leg rose and, as before, cocked, and uncoiled at Derk's head. This time Derk moved. As the kick brushed his shoulder, the momentum rolled him to his right. Some flashing lights coruscated through the parking lot and disappeared into the service garage. The man hopped on one leg to maintain his balance, but his leg buckled, as if he were injured. Derk rolled back the other direction and slid his legs into the man's ankle. It wasn't forceful but enough to fell him like a wounded giraffe. Derk scrambled to gain an advantage. They rolled over and Derk used his weight to pin the man. He hit him with a hard right to the face. The kid's head spun and retorted. On the rebound Derk smashed him again. The man's head bounced off the ground and fell silent. Derk

325

stayed on top of him until he was certain he wouldn't get up. He shook his fist in the air to relieve the pain. "Damn!" he said. He had never hit a human being that hard.

Through the music Derk heard a sound, "Mmmmmmmmmm!"

In the car, blindfolded and gagged, Kate had crawled over the seat and was trying to open the electric lock on the passenger side with her hands tied behind her. Derk reached in, turned off the radio, and put his hands on Kate's shoulders. Startled, the reflex of her head against his almost knocked him unconscious.

"It's Derk!" he shouted but she struggled. He circled her with his arms and held her so tightly she couldn't move. "It's all right. It's me, Kate. Stay right here a minute."

He unlocked her door. Then he went around to her side of the car and removed the blindfold and the gag. She gasped for air and fell into his arms, sobbing.

"We've got to get out of here," he said. He tried to help her from the car, but she grasped him again, this time longer.

"They grabbed me in the parking lot," she cried.

"I know, but we've got to get away from here," Derk said. He led her away from the car.

"How did you find me?"

He stopped to untie her hands.

"We've got to get Hope." She turned back to her car.

Two men emerged from the side door of the main building. One of them, in his mid-forties, about five-foot eight, with dark hair and olive skin was wearing an expensive suit and an anxious demeanor. He was picking something on his nose. The other was tall, thin, fifty-ish and had on a dated tweed three piece.

"Know those guys?" Derk said to Kate.

Kate recoiled when she turned around. "That's him!" she shouted. "He's got a gun!"

"Who the fuck are you?" Banker said as drew his weapon. They were headed straight toward Derk and Kate.

There was no escape route, and a .38 special was pointed directly at Kate. Derk grabbed her arm to keep her from running.

"You deaf?" the man in the expensive suit said.

"EPA, we're here for an inspection," Derk said.

"The fuck you are," Banker said. "Get your hands up."

Derk raised his hands and whispered to Kate, "Be cool. We're not alone."

"Check his ID," Fagan Miranda instructed his accomplice as they approached.

Before the men in suits reached them, a deep, gruff voice called from the garage, "Hey, Miranda!"

Derk didn't know whether he was witnessing an apparition or a reincarnation. As the flashing lights of the ambulance reflected off the walls inside the garage a huge, bald man in a white smock walked toward them. He was wearing a paramedic's clothes, but his pants weren't medical issue, and they were matted with sand and speckled with something white. His shoes were Italian loafers. His face looked like an overly ripe mango and there was a big chunk missing from one ear. He had the focus of an eagle and the disposition of an angry bull. Derk dropped his hands and took a reflexive step toward him, but stopped when he heard a gun cock.

The men in the suits glanced around as if searching for others. Maybe they thought the paramedic was with the EPA, too. The closer the man in the smock approached, the more obvious it became he wasn't here to rescue anyone. The man with the gun turned it from Derk to the paramedic. Then he swung it back toward Kate and Derk, then toward the paramedic.

"Who's hurt?" Miranda asked.

Without breaking stride, Gloves said, "Von Lleuwan sent me." He was twenty feet from them.

"To get the woman?" Miranda said.

"That's right," Gloves said.

"No!" Kate cried out and attached herself to Derk

Derk had never wanted to take a shot at anyone as much as he wanted to go head long at Gloves right now. But with Kate clinging to him like moss on a tree trunk and a gun waving recklessly at them, he glanced toward the office, anxious for his backup to appear.

"He was supposed to call," Miranda said. Gloves was within spitting distance when Miranda glanced at his hands. "Shoot him!" he ordered Banker.

Miranda threw up his hand to defend himself from the monstrous fist that the man in the white smock launched at him. Gloves opened his hand and clasped Miranda's wrist. In one movement he twisted Miranda's arm and swung it over his head as he did a three-sixty with his body. Derk heard the man's shoulder pop and the bones in his wrist fracture. Miranda screamed. Banker got off one round as his boss collapsed in the soggy refuse of yesterday's dreams and one more as Gloves reached to deflect his aim. Gloves didn't flinch.

As Derk rushed Banker, he noticed only what appeared as a puff of air buffet the smock Gloves was wearing at just about the kidney line. Derk's charge spun Banker around, but he didn't let go of the gun. Gloves swallowed Banker's outstretched hand, sandwiched the gun and Banker's hand into a fist and levered Banker's arm against his body. Just under his chin the .38 exploded. When Gloves released him, the man in the second-hand suit fell to the sod like spent coffee grounds.

Gloves leaned over Banker, maybe to see if he were dead, and Derk chopped him with both hands on the back of his neck. Gloves fell onto Banker's motionless body, and Derk kneed him in the ribs. Derk's next punch was aimed at Gloves exposed cheek, but Gloves raised one hand and deflected it, his strength great enough to topple Derk. While Derk was scrambling to right himself, Gloves grabbed

Miranda's neck and snapped it. They got to their feet and faced each other.

Kate yelled, "Leave him alone."

Derk stood his ground and contemplated his options. He could disable him by feigning resignation and then kick him in the groin. No, he was too big and too quick. He could go straight at him, boll him over, and gain a superior position, then pummel him. Not a chance. This man was a killing machine.

"If I have to deal with you, you won't like it," Gloves said, but his posture intimated something else. His face sagged and his eyes were more bloodshot than the spot on the soil now engulfing Miranda's lifeless body. His arms hung to his side like the limbs of an aging willow. This big dog was one weary puppy. Derk titled his head to one side and pursed his lips, a gesture to let Gloves know that their confrontation was now up to him. The man in the paramedic's smock sputtered and shuffled away.

Poppy Oliver had his gun drawn when he and Agent French burst through the side door. Police officers with guns drawn were rushing into the yard from both entrances. Two men in suits were lying on the ground several feet from each other. Neither was moving. Derk kneeled next to one of them, checking for a pulse. On Derk's left, about thirty feet away, was a huge bald guy with two pigtails and a white smock walking toward the lights flashing inside the garage. The two mechanics with hand tools, who were standing on either side the doorway, backed away as the bald man approached. Behind Derk was an attractive blonde with her hands tied who was trying to get a big, white dog from the rear of a wine-colored BMW. As she pulled it from the car, the dog's legs buckled, and like a domino she collapsed beneath it. On the hood of the car behind them a short, slender man in military fatigues was poised in some kind of kung-fu position. Blood, almost the color of the hair that stood on his head like strands on a wire brush, dripped from his nose and tracked across his lips.

"Derk! Behind you," Sandra yelled as the man leaped toward him.

Derk somersaulted forward and reached for the .38 Special, lying next to Banker's open hand. When the Kung-fu kid landed he was straddling Derk's supine body, in a position to chop him senseless.

Derk pointed the revolver at his chest and shouted, "Back off!"

"Fuck me!" the man said as Derk cocked the gun.

Voices from everywhere shouted, "Police! Back off now!"

The Kung-fu kid raised his hands and stepped back. Derk waved the officers to his side. "Tie his hands and feet, the little turd," Derk said.

Sandra and Officer Oliver ran toward Derk.

"Check on Kate," Derk told Sandra.

"Is that the guy who ran into Von Lleuwan?" Officer Oliver asked, pointing his gun toward Gloves. Derk nodded, already headed toward the garage. "How . . .?" the officer said, so bewildered he didn't finish his question. Officer Oliver followed Derk.

"Not so fast, Jimmy Swingle," Derk said. Gloves had reached the ambulance. "I've got something that belongs to you."

Gloves braced against the back door of the ambulance with one hand. The other covered his wound. He turned to face Derk. His lips parted, but nothing came out. He grimaced, turned away, leaned unsteadily against the truck, and shuffled like a drunk against the wind toward the driver's door.

Derk walked over, grabbed his arm, and spun him around. Derk squared off, ready for one of the burly man's powerful punches, but Gloves offered no resistance. There were four revolvers within point blank range beaded on him. Derk removed a rolled-up paper bag from his pocket and spilled the contents on the ground in front of the ex-wrestler. Gloves' face was a pale as porcelain. The entire bottom of his smock was stained a deep magenta. The blood seeped between his fingers, and he was too listless to stem the flow. Like Venetian blinds, his eyelids slowly draped his remaining consciousness. He reached down for the ear and hit the concrete like a coil of hemp cable. Jimmy Swingle had played his last match.

In the back of the ambulance, the paramedics were bound with surgical tubing but neither was hurt.

"Dam-o-sam!" Derk said, overcome by a cold shiver. Von Lleuwan was restrained on a cot, still wearing the tourniquets that had been administered in his own rain-soaked lobby. But another had been added. Gloves had tied one end of a suture around Von Lleuwan's neck and the other end around his scrotum. Each time Von Lleuwan had tried to relax, the weight of his head pulled the noose around his balls. If he had survived the loss of blood from his crushed legs he would have been castrated. "There really are no coincidences," Derk said to Officer Oliver.

Derk jumped from the back of the rescue truck and went to assist Sandra. Sandra had untied Kate's hands and freed her from the giant dog that had fallen upon her. They were kneeling next to the dog, Kate's arms wrapped around Hope's neck. She pleaded for him to get up. Derk squatted and put his arms around Kate's shoulders. She collapsed against him. Her lipstick had become rouge stains on her tear-streaked face. The fear he had noticed earlier had turned into despair. Self-preservation had been replaced with suffering. The rolling boil of loneliness had spilled over, and an ocean of tears erupted.

"It's over, Kate. They're gone. They're all gone," he said.

For Kate truer words have never been spoken. Everyone in her world was gone. She was completely alone.

Derk put his arm around Sandra. She leaned against him.

"Are you okay?" she asked.

"Thanks to you," he said and kissed her. "I've got to see my mom. Will you go with me?"

Derk escorted Sandra and his mother into his father's room and was depleted by one brief glance. Six months ago his father had clearly been suffering from the effects of Alzheimer's Disease, the shortened memory, the propensity to eat all matter of things, and the dissociated discourse that were common to the malady, but he was alive. Artificial arteries attached to essential organs seemed the only things pumping life into his now bleached and frail body. Gone was the raspy, overbearing voice that had never stopped demanding. Gone was the energy of a man driven by an unrequited yearning. And gone was the nervous gesture he repeated when he tried but usually failed to listen to Derk. Derk reached for his arm but, spotting the bruises, withdrew.

"Without the drugs he knows only pain," his mother said.

Derk left the room. In the hallway he paced, conflicted by anger, despair, and sympathy. His resentment had swelled like a black eye, and he couldn't vent it because his father was incoherent, medicated to the max.

"I'm sorry I couldn't get here sooner," he said.

His mother came out and took him by one arm. She motioned Sandra to stay there while she led Derk to a private seating area at the end of the hall.

"I know there's a lot you want to tell him, and you can't," she said.

Derk had a lump in his throat the size of a grapefruit. "Yeah."

The years had not been kind to Derk's mother. She was a tiny woman, never taller than five-two, and the osteoarthritis had shrunk her to a wispy five feet, but she had once been beautiful. Her gray hair was pulled back exposing a presence once capable of disarming a charging bull with a single smile. The lines in her face now revealed a host of ailments, the most severe of which was a broken heart. She and Derk's father had been separated off and on for many years, but she never divorced him. Derk never understood why.

He sat down, then rose and paced. "I'm sorry, Mom, but I know what you want and I can't do it."

"You can't change what's happened," his mother said.

He clenched his fists and released them as he paced. "It's not right. It's too easy. And maybe I'm not ready for him to go," Derk said, almost sobbing now.

"Sit down, sweetheart. I have something to tell you."

Derk sat down beside his mother. The only sound in the room was from the low hum of a window air conditioner. A man had entered the room and put some coins into the vending machine. Derk's mother waited while the coffee drained into a Styrofoam cup. Derk rubbed his eyes and inhaled the coffee's resuscitating vapors, but the aroma was overwhelmed by the pallor of death.

When the man left, she said, "You asked me if there was something that might have caused the separation between you and your dad?" His mother smiled, but it was a dour affectation.

He could only nod, made dumb by his emotions.

"I married your father when we were very young. I was head over heels in love with him." Her pride radiated like a roaring campfire. "He was a great catch, handsome, athletic and bright. I came from a poor family, and I knew he was the guy the day I met him."

"I know, Mom," Derk said. "You've told me this before, but he wasn't there for you."

"What I've never told you is this. He was very ambitious. He wanted to go to college and start his own business. He didn't want to marry me so I got pregnant."

"It happens and people adjust."

She shook her head. "He was going off to college and I was afraid of losing him."

"That's no reason for how he treated us."

She seemed to be holding back a dam of fear. "I've never told anybody this, but I'm the reason you and your father weren't close."

He held her arm. "Mom, you got pregnant, but it was his fault as much as yours."

She pulled away. "I'm still afraid."

"Of what? You've always been my rock."

"I saw how distant you were with your father, the resentment, how you pushed him away even when he tried." A trickle formed on her face.

"He wasn't there for you either."

"I didn't want to lose you, too." The tears burst across her weathered cheeks like a flash flood. He had never seen her so frail, so vulnerable. She fell into his arms. "I got pregnant to keep him from leaving."

He held her. "It happens, Mom. You're not the only woman…"

"No, I tricked him. He didn't know. He's not your real father."

The reality hit him like a piano from a third story window. He released her and backed away.

"I'm so sorry."

He shook his head, rose and paced. "No, no." He felt completely disconnected, a stranger to himself, and no one's child.

"He still supported us," she said and reached for him. He resisted. "Sweetheart, I love you, I always have, but you're just like him."

Her words struck him like an assassin's bullet. "Get away from me."

"You're driven. Your first wife told you that. He's in there dying and you couldn't come 'til you finished some case. You fought him so much. You're just like him."

"Jesus, Mom, how could you?"

"I did what I could and so did he," she said and pointed in the direction of the man he had despised for so long, thinking his father had abandoned him. Through a glass partition Sandra looked back at him. He wasn't sure if she were feeling empathy or sympathy, but her presence was the only comfort he felt.

"He didn't abandon us," she said. "I knew he would leave if I didn't let him pursue his dreams."

"He did leave us."

"For a while. To do what he had to do."

"But he had a kid to take care of."

"We had an agreement. We never lacked for anything."

"You gave up a part of your life."

"That was my choice. I loved him." Her shoulders slumped and she collapsed on the couch.

This wasn't what he wanted to hear. He needed his father to be at fault for his failed relationships, and his mother was taking that away from him.

"He was very proud of you," his mother said.

"How would I have known?"

"You wouldn't listen. You wouldn't give him a chance. You did the same thing he did. You only thought of yourself."

"If you want to blame someone, blame me." She took Derk's hand and led him toward her husband's room. They stood in the doorway looking at him. "Come on. He needs you."

It wasn't what he wanted to hear, but it made sense. He put his hands on his neck and wrapped his arms around his head. His sympathy competed with his resentment. He couldn't stop the tears.

They stood on opposite sides of his bed. Sandra took Derk's hand. His mother bent over the bed, placed her hand on her husband's forehead, and combed his thinning hair with a gentle stroke.

"Charlie, Derk is here to see you," she said.

Derk wiped the tears from his eyes, and took hold of the man's hand. He looked at him for an extended time, an introspective gaze from a new vantage point. His anger and his pride dripped onto the man's hospital gown as he leaned down. In a barely audible voice he said, "Dad, it's Derk. It's Derk. I'm here."

His father's chest rose and declined ever so slightly. Derk couldn't tell if he could hear or if he was even aware of his presence. He put his hand on his father's forehead. There was warmth but little else. He leaned close and whispered, "I love you."

Sandra held him. His mother came around and put her arms around each of them.

"What should I do?" Derk choked on his new found perspective, like a lump of rolled cotton that had formed in his throat.

"Let him go. If you love him, let him go," his mother said.

"What do you mean?"

"He wants us to take him to Oregon," she said.

Derk withdrew from his mother's grip. From resentment to detachment to enlightenment, he had known no despair of this depth. Oregon permitted assisted suicide. Once again he was stranded upon that high precipice drawn between principle and love, and he felt like damaged goods, wondering if he could love or be loved. Was this the ultimate test? His mother had shown him how to love, unyielding love, but it had come with such a high tariff. As his tears released years of conflict, Sandra French's sweet fragrance suggested that he might have been given another chance.

The bright Michigan sky cast silver slivers through the partially opened curtains in the room of the only man he had ever known as father. From their perches high in a silver maple, just beyond the window, he heard the unmistakable mating calls of a pair of starlings. Could it be the sound of renewal, serving notice to all in need that hope springs eternal? He wasn't sure, but this he knew with certainty, "There are no coincidences."

46

Sandra French invited Derk to stay with her for a few days while they finished the report on the Von Lleuwan case. Her lakefront cottage was modest but sunny, airy, and wonderfully feminine. He hiked around the lake with her, prepared dinners with her, and made love with her until his bones ached. He wasn't at all embarrassed when, curled up in her arms on the evening of his father's burial, he shed more tears than in all the days of his life combined.

His mother lived less than an hour away, and he called her on the days he didn't see her. It was difficult. Her loneliness was like a virus consuming what was left of her spirit. He left Michigan with competing emotions.

When the cab dropped him in front of the Elgar plant in Tampa, his heart spilled onto his boots. His bike was nowhere in sight. A woman in the office told him that the receptionist had taken off a couple days to visit her sick sister, but she thought one of the guys had put it in the warehouse. "Ask for Miguel," she said.

The wind was carrying the caustic aroma away from the warehouse, and he could breathe normally, but he couldn't stop peaking around each corner as he made his way through the stacks. He found the bike parked against a wall just inside the loading dock at one end of the building. He ran his fingers across the gas tank. Not a speck of dust. As he straddled the seat, a denim-clad Latino in his mid-twenties approached him.

"It's a beauty," he said with a distinctly Latin accent. "Hope you didn't mind I moved it in here so nothing would happen to it."

"Thank you," Derk said.

"It's a '49 Panhead, isn't it?" he said.

"You know your Harleys," said Derk as he ran his hand across his once swollen jaw.

"I have my eye on a '74 Sportster. I'd like to customize it like yours," he said and reached for Derk's hand. "Miguel."

"Derk Bryan," he said as he shook the younger man's hand.

"You must be proud, Mr. Bryan. It's a classic. Do the work yourself?" Miguel asked.

"Except for the engine," Derk responded, a subtle grin revealing some of the pride the kid's admiration aroused.

The key was in the ignition, but he decided to jump start it. "Potata, potata, potata" reverberated throughout the steel building. Once he was confident the bike would idle on its own, he reached into his pocket and handed Miguel a twenty-dollar bill.

"Thanks for taking care of it," Derk said.

The kid declined his offer. "It's what one Harley man does for another."

"You're absolutely right," Derk said and put the twenty in his pocket. "If there's anything I can ever do for you, let me know." He handed Miguel his business card.

Miguel's head bobbed up and down, "Si, I'd like to ride it sometime," he said, moonbeams glaring.

"When you get yours running, we'll go riding, *amigo. Adios*," Derk said.

The ride to Pass-a-Grille was melancholy. He was returning to life on the beach and leisurely runs to Frenchy's Café for a beer with friends, but life had changed. He had lost a parent but gained a new perspective. One love had finally come to an end and another had begun. As he wound through the gears across the Gandy Bridge, connecting south Tampa with St. Petersburg, he couldn't shake the doubts. A line from a Dire Straits song played in his head, "I'm tired of making out on the telephone," and he knew that the miles and the time that separated him from Sandra might take their toll. Some of the best times in his life, some of his oldest and closest friends, and some of his most intimate relationships were linked to the North, but he was now entrenched in different place. At another time he might have thrown caution to the wind, packed up everything, and moved to Michigan to be with Sandra. Experience had taught him that trading what he knew made him happy for the benefit of a relationship that might work was fraught with risk. He had even discussed it with his old friend and mentor.

Wally Twill had said, "Everything will work out the way it's supposed to."

"Maybe I'm getting too set in my way," Derk said.

Wally's answer was, "No, you're just finding your way. If your way and her way are the same, it will work out between you." That was advice he couldn't deny.

At the peak of the bridge, a few gulls circled overhead and a brown pelican dived in search of lunch. He faced the healing sun, sucked in the salty air, and allowed the tropical breeze to cool the layer of lubricant that the Florida summer had already summoned. Instead of giving in to rational objectivity, he preferred to lean on sensual bliss, and he wondered if the scent of Sandra French might still meander throughout his condominium. He smiled and headed home with that prospect on his mind.

The End

Afterword

The Food Quality Protection Act of 1995 overturned the Delaney Clause that was the last bastion of defense against the use of most dangerous chemicals in our food supply. It is still the law today. Since its passage in 1996 pesticide producers and large corporate farming interests have effectively lobbied Congress to minimize the protections that even this new law was designed to provide women, children and the rest of us.

Although this story is fictional and any similarities to any people or places is purely coincidental, the facts regarding the registration, regulation, laws, and use and abuse of pesticides in this country is entirely authoritative and taken from public records.

About The Author

G. Spencer Myers' specialty is the eco-political thriller, featuring Dr. Derk Bryan, college professor, obsessive environmentalist and intrepid EPA investigator who works only on cases involving environmental chaos and dead bodies. His blogs feature controversial issues from an ecological point of view.

His first book, <u>Pest</u>, featured a race against the clock to save his former lover from a fraudulent pesticide manufacturer and an ex-wrestler turned body guard with anger management issues. In <u>Dead Wrong</u> he exposes the link between a toxic spill, police corruption and a Johnny Cash look alike. His memoir, <u>A Letter to My Grandson</u>, inspired the 1st Palm Beach County Short Story Contest entitled, "In Search of Integrity."

<u>WE ARE PLAYING ROULETTE WITH YOUR FUTURE</u> is an update of A Letter to My Grandson calling upon all grandchildren to heed the challenge of global warming.

In <u>The Girl with the Red Nails</u>, the antagonist is Pendleton Danswirth III, but the real villain is plastics. Since its completion the EPA has chosen to regulate so called forever chemicals in drinking water. His recent article on sustainable cruising has appeared in newspapers throughout Florida under The Invading Seas series. A long-time environmentalist, he was the first person in the U.S. to put solar panels on a multi family home listed on the National Register of Historic Places.

Mr. Myers is a graduate of the University of Michigan, holds an MBA from Bowling Green State University and is Certified by the American College of Sports Medicine.

He is a native of Michigan but lives in Durham, NC where he is still in pursuit of par. Contact him at <u>Author@GSpencerMyers.com</u>.